DEATH'S GRIP

A CHILLING ESSEX MURDER MYSTERY

DS TOMEK BOWEN CRIME THRILLER SERIES
BOOK 2

JACK PROBYN

ISBN: 978-1-80520-036-9
First Edition

Visit Jack Probyn's website at www.jackprobynbooks.com.

ABOUT THE BOOK

Annabelle Lake thought she recognised the Ford Fiesta waiting outside her school, and the driver in it. She was wrong.

Her body is discovered some time later, dangling from a swing in a local playground on Canvey Island.

The post-mortem shows she's been fed, clothed and kept warm. That whoever was responsible had looked after her. But when another girl goes missing and is found in a similar fashion, that's where the similarities end.

Both girls have never met, they don't know each other, and they're from completely different backgrounds.

So what connects them?

DS Tomek Bowen and the team at Essex Police must find out before it's too late. And on an island that's below sea level, it's only a matter of time until the truth comes flooding out.

JOIN THE VIP CLUB

Your FREE book is waiting for you

Available when you join the VIP Club below

Get your FREE copy of the prequel to the DS Tomek Bowen series now at jackprobynbooks.com when you join my VIP email club.

CHAPTER
ONE

The last time Amelia Duggan saw little Annabelle Lake was when she'd waved her off from the school gates. The school day had finished, and hordes of children from Canvey Beck Primary School filtered out onto the streets with their parents. But not Annabelle Lake. She didn't need her parents to come and collect her. They lived in the small close opposite the school, a stone's throw from the entrance. A short walk along the road, cross at the lights, and then she was safe.

Amelia watched her do the journey every afternoon just to make sure she crossed the busy street and she set foot through the front door safely.

This afternoon was no different.

'Got your bag and coat?' Amelia asked.

'Yes, miss,' Annabelle replied.

'And you've washed your hands?'

'Yes, miss.'

'Are you sure? I heard you using the toilet a few minutes ago.'

Amelia, sensing that she'd been rumbled, giggled childishly and then hurried off to the toilet. The time was 3:30 p.m. School had finished fifteen minutes ago, but Annabelle had stayed behind, as she often did, to allow the upper years to leave the playground. She didn't like large crowds of people, they scared her. And Amelia was more than happy to spend the extra fifteen minutes with her to make sure she felt as comfortable as possible.

A few moments later, Annabelle Lake returned to the classroom, her hands wet. She held them in the air, and Amelia high-tenned her. They were the Two As. Amelia and Annabelle, and Amelia had been with the little girl ever since she'd joined the school in reception. She'd watched her grow from a timid, shy individual who hadn't wanted to be there, into a smiling, ebullient child who brightened everyone's day as soon as she skipped into the building. Despite the difficulties she would face in later life, she wasn't going to let them stop her from living in the moment, living in the now.

Carrying her bag for her, Amelia followed behind Annabelle as she made her way down the stairs and through a set of double doors. By the time they breached into the car park, the space was empty, save for a few parents who were waiting for their children to finish detention. That particular number had been increasing in recent years. She wasn't sure what was happening to the place. And as a teaching assistant she wasn't privy to the intricate details of how the school was run, of how it was being run into the ground. The latest Ofsted report had marked them as "Requires Improvement". She was certain some of the children's attitudes and behaviour was largely contributing to that. In all her previous roles, she'd never experienced children as disorganised, spiteful, vindictive and less keen to learn as she had with those at Canvey Beck, one of Canvey Island's better performing schools. Except Annabelle Lake, of course. Little Annabelle was the reason she came to work, the reason she looked forward to the shitstorm she would have to endure every day. A part of her sensed that the absolute downfall of the education services in the school – and the increasing violence she found in the playground – was due to the recent influx of immigrants and migrants on the island. With nowhere else to go, and no one else willing to help them, they'd sought refuge on the south side of the island in the various caravan parks and social housing, much to the chagrin of the remaining Canvey residents. She wasn't saying they were all racist, but with the Castle Point constituency being among the top three in the biggest percentage of Leave voters during the Brexit referendum, it was difficult to envisage any other reason than a racial one. The influx of Eastern European children in the school had unsettled and unnerved many of the children she supervised in her class, and just in the last week alone she had put an end to three fights, all of them involving the people who thought they deserved to be at the school and those they believed didn't. And the funny thing was, it was typically the ones who had nowhere else to go, the ones who fled their war-torn countries, that performed better in the classroom. It was worrying times for the school, but children like Annabelle Lake were her reason for hope. They inspired her to continue the job she'd loved for so long.

At the end of the staff car park they came to a stop at the school gates. Annabelle's house was visible behind a low row of hedges.

'I'll see you tomorrow,' Amelia said.

'Yes, miss. Love you, miss.'

Amelia replied that she loved her too, and then folded her arms against the cold as she watched the little girl hobble down the road, wait patiently at the traffic lights, and then cross. She spotted a few of the parents she recognised on the other side of the road waiting for their children, dressed in their body warmers and tracksuit bottoms, cigarette in one hand, phone in the other.

Annabelle sauntered towards her house, her oversized backpack bouncing with every step, weighing her down. As she approached the line of hedges, a car pulled up beside her and she stopped. The figure driving the car was invisible behind the glare from the darkening November sky and the reflections from the ominous clouds overhead that threatened a week of rain. Amelia surveyed the car in an attempt to allay her fears. It was a Ford Fiesta. Black, with blacked out rims, a subwoofer blasting music and tinted windows. She recognised it as Annabelle's uncle's car. He was always coming over to pick her up at random. Said it was because she would be staying with him that evening.

As she had no reason to suspect otherwise, she'd often let Annabelle go into her uncle's custody. And now was no different. All that was visible of the little girl was the pigtails on her head and the top of her backpack.

Amelia watched as Annabelle opened the car door and hopped in.

A moment later, the car pulled out of the junction and headed in the opposite direction.

The direction away from her uncle and aunt's.

The direction away from her entire family.

CHAPTER
TWO

Tomek didn't like cemeteries. Come to think of it, he couldn't imagine anyone that did. Except for those that were paid to work there, or volunteered to keep the grounds as clean and respectable as possible. And even then he didn't think *enjoyed* was the right word.

Tolerated seemed more apt. Yes, they tolerated it. The same way Tomek was learning to tolerate new things in his life. The daughter he didn't know he had that had landed on his doorstep one afternoon, the utter boredom he felt every day not being able to work while he was suspended, pending investigation. He even found tolerating daytime television a struggle. And then there was this. Southend Cemetery. One of the largest, if not the largest, collection of bones and dead bodies he'd been to. And he'd been to a few crime scenes in his time that had tried to top it.

He lowered his gaze and his eyes fell on the headstone.

Tony William Hunt. He liked his coffee colder than his climate.

The inscription brought a smile to Tomek's face. That summed him up to a T.

The man had been dead for four weeks, and on the first month anniversary of his death, Tomek thought it was about time he made an appearance. Whether it had been guilt or grief that had prohibited him from attending sooner, he didn't know. All he knew was he'd only just started to come to terms with what had happened, and how if he was going to continue his career, he would need to put it behind him. He couldn't continue to live in the past, in fear of what he'd done, and how it had happened.

A large leaf, brown and dirtied by the rain that had hammered it deeper into the ground, flapped against the bottom of the headstone. Tomek bent down to remove it, to tidy it. As he pushed himself up from the sodden ground, he heard footsteps and the sound of a parka coat rustling. It stopped a few feet from him. And if it was possible, he felt the air pressure and temperature drop a few degrees.

Then he sensed an icy stare burning into the back of him.

'No...' was the solitary word that came out of her lips. Followed by: 'No... No, you do *not* get to be here. No! Get away from him!'

Tomek didn't need telling twice. He also didn't need to turn round to find out who was lambasting him for being near Tony's grave. Ever since that day, the day which Tomek refused to discuss with anyone else except the voices of reason inside his own head, Susan Hunt had made her feelings towards him very clear. She'd publicly outed him on various Facebook groups, run his name through the dirt with the media, and helped add the explosives to the bomb that was currently in the process of destroying his career.

He could hardly blame her. He *had* been responsible for her husband's death. He could hardly fault her for capitulating all the stages of grief and channelling it into him in a destructive and vengeful manner.

'Hi, Susan,' Tomek said softly. He kept his hands in his pockets and tried to keep the tone of his voice as light as possible. He wasn't there to argue, he wasn't there to offend, he just wanted to pay his respects and go.

'Fuck off,' she told him. 'And fuck you.'

'I just wanted to pay my—'

'I don't care. Fuck off. You have no right to be here.'

That was true, under any normal circumstances. But this wasn't normal circumstances. Guilt had brought him here. Guilt at allowing her husband to die when he had the chance – no matter how minuscule it might have appeared at the time – to save him.

Tomek pulled something from his pocket. A sachet of Sainsbury's own instant coffee. Times had been hard of late, and he wasn't in a position to purchase the labelled brands – the brands that Tony deserved.

'I know it's his favourite,' Tomek said, pulling out a flask from his other coat pocket. 'But I thought we could have a coffee together. In this weather I don't suppose it'll stay warm for very long.'

'No!' she bellowed, her voice rolling over the graves, disturbing the dead. 'You do not get to go anywhere near him. I've told you. If I find you here again I'll have a restraining order put against you.'

Could you have a restraining order against a dead person? Tomek didn't know. But he certainly didn't want to hang around long enough to find out.

To be the only one in the world who legally wasn't allowed within a hundred metres of a corpse. That would have made his job even more difficult.

Dropping his head, he retreated from the grave onto the pathway that cut through the cemetery. Susan was standing there, firm, her body stiff, blocking Tomek's exit route. Forcing him to go the long way back to his car.

'I know you may never be able to forgive me, and I know you may never want to, but if you can, it would mean a lot if we could sit down and discuss what happened.'

'It would mean a lot to *you*, you mean,' she said as a statement rather than a question. 'This isn't about you, so don't try to make it. You're the one who let him die, and I hope you live with that decision for the rest of your life.'

Tomek was, and would continue to do so.

There hadn't been a single day where he hadn't thought about it, where it hadn't eaten away at him from the inside.

But he couldn't begin to imagine how she was feeling. She was missing a husband, her soulmate, her life partner. That was far more severe and devastating than the guilt he faced. Who was he to beg for forgiveness when it was the last thing he deserved?

Realising he was fighting a battle he'd already lost and that it had been a mistake to come here, Tomek turned his back on Susan and headed back to his car – where he would be going to meet the other mistake in his life.

CHAPTER
THREE

'You ready?' he asked her.

But the question never landed; the two white ear plugs lodged as far as they would go in her ears prevented it from getting to her. To attract her attention, he waved his hand frantically in her face.

'*What?*' she hissed as she held the earphones between her fingers, shooting him a derisive look.

'Shopping. We're going. Are you ready? Now.'

The air of discontent that came out of her nose was strong enough to knock him back a few paces, but in the last few weeks he'd learned to tolerate it. In fact, it was one of the few things he actually had.

'I don't want to go food shopping,' she told him.

'Do you want to eat?'

'Ye—' she started, then caught herself. 'No.'

'I can only take your first answer, I'm afraid. And if you want to continue to eat, then you will get up off the sofa, put your coat and shoes on and come with me to the shops.'

'You're not my mum.'

'No, you're right. I'm your father. Which is exactly the same thing, just with more hair on my body. And what I say goes.'

Kasia remained firmly planted on the sofa, staring up at him, locked in a battle of defiance until a winner emerged. At the beginning of the calendar year, he never thought he would be entering a daily stare-off and argument with a thirteen-year-old. In fact, he hadn't imagined a lot of things would happen. He didn't think he would have found love and wished he'd never found it in the space of a few weeks. He didn't think he'd ever be suspended from his role as detective sergeant, pending investigation. And he certainly didn't think he would find out he was a father – thirteen years too late.

None of those were on his bingo card for the year.

'Three...' he started, parenting the only way he knew how: from the strict Polish upbringing he'd been subject to before his parents had dismembered him from the family. 'Two...'

Still, Kasia remained steadfast, the defiance behind her eyes glowering.

'Don't make me get to one...'

Fortunately tonight she wasn't willing to test his patience. Nor was she willing to call his bluff. And so, with another gust of wind coming from her nostrils, she slid off the sofa and made her way to the shoe rack by the front door. She plugged the headphones back into her head, and they remained there for the duration of the journey to their local Aldi. Ever since she'd come into his life, she'd become one thing and one thing only: a burden on his resources. Financial, time, and everything else. She'd consumed his every waking minute. Ensuring she was awake and ready for school; that she had food for breakfasts, lunches and dinner; that she had enough credit on her phone to last her the rest of the month; that she had spare school uniform after he'd managed to spill pasta sauce down it as he'd dished her food up. It was constant, a culture shock of the highest order. For the last twenty-two years, ever since he'd moved out of his parents' house and lived in various places (with ex-partners and house shares with friends), he'd never had to worry about anything else other than himself.

Nobody had been dependent on him to survive.

But now that had all changed.

And he never felt it more than when he was wandering down the aisles of Aldi with her.

'What do you want for lunch?'

As usual, she was on her phone. Glued to the bastard device. She spent so long on it he was beginning to think that it had somehow become sutured to her hand.

'Dunno,' came the typical response with a typical shrug of the shoulders.

'Brilliant. What about this?' Tomek pointed to a jar of sauerkraut.

She paid it little heed, the content on her phone infinitely more appealing.

'Would you like a hundred pounds?' he said abruptly.

That, rather unsurprisingly, seemed to get her attention. Her face shot up to him and her eyes widened. '*Really?*'

'No. Not really. Now... the sauerkraut. Do you want some of that?'

She scowled at the jar. 'Ew... no. What even *is* that?'

'Delicious goodness,' he told her. 'You're a quarter Polish, so you eat Polish things. You live in a Polish household, so you *enjoy* Polish things.'

The voice of his dad echoed in his head. His old man Perry had said something similar to him many years ago, when Tomek had once protested against eating red cabbage for the tenth day in a row.

Parenting the only way he knew how.

'I want soup,' she said, taking him by surprise.

'Soup?'

'Yes. Do you know what that is? Do you have it in Poland?'

Tomek smirked. 'I think you're going to like Poland,' he said. 'If

we ever get a chance to go. Or even if I take you to see my parents –
your grandparents. They practically live off soup.'

That seemed to shut her up, and engaged her focus in the rest of
the food shop. Even if it was still at only fifty per cent, he would take
it. As they meandered their way through the aisles, she eventually
became helpful and pointed out the things she wanted to eat and
drink, rather than making everything into an argument. That was,
until they came to the toiletry section.

'Do you need anything from here?' Tomek stared blankly at the
wall of toiletries and hair care products. 'Hair gel? Shower gel?'

So much choice. So many unnecessary products. Each replete
with marketing bollocks that made no sense. Things he'd never heard
of, words he was certain had been made up. The worst of it had been
when he'd taken her to Boots so she could refill her make-up bag
(something he didn't entirely agree with for someone her age, but that
was the mother's fault, and another argument for another day). He'd
spent fifteen minutes trying to process the sheer amount of shit that
Kasia had to choose from. The different brands competing for space
when they all did the exact same thing. And when they'd got to the
skincare section, he'd almost had a brain aneurysm. Hyaluronic acid.
Peptide technology. Each purporting to do something else, something
unnecessary. De-stressing, de-ageing. Everything was de-something
nowadays, a total fucking waste of time, and it pained him to see her
falling for it at such a young age.

But again, that was the mother's fault and an argument for
another day. Another argument he knew he'd lose.

'Since when did people need fifteen "beauty blenders"?' he had
asked her. He'd placed the name in air quotes because he couldn't
believe there was a fancy name for what was essentially a soft sponge.

'They all do something different,' she'd replied harshly.

There it was. That *something different* again.

'What exactly? Does this one mean you can blend your left nostril
while you have to use the other one for the right-hand side?'

Kasia had sighed and barged past him, hurrying away from the display. 'You're a man, you'll never understand.'

'I'm trying to, that's why I'm asking the question.'

'No you're not. You're being an arsehole about it.'

That had been the first time she'd sworn at him, something which he hadn't minded calling her out on in the middle of the shop. He received a lot of abuse in his job, he wasn't going to accept it at home either. Since then, she hadn't uttered a word worse than 'crap', and that had been aimed at her homework instead of him.

Now, however, as they stood beside one another, looking at the wall of Aldi skincare, Tomek sensed another incipient argument. He retreated to the wall of toilet roll and closed his mouth.

'Deodorant?' he asked, unable to help himself.

She scowled at him then stormed off to the end of the aisle.

Tomek took that as his cue to follow, without launching any of the niggling comments on the tip of his tongue at her.

At the end of the aisle they joined the back of the queue and then paid for their food shop. On the journey home, the headphones had gone back in, and he was forced to unpack the food alone, while Kasia curled into a ball on the sofa, scrolling on her phone.

TikTok, probably. Or Snapchat. They seemed to be the rage nowadays, and he had no idea about any of them. Not in any sort of intricate detail, anyway. All he knew was that it definitely wasn't a safe place for her to be in. But he wasn't in a position to offer an alternative. Not unless she wanted to start looking at photos of dead bodies and read up on case notes about serial killers and murderers.

Once he'd finished unloading the shopping, he peered his head round the kitchen doorway and found her sitting at the desk by the window sill. She was staring at a piece of paper.

'You all good?' he asked her, somewhat tentatively.

'I... I've got cooking tomorrow.'

'Right. What's that?'

'Where we cook things in class.'

'And someone gets paid to do that, do they?'

She nodded.

'Right. What do you need me to do about it?'

'Well, I need a load of ingredients. Cabbage. Carrots. Onion. Mayonnaise.'

'Jesus. What're you making?'

'Coleslaw, I think.'

Tomek thought of the tub of coleslaw sitting in the fridge. Tried not to get annoyed, though he already sensed what was coming.

'Right...'

'Well I need the ingredients.'

'We don't have them.'

'I need them.'

'Tough,' he said.

'But if we forget the ingredients then Mrs Shaw said she's going to give us a detention.'

'Then perhaps you should have thought about that while we were in the shops. We're not going back. You'll have to explain to Mrs Shaw that you don't have the ingredients and that you will do next time.'

'But...' She tried to protest but the words fell out of her mouth.

Tomek knew that she'd done this on purpose. To get him back for something. Out of spite. To retaliate for whatever he might have said or done in the past few days. Or maybe it was just her way of slowly getting back at him for the thirteen years of her life he'd missed. The ones he hadn't even known. She wanted to make him out to be a bad dad, a shitty father who wasn't prepared to go back to the shops for his own daughter's education.

Not that learning how to cook really constituted an education.

And she was exactly right. He wasn't willing to go back to the shops, not when she'd known about it for a whole week.

Besides, this was his version of parenting. Making it up as he was going along.

Parenting the only way he knew how.

CHAPTER
FOUR

I n the weeks since Tomek had last seen DCI Nick Cleaves, the man had lost what little hair remained on his head, and the sound of his heavy, exasperated breath had deepened. As though he was sighing with every exhalation.

The meeting to discuss his suspension had been in Tomek's calendar for almost a week now, but he'd nearly forgotten. It had completely slipped his mind, thanks to the thoughts of cabbage, carrot, onion and mayonnaise swimming around his head the night before. It wasn't until Kasia had quite politely – and quite surprisingly – asked what his plans were for the day, that he'd remembered.

'Late again,' Nick commented as he opened the door to his office. 'I'd've thought during this holiday of yours you might've actually learnt how to time keep.'

Tomek closed the door behind him, muting the voices of his colleagues on the other side. 'I wouldn't call this a holiday, sir,' he said. 'More like a living nightmare.'

'Things that bad?'

Tomek seated himself opposite the man and placed his hands across his stomach, knitting his fingers together.

'I'm going mental at home,' he started. 'There are only so many times I can dust the window sill and clean the bathroom. I've nearly drowned my bonsai trees because I've been watering them so much. The bastard things are lucky to be alive after what happened to them, and now I'm nearly killing them because I don't know what else to do with myself. I've lost my sense of purpose.'

'Has that focus not shifted onto Kasia?' Nick folded his hands across his larger, bulkier stomach, mimicking Tomek. Nick's had been the result of years' worth of remaining sedentary behind a desk and an unhealthy addiction to sausage rolls, while Tomek's had been a result of the past few weeks. Sometimes he confused boredom with hunger, and found himself gorging on snacks and a cheeky beer in the evening if he was in the mood, which he usually was.

'Kasia's fine,' he replied.

'That isn't what I asked.'

'I know. But Kasia's fine.'

Nick sighed, bringing a smile to Tomek's face. It was one of the things he'd missed the most about his removal from the office: the famous Nasty Nick Sigh, powerful and audible enough for its effects to be felt on the other side of the world. Capable of causing cyclones in the west and moving tectonic plates in the east.

'How have the two of you been... *getting on*?' The hesitation in Nick's voice was apparent. Perhaps the conversation reminded him of his fractious relationship with his son, and his son's later decision to join the armed forces.

'We're getting on as well as can be expected. We're not the best of friends, but—'

'You're not supposed to be friends,' Nick replied. 'You're supposed to be father and daughter. A team.'

Not only did Nick have a son he no longer spoke to, he also had two daughters, both of whom were of similar age to Kasia. A part of

Tomek felt inclined to come clean and confess to the man he respected so much to ask for help and guidance. But the other part of him didn't want to admit he had no idea what he was doing. He didn't want to admit that he was beginning to resent Kasia and everything that she represented: his disastrous relationship with her mum, the upheaval she'd caused in his life, and the uncertain future to come for them both. He didn't want to admit that to his boss. Anyone but his boss.

'We'll get there eventually,' he told Nick, even though he didn't believe his own words.

'Hmm. I'm sure you will. In the meantime, I might be able to fill the black hole in your life that missing out on work has made...'

Tomek's face beamed, and all of a sudden the room seemed to get a shade lighter.

'Two days ago, a young girl was kidnapped outside a school on Canvey,' Nick started. 'A teacher watched her leave the school and then jump into the back of a Ford Fiesta, right outside her own house. At first she didn't think anything of it, but when the girl's mother came over to the school asking where she was, that's when they called it in. It's been forty-eight hours and she still hasn't turned up.'

Tomek nodded, his focus absorbed by Nick's words and the excitement bubbling away in him. The excitement that something terrible had happened to someone and he could don his superhero leotard and save the day.

'We have since managed to find the car she was abducted in,' Nick continued. 'It was dumped in a farm up in the Maldon area – Latchingdon, to be precise. The car's registered to a Bradley Baxter, though it appears to have been stolen. Mr Baxter reported the car missing the same day.'

'And I'm assuming there was no trace of the girl?' Tomek asked. As he'd been listening, his mind had conjured images of the little girl getting into the car and driving to the middle of nowhere. Then being taken out and... well, he didn't want his imagination to run away just yet.

'Yes, and no,' Nick replied. 'We found Mr Baxter's DNA in the car, as was to be expected. We also found the little girl's. We also found Baxter's girlfriend's DNA... and then there was one more, connected to a young woman. Turns out Mr Baxter had been having an affair with the young woman and his place of choice was the backseat of his car.'

Tomek sniggered. 'Who said romance was dead?'

'I think that tells you more about the youth of today,' Nick replied. 'Back in my day the cars weren't comfortable enough for that sort of thing.'

'I didn't think they had cars back in your day?'

Nick shot Tomek a look of contempt.

'So there was no trace of the kidnapper?' Tomek asked.

Nick shook his head. 'It was as though she'd got in the car herself and driven all that way alone.'

'What's her name?'

'Annabelle Lake.' Nick reached across to the other side of his desk and handed Tomek a thick file. Even though the case was only a couple of days old, the team had already gathered a wealth of information. 'Witness statements of parents and passers-by who were outside the school at the time she was abducted. Her parents, extended family. The DNA reports we've got done already. It's all in there.'

Tomek took the document from Nick carefully, almost ceremoniously, as though doing so jarringly might cause the folder to burst into flames at any moment.

'Does this mean I'm coming back?' Tomek asked, unable to keep the excitement out of his voice.

'Not yet.'

And then it came crashing back down again.

'Oh.'

'I'm only sharing this with you because we could really use your help. Just for you to have a read through, familiarise yourself with the notes.'

'Why me?'

'Because you're good with this kind of thing, given what happened last time. Saving children is your thing.'

Tomek tilted his head to the side and smirked facetiously. 'You're making me out to be some sort of child whisperer...'

'No, you're right,' Nick began. 'You didn't even need to say anything and Kasia landed on your doorstep.'

The mood in the room instantly collapsed. Tomek held his breath as he suppressed the anger that had just spiked in his blood.

'I... I'm sorry, mate. That was out of order.'

Tomek said nothing. Better to let him wallow in his own grief.

'What's happening about my suspension?' Tomek asked quickly. He didn't want to be in the room much longer.

'The IOPC are still deliberating. The only thing it's riding on is your word against Katie's.'

'I know all this. I thought you were going to have something more useful for me.'

Nick tilted forward in his chair and rested his elbows against the desk, the light reflecting off his bald head. 'Though I think there's an *unofficial* way that you can expedite the process and swing it in your favour... And I think you know what it is.'

That was going to take some doing. The Independent Office for Police Complaints, the independent body that investigated wrongdoing by serving police officers, was currently deciding between two things: the first involved a fake Instagram account that had been set up in his name and been used to send sexually explicit images of himself to an underage girl, while the second was whether Detective Inspector Tony Hunt had been dead by the time Tomek had found him, or if he'd let the man die in order to pursue the criminal. The criminal in question was Charlotte Hanton, or Katie Norton-Downs as he'd known her, the woman Tomek had let into his life and into his home.

The only one who could stop the investigation and swing it in his favour.

'I'll think about it,' he told Nick.

'Good man. Just swallow your pride and do what you need to. Then you'll be back in no time.'

CHAPTER
FIVE

A fter being told that he would need to confront the woman responsible for putting his career in jeopardy, Tomek felt the need for a drink. And so, on the way out of Nick's office, he had rounded up the troops and told them to meet him at the pub round the corner from the station.

The Last Post had been a regular haunt for Tomek during the early years of his career, and had been the last place one of his friends had visited before being murdered. But despite the negative emotions attached to it, he still found himself there in the evenings after a long and gruelling shift. Sometimes they'd find it completely empty, all the students and youngsters having moved on to the nightclubs, or they'd find themselves immersed in the excitement of it all. Surrounded by hundreds of drunk and loud teenagers, handling their alcohol badly and trying their best to flirt with as many members of the opposite sex as possible.

Tonight, however, was a school night, and all the kids with the fake IDs were tucked up in bed.

Tomek was nursing his second pint as the doors opened. In stepped DS Sean Campbell, Tomek's closest friend, DC Rachel

Hamilton, the team's latest recruit, and DC Nadia Chakrabarti, the woman he considered to be his office mum, despite her being a few years younger than him. Tonight they were dressed almost casually, in jeans and shirts, with the obvious exception of five months pregnant Nadia, who wore a dress above her baby bump. It was good to see them again, outside the office. Even though it had only been a few weeks, it had felt like several years. Several years away from his extended family.

Once they'd seated themselves in a booth, tucked away from the rest of the middle-aged men in that corner of the pub, Sean offered to get the next round in.

'You want a third?' Sean asked Tomek.

'Please.'

Nadia pointed to the half-drunk glass he was holding in his hands protectively. 'Been a tough day, has it?'

Tomek rolled his eyes. 'Like you wouldn't believe.'

'What did Nasty Nick have to say for himself?'

'You know Nick. He breathes more than he says anything. But on this occasion he was surprisingly talkative. He told me about Annabelle Lake, shared the case files with me...'

'Poor girl,' Rachel said, staring into the beer stains on the table. Her hair fell nicely off her shoulders and she had a new addition to her face: a pair of leopard-print glasses. 'I can't imagine what she's going through.'

'Have you had any word from the kidnappers at all?' Tomek asked. 'They made a ransom demand of some sort?'

Both women shook their heads. Then Rachel removed the glasses and tucked them into a small carry case. It was her very own version of letting her hair down. And good timing too, because a moment later Sean returned with the drinks. Another pint of Peroni for Tomek, a pint of Guinness for Sean and Rachel each, and a pint of Coke for Nadia.

'Are you the designated driver tonight?' Tomek asked her.

'For the next year and a bit, yeah. But don't think that means you can invite me every time just so you can have a lift home,' Nadia replied, and placed a hand on her bump.

'I'll bear that in mind.' He reached over and placed a hand on her stomach. It felt firm and strange to the touch, like a giant boil growing inside her. 'How's everything going?'

'Good,' she replied. 'Had an ultrasound the other day. Everything's perfect, everything's healthy.'

Just as he was about to respond, he felt something prod his hand. At the sudden realisation it was Nadia's baby kicking him, he pulled his hand away and screamed. 'It kicked!'

'No, no, no – not *it*. She... *she* kicked.'

'You're having a girl?'

Nadia nodded. 'Now I can come to you for advice when she's the same age as Kasia.'

There it was. Kasia. He wondered how long it would take for the conversation to move on to her. Record time. It was the only thing anyone ever seemed to want to talk about with him now. Nothing to do with Charlotte, nothing to do with Tony, nothing to do with the sleepless nights, nothing to do with the images he saw in his head every time he closed his eyes of his friend dangling there, bleeding to death, half naked, suspended from a rope. Nothing to do with the deterioration of his mental health. Nothing to do with his increased dependency on alcohol to help him deal with it.

Nothing like that at all.

Just Kasia.

All about Kasia.

'Come on then,' he began, accepting defeat. 'Let's get it over with.'

'Get what over with?' Rachel asked. The light overhead caught her brown eyes and made her long auburn hair glisten. It was either the alcohol talking, or his genuine feelings, but he suddenly thought she was quite attractive.

'Me and Kasia. Kasia and me. Get all your questions out of the way.'

A hush fell on the table as they considered the appropriate thing to say. In one clean gulp he finished off his second pint and turned his attention to the next one Sean had just bought him.

'This is your only chance,' he said, fighting down the burp.

That was enough to inspire them. Sean went first, and asked the obvious question.

'What's it been like living with her?'

'Shit,' came Tomek's response. 'The flat's not big enough for the both of us. I've had to spend the past four weeks sleeping on the sofa while she's living the life of luxury in my bed. Her stuff is *everywhere*, and my share of the wardrobe has been reduced to what I can fit on a single hanger. Her school books are all over the dining room table and my desk. I can't fart when I want to, I can't even eat my peanuts anymore because she's extremely allergic and just the sight of them sets her off. I can't watch what I want on TV because she's always got something she wants to watch – even if she's not watching it and is just glued to her phone instead. And that's another thing – she doesn't talk; she just spends most of her time scrolling on her phone. I don't think it'll be long before her eyes start to turn square. She won't tell me how her day was at school. She doesn't communicate with me. And we argue a lot. It's like when you first move in with your girlfriend. It's a *real* eye-opener.'

Tomek took another sip of his drink, longer this time, to calm himself down. He was glad to get that off his chest, felt like a weight had been lifted. They were all things he'd felt from the day she'd first moved in. Yet he'd been unable to express them to anyone. And he felt like he could trust these three, more so than Nick, or his parents, or anyone else he knew.

Sean placed his palm on the table, gesturing that he wanted to speak first. 'This may sound like a stupid question, but she definitely is yours, isn't she?'

As though she was an item of his possession.

'Yes,' he replied bluntly.

Shortly after she'd turned up unannounced at his doorstep, Tomek had felt compelled to validate his paternity with a DNA test. He'd found one online, taken the samples at home, and then sent them off for examination. Within twenty-four hours, he was ninety quid lighter, and an unknown daughter heavier. He didn't think the two cancelled each other out.

'Who's the mum?' Rachel asked.

Tomek hadn't wanted to get into that, but then he remembered that he had promised they could ask all the questions they wanted.

'Anika Coleman.' He took another gulp of the drink to help summon the courage to continue. 'We'd gone to school together and things just sort of went from there. She was one of the cool kids back then, had kids throwing themselves at her feet, and I eventually managed to end up with her. But it was the worst six months of my life. She treated me like shit, cheated on me with some random bloke, and then her uncle ended up killing two of my mates.'

'Wow...' came the muted response from Rachel.

'Oh, and then he also knocked me unconscious and dangled me over a railway bridge,' he added as though it was an afterthought, a minor detail to be added at the end. 'Fortunately I managed to escape from that little ordeal with nothing but a scratch, but I've not heard or seen anything about her uncle since. By the time I got back to the flat we were sharing at the time, Anika was nowhere to be seen, so I grabbed my stuff and got out of there. I hadn't spoken to her in thirteen years... until recently. Turns out she's in prison now for drugs charges and there was no one else for Kasia to go to.'

A stunned silence settled on the table. Tomek filled it with the sounds of sipping from his drink and setting the glass down a little heavier than he would have liked.

'I...' Nadia began. 'I don't know what to say, Tomek.'

'Not much you can really.'

'I'm stunned...'

'How do you think *I* feel?'

'No, not about that. I'm stunned by what you said before. How can you say those things about Kasia? She didn't ask to be in this situation. And yes, yes, I know you didn't either. But you're both in it now, so you need to shut up and get on with it. You know I love you and everything, but from what you've just said it sounds to me like you need to grow up and you need to grow up fast. This is a lot worse for her than it is you. You're an adult, you can process things, you can deal with them better than she can. She's just a child.'

Tomek couldn't bring himself to look her in the eye. Like a spoilt child that had received his first ever telling off. He couldn't bring himself to look any of them in the eye, in fact.

'Right now she's probably frightened and afraid. She doesn't have her mum anymore, and now she's been lumbered with you. Her dad. Whether you like that title or not. And right now you have to step up and sort your shit out. No one's asking you to be the best dad in the world – and she doesn't even know what that is, so her expectations aren't going to be too high. All you've got to do is be the dad she needs, not the dad she wants. And then I think you'll get along just fine.'

Tomek cowered into his seat slightly. It was only a small movement, but everyone else at the table picked up on it. He knew, deep down, that what she'd said was right. More than right, in fact. It was what he'd needed to hear. Now all he had to do was heed her advice and put it into practice.

Which would be easier said than done.

'I hate to say it, Nads,' he said. 'But if you're that hard on your kid, then I hate to think how successful it's going to be when it grows up.'

'*She*!' she screamed in his face, slamming her hand on the table. 'When *she* grows up!'

CHAPTER
SIX

I t had taken Tomek a little over a day to come to a decision. And then it had taken a further two days to get his appointment approved. In the meantime, Nick and the team were no closer to finding little Annabelle Lake and were beginning to feel like they'd exhausted all their options. Options which Tomek wasn't inclined to focus on. At least, not right now.

Not when he had a name to clear.

The alarm buzzed inside its cage overhead, alerting him that it was time to enter.

Visiting hours at HMP Send, in Woking, the maximum security prison in the heart of Surrey.

The door at the other end of the waiting room opened and Tomek, along with the rest of the visitors, shuffled through the door tentatively, a hint of trepidation and anxiety lacing the air, as though they were the ones that were about to be incarcerated.

Tomek ducked below the door and then scanned the visiting room. Charlotte Hanton, or Katie Norton-Downs as he'd once known her, had at one point been the love of his life. She'd stumbled into it by mistake, stayed there, made him fall in love with her, and then left, ripping his heart out as she went. Except it hadn't been a mistake at all. Rather, a clever and manipulative ploy for her to stay close to the triple murder investigation he had been working.

He spotted her. Sitting with her back to him, brown hair flowing down to the middle of her back, covering the grey tracksuit jumper she was forced to wear.

He made his way over to her.

As soon as he saw her face, he tried to suppress the soup of emotions he felt bubbling inside him. The anger, the resentment, the betrayal, the hurt, the pain. The residual love and affection that still remained somewhere in the pit of his stomach, even though he knew it shouldn't. Despite everything she'd done to him, he still felt sorry for her. The love of his life was sitting in prison. That wasn't how it was supposed to be. They were supposed to have stayed together, maybe even got married.

But their trajectories had gone in completely different directions.

'Tomek...' she said, her voice a tantalising whisper. She smiled at him, baring her teeth.

That smile. He couldn't. He'd always fallen for *that* smile...

'Hi, Charlotte,' he said, trying to sound as cold as he possibly could. 'You look well.'

'Thank you,' she replied, surveying her tracksuit as though making sure she was seeing the same outfit as him. 'That means a lot to me. I appreciate that. Especially coming from you.' She placed a hand on the table that separated them, palm facing up.

Tomek didn't dare look at it. Because if he did he knew the desire to touch it and envelope his fingers in hers would be too strong.

After a short while she got the hint and pulled her palm away a little.

'How have you been keeping?' she asked.

Tomek paused a moment, balancing on the decision to bring up the topic of Kasia in conversation.

'Bored,' he replied.

'I hear they suspended you?'

Tomek nodded.

'That must be driving you crazy. You were always so obsessed with your work.'

'And for good reason.'

'I also hear you've had a little surprise land on your doorstep.'

Tomek's heart faltered a moment. He held his breath. Contemplated...

How did she know? How could she have known?

'How...?'

'I hope you won't mind the intrusion,' she said, lowering her voice a fraction. 'But some of the women in here did me a favour. I wanted to see if you were okay. Fortunately they've got people on the outside who owe them a few favours, so they called them in. It's all very cyclical in this world.'

A dozen thoughts raced through his mind. He tried to think of anything suspicious he'd seen outside the house, somewhere along the street. The same face twice. The same car that had been sitting there for a few days. The same car that had no purpose being there.

He drew a blank on all accounts.

'You've been following me?'

'Only once or twice!' she said, as though that made it any better. 'I just needed to know you were coping.'

'I haven't had time to process it,' he lied. The evenings where he'd lain awake could testify to that.

'I'm not surprised.' The smile returned to her face, and she brushed a thick strand of hair behind her ear. 'You'll have to tell me all about her. I want to know her name, what she's interested in. You never told me you had a daughter.'

'*You* never told me you had a daughter,' Tomek replied, the venom in his voice starting to come through.

As he sat there he was becoming increasingly uncomfortable. One of the women in the room with him had sent someone to his house.

They'd seen him, they'd spied on him, maybe even listened to his conversations. They'd broken through his bubble of privacy and burst his safety. Not only that, they'd burst through Kasia's safety. There was no knowing what sort of deranged and insidious things Charlotte might have planned for them both. Christ knew she was capable of it.

'I don't want you or anyone else you know anywhere near my flat, or anywhere near my daughter,' he hissed. 'Do you understand? That's a big fucking no-no. And I will not tolerate it.'

Charlotte's pupils dilated, and her head tilted to one side. In that moment, she looked a few years younger – and a lot more attractive. 'Tomek, baby. I would never. I told you all along, I never wanted to hurt you. Only to teach you. Only to change you... And it worked, didn't it?'

Tomek dropped his gaze into his lap. That was a question he'd confronted himself with several times over, in the dead of night, staring up at the curtains that glowed a deep shade of orange as the light from outside tried to burst through them. She *had* changed him, yes. She had made him see how paedophiles and rapists were sick people, people who couldn't be helped, no matter how much help and advice they received. She had made him see that his colleague, whom she'd believed to be a part of the same evil group, had suffered from the same illness. She had made him change his beliefs so that he would leave the man there to die, to suffer the retribution he thought he deserved.

Tomek closed his eyes.

But he hadn't deserved it. Not at all. Tony hadn't been a paedophile or a rapist. He was the opposite. A hard-working and dedicated detective inspector who'd put himself in the difficult position of pretending to be a monster. He'd used himself as bait to lure the killer in. And he'd been the one to pay the price.

And so had Tomek.

He'd let someone die.

His own friend, his own colleague. And that decision would stay with him for the rest of his life.

He looked up at Charlotte, met her stare.

'You made me see a lot of things,' he replied.

'And that was all I wanted. I just wanted you to... *change*. Not everyone is capable of it, but you were. I knew you had it in you.'

'I still don't want you anywhere near me or my daughter.'

A light glistened in Charlotte's eyes. 'You'll have to tell me all about her. I want to know everything.'

'There's nothing you need to know,' he replied, rapidly becoming angry. The topic of conversation wasn't moving along, and he didn't like it. 'What about *your* daughter, eh? What about little *Caitlin*?'

At the mention of her daughter's name, Charlotte tensed and her demeanour dropped. She lowered her shoulders and turned her attention to the rest of the room, unable to meet his eye.

'We haven't spoken since I've been in here. They won't let me.'

'Do you know where she is?'

'Social services. A foster home somewhere.'

Tomek nodded thoughtfully. Though he held no sentimental feelings towards the girl, he still couldn't imagine what it must have been like for her. A life with no father. A life with two mothers who'd turned out to be murderers. And now a lifetime of loneliness and sadness.

'Why have you come today, Tomek?' Charlotte asked, folding her arms across her chest. The question took him by surprise. 'You've not come to see me, that's for certain. Not with the investigation still ongoing. I'm sure you've risked a lot to be here... so why are you?'

'To see if I can convince you to retract your evidence and your statement.' He switched on his professional hat and shut all emotion and sentiment out of his mind. It was time to talk business. 'My career is fucked, thanks to you. And I need you to make it right again. You owe me.'

Charlotte pondered this a moment. She kept her gaze fixed on his, their eyes locked in an invisible and unspoken battle. Tomek didn't falter, didn't break.

'What do you need from me?' she murmured.

'I need you to retract everything you've said, all the evidence you've put forward against me. I need you to tell them I never sent those messages, I never messaged that schoolgirl. And I need you to tell them that Tony was already dead by the time I got there. It's your word against mine, and so far yours is winning.'

Charlotte continued to ponder this, and this time he could see the cogs in her brain processing the decision, as her face became glazed over in thought.

'What do I get in return?'

Tomek rolled his eyes. 'For fuck's sake, Charlotte. There's nothing you can win here, nothing you can gain. You're stuck here. You're never getting out of this place. So what do you have to lose? If you still cared about me... you'd do this.'

The casual attempt at blackmail didn't go unnoticed.

'I want something in return.'

The sigh left Tomek's nostrils before he had a chance to stop it. 'What? *What* is it you want in return?'

'A message. I want you to pass on a message.'

Tomek froze as he listened, already aware of where this was headed.

'Caitlin,' she said. 'I need you to speak with my little girl. You're a dad now, you can imagine what it must be like for me to be without her. She's my baby, she's all I think about. I need to know that she's okay, and I need her to know that I love her. That I will always love her.'

'That's it?'

She nodded.

'So you're telling me all I have to do is find your daughter, tell her that you love her, and then you'll retract your statements?'

'Yes.'

It seemed too good to be true. But he wasn't in a position to barter with her. Considering the task was so minor, he couldn't see a problem with it.

But why did a part of him still feel like he was making a deal with the devil?

'If you do that for me, then I will tell them everything you ask me to. Before you know it, you'll be back at work, catching the bad guys again.'

Yeah, Tomek thought, fighting the smile from breaking onto his face. *Catching people like you.*

CHAPTER
SEVEN

The concept of good and bad had always confused Tomek. The line between right and wrong had been frequently blurred over the years as his perception of it had changed, not least since his decision to leave Tony dying in the middle of a small boathouse.

Did that make him a bad guy? Or did it make him the good guy because he was the one catching the bad guys? Like Charlotte Hanton and Sophia Wainwright, Charlotte's accomplice. They had both been raped by the same man and subsequently killed him. They had exacted revenge on the man who had destroyed their lives, and then the men who had ruined several others. They had done bad things, but only to other bad people who'd deserved it. Did that make them good? Had their acts of revenge been a service to the general public? Had they *done* good?

And then there was the topic of Caitlin, Charlotte's daughter. She'd been used as bait to lure paedophiles into her parents' trap. Did that make her one of the good guys, or one of the bad guys? For a seven-year-old, that was a massive burden to bear.

Her life would never be the same. Both women in her life, both purporting to be her mummies, were in prison, awaiting sentence at the end of their trial. She would, in all likelihood, never see them again.

Would she grow up to be a bad guy or a good guy?

As the product of a violent rape, and after the sorts of things she'd seen and encountered in her short life, it was difficult to think of her leading anything other than a life of violence, anti-sociable behaviour, potentially resulting in a career of crime. Following in her parents' footsteps.

It was the sort of thing criminal profilers and forensic psychologists studied for years, wrote books about, and earned their living from.

And yet, as he looked at her from across the room, playing with a toy dinosaur on the table, he couldn't sense any of that about her. She was sociable, allowing the other children around her to play, and she was talkative, friendly.

Either she would grow up to be a normal kid, or she'd already mastered the act of deceit and mental manipulation from the women who had raised her.

'She's had a tough couple of weeks,' a voice said beside him. It was the owner of the foster home. Mother Hen, she'd called herself when she'd been introduced to him.

Tomek didn't plan on calling her that, and had instead decided to go with her real name, Hannah.

Hannah was in her late forties and had explained to him that she'd never been able to have children of her own so had chosen to dedicate her life to those who didn't have parents. She felt an affinity to them, she'd said. As though they were the yin to her yang. The key to her lock.

'She's had a tough couple of years, in fact,' Hannah added as an afterthought.

'How's she been settling in?' Tomek asked. He felt compelled to make conversation, when in reality he just wanted to get in and get out again. He didn't want to outstay his welcome; Caitlin served as a constant reminder of Charlotte, of their relationship, and the less time he spent around her, the better.

But first came the inane small talk.

'Difficult at first,' Hannah began, shifting her weight from one foot to the other. 'She was very shy, timid. It took a while for her to come out of her bubble, but she's a tough little thing, is our Caitlin.'

'Hmm. That's good to hear.'

'Would you like to speak with her?'

He didn't have a choice. If he wanted his career, the one sense of stability he had in his life, to get back on track, he was going to have to.

'Has she had any visitors?' Tomek asked as they made their way over to her.

'Not since she's been here, no. Only social workers and people like yourself.'

'Any contact with her parents?'

'They've tried but we've blocked all communication. Letters, post, that type of thing. We don't think it's right that she has any interaction with them at the moment, not while she's getting settled.'

Oops. Tomek was about to burst their little bubble of safety and privacy. And they didn't even know it. Was it selfish? Possibly. Would it stop him? Well, he was here now.

There was that topic of good and bad guys again.

They came to a stop beside Caitlin, standing either side of her shoulders. If she noticed their presence, she made no effort to show it and instead continued to play with her dinosaur.

'Caitlin, sweetheart,' Hannah said as she crouched to the young girl's level. 'Someone's here to see you. He says you might recognise him.'

Caitlin kept her attention focused on the toy, lost inside her own imagination.

Tomek crouched down on her other side, ignoring the cracks in his knees and the pain in his hips. His lack of mobility in the past few weeks were ageing him faster than the job. And he seriously needed to get back out there and go for a run. Indecision and a hint of depression had crept in and prohibited him from feeling the sensation of the salty wind and sand battering his body as he jogged along the seafront. It was well overdue.

'Hi, Caitlin,' he started, a catch in his throat. 'My name's Tomek. Do you remember me?'

It was a long moment before she acknowledged him. She carefully set the dinosaur down on the coffee table and turned to face him. The look of recognition wasn't the only thing he noticed in her eyes. It was the darkness, the hollowness, the black hole that appeared to suck in and devour all emotion.

'Yes,' she said, her voice cold and callous. 'I remember you.'

Bad guy. Definitely a bad guy.

Or in her case, bad girl.

'Good. I'll leave you two to it then,' Hannah said, and wandered away. Except she only made it as far as the doorframe and monitored their conversation from there.

Tomek placed a hand on his knee to ease the burden of his weight on his joints.

'Caitlin,' he began, unsure how to continue. 'I've got something to tell you. I've spoken with your mummy. And there's something she wants you to know...'

CHAPTER
EIGHT

For the third time in thirty seconds, Kasia checked the time on her phone. It was 7:15 p.m., and the last of the meetings was taking place. And there was still no sign of Tomek.

Or father, as he called himself.

She still didn't think that they were at the Dad stage yet. She didn't feel comfortable enough. So far he'd behaved as though he'd had no choice but to look after her, as though she were a burden he regretted and lamented every day. So far he'd done nothing or given her any signs to suggest that he wanted to look after her, care for her.

And he was proving it right now.

Over two hours late to parents' evening. The evening where he would sit down with her form tutor and hear about how badly things had been going. Because they had been going badly, really badly. How couldn't they? She didn't know anyone at the school. She didn't like being there. In fact, she hated it.

More than she hated Tomek and her mum.

The only positive that had come out of going to school – and the part of it that had kept her in classes, rather than bunking and skipping out of the building before and after lunchtimes – had been

Sylvia, her only friend. They were in the same tutor group, and Sylvia had been one of the few people who'd taken the time to speak with her. Since then they'd become close friends. They were in most classes together, including science, English, geography, history and physical education. The only lesson they were forced to spend apart was maths, her least favourite subject. Sylvia made her lessons more enjoyable, as they sat there in the back of the room, doodling on the pages, asking stupid questions, pretending to not know the answers to things, giving the teachers attitude when they gave it to her.

She felt like they were all out to get her, all out to make her life hell. It was the same with Tomek. Why couldn't he have just taken her back to the shops to buy the ingredients she needed? Why couldn't he have been on time? It wasn't like he had anywhere else to be, or anything else to do...

A noise came from the classroom door. Janie Stephens, one of the most popular girls in school, stormed out of the room, followed closely by her dad who called after her. She didn't know how Janie looked immaculate every day, but she envied the way she was able to apply her make-up. The way she was able to make herself look attractive and have all the boys falling at her feet. She ruled the school and she knew it. And everyone else knew it too.

Kasia seriously envied her.

Then Miss Holloway came out of the room, looking grumpy like she always did. Tonight she was dressed in that pretty green dress of hers that flowed around her ankles. Kasia thought Miss Holloway was pretty, maybe even prettier than Janie. But she was also a bitch. With the telling off, the constant moaning. Just like Tomek, she made life at school difficult and miserable.

'Any sign of your dad yet, Kasia?' Miss Holloway asked.

Kasia pulled the earphone out and scowled at her teacher. 'He's not my dad.'

'Sorry,' she replied defensively. 'Tomek, then. Any sign of Tomek?'

The way she said it made him sound like he was her older brother, which was far worse.

'I don't know where he is.'

'I'm sure he'll be here soon.'

Miss Holloway checked her watch, sighed.

'You can go if you want, miss. He probably won't even show up.'

Miss Holloway folded her arms across her chest. 'I don't usually wait beyond half-seven, but I'm willing to make an exception in this instance.'

Oh good. More waiting. The last thing she wanted.

Kasia grunted and returned her attention to her phone. She'd been scrolling through TikTok for hours, losing herself in the videos of cats, dogs, reality TV shows and dance videos.

She'd tried to make some herself, when Tomek wasn't home (when he was doing whatever it was he was doing), but they hadn't gained any traction. The most views she'd had on a video had been fifty. And she was sure it was some of the girls at school sharing it round, laughing at her, mocking her.

The song on her Spotify changed, and she was now listening to Harry Styles. She loved him, had listened to him for years. In her old bedroom she'd had posters of him on the wall, but now they'd all been taken down and put in the bin. She hadn't been allowed to bring that much stuff over with her, and the stuff she did have wasn't allowed to go on the walls or anywhere because there was no room for it. The room that she'd been staying in – Tomek's bedroom – didn't feel like a room at all. Rather, a hotel that she was being forced to stay in.

The worst hotel ever.

As she listened to "Watermelon Sugar", she closed her eyes and wished that she could go back in time. Back to the good old days. With her mum, the school she liked, her friends.

CHAPTER
NINE

Tomek skidded the car into the school car park and parked sideways in the spot. He was running late. Very late. How long, he didn't know. But no doubt Kasia would insist on reminding him afterwards. The drive to and from the foster home in Kent had taken a little over two hours, and the traffic had been a nightmare on the return leg at the Dartford Tunnel. Rush hour, the worst possible time to do anything important.

He skipped up the steps to the school, headed down the corridors and made his way towards Kasia's classroom. He'd been there once before, after she'd first joined the school, and mercifully it hadn't been too far from the entrance, otherwise his sense of direction would have given up on him and he'd have spent another twenty minutes trying to find it.

Eventually he found Kasia lounging on a chair, headphones plugged into her ears, phone in hand. She looked a scruff. Top button undone, tie as small as her expectations of him, skirt halfway up her legs. Every morning he made sure she left the house looking presentable, respectable, but it was clear to see that changed the moment she stepped outside.

'Kasia,' he said, trying to hide the breathlessness in his voice. 'Sorry I'm late.'

At that moment, her teacher appeared from the classroom. Miss Holloway. Tomek remembered her from the induction. She was in her mid- to late thirties, always dressed immaculately, with her hair tied in a bun, a delicate layer of make-up applied on her face, and looked as though she still enjoyed her job, not something that could be said for some of the other teachers he'd met in the past few weeks. Tomek thought she was a good role model for his daughter. If only she noticed.

'Mr Bowen,' Miss Holloway said. She approached him with her hand outstretched. Tomek took it and looked into her eyes. 'Pleasure to meet you again.'

'And you. Sorry I'm late.'

Miss Holloway checked her watch. 'Just in time. I gave you until seven thirty, and you've got a few minutes to spare.'

Tomek's cheeks flushed with embarrassment. He hadn't realised he was *that* late.

'Sorry to keep you waiting, Miss Holloway,' he said, though he knew the damage had already been done.

'It's fine. You're here now. And please, call me Bridget.'

Bridget. He liked that name.

Before entering the classroom, Tomek flagged Kasia's attention with a wave of his arm and gestured for her to follow. Reluctantly, and with the normal attitude of a teenager, she stormed into the room, disregarding him as she entered. No warm welcome, no pleasant greeting. Just the muted stare of disappointment.

Tomek didn't know what to expect for his first parents' evening. It was uncharted territory for them both, and yet he felt a smattering of excitement; perhaps now he might finally find out how she'd been getting on at school.

'The way this usually works, Mr Bowen—'

'Tomek, please.'

'The way this works, Tomek, is I'll give you a brief rundown of how Kasia's been settling in, then we'll discuss her classes and any feedback from her teachers, and then we'll have a chance to hear back from Kasia and yourself if you have any questions. All make sense?'

Tomek nodded, bracing himself. He turned to face Kasia, who was sitting there with one headphone in still. He reached across and yanked it out of her ear.

'*Listen...*' he told her. 'This is important.'

Bridget offered an awkward smile before continuing. Right off the bat Tomek sensed this wasn't going to be as positive as he'd hoped.

'Firstly, I'd like to start by saying that Kasia is a considerate girl with a considerable amount of potential. I just wish she'd apply herself better. Unfortunately her attendance has been a cause for concern – her report card says that she's been late for ten lessons and has missed at least five of them in the past four weeks. That's considerably higher than a lot of other students. Most achieve those sorts of numbers in a whole school year, not in a month.'

'You make it sound like a good thing,' Tomek remarked.

'Trust me. It's not.' She turned to Kasia, whose attention had wandered onto something on the wall. 'It's a serious issue and one that I hope we can work together to improve.'

Tomek's knuckles whitened as he clenched his fists. 'Believe me, we'll work on it all right.' Then he turned to face her, unable to hold it in. 'Five lessons. *Five*? I can go to prison for that.'

'Not the only thing then, is it?' Kasia said, still looking into the wall.

Tomek was grateful Bridget was in the room with them, and judging from the look on her face, so was Kasia; he couldn't shout at her if he had a witness.

'It's a work thing,' he explained to Bridget, feeling the need to justify himself. 'Ongoing. Nothing to worry about. You were saying...'

'Oh. Yes. Attendance. It's not the end of the world, and I think it's something we can work on. If I'm being honest, I can understand why it's the way it is. I came to a new school during the term time, and right around your age, Kasia, as well, so I know what it's like. It's a bit daunting and there's an adjustment period you need to get through. But you'll get there soon enough.' She turned over the document in her hand. On it was a table of subjects, scores out of ten, and written feedback from her various teachers. 'Her strongest subjects are English and science, which is strange because we don't typically see students enjoying those two together, but we're not complaining. The area we seem to be struggling in, however is, maths. At the moment she's on track to get a three at GCSE.'

'A three... What's that?'

'Our new system. It's numbered from one to nine, with nine being the highest – obviously.'

'What's the equivalent to what it used to be back in my day?'

'The equivalent is a D at GCSE.'

'Right. And why did they decide to change it?'

Bridget shrugged. 'You're asking the wrong person. Someone probably smoked something they shouldn't have and thought it was a brilliant idea. Anyway... Maths. The score's a little disconcerting, as I teach Kasia in maths, but it's not a massive cause for concern – I can certainly see a lot of promise in there, and I think with a little bit of guidance we can easily get that up to at least a five or maybe even a six.'

Tomek made a note of Bridget's use of the term "we". As though she actually cared about Kasia's progress. As though she *really* wanted to help. But the cynic in him questioned why she would care about Kasia in particular when she had thirty other kids to care about and hundreds more that she taught every day? It was the same with his cases at work. The victims of crime probably felt the same way when he told them that he would do everything he could to help them. But the truth was he was too stretched, spread too thin. And that it was almost impossible to promise fast turnarounds. So would she be any different? Sadly, he began to think that it was all too good to be true.

'Is there anything you'd like to say about that?' Bridget asked Kasia. 'Is there a reason you don't like maths?'

Kasia chose not to respond.

'Is it because Sylvia's not in the class? I've noticed you two together at lunchtimes and in the classrooms. But she's not in our maths class, is she?'

Sylvia. *Sylvia, Sylvia, Sylvia.* Tomek ran the name through his head several times, attempting to recall if he'd heard it anywhere, if she'd mentioned it at all. The answer was a resounding no. He couldn't recall it at all.

'Is there a way that we can get them in the same classroom?' Tomek asked, and Kasia's head tilted a fraction towards the conversation.

Progress. Moving in the right direction. Proving to her that he cared.

'It's something I'll have to look into, but I'll do my best.'

Tomek offered her a warm smile by way of saying thank you.

'Aside from those three, Kasia seems to be performing really well in history and food tech.'

'Food tech,' Tomek said. 'With Mrs Shaw?'

'That's the one.'

'Interesting. Really interesting.' Tomek cast a quick sideways glance towards his daughter. Her cheeks had reddened and her gaze had fallen onto the table. The words "please don't look at me like that" were written across her forehead.

'Do you have a favourite subject, Kasia?' Bridget asked.

'History. I like learning about the Romans.'

'Very good. History was always my favourite subject as well. That and maths.' The effort to jerk a response from Kasia was commendable, if not a little misguided.

'Any subjects she's not doing well in?' Tomek asked.

Bridget consulted the sheet. 'Art, Geography and music.'

'Most of those are just colouring in though, aren't they?'

'Erm...'

'From what I remember geography was just painting by numbers. Art is, well... art. And music is the only exception.' He nudged Kasia on the arm with his elbow. 'At least I won't have to bank on you making it as a musician who draws with their feet while playing the piano.'

Much to his surprise, that little comment elicited a response. It was *little* in kind, but the ramifications it meant for their relationship were huge.

More progress. More moving in the right direction.

'I'm not too worried about those grades,' Tomek said. 'Mostly the important ones.'

The same ones his parents had been hard on him to learn. And then a thought occurred to him.

'What about languages?'

'Kasia's studying French.'

'Any Polish?'

'It's not on the curriculum.'

'*Kurwa mać,*' he replied.

It didn't take them long to work out what he'd said.

'Why isn't on there?' he asked.

'You'll have to ask the government.'

Tomek tutted. 'I guess I'll have to find you a tutor,' he said to Kasia. 'If that's something you'd like to learn?'

He had to remember that it wasn't about him. It was about her. Her choices, her decisions. He'd had the luxury of being born in Poland, and had learnt English at such a young age that he'd soaked it up with ease, like a sponge. Kasia didn't have those same luxuries, and while she might not be willing to entertain him as her father, she might be willing to entertain a part of her heritage.

'I'll think about it,' she replied.

It wasn't a yes, but more importantly, it wasn't a no.

'Is there anything you'd like to tell us?' Tomek asked, checking his watch. 'I'm conscious of the time and the fact I've kept you so late. So if you'd like us to go, then we'll be more than happy to. Kasia and I have got some colouring in to do. Tonight we're going to work on making sure we can keep it between the lines.'

Tomek didn't need to see his daughter to know that she was smirking to herself. And trying her hardest to hide it.

'Nothing more from me. Unless you've got anything you want to add?'

Both adults turned their attention to Kasia, who looked surprised, as though she'd just won a million pounds as a contestant on one of those shitty daytime TV shows he'd become enraged by.

'No,' she said tentatively. 'I don't have anything more to add.'

Tomek clapped his hands and rose to his feet. 'That's settled then. Thank you very much, Miss Holloway. Plenty of feedback for us to mull over. And thank you for your time.'

They shook hands and together he and Kasia headed out of the room. Kasia was already in the waiting room grabbing her bag from the chair she'd been sitting on by the time he'd reached the door. They made it halfway down the corridor when a thought occurred to him.

'You go to the car,' he said to her, reaching into his pocket and chucking her the keys. 'I'll be down in a second.'

Kasia didn't protest, and continued down the corridor, eager to get out of there as quickly as possible. Tomek made his way back to the classroom and poked his head round the door. He found Bridget tidying up her notes.

'Only me.'

His sudden presence startled her, and as she spun round, her dress flowed around her knees, showing more skin than he'd been expecting.

'Fucking hell!' she said, then covered her mouth immediately afterwards. 'I'm so sorry!'

'It's fine. She's gone. And she's heard a lot worse at home.'

'I can't begin to imagine what it's like for the two of you. The school have made me aware of your situation.'

The smile on Tomek's face told her that he didn't want to go there.

'I wanted to apologise,' he said. 'For the delay.'

'Oh, it's fine. You get used to it over the years.'

'I'm sure. And I wanted to thank you for everything you're doing for Kasia. It doesn't take a genius to work out that this is a massive adjustment period for her, and a genius I am not. But I'm slowly getting round to it all, we both are.' He hesitated as he stood there awkwardly, feeling like a teenager again asking out the pretty girl he saw at the under thirteen's social night. 'Earlier you mentioned about us helping her. *We.* I was wondering if you'd be open to the idea of helping Kasia with her maths. A sort of... tutoring?'

A chance for him to believe that she was serious about helping his daughter.

'Of course.'

'Are you sure?'

'Absolutely. I've done it before. Plenty of times.'

Tomek was stunned. 'Wow. I didn't even have to offer you any money.'

She opened her mouth to respond, but he beat her to it. 'Of course I'd make sure you're fairly compensated for your time and expertise. Christ knows she's costing me enough money as it is, can't imagine paying some tutoring fees is going to make much of a difference.'

Before leaving Bridget to gather her things and finally leave the school, after what had been a thirteen-hour shift, they agreed a date for Kasia's first tutoring session and a price.

It was a fair assessment, Tomek thought. And as he hurried down the corridor, he wondered whether she'd be willing to accept payment in the form of a dinner one time.

CHAPTER
TEN

It was all very exciting. And all very secretive. Very, very secretive indeed. She mustn't say anything to anyone. She mustn't venture outside. She mustn't even think of finding anyone else. Otherwise the game would be over, and she would lose.

And Annabelle Lake didn't like losing. It was the worst thing in the world. Ever since she could remember, she always needed to win. Even if she was playing against herself.

But for this game, she was clueless. She didn't know what was happening. All she knew was that she was looking forward to seeing how it all played out – if she'd win. It was important to win. Winning was more important than taking part, Daddy had said that. He said a lot of things, but that was the one she listened to mostly.

She loved her mummy and daddy. And sometimes she missed them, but she was so caught up in the excitement of it that she couldn't think about them too much. She hoped they wouldn't mind, that they would forgive her once this was all over. Especially Mummy, and especially Uncle Vincent.

Her favourite game, out of all the ones that she'd been given to keep her entertained, was connect the dots. She loved counting the numbers in her head while looking for them with her eyes, then tracing the direction her pen needed to move in with her finger. All the while her tongue stuck out, deep in thought. Then, as a reward, she was given a carton full of her favourite colouring-in pens.

Yes, pens. Not pencils. That had been a nice surprise. At home, Mummy and Daddy always told her to use pencils whenever she wanted to do any of her drawing or colouring in (although Uncle Vincent often let her use pens, so long as they kept their little secret between them). They were cleaner, safer, and she was less likely to stain any of the furniture, according to her parents. She didn't think so, but she didn't like to argue and upset them. They did enough of that anyway.

But here... here, none of that mattered. She could do what she wanted. Paint the table, the toilet, the walls, the ceilings. She could even paint the windows if she really wanted to. But she didn't.

Mostly because it might have been a trick, to test whether she actually *did* all those things she wanted to. If she coloured the walls, then it might mean she'd lose the game. And she didn't want that.

Not to mention that drawing all over something that wasn't hers would be considered mean.

And she didn't like being rude.

Miss Duggan's words echoed in her head.

It's wise to be polite, stupid to be rude.

Annabelle didn't want to be stupid.

No, she wanted to win, and she couldn't win if she was being stupid. Instead, she would have to win by being wise.

CHAPTER
ELEVEN

I t had been a while since Tomek had last burned the midnight oil and not felt slightly guilty about it. In fact, he couldn't recall a time when he ever had. Sure, Charlotte Hanton had protested about his working late and having to travel to other parts of the country as part of his job, but that had been during the middle of a serial killer investigation. How could she have expected any less?

But now was slightly different. Kasia was home, and he should have been spending quality time with her, making up for the past thirteen years of not knowing she existed. Except for the fact it was already well past her bedtime. While she may have gone to bed a little over half an hour ago, he was almost certain she wasn't asleep. Probably more endless scrolling on that braindead app of hers or watching something on Netflix. If she kept it up, he might have to confiscate the device from her so she could get to sleep at a normal time.

Times had changed since he'd been a teenager. He hadn't had any of these distractions. All he'd had were his comic books and the almost invisible glow from the street light outside illuminating the words and illustrations. Hiding under the duvet covers every time his dad wandered near his and his brothers' bedroom. There had been none of this streaming stuff. Instant access to Netflix, Prime Video, Disney+. All the shit that was on YouTube nowadays – so-called influencers reacting to videos of other people reacting to something. Soon we'd all be stuck in a perpetual cycle of acting and reacting, creating false personas for the benefit of likes, views and a large follower count. Tomek lamented the idea of it, but he was still considering the possibility of creating various social media accounts for himself and forcing Kasia to befriend him. That way he could keep an eye on what sort of things she was posting and liking. The sort of people she was communicating with and messaging. The whole reality of life as a teenager nowadays was a complete mindfuck to him, and one he couldn't get his head round.

Fortunately, he wasn't having that problem with the documents right in front of him.

The abduction of Annabelle Lake.

He'd kept the files Nick had given him close to his chest, and hidden in a secret drawer in his desk. The last thing he had wanted was Kasia seeing and worrying about the sort of things he got involved with.

By now, little Annabelle Lake, the nine-year-old from Canvey Island, had been missing for over five days. In that time, the team had spoken with her family members several times, her teacher who happened to be the last person to see her, and a handful of witnesses around the area. They'd conducted the house-to-house enquiries of the quaint cul-de-sac where she lived. They'd searched through ANPR records and CCTV cameras for any vehicles behaving strangely on the road at the same time she'd been abducted and during the time they suspected the Ford Fiesta had been ditched – and nothing. There were no demands from the kidnappers, nothing. It was as though she had just vanished from the face of the earth. And that was exactly the way her kidnappers had intended it.

At the top of the folder Nick had given him was an enlarged

photo of Annabelle. A pair of slightly stained wonky teeth grinned at him. Her eyes were enlarged behind a set of thick glasses that made her look like she was permanently surprised. Her brown hair had been tied into pigtails that hung either side of her head. And a dozen or so freckles covered her cheeks and nose. On the top of her left cheek, just below the frame of her glasses, was a small scar. The background of the photo was a sky blue, and she was dressed in her school uniform. The photo had been dated three months prior, taken at the start of the school term. It reminded Tomek of the photo at his parents' house. The one of him entering secondary school. Two years after his brother had died. That one didn't contain the same innocence and childlike sweetness that Annabelle possessed. It was etched into every contour of her face, whereas Tomek's had looked depressed, sad, both emotions seeping through the pores of his skin and hair follicles. Even the lighting had been off, as though the photographer had known what had happened, and had tried to get all artistic with a school photo. Tomek couldn't recall the last time he'd seen the image – it wouldn't surprise him if his mum and dad had disposed of it long ago.

Pushing those particular thoughts to the back of his mind, Tomek turned the image over and laid it face down on the desk. Then he turned his attention to the witness statements. Spent the next couple of hours trawling through the minutiae of the evidence that had been gathered. Continued reading until his eyes felt heavy.

He called it a night shortly after 1 a.m. But sleep evaded him. One of the bars in the sofa bed he'd been forced to purchase soon after Kasia's arrival had snapped at one end and so the top half of his body sunk a few centimetres when he lay on his side. He'd tried swapping ends but it was even less comfortable.

As he lay there, he looked out upon the living room that was now tilted a few degrees. At the absolute bomb site. At the clothes on the floor, at the boxes that had been moved down from the loft to accommodate Kasia's items. At the plants that had been pushed into the corner away from the sunlight. At the bonsai trees that were becoming squished on the window sill. At the documents and school folders overflowing the desk and spilling onto the floor.

The flat had barely been large enough for him when he'd lived alone. And now it certainly wasn't.

Perhaps what they needed was a change of scenery. A new place. A fresh start. A reset. Perhaps that was what Kasia was crying out for in her own way. This was *his* house, and he often wondered whether she felt like an intruder, disturbing the status quo (which, of course, she had...). But if they had a new place for them to begin their father-daughter adventures together, then perhaps that would reset everything, put her at ease.

Yes, he would do that. Tomorrow he would look for a new place to live. But until then he would have to put up with the broken sofa bed, despite the pain he often woke up with in his neck.

CHAPTER
TWELVE

The two-bedroom flat was situated a little further inland than Tomek would have liked. For the past thirteen years, ever since he'd broken up with Kasia's mum, he'd been living in the same flat, less than five minutes' walk from Old Leigh and the beach. It was what he'd been used to, what he'd known. But as he'd come to learn, after a quick Internet search on Rightmove and some of the various local estate agents, house prices in the area had become unaffordable – laughably so. And so he was forced to turn his back on the water, and focus his attention on the mainland of Leigh. And there was the real possibility that he might even be forced to look further afield. Southend. Hadleigh. Maybe even Basildon.

The first of several viewings he had lined up for that week was on the north side of Leigh. The estate agent, a man who'd introduced himself as James-but-you-can-call-me-Jimmy over the phone, was waiting for him outside the flat, resting against the bonnet of his car, as though he was a shitty undercover officer in a seventies spy movie. Despite the obvious attempts to look cooler than he actually was, the man was immaculately dressed. His hair was well-greased and combed backwards, making his forehead appear a few inches taller than it was, and his three-piece suit was well-pressed and tight against his slim frame. It was obvious to see a considerable amount of time, effort and money had been spent on it, and Tomek was dubious whether it made a difference or not to his selling abilities. Whether it gave James-but-you-can-call-me-Jimmy any special powers – the power to not be a sanctimonious prick.

Tomek's albeit *limited* experience with estate agents was that they were all sharks, ravenous blood sniffers hunting out their prey, desperate for their commission. Every property they set foot in was perfect, had untold amounts of character, and with a little bit of TLC and a lick of paint, could be made into the most beautiful home for Tomek and his family. Back then, it had been a family of one, and he'd seen right through the bullshit and focused on the aspects of the house that were important to him – a decent-sized bedroom, a kitchen with all the right appliances, and a window sill large enough for his bonsai trees. But now it wasn't just him. He had a family of two to consider, someone other than himself. So he wondered if he might fall for the bullshit.

'Mr Bowen?' Jimmy said as Tomek approached. The man spoke with so much confidence that, even if he wasn't Mr Bowen, Tomek would have been convinced he was.

'Good to meet you.' Jimmy pushed himself away from the car bonnet and extended his hand, smiling. The brightness of the man's teeth almost blinded Tomek, and as he approached he was so focused on them that he completely missed the man's hand.

'Sorry about that,' Tomek said, hiding his blushes, still unable to pull his gaze from the man's dazzling gravestones. They were so... perfectly aligned. Tomek nodded to them. 'Are you plugged into the mains or have you got a solar panel stuck to you somewhere?'

At first, Jimmy didn't understand what Tomek was referring to. Then he pointed to his teeth and, in an act of pride, opened his mouth wider, showing Tomek more of the ones at the back. 'Oh, you mean *these*? You like 'em?'

'I'd like them a little bit more if I didn't need sunglasses to look at you.'

'Ha! Good one. Got 'em done in Turkey a few months ago. Turkey Teeth, they call 'em. You shoulda seen what they was like before. As yellow as the end of a cigarette, and I don't even smoke.'

'Then why'd you get them done? You lose a bet?'

Jimmy shrugged, as though he'd never questioned his own decision. 'Just wanted to get 'em done, see what all the fuss is about. First they file your teeth down until they're like a sharpened pencil, and then they mould the new set to your mouth and jobs-a-gooden, you're all set. Everyone's happy.'

'Except for your bank account, I'm sure.'

'That's why you get 'em done in Turkey, mate. Cheaper over there. Mate o' mine got a hair transplant done for next to nothing couple months ago. His hair's already longer than his missus'.'

Tomek was struggling to keep up. Since when had people been so fascinated with having the shiniest teeth and the thickest hairline? Sure, he knew that balding was a concern for many men (fortunately, he'd been blessed with a good hairline and thick black hair), and so could understand the desire to improve it, but the *teeth*? That was a step too far. He worried about the next generation. If they weren't careful, none of their body parts would be natural, and they'd all be walking around like life-sized versions of Barbie and Ken.

'I hope you haven't been waiting too long,' Tomek said to fill the awkward silence.

'Only a few minutes. No bother. Shall we?'

With that, Tomek followed James-but-you-can-call-me-Jimmy down the side of the flat conversion and up the small set of steps leading to the front door. As they entered, Jimmy began reeling off the script he'd no doubt committed to memory. The same one he probably abused at every viewing.

'This gorgeous flat has been recently added to the market, just last week in fact. The seller is looking to sell up pretty quickly, and we've already had a lot of interest.'

Of course they had. Got to plant the scarcity seed early on, make him ponder on it for the rest of the viewing.

'The flat is valued at three hundred and thirty thousand, and is only a stone's throw from the town centre, with good transport links into Southend and London. You've got two bedrooms, both approximately a hundred square feet, with plenty of space for wardrobes, beds, cabinets, TVs, desks.'

Jimmy opened the door and stepped in. Tomek followed shortly behind.

'This is the hallway,' Jimmy continued. 'Immediately ahead you've got a small bathroom, complete with toilet and sink...'

That was a good start. All the essentials.

'The boiler's in this small cupboard here, along with a place for all your coats and shoes and umbrellas. The door to your left is the living room...'

They entered the large space. It was slightly smaller than Tomek had been used to, but mind you, everything in the flat seemed to have shrunk in size since it had been replaced with a lot of Kasia's stuff. He looked out upon the open space and imagined a section for his desk, the sofa, coffee table and the space for a TV. All the essentials.

'The bay windows are double-glazed, and as you can see, they let a lot of light in. This part of the house is south-facing, so you've got light pretty much all day round.'

'Do you come with the flat then?' Tomek asked.

The joke didn't land. Tomek wondered whether he got the same sort of grief from his mates or colleagues at work. And then he wondered whether they were all the same. In which case Tomek would need to remember a pair of sunglasses if he had to venture into their offices to sign anything.

Jimmy continued: 'The windows were fitted a few years back, so you're still under warranty for them. And what's great about this is that there's no onward chain, so you can move in pretty quickly...'

But Tomek wasn't listening. He was looking for the most important space. A window sill large enough for his bonsai trees.

'If you come this way...' Jimmy pulled Tomek away and into the kitchen. 'This is a place I imagine you'll be spending a lot of your time, or maybe none depending on your preference. But as you can see, this area is large enough for the two of you to cook at the same time.'

'Two of us?'

'You and the missus?'

Tomek pursed his lips. 'Not quite. Me and my daughter.'

'Oh. Sorry.'

'Never assume, mate.'

'I know, I know. It makes an ass out of you and me.'

'Not just that, makes you look like a tit.'

But not nearly as much as the teeth and shocking hairline did.

After seeing the kitchen where – and James had been right on that one – he would be spending a lot of his time, they made their way to the two bedrooms at the back of the house. In Tomek's modest and quite frankly inexperienced opinion, they were large enough for both his and Kasia's needs. To be fair, anything was better than the cramped conditions they were living in currently. Each room came with a small alcove for a wardrobe, and enough space for either of them to comfortably move around their beds. However only one of them contained the Holy Grail. The precious window sill. Tomek bagsied that one as his own.

The last on the shopping list of rooms to look at, and nod noncommittally at, was the bathroom. It had everything he'd come to expect of bathrooms: a shower, a toilet and a sink. Except there was one minor alteration he wasn't too keen on.

Tomek pointed to it. 'What's that doing there?'

James-but-you-can-call-me-Jimmy looked down at the bidet that had been tucked into the corner of the bathroom beside the toilet. 'Not too sure on that one... Think the previous owners are from the continent somewhere... Can't say I've ever used one myself before. But never say never!'

The first thought that occurred to Tomek wasn't about what he would do with it if he decided to put down a deposit on the place. Rather, it was whether the colour of it was what Jimmy had modelled his teeth on.

'So,' he asked, blinding Tomek with them again. 'Whaddya think?'

'I don't think you'd look too out of place,' Tomek replied, but moved the conversation on before he offended Jimmy some more. 'What are the next steps?'

'Well, if you're interested, let me know and we can secure the deposit first. After that, we'll handle the sale of your existing property at the same time as we handle all the paperwork for the new one.'

It sounded simple in theory, but Tomek guessed that was the way Jimmy had intended it to sound.

'Sounds too good to be true.'

'Usually it is, but not with us. That's why we're rated number one on Trip Advisor.'

And there it was. The scarcity at the beginning backed up by the social proof at the end. They'd come full circle.

'I mean, I like it. It's big enough for what we need, but I'm not there yet.'

'Oh?'

'Yeah. I've got to go home and speak with the boss. See what she thinks about it first.'

On the way home, Tomek stopped off in Leigh High Street to grab a few bits from the local Co-op. On the menu tonight was pizza, he decided. With a bottle of Coke for Kasia, and a crate of beers for him. Something to celebrate.

As he headed back to the car, the bottles of beer jangling against his leg, his eyes darted to the other side of the road. Stopped as soon as they landed on the school uniform shop wedged between a gift shop and a coffee shop. Tomek had tried his hardest to avoid "Too School For Cool" for as long as possible. Yet it was still there, untouched, closed. The police notice notifying everyone that it was part of an ongoing investigation was still hanging on the door. Tomek couldn't look at it for long. It brought back images and memories he'd tried his hardest to suppress. The ones of him and Charlotte in bed together, kayaking along the marshes of Tollesbury, at the Roots Hall football stadium watching the Mighty Shrimpers. And then the darker ones returned. The images of her slaughtering three men, slicing their genitalia off and shoving them in their respective mouths. Of slicing their throats and undressing them.

He turned away and continued back to the car, though he was unable to shake the images that played in his mind like a cinema.

The drive home was brief. A couple of left turns, a few more right ones, and he was there. Because the street was packed with narrow, terraced houses, there was little to no room for parking. Which meant finding a space was like trying to find a strawberry seed in the dessert. Almost impossible. Sometimes he had to park the next road over and walk. Others he was forced to wait for his neighbours to shake their arses into gear and move out of the way. On the odd occasion that he was able to find a space with ease, it was typically made more difficult by the bellends parking at terrible angles and leaving no space for his car.

It was often at its worst when he came home late after a long day of trying to rid the streets of criminals. It wasn't that he felt he deserved a permanent space for the job he did but... Actually, he did want a permanent space. A nice big, juicy space with enough room either side for him to do star jumps in. That way it wouldn't take him an extra ten minutes trying to find somewhere.

Like he had done just now.

Parked on the street round the corner in the only available space, several hundred yards from his home.

He sauntered along the road as a light rainfall began to tickle his face. Tucking the beer and cans of Coke under one arm he pulled the hood over his head and increased his pace.

But he was brought to an abrupt stop when the figure came into view. A man, thick, heavyset, braving the elements. Standing outside his flat, staring up at the bonsai trees on the window sill.

Immediately Tomek sensed his body switch into fight mode. His shoulders and core tensed, preparing themselves for an altercation, if only verbal.

As he approached, his arrival registered with the man and he turned. The straight jawline and chiselled chin belied the animosity in his expression. The man was both a hunky model and an insane-looking bloke rolled into one. It was the eyes, predominantly. Sky blue. Dazzling and overwhelming. Yet more fuel to the fire of confusion that raged in Tomek. He looked as though he had a photoshoot during the weekdays and a football hooligan fight to get to on the weekends.

'Can I help you?' Tomek asked as sternly as he could manage.

'Tomek, is it?'

The man kept his hands in his pockets, which unsettled Tomek. He'd have preferred to see what they were holding, if anything.

'Who wants to know?'

'A friend of a friend. They just wanted to make sure you've kept up your end of the bargain.'

Charlotte. The message. Caitlin.

Surprise registered across Tomek's face.

'How did you find this address?'

'A friend of a friend of a friend.'

Tomek wondered how far the bloke's friends list really went and whether he knew anyone in the Royal Family.

'I've done what I needed to,' he replied.

'Good. Then so have I. Have a good evening, Mr Bowen. Hopefully I won't have to see you again.'

Before he knew it, the man was out of the porch and heading down the street in the opposite direction, walking headfirst into the hardening rain. Without wasting any time, Tomek hurried to the front door, fought frustratingly with the lock that still needed fixing, and dived into the living room. He hadn't realised it, but his pulse was through the roof, and he bent double as he struggled to get it back.

Charlotte had been true to her word, all right. But that posed a new sort of problem. Her and her criminal friends, along with all *their* criminal friends, knew his address. And if they knew his address it meant they were susceptible, vulnerable. More importantly, *Kasia* was susceptible and vulnerable.

He left the shopping on the kitchen counter and reached into his pocket. Then he called James-but-you-can-call-me-Jimmy.

'Hello?' came the cocky voice on the other end. From that word alone, Tomek could sense the man was smiling; he could almost hear the sound of his teeth radiating radioactive material.

'James? I mean, Jimmy. It's Mr Bowen, from the flat earlier.'

A moment to process the name.

'Ah, Mr Bowen. Good to hear from you. What can I help you with?'

'We'll take it.'

'Already? Have you had a chance to speak with your daughter?'

'No. I just... don't want to miss out.'

'Excellent. I'll get that all squared away.' If it was possible, Jimmy's telephone manner was more convincing than his in-person manner.

'Thank you.'

'Did you still want to visit the property tonight at all?'

'Please. She'll need plenty of time to work out where all her stuff's going to fit.'

A slight chuckle. 'Of course. Well, thank you for letting me know. Leave it with me, and I'll get everything sorted for you. Pleasure doing business with you.'

Of course it was. Anything was worth it for the one percent.

Tomek chucked the phone on the counter and began unloading the shopping. He was halfway through opening his bottle of beer – the liquid had just *psssed* as he yanked the cap off – when his phone rang. The device vibrated angrily on the surface. He answered without checking the Caller ID.

'Hello?'

'You busy?'

Nick. Good old Nasty Nick to settle the nerves.

'I can talk.'

'Was worried I might have found you with your hands down your trousers. All that free time you've found yourself in, n'all.'

'Nope,' Tomek replied.

'Good. Then I have some news for you.'

'You're retiring?'

Nick mock-laughed. 'Funny.'

'I'll have to be careful about when I phone *you*.'

A signature sigh echoed through the phone. 'Do you want the good news or not?'

'Don't see what the harm is. Let's have it.'

'You're coming back.'

'What?'

'Miraculously, Charlotte's statements – about Tony and the Instagram account – have been withdrawn and there's no case against you. The IOPC have dropped the case and your suspension is finished. We'll see you tomorrow.'

'*Tomorrow*?'

'Unless you've got plans?'

'Not that I can think of. Just means now I'm going to have to shave and make myself look presentable.'

'I didn't want to say anything the other day...'

'I've not wanted to say anything for the past few years but you don't hear me complaining.'

Nick didn't reply.

'That, sir, is what I believe the youngsters nowadays call a *clap back*.' To highlight the meaning of the word, Tomek wedged the phone between ear and shoulder, and slapped his palm with the back of his hand.

'Carry on, mate,' Nick began, 'and I'll sit you with Chey for the next six months. See how funny that is then.'

Chey, even though there was nothing wrong with him – no weird personality defects, no awkward behaviour – was notorious in the office for farting and emitting a constant aroma of shit. It was one of the reasons he was the butt of the jokes. That, and because he was the youngest.

'No need for that, sir,' Tomek said, smiling to himself. 'Forget I said anything. I'll see you tomorrow first thing.'

CHAPTER
THIRTEEN

After finishing his shift, James-but-you-can-call-me-Jimmy had dropped off the keys to their new flat. He trusted Tomek enough – "you are a *police officer*, after all" – to do the right thing and return the keys without issue within the next couple of days. In the brief exchange, Tomek had picked up some bizarre sort of sexual tension in the room. The majority of it had come, quite rightly, from the Coleman side of the family. As soon as she'd laid eyes on Jimmy, Kasia had become curt and shy, timid almost. Hiding behind her phone while making it abundantly obvious she was watching his every movement.

She was at that age when her hormones were beginning to fire into gear, and the world was beginning to change to a different colour. Tomek couldn't blame her for being interested in Jimmy. He could see the appeal. He'd been a teenager once, he knew what it was all about. Except for the teeth. That hadn't been a *thing* when he was that age. If it had, then he feared he might have been looking like a floodlight every time he opened his mouth by the age of eighteen.

Once Jimmy had left, they finished their dinner, grabbed the essentials and left. The rain had eased slightly, though the traffic in the town hadn't received the same message. It took them twenty minutes, the same as if they'd walked. They pulled up outside the flat and Tomek killed the engine. The lights were on in the living room and kitchen, presumably left that way by Jimmy in preparation for their visit.

'What do you think?' Tomek asked.

'Looks exactly the same as our one at the moment.'

'Brilliant,' Tomek said sardonically, though his mind focused on the two words that had come out of her mouth.

Our one.

Our. Our flat. Our space. Our home. For the first few days of their father-daughter relationship it had always been *his* flat, *his* home.

It was only a minor step, but it was a step in the right direction, at least.

Tomek was first out of the car and he made his way to the front door. Yesterday's altercation with the model-cum-football hooligan had played in Tomek's mind since. If ever there was an incentive to move out of your home (if being reduced to sleeping on the sofa so your daughter had somewhere comfortable to sleep wasn't enough of an incentive already) then the prospect of being watched and being made to feel like you were in danger would certainly do it. There was no doubt in his mind Charlotte had no intention of leaving him alone. She herself was going nowhere, and so she needed to keep herself entertained, busy. She wanted to have her own episodes of *Keeping Up With The Bowens*. Charlotte wouldn't leave them alone so long as she had the power, the contacts, and the access to do so. If moving house, albeit only a few hundred metres away, was a preventative measure he needed to take in order to protect his family, then he was willing to do it.

He shoved the key into the lock, and with a simple turn, he was in.

'This place is worth it for front door alone,' Kasia remarked. 'I fucking hate the one we have.'

Tomek stopped dead in his tracks, scowling at her. 'What have I said about that type language?'

Her face dropped and she lowered her gaze. 'You do it all the time.'

'And when you turn eighteen you can do it as well. If you make it that far... But while you're under this roof...'

'Fine.'

The first room Tomek showed her was the shoe cupboard. When he told her that was where she'd be sleeping, she glowered at him, her eyes narrowing. The next room was the living room. All the preconceived plans and ideas he'd had for the space were immediately broken down as she changed everything. The layout, the organisation, the amount of new furniture they would need. He quickly realised that this was her house, and he would just be living in it.

The bedroom discussion was no different. Mercifully, she'd opted for the smaller space, without his insistence, and had already figured out how to arrange a bed, wardrobe, make-up table, desk, and chest of drawers in the small space. To Tomek, it was like asking him to complete the Rubik's Cube while being told what to do with the instructions right in front of him. It still didn't make sense to him, but it made sense to her. And that was important. To give her the freedom to choose what she did with her own space.

'You want to see the best part of the house?' Tomek asked excitedly.

'It's not going to be exciting, is it?'

'*I* think it is.'

Tomek pulled her by the arm and showed her his new bedroom. The window sill. The sheer size of it.

'Beautiful, don't you think?'

'That's not a word I'd use to describe it.'

'What word would you use?'

She looked up at him. 'You'll have to wait till I'm eighteen to find out.'

That brought a smirk to his face. He wandered up to the window sill and rested against it, looking out at the road below.

'I got a call today,' he began.

'Okay...' The caution in her voice was apparent.

'I'm going back to work tomorrow.'

'Oh. Okay.'

'Which means you'll have to look after my bonsai trees,' he said, his smirk having turned into a grin. 'They need watering once every couple of days, preferably in the evening. When we get to summer you'll need to do it a lot more.' Kasia's gaze pivoted to outside the window, staring at her reflection. 'On a more serious note,' he continued, 'it also means I'm not going to be home as much as I am at the moment. I'll still make your breakfast and lunches for school as often as I can. I'll still drop you off at school when I can. But on the mornings I can't, then this place is about equidistant to where we are at the moment so you should be all right. The only problem will be your dinners. Sometimes I might have to work late. If that's the case then I'll leave you instructions on how to make dinner.'

'I already know how to cook,' she said, her voice devoid of emotion, as though the last of it had been sucker-punched out of her by Tomek's announcement.

'If your report card from Mrs Shaw is anything to go by...'

'Not because of that,' she said. 'I learnt to cook for myself when mum wasn't around. She'd go for days at a time sometimes. Leave me nothing to eat so I had to find it for myself.'

This was the first time Kasia had brought up living with her mum. He'd decided not to push her too much on the topic, rather wait for her to explain things in her own time. Now that she had, he felt privileged that she trusted him with it.

'I'll try to be home as much as I can,' he told her.

'Can I have Sylvia over after school?'

Tomek hesitated. Considered the decision. 'Yes, I don't see a problem with that. Just let me know the days and I'll remember to hide my dirty underwear and pick up my socks.'

Kasia chuckled to herself. For a brief moment, Tomek thought she was about to nudge him lovingly, place a hand on his arm affectionately, but she didn't. Instead she pulled out her phone and read a message.

'She's asked if I want to go over for a sleepover this weekend, actually,' Kasia said.

'Sylvia?'

'Yeah.'

'Hmm.'

Now, *that*, Tomek wasn't so keen on. He didn't mind the idea of having a friend come over to theirs. It was familiar territory. A safe space. But Kasia going over to Sylvia's... It was a decision he would have to think about.

'Not so sure on that one,' he told her. 'If everything goes as quickly as James – I mean *Jimmy* – says, then we should be able to move in by next week. I'll need all the help I can get with packing.' He paused a beat. 'How about... you can only have a sleepover with her when you get your maths grade up?'

That'll do it. Bribery. Give her a reward by the end of it.

Parenting the only way he knew how.

'What?' she asked, incipient anger rising in her voice.

'Which reminds me,' he began, making his way towards the exit. 'I've spoken with Miss Holloway and she's agreed to come round in the evenings to give you tutoring lessons.'

'What? Are you shitting me?'

Tomek swivelled on the spot. 'Language! I had originally planned for her to stop once your grades improved but I can get her to do the full year if you'd rather?'

Kasia rolled her eyes and puffed out a large wave of air through her mouth. '*No.*'

'Good. Then stop fucking swearing.'

CHAPTER
FOURTEEN

The games weren't fun anymore. They'd stopped being enjoyable after he'd hit her. Hard. Really, really hard. Annabelle didn't know why he'd done it, but things had become tense ever since. They were arguing a lot more, shouting at each other, getting close and confrontational. Meanwhile, Annabelle just stayed on her chair like she was told to. She didn't want to get hit again. No, sir. That wasn't a part of the game she liked.

It hurt so much she couldn't move her mouth for what felt like days, but had only been a few hours. And it still hurt now, ached like that time Will Robbie had punched her in the arm at school to see if it hurt. She had told him that she couldn't feel pain, that she was superhuman, that she was unlike any of the other kids in the school. But it had hurt. So much, in fact. And her arm throbbed with phantom pain as she thought about it now.

Time had become a tricky thing to manage. She was usually so good with looking at the numbers going round and round in circles. She didn't always know what they meant, but her favourite number was twelve, and whenever the big hand reached her favourite number she knew that a whole hour had moved forward. Miss Duggan had told her that. Miss Duggan told her lots of things. Annabelle liked Miss Duggan, and she thought about her now as she sat in the chair, staring at the television opposite.

They were still arguing, but she blocked it out. Annabelle watching a *SpongeBob SquarePants* episode on DVD. Because it wasn't one of her favourite episodes – she was very particular about her SpongeBob SquarePants – she drifted off and continued thinking about Miss Duggan. The prettiest lady she'd ever seen.

It was a shame she didn't have a boyfriend.

Though it wasn't through a lack of trying, Amelia had told her. Whatever that meant. Annabelle assumed it was a bad thing, yet still couldn't work out why she was single and lonely.

'You must be really lonely, aren't you, miss?' she'd asked one lunchtime. While the rest of her class were playing outside, she was busy playing Disney Princess Top Trumps.

Her favourite card game with her favourite teacher.

'I don't get lonely,' Amelia replied. 'I've got my cat and I've got lots of friends who I hang out with at the weekends. Do you get lonely, Annabelle, as an only child?'

At that, Annabelle had shaken her head. She didn't get lonely, *could* never. Not when she had her friends by her side: SpongeBob, Sandy, Patrick, Mr Krabs. Even Plankton was one of the good guys if you got to know him. She liked them because they all spoke to her when she was down and helped pick her up again. No matter what mood she was in, she was always happy to see her favourite people.

Her attention was pulled back to the present by a loud noise. She turned to face them. They were still arguing, except now they'd started to whisper to one another, talk in hushed tones. Annabelle had seen that enough times to know they were talking about adult things, things they didn't want her to hear.

Then they stopped and made their way towards her. They crouched either side of the chair and looked her in the eyes.

'Are you okay, Annabelle?' *She* asked.

Annabelle nodded.

'You're not in any trouble.'

That was good. Annabelle didn't like being in trouble.

'We're sorry about earlier,' *He* began. 'It was an accident. Does it hurt?'

Annabelle shook her head. Now was the time to be brave, like that time she hadn't told anyone when Will Robbie had also tried to put his hand up her skirt.

'We're going to go out for a walk now. Would you like to come?'

Annabelle hesitated a moment before nodding. Her legs were really tired. She hadn't stretched them in what felt like weeks. The space was so cramped and confined. At first she thought it was exciting being in there, all snug as a bug in a rug, but now she wasn't so sure.

'Get your coat and then we'll go.'

Annabelle didn't need to be told twice. She leapt off the chair, grabbed her favourite coat from the back of it, and was waiting by the door before they were ready.

The first thing she noticed was the cold. Winter wasn't her favourite month – except for Christmas, she *loved* Christmas – and she never looked forward to the chilly temperatures and the darkness.

The darkness was the scariest part.

And tonight was no different. It was pitch black out there. Not even the street lights were strong enough to fight against the encroaching envelope of despair.

As she wandered along the road, walking with both hands being held, she imagined the darkness in a battle with the street lamp. Two long figures with big metal arms punching and kicking and biting each other.

Then they all took a turn through a gate and the lights disappeared. The field they'd just entered was on a different level of darkness. Darker than the darkest dark she'd ever seen.

It frightened her, and she clung tightly to the hands wrapped around hers.

'Don't worry,' a voice came from above but she was so afraid that she couldn't work out who had said it. 'Look up at the sky. Can you see all those pretty stars?'

Annabelle craned her head skyward and nodded. Dozens of holes appeared in the blanket across the sky, like God had grabbed a pin and jabbed it for fun. Maybe he'd been playing a game as well, she wondered.

God must have played loads of games. Especially on people. Like when Mason Jones had tripped over air in the school playground and everyone had laughed at him.

God must have had the best games. And as they traversed the field, she wondered if he had any of her favourites.

She bet he did.

After what felt like hours, they eventually came to a stop outside a playground. Annabelle had been to loads of them before but never this one. It had everything. A swing, a slide, rocking horses, seesaw, a merry-go-round. All her favourites.

But the one favourite she loved more than most was the swing. The way she could go up and down, up and down... up and down. The way she could get close to the stars and close to God and his games.

'In you go,' *He* instructed her.

Like a greyhound that had just been let off the lead, Annabelle sprinted towards the swing, leapt onto it, and started propelling herself backwards and forwards, increasing her momentum each time.

Higher and higher...

Up and down...

Looking into the stars. Connecting the dots and pretending she was colouring them in. This time she had no trouble keeping between the lines.

And then it stopped. On the way back down to earth, she crashed into something solid and almost fell off. Before she had a chance to react, the chain that her hand had once been holding onto started wrapping around her throat, like a python ensnaring its prey. The thick, metal chains cut into her skin and started constricting her breathing.

The python's grip became tighter, tighter...

Death's grip...

Tighter, tighter, still...

Annabelle tried to jam her fingers between the chain and her throat, to wedge a gap between life and death, but it was no use. It was too tight.

And soon the world started to darken. The pinpricks of light started to fade. The sound of the wind began to dampen.

And within what felt like minutes, Annabelle Lake's world turned completely black. And as her eyes closed, the last thought that occupied her mind was one of excitement. Because at least now she would get to play the same games as God.

CHAPTER
FIFTEEN

That morning, when Amelia Duggan left the house, she had no idea that her life would turn upside down. Like every other morning, she was rudely awakened by Mister Whiskers, who'd insisted on screaming at 4 a.m.; climbing on the headboard and scratching the side of the bed at five; and then suffocating her at 6 a.m. by sitting on her face. Her feline alarm clock. The selfish fur-baby bastard only woke her up in such a manner because he was hungry and begging for food. And Amelia was in no position to refuse him – she could hardly allow him to continue suffocating her. In the past she'd tried throwing him onto the floor and rolling her face into the pillow, burying into the cushion so that it was out of reach. But that had only seemed to antagonise Mister Whiskers, who'd proceeded to scratch and bite every bare bit of flesh on her body that had become exposed from beneath the duvet.

The selfish fur-baby bastard.

As she'd left the house, he'd sat in front of the doorstep and pleaded with his eyes for her to stay. For her to continue the endless supply of wet and dry food that his bulging stomach didn't need.

'I'll be back as soon as I can,' she told him. 'You be a good boy. Love you.'

The same routine every morning, without fail. It was a miracle she ever got any sleep. And as she left, she gave one last look at herself in the mirror. The dark clouds hanging below her eyes were enough to make her rue the decision to buy him. The lack of sleep, the constant need for attention. The selfish fur-baby bastard was gradually wearing her down, and combined with her increasing workload, she wasn't sure she could handle it anymore. But then she checked the time on her phone, and saw the image of Mister Whiskers on his first birthday appear on her wallpaper, and all was right again.

How could she ever get rid of him?

She often wondered whether it was the same with parents. Whether they found their child so infuriating, so frustrating, that they felt compelled to dropkick them in the face now and then. But then all it took was a cute moment – a smile, a giggle, picking up the crayon and then putting it down instead of drawing on the walls or shoving it up their noses – and they instantly fell in love with them again.

During school, she was only with the children for a few hours a day, when they were typically on their best behaviour, locked in the mindset of learning, where distractions and technological devices were kept outside the classroom. For the most part, the children she encountered in her lessons were golden. Sure, they put up a fight and argued at times, but they were in a different setting. The unspoken rules that governed every child the moment they entered the school gates was in full effect. They had a level of respect, a level of professionalism. Even the little racist ones in Year 6 who came in with their trainers and vape cigarettes and picked fights with the Eastern Europeans.

It would have been a nice dilemma to have, having children. She didn't think she could ever hate her own child, ever despise it or want to hurt it. In fact, she longed to have them. Had done ever since she became a teacher. They were all unique, special in their own little way. And she loved it, and she'd love to have one.

The only problem was finding someone brave (or was it stupid?) enough to have one with her. Now *that* had been a war she'd ventured into many times and lost. Online dating, speed dating, meeting people on nights out – she'd tried them all. But to no avail. No man was willing to commit. Instead they were all after one thing, and one thing only. Something which she wasn't prepared to give them. She'd made that mistake too many times in the past and been stung before. No, she needed the right man, the perfect man.

Like Mister Whiskers... when he wasn't being a complete arsehole.

Amelia locked her front door and started the forty-minute walk to school. It was still dark outside, and with any luck by the time she finally arrived at the school gates the sky would have lightened a little. To get there, her journey consisted of a twenty-minute walk across a field near the golf course, a ten-minute walk through a suburban part of town, followed by the final stretch along the busy street. She enjoyed the walk, and come rain or shine, she would do it. It was good for the soul, good for the body, and good for the mind. The steady rhythm of her feet on the different surfaces allowed her to decompress, to process yesterday's events, and to plan the day ahead.

First up was the scariest part of the walk. She dreaded it both in the morning and in the evening, particularly in the dark months. The park. She'd heard horror stories of young women being attacked and raped in there, and as a result she'd signed the petition to ensure that more street lamps (or lighting of any kind) were installed across the path that cut through the field. That had been ten months ago, and still nothing had been done about it.

This morning, the soil was damp, sodden by a rainfall that had fallen overnight. In the darkness, she was only able to see fifty feet in front of her. For this part of the journey, she removed her headphones and hurried her pace, almost into a jog – a pace that would give speed-walkers a run for their money.

At the halfway point, she came up to the playground that had been installed a few years back. As usual at this time in the morning, it was deserted. But Amelia had even been through there in the middle of the day, or shortly after school, and it had still been empty. As though there was an aura around the place that prohibited people from entering. An invisible warning that scared them off.

Her eyes flitted towards the slide. The towering feature, silhouetted vaguely in the darkness, was the place where, a few months before, a twenty-four-year-old had been attacked. Fortunately, the woman had been saved by a passer-by, and the attacker had been caught.

But it didn't make her slow down any.

Instead, she did the opposite.

Until something caught her eye.

Something odd, something that shouldn't have been there.

A figure, sitting on the swings...

No, they weren't sitting. They were... dangling?

Yes, dangling. But who? A small figure. A child perhaps.

Immediately, Amelia leapt into action and sprinted into the playground. Her coat got caught on the gate handle and pulled her back, delaying her a fraction. She swore aloud, then yanked it free, before hurrying over to the figure.

Even in the low light, she didn't need to see who it was to know.

She'd recognise those pigtails anywhere. And the coat. And the little Converse shoes that the school had made an exception on.

Amelia's heart jumped into her mouth as realisation slapped her across the face.

Before anything else could register in her brain, her scream filled the air and rolled across the field where it was drowned out by the traffic on the other side of the fence.

CHAPTER
SIXTEEN

Tomek tried to avoid Canvey Island as much as he could. It was grey, depressing, full of Nike-clad teenagers and idiots racing Vauxhall Corsas and Ford Focus', and was largely considered to be the arsehole of Essex. Over the years local businesses and the council had tried to attract more people to the island with the addition of a cinema, a bowling alley, a small theme park by the coast and a retail park that boasted the likes of B&M, M&S, and a Costa Coffee – the hallmark of Sunday afternoon shopping. But despite that, it hadn't been enough to tempt him.

The island was at an ever-present and increasing risk of flooding, and was infamous for lying below sea level. In the sixteen hundreds, the government had lured in a Dutch engineer by the name of Cornelius Vermuyden (who they'd later honoured with a school in his name) and tasked him with developing the sea walls around the island to protect it from the rising waterlines. So far the defences had survived and withstood the battery of the tide for four hundred years, but if the scientists and experts were to be believed, then it was only a matter of time until the walls gave way and the sea claimed the land for its own.

The field Tomek currently found himself in, however, was one of the nicer parts of greenery he'd stepped into on the island.

The bad part about it, though, was the dead nine-year-old dangling from the swing.

There was no doubt in Tomek's mind that the little girl was Annabelle Lake. He recognised the pigtails and the scar on her cheek from the photos he'd studied the night before.

'What a way to start your first day back.'

Tomek felt a slap on the back from Sean as the loveable giant joined his side.

'It's almost as bad as having to be on Canvey,' Tomek remarked.

'Still, could be worse.'

'Oh yeah?'

'We could be doing this in Tilbury.'

Tomek shivered at the thought.

'I heard that!' The high-pitched shrill came from Lorna Dean, the Home Office pathologist that had been assigned to the case. Tomek had worked with her on several occasions, and enjoyed each time. She was one of the most down-to-earth, humble and intelligent people he knew. And for someone who dealt with dead bodies on a daily basis, which made her an odd person by default, she had a relatively good outlook on life.

'Can I help you?' Tomek asked playfully.

'Watch what you say about Tilbury,' she called from the other side of the cordon. 'That's where I'm from.'

Tomek and Sean shared a glance that said "tells you everything you need to know".

'Maybe don't go around spreading news like that,' Tomek said to her. 'People might begin to think you're not qualified for the job.'

Lorna shot him the middle finger. 'Do you want to know anything about the dead girl or not?'

Tomek couldn't argue with that, and so he gestured for her to come over. A few moments later, she ducked beneath the cordon and shuffled towards them both.

'Good to see you again, Tomek,' Lorna said, lowering the face mask under her chin. 'See they finally let you off, did they?'

'Eventually.'

'I hope they were right to. I've got a teenage daughter who saw those images of you.'

Christ on a bike. It hadn't occurred to him that the unsolicited nude photos that Charlotte had taken of him while he'd been sleeping were out there on the internet now, out there for the whole world to see. Including Lorna's daughter.

'Where? How?'

'Instagram.'

'For fuck's sake...' he said. 'Remind me to never come into contact with your daughter. Ever. Please.'

'My fucking pleasure.' Lorna lowered her hood, revealing a flock of flame-red hair. On a bright day, it was strong enough to burn through the fabric of her suit, but in the low light, Tomek had almost forgotten the colour of it. It had been a while since Tomek had last dealt with her.

'So...' he said, keen to move things along.

'So, your little girl.' Lorna moved a strand of hair aside. 'Do you have any idea who it could be?'

Tomek nodded. 'Annabelle Lake. Nine years old. Abducted almost a week ago from her school.'

'Excellent. Well, not *excellent*. But it's good that you've got an idea who she is. That'll save me some time.'

'How did she die?'

Lorna swivelled on the spot and pointed to Annabelle's small frame. 'I think she might have been trying to practise the art of levitation... From what I can see, the chain wrapped around her neck was enough to do the trick. There doesn't appear to be any other signs of strangulation, though I won't know more until she's on the table.

And even then it might be too difficult to tell – the marks on her neck from the chain have left deep indentations in her throat, so it might not be possible to see anything else.'

'How long's she been there?'

As he said it, the ominous grey clouds above opened up and heavy rain started to fall. Perfect. Just the thing to spoil his impression of Canvey even further.

'Overnight,' Lorna replied. 'I'd say the early hours of the morning. Under the cover of darkness.'

'It gets dark around five p.m. ...' Tomek noted.

'But this place is usually empty,' Sean added.

Tomek turned to him. 'How do you know?'

'I've got friends that live here.'

'Friends? Other than... me?'

A smirk grew on Sean's face and he patted Tomek on the back patronisingly.

'Do you two need a moment?' Lorna asked.

'No. We're fine. Continue...' Tomek said, shaking Sean off him.

'As I was saying, she was most likely murdered in the early hours of the morning. When I got here her body was wet, and from the meteorological reports I read, it supposedly rained overnight. Stopped at about four-ish.' She looked at the field around her, squinting against the wind and rain that battered her head-on. 'Nothing since... Except for now, of course.'

'Of course,' he said.

Conscious of the rain and wanting to get out of it as fast as possible, Tomek asked if she had anything else to offer them at the moment.

Lorna shook her head. 'Sadly not right now, boys. That barrel of fun is coming later on when I get her on the table.'

Tomek couldn't wait. Before leaving, he paused to watch the Scenes of Crime Officers frantically racing in and out of the field in order to preserve as much of the evidence as possible.

After thanking Lorna for her time, Tomek and Sean headed back to the car. As they made their way across the mud-covered path that cut through the field, Tomek's foot slipped and he landed face first in a puddle. Muddy, dirty water splashed in his hair and onto his clothes. Around him, he heard the sound of laughter.

Then came Lorna: 'Serves you right,' she said, her voice carried quickly by the wind. 'That's what you get for slagging off Tilbury.'

CHAPTER
SEVENTEEN

The sound of Tomek knocking on the door echoed around the small cul-de-sac where Steven and Elizabeth Lake lived. From their doorstep, he could see one of the buildings from Canvey Beck Primary School and the red metal fence that ran around it behind the hedge.

It was time for school drop-off, and hordes of tiny humans with oversized backpacks that seemed to drag along the concrete trundled towards the gate, being pulled along by their parents.

A moment later the front door opened and Tomek swivelled on the spot to find a woman in her thirties staring back at him. She was dressed in a thin hoodie that hung off one shoulder, its drawstrings lopsided, and the zip undone to her chest, revealing more skin than Tomek had bargained for at 9 a.m.

'Mrs Lake?' Sean asked.

'Yeah...?' Her voice was gruff, deep, as though she'd already smoked thirty cigarettes by the time they'd arrived. And then realisation settled into the pores of her skin and set up camp. Her mouth widened, revealing a set of teeth the same colour as mud, and she retreated into the house. Babbling, inconsolable, the vowels and consonants coming out of her mouth incomprehensible.

'Mrs Lake,' Tomek began, 'is it all right if we come in?'

But when she didn't respond, too busy hyperventilating like a four-year-old, Tomek looked to Sean. They shrugged at one another and then made their move. Tomek bit the bullet and stepped in first. He'd expected a verbal assault, a stream of spittle-filled expletives telling him to leave and never come back. Like they were in a domestic. But it hadn't come. Instead, Elizabeth stumbled backwards to the bottom of the stairs, clawing the air wildly for support as though searching through the darkness. When she eventually found the stairs, she drew her knees up to her chest and curled herself into a ball.

Tomek made a move to approach but Sean held him back. 'You make the tea,' he said. 'I'll deal with this. Kettle's through there.'

Without arguing, Tomek headed towards the kitchen and briefly surveyed it before switching on the kettle. There was nothing of immediate note. No cable ties or rope or chair in the middle of the floor with blood on it. No potential murder weapons or torture devices. Just an assortment of horrific drawings that looked as though they'd been done by a two-year-old, and a collection of letters from the government. When he finished the teas, he left the kitchen and crouched in front of Elizabeth Lake in the hallway.

'Here you are, love,' he said, handing the Minnie Mouse cup across. Then he passed the Mickey Mouse mug over to Sean. Tomek had seen the collection in the cupboard – a vast array of Disney-themed drinking apparatus – and opted for his favourite for himself. Pluto.

'Am I right in thinking these are all Annabelle's?' Tomek asked, wagging his finger between their mugs.

'Yeah...' Elizabeth said, a lump the size of a baseball caught in her throat. 'She loves Disney. Adores it.'

What nine-year-old didn't? In fact, what *person* didn't? The franchise had been going for over a hundred years for a reason.

Tomek suggested they take the conversation to the living room. With a reluctant nod, Elizabeth agreed and showed them into the small space. The majority of the room was taken up by two large sofas that had been shoehorned in, and the first hurdle Tomek faced was squeezing his thick thigh through the thin gap. The next hurdle was making sure he didn't spill his drink on the carpet. But at least it wasn't as bad as Sean's attempt: after trying to fit his leg through unsuccessfully, he eventually lifted his other leg over the sofa and hopped into the space. Once they were both behind enemy lines they perched themselves on the end of the sofa closest to the window. Elizabeth, with the dexterity and grace of a gymnast, stretched her legs over the side of the chair and slotted herself onto the sofa with ease.

'Mrs Lake,' Tomek began.

'Beff. You can call me Beff.'

Beth with an F. As though the few missing teeth in her mouth prevented her from speaking properly.

Tomek then explained to her that her daughter's body had been found. It took no time at all for the tears to begin again, and after a few minutes, Elizabeth removed her phone from her pocket and began typing. Like she'd got it out of her system and had moved onto the next train of thought.

'Is there anyone else we need to inform?' Tomek asked. 'What about Steven?'

'He's at work.'

'Would you like us to have someone tell him?'

She held a finger up at him, instructing him to wait. 'I'm texting my brother. He needs to know.'

Tomek recalled the notes from the files Nick had given him. Vincent Gregory. Beth with F's brother. A comment had been made that, during the first few days of the investigation, he'd been insufferable. A nasty piece of work who'd harassed and shouted at members of the team, calling them inept and threatening legal action if they didn't find Annabelle. Most notably at Sean.

'You're telling him over your husband?'

'He has a right to know. As much as anyone else.'

Tomek didn't think that was strictly true. Broadcasting it from the rooftops wouldn't achieve anything.

When she'd finished, she finally turned her attention to Steven and gave him the call that was over within thirty seconds.

'He's on his way,' she said. 'He's just finishing up a job.'

As Tomek listened he couldn't help think that she'd made Steven Lake out to be some sort of hitman.

The hitman arrived ten minutes later, bursting through the door. He looked nothing like a contract killer, and was instead dressed in electrician trousers, wore a dirty navy polo, and his arms and fingers were covered in dirt and filth. If the words 'Lake Electrical Services' weren't emblazoned on the breast of his shirt, Tomek would have assumed he was a builder of some description.

Steven Lake ignored Sean and Tomek as he headed straight towards his wife. They gave each other a brief hug and then he sat beside her. He placed both hands on his knees and leant forward, as though watching the climax of an action thriller on the big screen.

'Please don't say it's true,' he said. 'I got here as fast I could, please don't say it's true.'

Sean swallowed before responding. Before sitting down with the family, they'd agreed the news was better coming from someone they'd met before, someone they'd got to know, rather than the stranger who'd turned up on their doorstep with him. As he listened, Tomek studied Annabelle Lake's parents. Their movements, their reactions. In theory they would have been more relaxed, more open, more *trusting* of the news as it was coming from Sean – and as a result more likely to give something away if anything.

But that wasn't the case. Both broke down into floods of tears, crying into their own hands at first, then finding some solace in each other. Steven had leant across and was sobbing into Beth's lap, enveloped by her arms.

'We're going to do everything we can to find who did this,' Tomek said. 'I know we've never met, so I guess this is the best time to introduce myself.' Tomek waited a moment; they both looked up at him, appalled for the horrible lack of timing. 'I'm DS Tomek Bowen,' he said. 'I work with Sean and the rest of the team and have been drafted in to—'

'*Tomek?*' Beth asked.

'Yes. That's my name.' He turned to Sean and asked, 'That is what I said, right?'

'Yes,' Sean confirmed with a dip of the head.

'That's not an English name, is it?' Beth said.

'No. How astute of you.' He could feel his back getting up. 'I'm half Polish.'

A look of surprise, followed by anguish, settled on Beth's grey eyes. 'You can't be here...'

'Excuse me?'

'It's bad enough you being here as well...' Beth continued, looking directly into Sean's eyes.

'What?' Tomek asked, his back stiffening with each second.

'It's her brother,' Steven added.

'What about him?'

'He... How can we put this? He...'

'He has certain views on certain things...'

'Oh, you mean he's a racist?'

That word took Beth by surprise, as though no one had said it about her brother before. Or perhaps they had, and she just ignored it. If there was one thing he knew about belligerent arseholes like her brother, it was that that particular word didn't exist to them.

'My brother isn't racist...'

Tomek could see the hole getting deeper the longer it took her to complete her sentence.

'He's just opinionated about these things.'

'About *what* things?'

'People who aren't... you know, English.'

'And what's *your* opinion?'

'I... I don't have one.'

'Well I'm half English, so does that not count for anything?'

Beth pursed her lips and shook her head imperceptibly.

The rod up Tomek's back was well and truly at full mast. Not even an earthquake could knock him down.

'Does your brother have swastikas in his house? Do you want to know if I'm Jewish as well?'

Beth babbled, her top lip quivering.

Go on, Tomek willed her. *Do it.*

Say it.

I dare you.

'A-Are... Are you Jewish?'

A smile leapt onto Tomek's face. 'No. No I'm not.'

He wasn't Jewish. He didn't practise any religion – much to his mother's despair – but that wasn't going to stop him from making her believe that he did.

Tomek cast a quick glance to Steven, who was no longer sitting with his head on Beth's lap. By now it was resting in his hands, embarrassed, his body positioned away from her. Their body language looked like they were sitting in a couples therapist's office, deep in conversation as to why they hated the other.

What had Steven married into? Tomek wondered.

And from the look on his face, the electrician had wondered the same thing.

'Guys...' Sean, the friendly giant, mediated. 'This is not what we're here for. We're here to discuss Annabelle.'

'You're right,' Tomek said. 'And while we wait for your brother to get here, we have some questions to ask you.'

'Like what?' Beth asked.

'Where you were last night?'

'Here. Both of us. We was asleep by about ten. Steve had work early.'

'Really? Where?'

'I start most mornings about seven or eight-ish. I'm self-employed so time I'm not working is time wasted.'

'And what do you do for work, Elizabeth?'

'I'm a part-time sales assistant at Dorothy Perkins in town. I spend the rest of the time looking after Annabelle.'

Tomek knew all of this, of course, he knew almost everything about them, but he wanted to hear it directly. He wanted to hear it straight from the horse's mouth.

Then he moved the conversation on to the events leading up to Annabelle's death. Their movements, their behaviour, if they'd noticed anything strange outside the house.

They hadn't. They'd seen nothing.

And during the time of Annabelle's abduction, Steven had been working in Southend, while Elizabeth had been in the store.

'Steve's been getting a load of work up in Southend recently. Business has been good. I'm so proud of him.'

Judging by the look on his face, Steven was prouder of himself than she was. In fact, he looked as though he'd have been happier to hear Tomek say he was proud of him.

'Congratulations,' Tomek replied.

The smile on Steven's face proved his point. 'Thanks. Taken a couple of years and a lot of hard work but I'm finally getting there. Putting a little extra away here and there...'

The man smiled but it quickly fell away and revealed his true feeling. That he was broken and hurt – whether by the death of his daughter or the constant pressure of providing financially for his family, or most likely both. Tomek didn't know. Though he could sense the feelings weren't going away anytime soon. He'd seen it happen before. The victim's father internalising the suffering and pain of death. Soaking it up like a malevolent sponge that had been glued to him and the only way to get it out was to rip it open.

And that was the way some men dealt with it. Ripping themselves open in the only way they knew how: exterminating the problem so it was no longer a concern for their families.

A short while after, Elizabeth's brother turned up. Vincent Gregory was exactly the way Tomek had expected him to be. Based on the one (and quite frankly vital) piece of information he knew about the man, he suspected his hair would be cut short so that there was very little of it left on his head, his face would be as round as his stomach, and he would have at least one, if not two, tattoos on his neck. Tomek had been right on the first two. As for the third, he'd missed the count by one. Vincent Gregory had three tattoos on his neck. The first was of a snake wrapping itself around his throat. Between the ribbons of skin and scales was a small boat that looked like it had been stencilled from the film *Pirates of the Caribbean*. The missing piece of the collage was the name 'Annabelle', with its jagged lines and poor attempt at bubble writing. There was no identity behind it, no clear style, and looked as though Annabelle herself had drawn it. In which case, fine. But if not, then Tomek thought it was about time Vincent find himself a new tattoo artist.

'Vinnie,' Elizabeth said to him as soon as he entered the living room.

'Oh, Beth, babe, I'm so sorry.'

The two embraced, their bodies colliding in a dull *thud*, and they stayed there for a moment longer than was socially acceptable. While the rest of them stood at the edge of the room, staring awkwardly as they watched Elizabeth and Vincent's hands massage the folds in each other's skin.

'I'm so sorry...' Vincent said as he pulled away from her and stared into her face, oblivious to the rest of the room.

'I know,' Elizabeth replied, then turned to Sean and Tomek. 'These are the detectives that are going to help find her killer.'

It took less than a fraction of a second for disgust to register on Vincent Gregory's face. Not because of Tomek – who looked no different to Steven Lake – but because of Sean. The only black man in the room. His face contorted and his mouth opened, but he caught himself at the last minute. He took a step forward and inflated his chest, as if squaring up to Sean.

'You *two* are the ones in charge of finding out who killed my niece? What happened – no one else available? I dunno what you're doing here...' he said to Sean. 'Thought I told you about coming back...'

Sean bristled as he fought the urge to grab the man by his throat and ram his fat head between the gap in the sofas.

'Mr Gregory,' Tomek said, jumping into the conversation before any sort of conflict could arise. 'Vincent... Vinnie... There's something you should know about us.'

'Oh, yeah – what's that?'

Tomek placed his palm on his chest. 'My name's Tomek. And no matter what you say or do, we will not stop until we find out what happened to Annabelle.'

As Tomek's name registered in Vincent's tiny head, his pupils dilated and his mouth opened wider.

'That's right,' Tomek continued. 'You've got a Polish man and a black man on the case. The best of the best, if I'm being honest. I don't know about you, Sean, but I can't think of anyone else I'd rather have helping out little Annabelle.'

'Absolutely,' Sean concurred.

They both kept their gaze firmly planted on Vincent Gregory

who, standing before them, seemed to have shrunk in size considerably.

'We're the best chance you've got,' Sean added.

'What about the... what about the woman that was here the other day? Anna, wasn't it?'

Triple Word Score? DC Anna Kaczmarek? The constable with the most Polish name possible?

'She's our family liaison officer. She'll still be coming over to update you when necessary.'

'Can't she do... more? I liked her. I thought she was... helpful.'

Of course you did, you racist fascist prick, because she didn't tell you her full name.

Or maybe you're not a racist fascist prick when it comes to women, you racist fascist prick.

Instead of voicing the thoughts inside his head, he offered the man a warm smile and returned to his position on the chair. 'If you don't mind we've got some questions to ask you, Vincent.'

'It's Vinnie.'

'Okay,' Tomek began. 'Well, Vincent, firstly, I'd like to—'

'You deaf?'

'Excuse me?'

'I said it was *Vinnie*.'

'And I said *ok-ay*. Just because I understood what you said doesn't mean I have to agree to it.'

A lot like your opinions...

'Now if you don't mind,' Tomek continued before Vincent could protest, 'we've got a lot to be getting on with.'

'Like taking our jobs?'

And there it was. Tomek felt the urge to check his watch. To see how long it had taken for the man to reveal himself in all his naked splendour. He supposed it was less than a few minutes, a new record.

'Which jobs would those be, Vincent?'

Vincent wagged his finger at them. 'Your lot...' he said in the end. 'Taking our jobs.'

'Which jobs have we taken, Mr Gregory?'

This was a topic Tomek had no doubt the man could wax lyrical about. Most racists could. They could argue and argue, but it was all vague, superfluous waffle that never came up with any facts or examples. It was all a malicious hatred fuelled by a growing divide in social and economic circumstances.

'Uh... Well, I work in Southend Hospital, right? Cleaning the floors and mopping up people's piss, and that. And all the people I work with are foreigners, right? They've come over and started working here...'

'Yes. Okay. But have they taken your job?'

'Uh... No but I can't get no other jobs anymore because the rest of them have taken them.'

And, naturally, it had absolutely nothing to do with his abilities, his skills. It was always someone else's fault.

Tomek decided that he didn't want to entertain the conversation any longer. The best way to beat a bully was to walk away and let them run out of steam. That way there was no confrontation and no risk of losing his job. Not only would that have made Vincent Gregory a very happy man, it was only his first day back and he couldn't risk going back to sitting around the house doing nothing again. Not for a long time, at least.

'I think that's everything for now,' Tomek told them, but spoke directly to Steven Lake. 'We'll be in touch if we need anything in the immediate future.'

On the way out, Tomek brushed past Vincent Gregory and received an apologetic smile from Beth with an F. As they headed back to the car, Tomek sensed Vincent opening the curtains and glaring at them through the window. He had half a mind to turn back and wave, just as a little reminder that he wasn't going anywhere, but then thought better of it.

He wasn't that childish.

Maybe...

'What did you make of all that then?' Sean asked as they climbed into the car. 'He's a nasty piece of work, isn't he?'

'No,' Tomek replied, plugging in his seat belt. 'There's nothing nasty about him. He's just a cunt.'

CHAPTER
EIGHTEEN

Tomek gently closed the door to DCI Cleaves' office, shutting out the soft drone of the incident room behind him. Nick had summoned him the moment he'd arrived in the car park. This morning, the chief inspector wore a look of consternation on his face, an expression Tomek had never seen before and, even though it had been less than a week, Tomek was sure the man had put on some weight since he'd last seen him.

'Something up, guv? You look like you've just had some bad news.'

'That's one way of putting it, Tomek.'

Tomek didn't like the sound of that. Not one bit. Something was coming his way, and the summation of his experience taught him it wasn't going to be the offer of promotion.

'I guess, firstly, I should say welcome back. Nothing like chucking you back in at the deep end, is there?'

'You chucked me in right in the middle of Canvey, sir. That's far worse.'

'I heard about your little fall...' The sides of Nick's mouth flickered into a smirk, though he tried his hardest to suppress it. 'That you went over like a sack of shit.'

'Happens to the best of us.' Tomek looked down at his arm and brushed a chunk of dried mud from his blazer.

'Poor little Annabelle...' Nick continued, his gaze falling onto the table. 'Devastating...'

It was the first time in a while that Tomek had seen Nick show any semblance of emotion over a case. Usually he was rigid, ambivalent, a master of hiding his true feelings. But this was different. And Tomek wasn't sure how to react.

'You all right there, sir?' he said. 'Need me to get you a tissue?'

The look he'd come to expect from Nick – the sinister glare, the upturned nostrils, the furrowed brow – returned with aplomb.

'Fuck off. I'm fine. Just sad to see. You must get that, now you've got Kasia in your life?'

Tomek hadn't thought about it like that. In fact, he'd tried not to. That the age difference between Annabelle and Kasia helped him come to the conclusion it *wasn't* the same and it *wasn't* possible for something similar to happen to his daughter.

'I guess,' he replied with a shrug of the shoulders. 'But I'm trying not to think about it.'

'Probably for the best.'

A long moment of silence wandered through the window and sat between them. Tomek shifted uncomfortably in his seat and surveyed the room to fill the time – the room he'd seen countless times and had started to feel like he knew every square inch of. It contained the usual fixtures and furnishings of an office: a chair, a desk, shelves, a whiteboard, even a chest of drawers reserved for the top secret parts of the job Nick wouldn't share with him, no matter how much he begged. But there were no home effects there, nothing to make it feel like a warm and welcoming place. Though Tomek didn't think he could have done any better if he'd had an office of his own. Except maybe for a plant. Definitely a plant. Perhaps even a bonsai...

Now there was an idea. Nick's birthday was coming up in a couple of months.

Eventually, after what felt like a minute, Nick continued: 'As part of your return to work you've got to do some boring welfare shit. The guys in HR will help you with all that, but I can't imagine it'll take you too long. You've already hit the ground running and it's only been two minutes.'

'You might have to start calling me Usain Bowen,' he said. 'Fastest man in the team.'

'Your arse alone must weigh about fifty kilograms. Think of the drag.'

Tomek had never been one to admit it, but in the team there'd been a running joke that, out of all the men, he had the biggest arse. He slotted it down to his morning runs, but in truth, it had always been large, and he often struggled to find a pair of jeans or trousers comfortable enough for both it, and his even thicker thighs, to fit into.

'Even with the drag, still quicker than you and that stomach of yours,' Tomek replied.

'What are you talking about?' Nick looked down at his belly with a scintilla of triumph flashing in his eyes. 'I've got the body of a God.'

'Shame it's the Buddha.'

'Good one, but the Buddha isn't a God... *actually*.'

Tomek held his hands up in defeat. 'Didn't realise we had two Captain Actuallys on the team...'

Another moment of silence, this time briefer.

There was something on Nick's mind, but he was too afraid to say it. Filling the gaps of indecision with awkward silence. And Tomek wanted to know what it was. He opened his mouth to find out, but was beaten to it.

'How are you finding the investigation so far? Any ideas? I trust you had a chance to review all the notes before you came back.'

Tomek nodded. 'Nothing better to do with my time, sir. Only so much daytime TV I can watch before I start thinking about wanting to hang myself.' Tomek plugged a finger in his ear and wriggled it around, then pulled it out and wiped the contents on his trousers without looking. 'Though I've been meaning to ask: who's been running the investigation so far?'

'Inspector Orange.'

'Orange...?'

'Yes. You got a problem with that?'

'That's her actual surname?'

'I know you find it hard to believe, but yes.'

Tomek sucked on his bottom lip. 'At least I don't think we'll struggle to come up with a nickname for her. Though we might struggle if we want to find something that rhymes with it.'

'You will do no such thing. She's only just started, and I won't have you winding her up by making fun of her.'

'We'll be laughing *with* her, sir. Not *at* her.'

'I don't give a fuck. It all amounts to the same thing.'

Tomek couldn't argue with that. As the instigator for many of the nicknames in the office – Captain Actually, Tepid Tony, Chey-enne Pepper, to name a few – he sometimes wondered whether he took them too far, whether they crossed a line at all. But since no one had pulled him up on it or complained to him about them, he'd never considered them to be a problem.

'I'll introduce you to her after this,' Nick said, pulling Tomek out of his thoughts. 'She's lovely, and knows what she's doing.'

'You sure?'

Nick's eyebrow rose and he tilted forward on his chair. 'Sergeant? Do you want to think carefully about your next few words?'

Tomek didn't want to get on the wrong side of another inspector within the team. Especially one he hadn't met yet. But there were some things he needed to say.

'Nothing, sir. Well, nothing terrible. Just that... I think things could have been done a bit better, that's all.'

'Better?'

'Faster. More efficient. Annabelle Lake had been missing for two days when you gave me the case file, and based on the information inside it, I'd say it was about half the amount of work that could have been done to find her.'

'And you're the expert in finding small children?'

A wry smile made its way onto his lips. 'Like you said yourself, sir, they have a habit of finding themselves on my doorstep.'

Then immediately wished he hadn't said that. Not because it was egotistical or big-headed, but because it made him seem like something he wasn't. And he wasn't prepared to go down that route again.

'What would you have done differently?'

'I... I don't know. I just would have been more... proactive. I didn't even see her face get shared on our social channels...'

'That's because you don't have them.'

Tomek ignored the comment and continued. 'Dare I say that I feel like I could have done a better job.'

'Really?'

'No need to sound so surprised, sir.'

'I'm not. It's just that I've never heard you say anything like that before. Are you feeling okay? Do you need me to schedule the HR return to work for five minutes?'

'No.'

'Go on then, hotshot. Out with it.'

Tomek massaged the palm of his hand with his opposing thumb, rubbing away the stress. 'The past few weeks have given me a lot of time to think, to reflect. I know it's something you've tried to push my way in the past, and I've always been reluctant for some reason. Some might argue it's fear, nerves. I might argue it's comfort. I'm used to following someone else's lead, rather than taking my own initiative. Which is why I've been thinking about the inspector's exam.'

'Oh, right?'

'And for that, I thought I could help lead this murder investigation in some way. Take over the reins.'

A look of surprise, as though something Nick had never seen before had just crept along his desk. 'For the first time since I've known you, I'm speechless. You're growing up,' he said. 'Kasia must have changed you in more ways than you can imagine.'

'Most notably my bank balance, Nick. I've got to fund the next five years of make-up, phone bills, clothes and social nights somehow. And not to mention the black hole my money will sink into if she thinks about going to university.'

'They only get more expensive as they get older,' said Nick, spoken like a man with experience.

'Don't suppose you fancy giving me some of your money, instead?'

Nick didn't think so. But he did think that he would consider it. The only problem was, there was a catch.

'That's why I brought you in here...'

Oh good. Here we go.

'What have I done now?'

'After you left the Lake family household, I received a phone call from Vincent Gregory...'

Nick didn't need to say anything else; Tomek could see where this was going already.

'For reasons he made very clear over the phone, he doesn't want you on the investigation anymore.'

'Which reasons are those?'

'I'm not prepared to say, but he made his thoughts on the matter very clear.'

'So now what?'

'I don't think I can have you running this investigation. If the family don't want you anywhere near it, then there's nothing I can do.'

'What reasons did he give?'

Tomek's mind swelled with a red mist that rapidly began to fog and blur his rage.

'Your attitude,' Nick replied. 'And we'll leave it at that.'

'Bollocks. I know the *real* reason. And so do you. Has he asked for Sean to come off the team as well?'

Nick failed to meet Tomek's gaze.

'Brilliant,' he spat. 'So now what?'

'You'll have a limited role. More back office, rather than front of house.'

'So I'm being kept indoors like a fucking dog?'

'No different to what you've been used to for the past four weeks.'

Tomek breathed heavily through his nose, letting all the frustration dissipate out of him. Though not everything left his body. Not entirely. Not while he continued to think about that stumpy, pompous, little fuckwit bastard.

'The guy's a racist,' he said, censoring his word choice.

'We don't know that.'

Tomek gasped in shock. 'We do, and you know it.' He shook his head and turned his attention away from Nick. 'I can't believe we're doing what he wants. Fuck him, the scumbag!'

Nick held his palm in the air to placate Tomek. 'Carry on talking like that and you definitely won't be allowed anywhere near him.'

'I've just come back, and now this... Now *this*!'

'It's not like you won't be without work. You just won't be dealing with the family in a personal capacity.'

Tomek folded his arms across his chest and huffed. He'd said everything he needed to say – without further running the risk of losing his job – and decided to keep quiet. There was nothing more he could do or say that would convince Nick to change his mind. The man was stubborn at times, and he had every right to be.

'Now what?' he asked like a child.

'I think it's about time we met your new colleagues.'

Tomek was in the least agreeable, least open and friendly mood when he'd been introduced to Detective Inspector Victoria Orange and Detective Constable Martin Brown. So much so, in fact, that he hadn't even bothered to make a reference to the fact their surnames were both colours, and that the office was one colour on the rainbow away from completing the make-up of a Jaffa cake.

Victoria Orange was younger than Tomek and had fast-tracked her way to inspector. Her goal had been to achieve the rank before she reached forty. After only ten years in the job, she'd accomplished it. Tomek hoped that the role hadn't gone to her head. He'd met her kind before: rank didn't always equate to experience, and sometimes there were gaps between the two. Gaps that he'd already begun to notice.

DC Martin Brown, meanwhile, was an unassuming man in his early thirties. Medium height, medium build, with a beard that Tomek could only dream of growing for himself. As a result he became slightly envious, and thought Martin Brown looked like the type of man to order his steak well done. He was dressed in a blue-and-white flannel shirt and a pair of chino trousers. Not quite the standard uniform, but if Nick didn't mind, then Tomek didn't have a leg to stand on. Martin had transferred from Colchester, thanks to the better transport links and also the new challenge, and had been with them for a little over two weeks.

'Welcome to the team,' Tomek said briefly.

'Thanks.'

'How you settling in?'

'Good. Though I knew I should have bought the nicer keyboard. Don't get me wrong, this one's good, but it isn't half straining on the old wrists.'

It wasn't until Tomek looked down at the man's desk that he

realised he was using his own computer keyboard. A wireless one with small keys.

For a moment he wondered whether he was really about to enter a conversation with a grown man about keyboards, but then realised that it made sense – that Martin seemed like the neurotic type to have one on standby in his backpack, a portable one ready for any occasion.

He could feel a nickname coming on...

After he'd finished with Mr Keys, Tomek turned his attention to DC Anna Kaczmarek – or Triple Word Score as she was known thanks to her long, and for some, unpronounceable surname. The family liaison officer was busy on her computer when he found her, sipping on a can of Coke through a straw to protect her lip balm from rubbing off.

He pulled the chair out from beneath the desk beside her and dropped himself into it.

'Hope I wasn't distracting you from anything,' he said.

'That's never stopped you before,' she replied.

As the only two Polish people in the team, they had a particular connection, a bond, that he didn't share with anyone else. He often thought of her as an older sister, and she fit the stereotype of a Polish person well – no-nonsense, serious, and the most part liked to keep herself to herself. She seldom joined them at the pub, and as soon as her shift was finished she went home to her husband and son. But when she spoke with Tomek, it was as though she came alive, stepped out of her shell and showed Tomek the real her. Whenever they spoke it was usually in Polish – the language she felt most comfortable with. And the other added benefit was that they could gossip and slag off other members of the team.

'I've got one word for you...' he began.

'Yeah?'

'Vincent.'

Anna rolled her eyes behind her heavily applied make-up.

'He's a bit of a scumbag, isn't he?'

'You want me to write that down on his profile?' she asked.

'If you could... Just make sure you don't attribute it to me. I can't be the only one who seems to have that impression?'

'No, you're well within your rights to think that."

'He seems to like you though,' Tomek said, recalling the conversation he'd had in the living room. 'Which I can't get my head around, for a man who doesn't like *our lot.*'

'I told him I was married to a Polish man. He doesn't like it, but it's... *better.*'

'Better than a Polish native and a black man?'

Anna nodded solemnly. 'You should have seen the way he approached me when I went round there the first time. It was like he was going to strangle me.'

Tomek pondered on the interesting choice of words for a moment.

'He was aggressive?'

She nodded again.

'In what way?'

'The way that suggested he was going to be violent. What other way would there be?'

Good point.

'And this was the first time you saw him?'

Another nod.

'And he made you feel like you had to lie to him to protect yourself? Tell him what he wanted to hear?'

And another. If only someone had warned him, he might have been able to do the same thing. Told them that his name was Tom instead of Tomek.

'And when you first saw him, was he already at the house?'

She shrugged. 'Yes and no. He was on his way over when I got there. Beth had called Vincent and asked him to come home from work.'

'What about her husband?'

'Not sure. Think she tried Steven afterwards.'

'So she called her brother about her missing daughter before she called her husband?'

'Yeah, I guess.'

Tomek took a moment to consider this. Images of the hug that the two siblings had shared, leaving Steven Lake to sit on the sofa like a lost child, appeared in his mind. The hands getting lost in the folds of each other's back. The way they looked like they were *enjoying* it.

'I take it they're a close family?'

'Close is a bit of an understatement. Vincent and Elizabeth were foster children. They grew up in various homes. They were inseparable from one another – her words, not mine.'

'Big word for her,' Tomek noted. 'She doesn't strike me as the type to know what it means.'

'Clearly she does. And they're still inseparable to this day. Vincent's always round there, coming over for a chat, having lunch, dinner. It's strange. And I'm fairly sure he's even got a key.'

'So he comes and goes as he pleases?'

'He comes more than he goes.'

Another interesting choice of terminology.

'What about Vincent's wife?' he asked.

'An unhappy marriage, as far as I can tell.'

'How so?'

'Why else would he be over there all the time?'

Why else indeed?

Tomek peered his head over the computer screen and nodded in the general direction of DI Orange, who was sitting in her office, staring at the wall.

'What's she saying about him?'

'Nothing. Don't think she's considered him a suspect.'

'Hmm. Well, maybe it's about time she did.'

CHAPTER
NINETEEN

It was nearly six o'clock by the time Tomek left the incident room. Rush hour. Which made a twenty-minute journey into nearly an hour-long affair. As he gradually progressed through the stop-start of the Southend traffic lights, wincing every time the suspension of his car bounced in and out of a pothole, he checked his phone repeatedly. He hadn't heard from Kasia all day. He'd messaged her in the morning to see if she'd got to school okay; same again at lunchtime (and if she'd remembered to pack the food he'd made for her); and then again at four when she was due home. And yet he'd received no word, no reply, no answer to his several phone calls. To say he'd started to worry was an understatement.

She was glued to the bloody thing, so it was impossible for her to not have seen the messages or the missed calls. Either something serious had happened to her, or she'd seen them and chosen to ignore them.

If it was the latter, he couldn't think why she would be choosing to ignore him. Had he done something wrong? Said something inappropriate that might have upset her? It was possible, but nothing came to mind. Or was she more upset about him going back to work than she'd let on?

And still, by half-seven, after he'd been home for just under an hour, pacing about the house, calling her several times, he'd had no word from her.

Until the doorbell rang a few minutes shy of 8 p.m.

At the sound of it, Tomek vaulted down the stairs, skipping them two at a time. At the bottom, he thrust open the door, almost losing his grip on it and smashing it into the wall. The light from the stairwell bathed the three women standing in front of him in an almost pure white. One he recognised. The other two he was unfamiliar with. The girl to Kasia's left was of similar age and looked almost identical, with her brown hair, young face, and school uniform. Whereas the woman standing behind them was older, more mature, and appeared happier to see him than Kasia was.

'Where have you been?' he asked her, ignoring the other two.

'That's my fault,' the woman said. She wedged herself between the two girls and held out a hand. 'Sorry about that. My name's Louise... I'm Sylvia's mum.'

Sylvia. The girl he'd now heard so much about. The one who had the cat that was the most adorable thing in the world. The one who spoke to four different boys at once and had them all on tenterhooks. The one who was much better at sports than Kasia. The one who was really funny and the only one who was nice enough to introduce herself to Kasia on her first day.

Tomek had known what that was like. To be lonely, isolated and without any friends at a new school. As a five-year-old, he'd been forced to go to a British school without speaking the language, without knowing anyone on the playground, and sitting in the corner of the room of his own. It hadn't been until little Saskia Albright had come up to him and asked if he wanted to be friends. All it took was one act of random kindness to change the trajectory of someone's life.

'Nice to meet you. I'm Tomek, Kasia's father.'

The words still felt strange to say – even stranger to hear – and he didn't know if he'd ever get used to them.

'I know who you are,' she said, smiling warmly at him with her eyes. 'I wondered if we might come in?'

Tomek stepped aside and let the girls enter first, then Louise. Tomek followed behind and shut the door after them. When they reached the top of the stairs, Louise suggested the girls go into the bedroom, while the adults stayed and had a chat.

'Cup of tea?' Tomek asked, more out of politeness than anything else.

'Please,' she said. 'Milk, no sugar.'

As soon as he'd finished making the tea, Tomek handed her the mug and they both rested against the kitchen counter, the furthest point from the bedroom.

Also the cleanest.

'Sorry it's a mess,' he said. 'I wasn't expecting company.'

'That's fine. Kasia mentioned you've got some unusual sleeping arrangements.'

She could say that again.

'I've given Kasia something to eat,' Louise began. 'Just a pizza. It was all we had in the freezer. So you don't have to worry about that.'

'Thank you. I appreciate it.'

Though I'd appreciate you telling me why I haven't heard from her all day, he thought, but couldn't bring himself to talk to her like that.

Louise sipped delicately from her tea, and looked out of the kitchen window. 'Sorry I didn't bring her home sooner,' she said.

'I tried calling her about fifty times.'

'You didn't know where she was?'

Tomek shook his head. 'No idea. I thought something had happened to her.'

'Oh. Well, she told me that you knew where she was and that you were fine with it.'

Tomek offered her a smile that said he definitely wasn't fine with it.

'Well, I'm sorry about that.'

'It's all right. Not your fault.'

'Though we would have been here sooner, mind. Took us twenty minutes alone to find a parking space.'

'Tell me about it. You've got more chance parking in London and walking back before you find a space down here. It's a nightmare.'

'I bet you'll be glad to move...'

Oh. So she knew about that then, did she?

So not only had Kasia lied about her whereabouts, but she'd also let slip that they were moving house. Tomek wondered how much more Kasia had told her.

'It'll be nice. A new start for the both of us,' he replied, aware he was coming off as cagey. 'I'm looking forward to having my own space, more than anything.'

'A room of one's own...'

The reference was lost on Tomek, but he didn't want to come across as stupid, so instead he agreed and nodded, hiding his brief embarrassment behind the mug.

'I guess you're wondering why Kasia came round ours this evening,' Louise said, her voice soft.

'The thought had crossed my mind, yes...'

She set her mug on the counter. Tomek prepared himself. His mind racing. Thinking of the worst possible scenarios. That she'd been truanting, that she'd got herself into a fight, that she'd got herself expelled somehow.

'She's had a rough day,' Louise continued. 'Nothing serious. Sylvia went through it only the other week, so we were primed to help.'

'Went through what?'

'Kasia's period started today. Her first one.'

Tomek felt like the wind had been knocked out of him. This

wasn't what he'd been expecting at all. Of course, he knew that she hadn't started yet, that it was bound to come in the next few months or so, but he still wasn't prepared for it. Bunking from school, getting into fights, getting into trouble – he could deal with those things, he felt qualified for those. But this... he had no idea where to start.

'Sylvia called me during their lunch and asked if Kasia could home with her. I said that of course she could, that she was always welcome. When they got there I sat Kasia down and explained how it all works. I know they have these sorts of classes in school nowadays but it's not the same until you've experienced it. Fortunately we had all the necessary stuff in our house, so we were equipped to assist her. Do you... do you have sanitary towels or tampons here?'

The blank expression on Tomek's face answered her question.

Smiling, she reached into her bag and produced a pack of tampons.

'I know it's awkward, especially given... well, everything, but these are the ones she said she feels most comfortable using.'

Tomek took the box from her and held them at arm's length, like he'd just been given a bomb to hold.

'How...? How...? Thank you.'

'You're welcome,' Louise said with another warm smile. 'She asked me to come over so we could discuss it together. I think she finds it a bit awkward at the moment, which is only natural.'

She wasn't the only one.

'It's going to be a strange time for her. What with everything else that's going on. Now all her hormones are going to be out of place. Right now she's feeling a bit fragile.'

'What can I...? How do I...?'

The words just weren't coming out.

'How do you help her?'

Tomek nodded. He could tell he was going to need as much hand-holding as possible.

'I find that chocolate gets me through it,' Louise said. 'Lots and lots of chocolate. Same for Sylvia. The cheaper the better.'

'That explains why she bought so much of it when we went food shopping the other day.'

'And there's your first lesson.'

'How many more are there?' he asked, hopeful.

'If I knew the answer to that, I'd be able to help you.' She took a step closer to him, placed a hand on his forearm. Tomek looked down at it, searching for a wedding ring. There was none. Louise continued: 'Don't think you should blame yourself for any of this. It's new to all of us at one time or another. You'll get there, eventually. And so will she. Just give her time.'

CHAPTER
TWENTY

The following morning, after what had been a tumultuous night's sleep on the upside-down sofa bed, Tomek found himself in the major incident room by 8 a.m. By the time he arrived, he was surprised to see he was one of the first there. With him in the room were his two new colleagues, DI Orange and DC Brown, speaking with someone Tomek didn't recognise. New names and new faces were all too common across the wider teams in the station, but not for their team in CID. They were close knit, and so it felt strange to see someone potentially muscling their way in. That being said, he didn't know who the unidentified female was, and he wasn't too arsed about finding out either. Rather leave that up to the two-thirds Jaffa cake and find out afterwards.

As he watched them giggle and whisper with one another, the cynic in him told him he should have been paying attention, but he was too tired to think about it. It had been a terrible night's sleep, one of the worst in ages. There had been another nightmare. This time new, different. The darkness taking on different forms. Until Tony's death, Tomek had been plagued with nightmares regarding his brother's death – the park, the blackness, the playground, the blood –

but now they'd been replaced with images of water, of marshland, of Tomek paddling in a kayak, searching for the abandoned shack in the distance, of Tony dangling there...

Each nightmare was a different retelling. A new narrator. A new plot twist.

Last night's had been particularly grisly. Instead of dangling from a rope, Tony had hung there by a thick chain. And the blood. There had been more blood – so much more. It had adorned the walls of the shack, seeping through the wood and into the marshland outside. Splashing onto his legs and in his shoes with every step. And then Tony's head had lifted, a demonic gaze sprawled across his bloody and battered face. Lips moving, wheezy air falling over his teeth. And then it became legible, audible.

Why didn't you save me?
You could have saved me.
You could have stopped this.

And then, during the nightmare, Tony's face had changed into a sort of metamorphosis of Kasia and Annabelle Lake. The same brown hair, same colour eyes. But the features had been different, merged. Kasia's larger, more protruding nose, with Annabelle's small lips.

Tomek was no dream expert – he'd only Googled his dreams a handful of times to make sure he wasn't going completely insane – but he was certain the events of the day before were getting to him, wreaking havoc with his subconscious.

The sound of the door opening behind him brought his attention back to the present. DC Rachel Hamilton and DC Chey Carter entered, said good morning to him and then headed straight to the coffee machine – with Tomek's order. They returned a few moments later, finding him with his eyes half closed.

'Easy, tiger,' Chey said, handing the drink across. 'Calm yourself down, yeah? Can't be having you this excited first thing in the morning. Putting the rest of us to shame.'

'Says the one whose mum still wakes him up every morning.'

Chey fell silent and drank from his drink. He knew when he'd been beat. Which was most of the time.

Tomek turned to Rachel. Her make-up had been hastily applied this morning, and her eyes were bloodshot and swollen.

'Do you feel as bad as you look?' he asked.

'Charming.' She scoffed and took a large gulp of her drink, more to cover her face than out of any real thirst.

'Late one, was it?'

'Only a few.'

'Heard that before. Where'd you go?'

'Just the Last Post.'

'Who'd you go out with?' he asked nosily.

Rachel hesitated before responding. 'Sean... Chey... though his mum wanted him back by eight—'

'Shut up!'

'—Nadia came for a Coke, and so did Martin.'

'The whole crowd was there then...'

'Yeah. We wanted to invite you but you said you had to go. We figured that you needed to get back for Kasia.'

Tomek couldn't argue with that logic. In fact he couldn't argue at all. They'd been absolutely right not to invite him. His priorities had changed. Had this discussion taken place six months before, he might have felt a raging case of FOMO, the fear of missing out. But now... now he wasn't as bothered. Sure, it would have been nice to have received an invite (just so he could have had the privilege of turning it down and saving his pride for a later date), but he didn't feel as upset as he usually might have. There were more important things to worry about than getting drunk with his friends now.

Like worrying about Kasia at school. Making sure she had everything she needed to be as comfortable as she could during her classes.

A few minutes later, and everyone in the team had arrived. Sean and Nadia had both turned up late, and slipped through the doorway without further reprimand. It was interesting to see that Inspector Orange wasn't willing to lay down the law just yet. Though if she wanted to embed herself as a hard arse who took no prisoners, Tomek thought she'd lost a little credibility already. If she'd come in, guns blazing, then the team might have toed the line more, followed the precedent. But now he wasn't so sure. Instead, she gave them both their last warning before continuing the meeting.

'All right everyone,' she began, regaining control of the room quickly. 'I want to begin today by discussing yesterday's events and bouncing ideas off each other. Then we can better pivot our priorities for today.'

As the discussion began, Tomek reshuffled in his seat and began paying closer attention. Chey was first up. He brushed away a few crumbs from an earlier pastry and cleared his throat.

'Not good news, I'm afraid,' he said. 'The two roads that run around the crime scene don't have CCTV. Well, they do – just not in the two entrances. They're by the roundabout instead. Similarly we don't have any home surveillance footage because the nearest house is about a ten-minute walk away.'

'So you had a pretty quiet afternoon then, eh?' Tomek commented.

Chey chose not to answer, though his embarrassed expression confirmed the truth.

'Do we know Annabelle's final movements?' Victoria asked. 'Do we have any working theories?'

As she spoke, her face flushed a deeper shade of red which, combined with her make-up, made Tomek think she was Orange by name, orange by nature.

Chey reached into his bag and produced his laptop. Then he called the screen up to the monitor on the other side of the room, a technological feat Tomek had only mastered a few months before. On the television monitor was a map of the park in which Annabelle had been found and the surrounding area. At the top was the river that separated the island from Benfleet, denoted by a blue line that snaked its way through the marshes. Beneath it was a marina and boatyard in grey. Beneath that was a park, a large expanse of light green. And running through the rest of the image were dark grey lines to signify roads. Chey moved the cursor to a small cluster of narrow lines, then to another smaller cluster.

'These are the two nearest places of residence that I reckon she could have come from. They're both about a ten-minute walk from the field. My guess would be that she was kept in one of the houses in these areas and then marched to her death.'

'We don't think she was driven or dropped off?'

Chey shook his head. He moved a red pin to the middle of a dark grey line, and replicated the movement further down the map.

'This is the main road that runs round the park, and there's the roundabout. These points are where the CCTV cameras are. I've reviewed them and there are no cars coming or going at the time of death.'

'So she just appeared out of nowhere?' Sean asked.

'Maybe. Or like I said, someone in these houses walked her there...'

Victoria considered a moment. She turned to face the screen and ran her finger along the white lines.

'Where does the teacher, Amelia Duggan, live?'

Chey pointed to her house with another red marker. He dropped it on the residential street to the left of the park.

'Interesting...' Victoria said. 'Good work, Chey. I'm impressed.'

Chey's face beamed with the innocence of a child, then he sat down.

'What you thinking, ma'am?' Tomek asked. 'Amelia Duggan's got something to do with it?'

'Possibly. Maybe. It's just that she's there when little Annabelle goes missing – she sees the car but not the person. And then she's the one to find her in the playground. What are the odds of both those things happening?'

'In Canvey... probably not that high at all,' Sean noted. 'But I see your point.'

It was a good point, but one that Tomek wasn't sure he agreed with. Yes, the chances of her being involved in both the disappearance and the sudden reappearance of Annabelle Lake were in the atmosphere, but Canvey was a small place, with a population of over thirty thousand, and chances were the killer knew of Amelia's close relationship with Annabelle and could have used that information to set her up, to make it seem like she'd had a role to play. More often than not these abductions and killings were related – the victim knew the killer and vice versa – and while it might not have been Amelia Duggan, it might have been someone who knew them both.

Tomek pitched the idea.

'Any names come to mind?' DC Martin Brown asked as he stroked some hair behind his ears.

Tomek shrugged. 'You know more about this investigation than me.' He hesitated. 'Is there a connection between Amelia Duggan and Vincent Gregory?'

Tomek had been waiting to get that name in since the start of the conversation. More out of spite than anything else. That little racist fascist bastard...

'Not that we've been able to pick out,' Rachel murmured, turning to address him as she spoke. 'But we can certainly dig deeper into it if you think it's worth the time, ma'am?'

Victoria picked at her fingernails as she listened. The nerves of speaking to a new audience were still clearly getting to her. Then he realised that she'd been working with the team for the past two weeks, and that the only anomaly to that group was himself. Perhaps it was he who was making her nervous...

'I think not... not for now. He's definitely on the radar, as are the rest of the family, so we'll keep a keen eye on them until I think it's pertinent to do otherwise.'

A knock came from the door on the other side of the incident room. All the heads in the room pivoted towards it. Gradually, it opened and Lorna Dean, the Home Office pathologist, peered her head round, fiery red hair dangling by her shoulders.

'Not interrupting, am I?'

'Yes,' Tomek said. 'How rude of you. Do you think you could come back in about thirty seconds?'

Realising that the remark had come from him, and that she was under no circumstance to take it seriously, Lorna stepped into the room and shut the door behind her.

'I've got my report if you fancy listening to it,' she said.

'Absolutely. Couldn't have come at a better time.' Victoria moved aside to allow Lorna through. The excited look on her face suggested she was happy for the interruption. Either because it was an important part of the investigation process or because it allowed someone else to speak for a change and took some of the light away from her.

Or perhaps both.

At the head of the room, Lorna scanned each of their faces before speaking.

'Annabelle Lake,' she began. 'Nine years, four months and fifty-five days old. Struck down in the prime of life. How? Well, she was strangled. Strangled by the same chains that she may well have once played with. She was hanged, left to dangle a few feet above the air. How long did it take her to die? I'm glad you asked: not long. It didn't take long at all for the chains to eventually starve her tiny brain of oxygen. Less than a minute, in fact. In that time our killer had plenty of time to flee the scene and leave poor Annabelle Lake at the hands of gravity. Any questions so far?'

Tomek didn't know why she was speaking to them in such a way, as though he was witnessing a theatrical production, but he was loving it, and he felt overcome to raise his hand.

'Have you firmed up the time of death?'

'Good question! Though I shall answer that with another question: when do you think she died? And not Tomek or Sean – they've already heard all this.'

'At some point in the middle of the night,' Chey said, the hint of excitement strong on his voice. 'That's when these things usually happen. Surprised it wasn't a dog walker who found her either...'

'As I'm sure is the dog walker. Alas, you would be wrong. I estimate her time of death at roughly five a.m. to six a.m.'

A collective gasp and a few 'Ooos' rolled throughout the room. At least they were all getting behind Lorna's performance. Something to brighten up the morbidity of death.

'Interesting, isn't it? Which means she was still relatively warm by the time we got there. Though the weather had started to have its way with her...'

Sensing the hook dangling in front of him, Tomek was next to speak.

'Speaking of which,' he said, 'were there any signs of sexual assault or molestation?'

The words, which would have once rolled off his tongue without any further thought or consideration, now came out like vegetable soup. Clunky and a proper mouthful.

'Glad you picked up on that one, Tomek,' Lorna started, then asked: 'How was the trip yesterday? Didn't get too muddy did you?'

Tomek shot her a facetious smile and waited for her to continue.

'I found no evidence to suggest that Annabelle Lake had been molested or penetrated, no.'

The room considered this for a moment. If she hadn't been injured or harmed in the process of her kidnapping, and if she hadn't been sexually assaulted or violated, and if there had been no ransom demand placed on the family – then what the fuck was going on? What was the motive? What was the reasoning behind her abduction? Could it have been as simple as someone taking her and killing her? Could it be so black and white? In Tomek's experience, he'd come to learn that it was never that clear-cut.

'Is there anything else we need to know?' asked Victoria from the back.

'A couple of things. The first is that I found some sand and dirt in her shoes and on her feet which has been sent away for testing. And, I'm not sure whether it's of any use to you, but the contents of Annabelle's stomach contained a lot of fish products. Fish food. Like salmon... tuna. It fucking stank, I can tell you that much, but—'

The sound of papers rustling frantically brought Victoria to a steady halt. She, along with everyone else in the room, turned their attention to the source of the noise.

Anna, who had been last in before Sean and Nadia, grabbed a sheet from her pile and waved it in the air triumphantly.

'Fish!'

'Said the caveman,' Chey noted. Then added: 'Or cave*woman*.'

Anna shot him a Polish look of derision, much fiercer and intimidating than anyone else in the room was capable of. 'Yes, thanks for that, Chey. But what I mean is, fish. Annabelle *loves* fish.'

'Can't say I ever did,' Chey continued, without reading the room. He then quickly realised that they were all eagerly sitting on the edges of their chairs, waiting to hear what Anna had to say.

'Elizabeth Lake told me that Annabelle loves fish. But she's not allowed it when she's at home... Steven doesn't like it and thinks that the industry behind fishing is corrupt and tarnishing the planet.'

A socially conscious electrician, that was a new one for Tomek.

'But when Annabelle goes over to her uncle's, Uncle Vincent's, she says that she can have as much fish as she wants. He even buys packets of salmon and tuna especially for her.'

Anna let that sit for a while as they computed the severity of it.

'I think that means perhaps we should bring Mr Gregory in for a chat,' Victoria said as she returned to the head of the room. 'Don't you?'

CHAPTER
TWENTY-ONE

T hanks to the complaint that had been made about him, Tomek was allowed nowhere near Vincent Gregory. Neither was Sean. Something which both men were deeply unhappy about.

Tomek wanted nothing more than to sit across the other side of the table from that rotund little bastard and help him dig his own hole. He wanted to watch the man's face crumple and whither as he realised his time was up.

Instead he would have to put up with watching it in the incident room via a live feed. But the only problem was, however, the team couldn't find him. They couldn't find him at his place of work in Southend Hospital, nor could they find him at his home or his sister's. The man had either gone into hiding, or he was just ignoring their many attempts to contact him. Either way a team of uniformed officers, with Martin's help, had been sent to look for him.

While he waited, Tomek had decided to fill the time by venturing down to Canvey again to speak with Miss Amelia Duggan.

He hoped this would be the last time he was forced to visit the island, but something in the back of his mind sensed it wouldn't be. That he would be coming here a lot more over the next few days, weeks. Perhaps it wasn't the island itself he hated, just the people in it. And if the rest of them were like Vincent Gregory, then he had every right to want to avoid it as much as possible.

Amelia Duggan had been given the day off from work, while the rest of the week was her prerogative. She'd been through a lot, and it was only fair she have time to recover from that.

'That's generous of the school,' Tomek noted.

'I know,' she said as she set a cup of tea down on his knee. 'It was the last thing I expected. We're massively understaffed as it is. They can't really afford for me to have the rest of the week off, but I guess they had no choice.'

Tomek lifted the cup to his mouth and took a sip. He could already taste the extra spoonful of sugar he hadn't asked for tingling his tastebuds. And he hated to admit that it was possibly one of the best cups of tea he'd had. He had met many teachers in his time – headteachers also – and there was one thing that he'd come to learn about them, one thing that Amelia Duggan had just proved, and that was that they made a blinding cup of tea. Some of the best he'd ever had. As though they tried to squeeze as much of the caffeine and taste out of it the same way they pressed their students for application and hard work.

'Do you think you'll go back this week?' he asked, setting the cup back on his knee.

'Probably. I could do with the distraction, if I'm being honest. I've done nothing but sit in here staring at the wall for the past twenty-four hours.'

'I know what that's like,' Tomek remarked. 'It's only worth doing if you've got something fun to look at. Best to get yourself out there as much as possible. Even talking with friends or neighbours or family members can help.'

'They're all busy. Especially my teacher friends.'

'And I guess going for a walk is off the cards...'

The comment didn't land in the way he'd hoped, and it was clear to see from her unimpressed expression that she was still a long way from coming to terms with what had happened.

'I think I'll get a cab – or a lift – next time I go in.'

'That's probably for the best.'

Tomek paused as he thought of a way to navigate the conversation onto the topic of Annabelle Lake and her family without making it so abrupt and jarring.

'I understand you were close... with Annabelle,' he began, hoping he was treading lightly enough for her.

Amelia nodded slowly and turned her gaze towards the window that looked out onto the busy residential street below. It was a while before she opened her mouth to speak. 'She was the best. She... she was different. She was special. I adored her as though she was my own. The sweetest little thing.'

'And were you close with the family? Or did you not really have any interaction with them?'

'Yes and no,' she said, gradually turning her attention towards him, like a slow-moving lighthouse. 'Because she lived so close to the school I hardly saw them. She always made it home safely, so there was no reason for them to come and pick her up.'

'And on the odd occasion that someone did need to, who was it typically?'

She turned to face him now, dead centre. 'Her uncle. Uncle Vinnie, she called him. He was always there, waiting outside the school gates, or waiting on the other side of the road for her to come back. I'm sure he dropped her off in the mornings a couple of times as well.'

Before and after he started work at the hospital, perhaps.

Tomek swallowed. 'And how would you describe their relationship?'

'Weird.'

That was all he needed. Weird. The same word that he'd thought the moment he'd seen the man enter Steven and Elizabeth's living room.

'Weird as in close? Or weird as in wrong?'

'A combination of the two. I don't know the specifics, but I don't think Vincent and his wife could have kids – Annabelle was always talking about Vincent calling her a "special little girl" – so I think he always treated her like his own daughter. But, even so... it was just a bit... *weird*.'

That word again.

'Was there ever any cause for concern? Any reason for their relationship to be flagged to social services that you know of?'

Amelia shook her head. 'I can't say I ever noticed anything wrong in that respect. I don't know... it was just...' She paused to sip her tea. 'You know when you look at something and think it doesn't look quite right.'

'Like a fifty-year-old going out with a twenty-year-old?'

Amelia smirked and giggled to herself. Probably the first time since the day before.

'Yeah. I guess. Like that. I mean, he was her uncle though, so he wouldn't have done anything... he wouldn't have done *that*, would he?'

'There was no evidence to suggest she'd been sexually assaulted, but that doesn't mean to say it didn't happen in other ways.'

And for that it put Vincent Gregory at the top of Tomek's list.

'Right now we don't have a whole lot of evidence to go on,' he continued. 'Which is why your help is greatly appreciated.'

Amelia's face seemed to light up, as though the thought or idea of her helping was the first step on her road to a full mental recovery.

'Is there anything else you'd like to know?' she asked, this time with more vigour and eagerness in her voice.

'Only whether anything else about the day of Annabelle's disappearance has come to mind? Sometimes these things take a while to unearth, once all the mess has settled.'

He wasn't sure he entirely believed that. It had been thirty years since his brother's death and, though the dust had settled on that event in his life a very long time ago, he was still no closer to *seeing* who was responsible.

Still, Amelia didn't need to know that. She would have to find out on her own.

As expected, she shook her head. 'Sorry... Nothing. I've already told your team everything I can remember.'

'What about anything before her disappearance?' Tomek asked.

Confusion wrapped itself around her face. 'What do you mean exactly?'

'If this was a targeted kidnap, looking out to get Annabelle specifically, then it would have taken some planning – a lot of it. Which means there might have been some unusual and unfamiliar faces around the school, either at the start, lunchtime or home time. People hovering, watching Annabelle's movements. They would have more than likely been in a car or well out of sight. I just wondered whether you'd seen anything like that?'

Amelia turned her attention to the window again, as though the answer was standing outside.

'I'm sorry,' she said with a shake of the head. 'Nothing immediately comes to mind, but if I think of something I'll call you. Do you have a card?'

Tomek did, and he handed it over to her. As he made his way to the living room door, he said, 'Thanks for the tea, by the way. Best I've had in a while.'

'You're welcome. Secret of the trade. We just put a load of cocaine in it. Helps us get through the day.'

A smirk had returned to Amelia's face. A genuine smile. From before. Before the disappearance, before the death. Before... when everything had been right with the world.

'Thanks for the tip. I think you might be onto something there...'

As he hopped into his car and waved goodbye, he knew that she would be fine. They always would eventually. Get over it within a few months. Maybe even a year.

But not everyone was as lucky.

Especially the little girl who was lying on her back on a metal table in the mortuary.

CHAPTER
TWENTY-TWO

Tomek made it back to the station just in time for the main event.

Vincent Gregory's hanging.

Or what would be as good as.

Accompanying Vincent through the ordeal were Chey and Rachel. Meanwhile Tomek and the rest of the team were sitting in the incident room, gawping up at the TV. The chairs had been arranged in a semi-circle, all directed to the screen, and Tomek had fought his way to the front for the best seats in the house. He'd even had time to make another cup of tea (though nowhere near as nice as Amelia's).

'I think we're about one microwave bag of popcorn away from this being the best cinema I've ever been to,' he said.

'Want me to turn the lights off and hook up all the computer speakers for the full experience?' asked Victoria Orange with a hint of playfulness in her voice.

Tomek swivelled on his chair to see her smiling at him. That was good. A step in the right direction. She was coming down to his level, feeling more at ease with him and the rest of the team. And if stupid humour was the way to do that, then he was more than happy to indulge her.

Five minutes later, the main event began. It was Chey who kicked off proceedings.

'Mr Gregory,' he began, his voice tinny over the TV's speakers, 'thank you for coming in this morning. We've spoken with your employer and they've cleared you for the rest of the day.'

'I ain't dun nuffin',' he replied, suddenly sounding more Essex in his speech.

'That may be the case, but the reason we've asked you to this voluntary interview is because we'd like to ask you a few questions about the events leading up to Annabelle's death.'

'I ain't dun nuffin',' Vincent continued. 'You can't arrest me like this when I ain't dun nuffin'.'

Tomek rolled his eyes and clenched his fist until his knuckles turned the colour of chalk. This was painful to listen to; he wanted to reach through the screen and grab the stumpy little racist fascist bastard by the neck. He could only imagine what it felt like for Rachel and Chey, who both had the luxury of sitting a few feet from the man. They could easily reach across and slam his annoying face into the table repeatedly until—

'You're not under arrest,' Chey continued, distracting Tomek from his thoughts. 'As I *just* mentioned, this interview is voluntary, which means you're here of your own accord, and you're free to leave at any time, but it's probably in your best interests to stay. Do you understand?'

From the angle of the camera, Tomek was just able to make out the look of desperate confusion on Vincent's face.

'Do you understand what I've just said, Mr Gregory?'

Either he didn't get it, or his mind was rapidly trying to come up with a back story, a version of events that suited him and would lead Tomek and the team up the garden path.

'I understand,' he said carefully. 'But what's all this about? Have you found the person who dun this to my niece?'

'No,' came the blunt response from Rachel. 'It's ongoing. That's why you're here...' She inhaled deeply, the sound coming over the TV speaker as she let it out. 'We just wanted to ask you a few questions, that's all.'

'I still ain't dun nuffin'.'

Tomek was grateful he wasn't in there with him, otherwise his face might have been battered a long time ago.

'Is he high or something?' he asked the room.

'Either that or he's got a few brain cells missing...' replied Sean with vehemence in his voice.

'Do you always talk during films, for fuck's sake?' asked Nadia, sitting directly beside him. 'I hate to imagine what you're like in the *actual* cinema.'

'I'm on my best behaviour,' he said. 'Always.' Then raised three fingers in the air and placed a hand on his chest. 'Scout's honour.'

As he turned his attention back to the interview, he caught the end of a question from Rachel.

'I leave for work about six sometimes, sometimes later,' came the response.

'And you drive to work?'

'I can't exactly walk, can I? I could try and take one of them short cuts along the seafront, but I ain't quite mastered the ability to walk on water yet, y'know.'

Chey removed a couple of sheets from a folder and placed them in front of Vincent. 'These are still images taken from CCTV cameras along the road that leads round the park where Annabelle was found...'

Tomek looked at the map that had been printed and placed on a cork board on the other side of the room. The two red dots signalling the CCTV cameras were still there.

'These images were taken at precisely 6:13 a.m.'

'And? I was driving to work.'

'We believe this was the same time that Annabelle was killed. And yet we have you driving past the scene of the crime?'

'You mean I drove past Annabelle while she was being *killed*?'

Vincent's face constricted into a mess. He dropped his head into his hands and began sobbing quietly in the chair. Silence fell on the room as they waited for him to stop.

'I can't believe it...' he whispered, a catch still in his throat. 'I could of saved her... I could of helped her...'

'So you deny having had anything to do with this?'

Vincent slammed his palm on the table. The sorrow in his voice was as far removed as the possibility he could walk on water. 'Course I fucking din't! I'm her uncle, in't I? Why would I ever do summin' like that? I loved her...'

'Are you sure you didn't take the love too far?'

It took a moment for the insinuation to settle in Vincent's mind. Eventually, he said, 'What are you fucking talking about? What are you fucking accusing me of?'

'Nothing, sir,' Rachel said, shutting that avenue down before it became too out of hand. 'Can you explain what you meant when you said you loved her?'

Vincent's head pivoted between Chey and Rachel. 'Are you lot dumb? You lot never loved anyfin' before? I already dun told you, she was my niece. But I loved her like she was my daughter. Poor little fing... Me and my wife can't have kids, so I... I always tret her like she was my own.'

Tomek grimaced at the man's use of the past tense.

'And what about your relationship with your sister? Do the two of you get along?'

'What sorta question's that? You know how much the two of us bin through? We get along more than you could ever possi'ly know.'

The intonation in Vincent's voice suggested that was all he was willing to say on that particular matter. Tomek willed them both to probe further, but in the end they didn't.

'Talk to us about your relationship with Steven...' Chey approached that avenue with trepidation. So far he'd impressed Tomek; he'd spoken slowly, confidently and eloquently. He'd not been intimidated or felt pressured by Vincent's outbursts. He would make a fine detective one day.

And one day Tomek might tell him that.

'Don't even get me started on that waste a space. He's a fucking deadbeat, a layabout who's no good for my sister or my niece.'

'You're very protective over them, aren't you?' Chey asked, gently probing.

'Course I am... they're my flesh and blood. I ain't gonna neglect 'em, am I? Gotta look out for 'em.'

'Why the disapproval of Steven? From what we've been able to gather he provides for them both and cares for them... What are we missing?'

'The fact he's hardly there. He's always working, in't he?'

'That's typically how providing for your family works, Mr Gregory.'

'Yeah, but it's just the way he does it, you know? I ain't like his line of work. He's a conman. The cheeky fucker wanted to charge me full price for a boiler that I ain't even have to pay for – the council were gonna fix it. The cheeky fucker.'

'How long have you known Mr Lake?' Rachel asked this time.

'Since he started going out with my sister.'

'You didn't know him before that?'

Vincent shook his head. 'Never met the cunt.'

'When would you say your relationship started to turn sour.'

'We ain't ever liked each other. We just don't get on. Simple as that. He don't like me and I don't like him. He's always saying I'm too close with my sister, that I'm always round. But let me tell you, if you knew what we bin through in our lifetime you'd know exactly why that is. Can you believe the little cunt tried to stop me seeing my sister and my niece?'

And there it was. Finally. The root of their evil. The real reason Steven and Vincent didn't get on. A frightened and insecure father doing everything he could to protect his daughter and wife from the strange and overbearing brother-in-law.

Tomek felt the parallel.

Minus the strange uncle.

Rachel cleared her throat on the microphone. 'If you wouldn't mind, Mr Gregory,' she began, 'but we'd like to turn our attention to fish for a moment.'

'Fish?'

'Yes.'

'What about them?'

'During the post-mortem report, Annabelle's stomach was found to have contained a lot of fish, which implies her last meals, while she'd been held in captivity, had been fish. Mostly salmon and tuna.'

'You gotta be fucking kidding me.'

'As we understand it, you're the only one in the family who lets her eat fish.'

Vincent threw his hands in the air and brought them down on the table in a loud bang. 'I ain't dun nuffin'. I ain't kidnapped my niece from school, I ain't kept her in some place, I ain't fed her fish, I ain't killed her. I... ain't... dun... nuffin'.'

CHAPTER
TWENTY-THREE

On the way home that evening, Tomek made a quick pit stop into the local Co-op to purchase some essentials. All the essentials Sylvia's mum had told him about. Namely chocolate, chocolate and more chocolate. Though as he'd stared at the shelf, looking at the overwhelming number of different brands, Tomek felt spoilt for choice. That and because he had no idea what to buy for her. He'd totally forgotten to ask which chocolate Louise had given her, and he'd never thought to ask Kasia herself. Sure, she chucked the brands into the shopping trolley when she was with him at Aldi, but he never paid attention to what he was buying – that was a battle he'd fought and lost very quickly. Besides, this was supposed to be a surprise... Some surprise it would be if he called her up to ask what she preferred.

"Hey, it's your dad. As you know, I'm useless at all of this stuff and have completely forgotten which chocolate you like. Don't suppose you could tell me and then act surprised when I give it to you? I'm trying to do a nice thing but am afraid it might backfire..."

In the end, he settled on an assortment of *his* favourite brands. Galaxy, Kit Kat, Aero and a Freddo (well, six of them). In the hope that, because they were flesh and blood, they were bound to have some of the same tastes, that there would be some crossover in chocolatey palate preference.

As he hopped into his car, he helped himself to a sneaky Freddo. He was appalled that the cost of two of them had come to the same price as the Galaxy bar. Out of spite he'd bought the other four and swallowed the extra cost. The froggy little bastard had skyrocketed in price since Tomek had last had one. He remembered when they'd been a couple of pennies, and he and his brothers had been sent to the corner shop with their allowance and ransacked the sweet counter, returning home like kings, pockets bulging.

Now Freddo had grown up, got himself a family of five, an expensive car, and a mortgage, and was passing the debt on to the customer.

And he was sure the little bastard had shrunk in size as well.

By the time he got home, the Freddo was gone. As he entered the living room, he called out to Kasia. A grunt came from the bedroom on the other side of the room. He sauntered towards it and knocked gently. The soft sound of music coming from her laptop echoed from behind the door.

'You can come in,' she said.

Tomek wrapped his hand around the door handle and peered his head through the gap. Kasia was sitting on her bed, dressed in her jogging bottoms and a thick hoodie that dwarfed her body. The hood was pulled over her head and beneath it her face was barely visible. Her knees were pulled up to her chest, with her laptop resting on top of them. The fairy lights they'd fought over in Primark (Kasia had wanted them while Tomek had point-blank refused as he considered them a total waste of money) dangled from various points along the back wall. To his right the desk that had once been his and had now been converted into a make-up dresser shone brightly, and he caught his reflection in the mirror, scaring the shit out of him. His bedroom – *her* bedroom – was unrecognisable. What had once been a bachelor pad filled with only the essentials had now been replaced with things that had forced him to go into shops he'd never set foot in before.

A whole new world to him.

'How was your day?' he asked, hovering awkwardly in the doorframe, trying to keep the Co-op bag out of sight as much as possible.

'Fine...' she said.

'Learn anything fun?'

'Nope...'

'Get much homework done?'

'Bits...'

'How was your tutoring with Miss Holloway?'

'Okay...'

'Was it helpful?'

'Yeah...'

Okay, so that's how it was. Monosyllabic answers. He could handle that. So long as she wasn't pissed off with him for some reason...

'How are... how are you feeling?'

She shrugged. 'Fine.'

'Do you... do you wanna talk about it?'

'Not really.'

'Okay, good.' Tomek breathed a deep sigh of relief. 'Did you like the pizza I left out?'

'It was all right, thanks.' She reached over to the bedside table and grabbed a cup of tea. Freshly made, the wisps of steam still rising from the top. 'I just made one, so the kettle's still hot if you want your own.'

Tomek smirked. 'Thanks.' Then he raised the Co-op bag in the air, feeling like a drunk walking along the high street with his entire life's possessions contained inside, and made his way to the end of the bed. 'I got you something. It's not much but... Sylvia's mum said chocolate was the best cure for your... you know.'

'I know.' Her open smile and expression told him to continue.

'And I forgot which ones you like, so I picked up an assortment...'
Tomek placed the bag in front of her and allowed her to open it.

With trepidation, she folded her legs on the bed and carefully opened it. Then she peered her head inside. Looked up at him. Grinning.

Tomek was unable to discern whether it was a genuine, "thank you so much these are the best chocolates in the world and you're the best dad in the world" smile, or whether it was a more strained, "I don't like any of these but I'm going to smile and pretend I like them anyway" sort of smile. Like a kid who opened a Christmas present they neither wanted nor asked for.

Ungrateful little shites.

'Thank you,' she said, reaching into the bag and pulling out a Freddo.

'Go easy on those,' he told her. 'The tax man'll be after me if they're gone too quickly.'

She surveyed the little frog as though it was the Crystal Skull Indiana Jones found in his fourth outing in the franchise. A precious and valuable relic to be treated with the utmost care and respect.

'What... what is it?'

Tomek's jaw had never dropped as hard as it did in that moment.

'You've... you've *never heard of or even tasted Freddo*?'

Kasia shook her head unapologetically.

'They're only the best chocolate in the world. Like little nuggets of pleasure. They taste so...' He stopped himself, the saliva in his mouth growing to an unnaturally high level. 'You just have to try one.'

Ever since Kasia had first moved in, he'd been forced to completely remove any and all nut products and their nut-related derivatives from his diet – peanuts, cashews, pistachios and even the Thai Sweet Chilli coated nuts that he'd discovered one afternoon while perusing the aisles of Lidl (don't tell Aldi). She was extremely allergic to them and couldn't be within a ten-foot radius. He couldn't even enjoy them at work and come home several hours later, because the smell would still be on his breath and the poison would continue to secrete from his pores. Since then Tomek had experienced several withdrawal symptoms and struggled to find himself a replacement, a bag of snacks he could have on his desk at work or leave in the cupboard for when he got peckish.

Until now.

As he watched her delicately tear the top of the packet off and nibble on the end of Freddo's hairline like a hamster, he seriously considered the possibility of buying the little business owner and family man in bulk.

He couldn't, could he? Surely that wasn't a thing? And if it was, then he'd certainly have to start finding the time to go back on his runs again. Or he could just gorge himself on the chocolatey goodness instead.

Fuck it. *You only live once*, he thought. YOLO. That was what the kids said nowadays, wasn't it?

'What do you think?' he asked, failing to contain the excitement in his voice.

She nodded as she shoved the frog's legs into her mouth. 'Not bad,' she mumbled. '*Really* good actually.'

It was settled. Now he had no choice but to buy them in bulk. If not for himself, then at least for her.

'Thank you,' she said as she tore off the wrapper for another one.

'Easy, tiger!' he yelled. 'Wish I'd had more than one now!'

Kasia chuckled to herself. She then ripped the top half of the frog's torso from his body and handed him the bottom half.

'You're a savage,' he said.

'I'm not used to sharing,' she replied. 'But here you go.'

Tomek felt privileged.

'It's fine,' he said, then pushed her back. 'You have it. I was joking.

I've gotta watch my weight. You start to notice these things when you hit forty.'

'I didn't wanna say anything...'

Tomek mocked being offended and snatched the rest of the chocolates away from her. 'You won't get these until tomorrow now. Congratulations. I hope you're happy!' He looked inside the bag. 'Do you even like any of these?'

She shook her head. 'Only the Galaxy. I *love* Galaxy.'

'Sorry.'

'It's fine. It was nice. Thoughtful of you. Thank you.'

Tomek took a moment to absorb those words. His body warmed and a combination of pride and ego swam through his veins. She'd acknowledged his gesture, appreciated it. He'd done something his parents had never done to him, not since Michał's death.

He'd shown that he cared.

Maybe that was the way forward. To break from what he knew and go rogue, off the books.

Parenting the way he *didn't* know how.

'Are you all right?'

She waved a hand in front of him.

'Yeah. Why?'

'You just looked like you were having a stroke.'

'Nearly.'

'What are you smiling for?'

'No reason,' he said, shrugging his shoulders. Then he made a move to leave but stopped in the door when Kasia called him back.

'Tomek...' she started as she began fiddling nervously with the wrapper in her hands. 'I know you said about going over to Sylvia's one night when I finish my exams and everything. But I was thinking...' She took a long pause. Tomek braced himself for what was to come. 'I was wondering if I could... if I could maybe go and see Mum. In prison. One time at the weekend or maybe during a school day. I miss her, and I would like to see her...'

Tomek's initial reaction was to say no. However nothing but air came out of his mouth and he froze in the doorframe, rooted to the spot. As though something was holding him there. He knew the answer to the question already, but he didn't want to make a rash and unfair decision.

It was just a shame that his brain couldn't communicate with the rest of his body.

'You're having another stroke again,' she said.

That made him come to. He shook his head gently and whistled out of his lips.

'It's... That's a tricky one,' he said. 'I'll... I'll have to think about it, okay? Give me some time to think about it and I'll let you know.'

As he closed the door behind him he recalled the countless missed phone calls he'd had from Anika Coleman inside prison in the past few weeks. The same phone calls that had escalated in frequency.

The same phone calls he'd ignored just as religiously.

CHAPTER
TWENTY-FOUR

The car engine sat in idle, quietly ticking over, purring beneath his feet. Warm air blew from the air vents, gently caressing his face and making him regret the decision to wear a sweater. A T-shirt was more than enough, but he continued to wear it because he needed something to hide the sweat stains.

The sweat stains of dread and regret.

This wasn't his decision. Not entirely. But he had no choice now. He was too far gone to turn back.

Besides, a part of him had enjoyed it the last time. The "not entirely" part. Taking a life had been easy, a sudden inducement of energy and power. Power over a little girl who'd deserved it.

And that was the same with tonight.

She *deserved* it.

Through the windscreen he saw her standing there, half naked, literally *begging* for it on the corner of the road. She was dressed in a small skirt that covered less of her arse than a pair of his underwear would have done, and a small crop top to match. More skin on show than a Dutch sex show. Her hair had been tied in a bun, and several layers of make-up had been plastered onto her face.

Seventeen, she was. Seventeen and she'd resorted to this. Selling herself for the pleasure of men, scumbags like himself.

But now wasn't the time to have an identity crisis.

Now was the time to act.

He slipped the car into gear and rolled up to the road beside her. She was hidden behind a closed fish and chip shop, just off the main street. Difficult to find. But not if you knew where to look...

As he approached, he lowered the window and rested his arm on the frame.

'You all right there, darling?' she asked, waddling over to him in those high-heel boots that were far too tall for anyone let alone a seventeen-year-old girl. 'You lost or anything?'

He shook his head. 'I'm looking for a good place to sleep tonight.'

The code word had been given to him by a friend of a friend of a friend, several layers deep in the social circle. Untraceable, as far he knew. And hoped.

'What sort of place you looking for?' she asked. 'All-inclusive or just bed and breakfast?'

'All-inclusive, if that's all right?'

He kicked himself. *If that's all right*. If that's all right! Who in the history of prostitution had ever asked that question? It was a part of the deal. It was all an unwritten agreement. Everything that happened between them was *all right* – so long as he continued to pay for it.

'All right, darling,' she said gently. 'I can sort that out for you.'

Without saying anything else she made her way round the bonnet, dragging her red acrylic fingernails over the body work, and into the passenger seat beside him.

'You know how much it'll cost?'

He hadn't noticed it, but she was chewing on a piece of gum. Loudly. The insufferable noise amplified by the confined space. He could smell it oozing off her breath. That and all the cock she'd had in there already. He didn't even want to think about that.

'Yeah, I know how much it'll cost.'

Sadly, *she* didn't know the true cost.

Her life.

He slipped the car into reverse, pulled out of the alleyway and then returned to the main road, heading back the way he'd come. As he drove along the street in the dead of night, the orange light from the street lamps bouncing off their faces intermittently, he rubbed his hands repeatedly on the steering wheel. Too afraid to remove them, lest they show the sweat marks beneath.

'You had a good evening so far, darling?'

He winced at the sound of her voice. So young, yet there was a tinge to it, a level that denoted the experience she'd had. He knew all about what had happened to her in her life, and he wasn't surprised to hear she sounded older. Much older.

'It's been all right,' he said, not wishing to engage in too much conversation.

'About to get even better,' she said. 'You ever done anything like this before?'

'Can't say I have.'

'Don't worry.' She placed a hand on his thigh and gave it a gentle squeeze. 'I can be delicate when I need to be.'

He made a little noise and turned his attention to the road again. By now they were on the south side of the island, gradually making their way round clockwise back to the safehouse. The roads were still empty, save for the odd car here and there, but the main thing was that there had been no sign of the police. He'd worried that they might have prowled the area, looking for girls like her so they could protect them and keep them off the streets.

But of course that didn't happen. The police had already proven they cared for girls like her as much as they cared about Annabelle Lake. Not at all.

Eventually, he came to a stop down Northwick Road. The place where he'd once learnt to drive. A long, straight stretch of road that led to a recycling centre and a quarry several hundred metres away.

The road was pitch black, save for the headlights that illuminated all the potholes and small mounds of gravel and dust that had piled up over the years. It had been a long time since he'd last been there, and it was the perfect place for what he needed to do.

He switched off the engine and killed the lights, suspending them in the darkness.

'There's nothing to be ashamed of, sweetheart,' she said. 'I've seen it all before.'

'I'm sure you have.'

Without needing to be told, she moved her hand from his thigh to his crotch, and began undoing the buttons. One by one. Until she wriggled his jeans free, and then his boxers. Leaving them by his knees. Then she cupped his penis in her hands and started massaging until he stood to attention.

At first he'd hated it, hated himself for allowing this to happen, for it to get this far. But now that he was here, now that this was happening, he was beginning to enjoy himself.

Because this was nothing compared to what they had planned for her later on.

CHAPTER
TWENTY-FIVE

Tomek's first day off since his return to work.

The investigation into Annabelle Lake's disappearance and murder had stalled. Without any real forensic evidence or leads for them to pursue with any sort of conviction, there was little for the team to do except focus on catching up on their admin and hoping something might come in.

And with Tomek's semi-exclusion from the investigation that meant there was even less for him to do.

As a result, DCI Cleaves, with the help of Victoria and a gentle nudge from the lovely bunch down in HR, had given Tomek a day off. To recover, they'd told him. Apparently, he'd jumped back into work after weeks off during the middle of an investigation. A shock to the system, they'd said. The decision baffled him. It wasn't like he was coming back from the brink of death and needed six months to embed himself back in the team. He'd only been sitting on his fat arse for a few weeks. The only "rest and recovery" he needed was from lounging around doing nothing all day.

Fortunately for him, he had a teenage daughter to keep him busy on a weekend. Later in the afternoon, he would be taking her to a karate lesson in Hadleigh. The local dojo had an introductory offer where the first lesson was free and open to all – men, women, children of all ages. Apparently it was something she'd always wanted to do and was something she'd been considering for a while, but had neglected to tell him until the very last minute – namely, the late hours of the night before. When asked why she hadn't mentioned it sooner, she'd said that it was because she hadn't felt comfortable, and that she hadn't been sure she'd wanted to do it in the first place. So instead she'd chosen to sit on the decision for a few weeks, internalising it, like waiting to call the GP about the pain you know isn't right.

Tomek was pleased to see her becoming more open with him (even if it did have a lead time of a few hours). It meant they were making progress, and that his efforts with her were having a positive impact on her life. He was also pleased to hear her say she wanted to try something new, something different. Something he expected no one else in her school did. That she was putting herself out there and meeting new people, rather than staying indoors all day losing brain cells as she continued to scroll, scroll, scroll...

But that was later.

Right now he had to think about what to say.

In front of him was his brother's headstone.

His second visit in as many months. During his suspension, Tomek had planned on coming more frequently, sitting there, using his brother as a sounding board for his thoughts and concerns about Kasia, his career... everything. But he hadn't come.

Fear. Guilt. Shame.

They'd all tricked him into staying at home and using his daughter as an excuse. It seemed he could only be bad at one thing at a time: bad brother while he was trying to be a good parent; or bad parent while he was trying to be a good brother. All the while he had to handle his career in the best way possible. It wasn't easy, but then who said life would be?

Tomek perched himself on the bench nearby and watched as a flock of seagulls flew in from the shore, squawking as they went. Probably telling him off in their own language for neglecting his brother for so long. Or being a shit dad.

Of being a shitty person in general.

'Been a while, eh mate?' he said, unable to bring his eyes level with the stone. 'A lot's changed since I last saw you. You wouldn't believe it if I told you but I found out I've got a daughter. Mental, I know. Well, *she* isn't... but the situation is. I would say it's funny but it's not really. It's all a bit fucked up, to be honest with you.

'I'm not cut out for it, this whole parenting malarkey. None of it makes a blind bit of sense, but we're here now, and these are the cards I've been dealt. I've either got to play them or fold – and I don't want to see the sort of damage *that* decision can do.'

A robin, chest puffed and full of singsong, landed on the arm of the bench beside him. Tomek was never one to believe in ghosts or spirits or signs of the supernatural, but something about that bird told him it was his brother, coming to see him.

'I appreciate you taking time out of your busy schedule to talk to me,' he said sarcastically. 'Must be a million-and-one things to do up there at any one time. And you've chosen to spend it with me.'

The bird bleated, staring up at him expectantly.

'Cheers, mate. Appreciate it. If you see Tony up there, or on your travels, don't reckon you could pass a message on to him for me, could you?'

The bird hesitated before responding. This time the message was brief and succinct, and Tomek knew it was his brother's way of saying, "Tell him yourself, you lazy prick." Classic Michał who, even for eleven, had learned a fair amount of foul language. All of which had naturally rolled downhill and landed Tomek in a lot trouble. Michał and Dawid, his eldest brother, were often the ones teaching him the bad words and daring him to use them in front of Mum. On the two occasions he'd done it (he'd quickly learnt his lesson after that), he'd found himself grounded for two weeks at a time. A total of four weeks he was never going to get back. Just so that his brothers would treat him like one of them.

Sadly it was nothing compared to the lifetime Michał would never have. The one that was stolen from him too soon.

The thought made him think. That life was too short. That Kasia could do what she wanted. That perhaps he shouldn't stop her from seeing her mother, no matter how much he disagreed with the idea. Because he didn't want her to have any regrets. If she went there and hated every minute of it, then at least she could say that she'd tried and made the effort. But on the other hand if she visited and rekindled the fractious relationship with her mother, who was he to intervene? It was a win-win for everyone.

The thought made him think. About regrets. About how he needed to make sure he didn't have any either...

As he was about to reach inside his pocket for his phone, he realised the robin had flown away. His brother's work done for the day.

'Hello, Mum?'

'Yes,' came the slightly warm response. 'Is everything all right?'

'Yeah. It's fine. I just wanted to check – does the invite still stand for tonight?'

'Of course it does. You know it does.'

'Great. Then make space for one more. There's someone I'd like you to meet.'

CHAPTER
TWENTY-SIX

The appointment had been in his diary for months, years if you counted the fact that it had been an annual event in the family calendar for over thirty years. The anniversary of Michał's birthday. An event that he'd often neglected and avoided at all costs. But tonight he was willing to try. Especially after the last time they'd been together as a family to celebrate the anniversary of Michał's death. He had taken Charlotte with him, and the night had ended in an argument and left a sour taste in everyone's mouth. Since then he'd had very little contact with his brother, but relations had improved with his parents.

Hopefully it would stay that way.

With him, sitting in the passenger seat, was Kasia, who looked as nervous as he felt. And she was probably more so than him.

He'd sprung the news on her that they'd be attending after she'd finished karate. She had just left the training lesson with a beaming smile on her face, which had disappeared the moment he told her.

'You good?' Tomek asked.

'I'm fine,' she replied.

Which meant she definitely was not fine.

'There's no need to be worried,' he said. 'They're your family. Your grandparents. And if at any point you feel uncomfortable or scared, or maybe you've just had enough, then you let me know and we'll come straight home, all right? And if it all starts kicking off and you're feeling brave, you can always bust out those karate moves you just learned.'

She turned to face him. 'Funny.'

'This is going to be as awkward for me as it is you, you know that, right?'

'Why?'

And then Tomek told her. Firstly about how his parents didn't know about her existence. And then he moved to his brother's death. About the missing second suspect. About how he'd been the one to give his mum hope that the killer was still out there, meanwhile the killer's identity was still locked in his brain, perpetually out of reach. About how it had caused a rift between them. About how he hadn't spoken to them much or seen eye to eye with them since. About how they'd not been a proper family.

'I'm... I'm sorry about your brother,' she said at the end of it, and turned to look at the passing trees outside the window.

'It happened a long time ago, and it's just one of those things you never quite get over, I don't think. Your grandma, especially. So if she acts a bit strange or a bit stand-offish, then try not to take it personally. Only *I'm* allowed to do that.'

A smile. Brief, just a flicker. But a start.

'And if you want something to keep you entertained while we're there...' he leant over the console between them, 'then count how many times your uncle flares his nostrils...'

'What?'

'He's got a nervous tic. Started when he was about fifteen, I think. Got really self-conscious about it when it first started. Obviously it didn't help when I kept taking the piss out of him for it. Had loads of help from doctors and psychologists but it's never stopped. We used to call him *świnia*, which is pig in Polish.'

Another smile. Bigger this time.

'And if you want to embark on a top secret mission, then count how many times the three boys – your cousins – hold their pants and jump up and down before they go to the toilet. They're only a few years younger than you, but they can't stop it, and I think they'll be doing it until they're about my age. And I'm fairly sure they still wet the bed.'

'Ewwww...'

'Too far? All right, you just bully your uncle then. Leave the three boys to me...'

———

They arrived a little under forty minutes later. The drive had given them a chance to catch up on the important things. Like how Kasia had found her first attempt at karate, whether she wanted to do it again: she had enjoyed it, and she did. On a weekly basis, every weekend, at 2 p.m. Between them they'd have to work out the logistics, but he was willing to make it work.

'Who was that woman I saw you talking to when you dropped me off?' Kasia had asked after he'd finished reminiscing about the one time he'd beaten up Frankie Hargreaves in Year 11 outside the school playground for being racist to him – a story which she didn't seem too interested to hear.

'I wondered if you saw that,' he'd replied, sighing. 'Amber Wilson. She was an old school friend. Like, way way back. So long I try to forget the date. We were in a couple of classes together, I think. Maths and science.'

'Did anything ever happen between you two?'

Before responding to that, Tomek had given her a concerned look with a raised eyebrow. 'No. Nothing ever happened between us.'

'Maybe you should get in touch.'

Tomek had scoffed. 'I don't need relationship advice from a thirteen-year-old, thank you very much.'

'From the looks of it, you do.'

'Excuse me?'

'Miss Holloway... didn't you see the way she was looking at you the other day during parents' evening? She couldn't take her eyes off you.'

Tomek hadn't noticed. He'd been so preoccupied with arriving on time – on actually *showing up* – that he'd completely disregarded any signs or signals Bridget Holloway had been sending him.

'Maybe you should...' Kasia had started, but then stopped herself. 'Actually, no. I take that back. You are under no circumstance to start going out with my teacher. *Please.*'

Tomek smirked at her, smug.

'No. Please. You can't. I don't think I could handle it at school. You going out with one of my teachers...' She visibly shook with fear. Or was it disgust?

'I'll bear that in mind,' Tomek said right as he pulled up to his parents' house.

Getting involved in a relationship wasn't something he was looking for right now. Not when he kept thinking about Charlotte and what had happened between them. Not when he kept playing the "what if?" card and wondering what could have been. His heart was still looking into the past, and he wasn't sure when it would begin to look forward.

Kasia kept her distance behind him as he stepped up to the front door and knocked. When the door eventually opened, she was hiding in his shadow, keeping her head down.

'Hi, Mum,' he began.

The woman in front of him had changed drastically since he'd last seen her. She'd dyed her hair a light shade of pink – to match her nail colour – and she'd shaved it short. For a woman well into her sixties it was the last thing he expected to see. But he liked it.

'You look good,' he told her. 'Funky. Not sure it would suit me, but I like it.'

'Thank you.' She hopped down the step and embraced him for longer than she had done in a while.

As she pulled away, she said. 'Where's your date?'

Smiling, Tomek stepped aside and wrapped his arm around Kasia's shoulders. He could feel her small frame trembling beneath his grip.

'Oh, Tomek... No. No, you can't be...' She placed a hand on Kasia's. 'How old are you, dear?'

'Shut up, Mum. It's not like that at all. Kasia's not my girlfriend, for fuck's sake!'

'*Kurwa mać*. You nearly gave me a heart attack! If she isn't your date then... who is she?'

Tomek gaze Kasia a gentle nudge in the back and gestured for her to step into the house.

'I think we should all go inside,' he said. 'There's something I need to tell you all.'

———

The smile hadn't left his face since the moment he'd laid eyes on Izabela and her new hair. Nor had it waned after he'd told his family about his daughter and received their muted, concerned glares. At first they hadn't known how to take the information, how to process it. But after launching a barrage or police-style questions – when did this happen, who was it with, where were you at the time – they gradually came to terms with it and began to understand it. He knew it would be a long time before they could accept it as fact.

'It's taken me a while to get my head around it myself,' he told them. 'But we're slowly getting used to one another. We're even moving into a bigger flat with more space.'

'We finally get a room each,' Kasia said. The longer she stayed there, the more confident she felt. And, now and then, Tomek had seen her staring at his brother Dawid, waiting for his tic to kick in.

'Has he been making you sleep on the sofa, the selfish bastard?' Dawid asked.

'Shut up,' Tomek said, jumping to his own defence. 'I'm not a monster. I've been shacked up on the sofa while she's had my nice double bed.'

Dawid placed his hand to the side of his mouth, as though speaking with her discreetly so no one else could hear. 'I bet he still smells though, doesn't he?'

Kasia giggled at that. Tomek rolled his eyes.

This was the first time in over a decade that they'd all been getting on like this. Last time with Charlotte had been different, the ice well and truly frozen over. But now... now it was beginning to thaw and the loving qualities of being in a family were beginning to shine through. Tomek even found himself tolerating the triplets, Kristian, Patryk and Jakub, for a change. Though he hadn't seen any of them need the toilet just yet.

It was 9 p.m. by the time dinner was ready and they were all seated around the table. On the menu tonight was one of Tomek's favourites: *pierogi*.

'You know them as dumplings,' Tomek said to Kasia as he spooned a healthy dose of gravy onto her plate.

'That'll do,' she told him, pushing the spoon away.

He ignored her and poured an extra half onto her plate. 'In this family, you have to get there quick and by any means necessary. Growing up we never used to share – especially when it came to food – and we always fought over the scraps at the end.'

'Is that why you always eat my leftovers?'

'Partly. Partly that, and partly because I don't like good food going to waste.'

'That's because he always used to lose,' Dawid said, butting in, his little nose wagging. 'Your dad was the last one to everything so he always had less food to eat.'

At that point, Kasia dropped her head to the table and played with her dinner. Tomek sent his brother a scowl and then a shake of the head.

The D word hadn't been uttered between the two of them yet. The conversation had been a difficult one for him to approach. He'd never called himself her dad and she'd never called him it either. Always 'father'.

I'm her father. She's my daughter.

But never *dad*. Dad was informal. Dad made it real, a solid, tangible thing that couldn't be taken back, like a broken vase that could never be fixed.

Picking up on the awkward atmosphere that had descended on the table, Dawid's wife, Kristina, said, 'How are you finding your new school, Kasia? The boys are about to start secondary school soon. Have you got any advice or tips for them?'

'Don't go,' she said bluntly. 'The lessons are boring, they're much harder, and the teachers are a lot stricter. But it can sometimes be fun.'

'Oh... So it sounds like you're enjoying it then?'

"Of course she fucking isn't" is the message Tomek hoped was implied by the look on his face. Kristina appeared to notice it, and then returned her attention to her food.

As the evening progressed, the topics of conversation ebbed and flowed, moving from Kasia's school life to Tomek's work and the reinvigoration of his career; from the latest thing his dad was building in the garage (a common ploy Tomek suspected he used to get away from his mum for as long as possible) to Kristina's career in law. It was all very interesting and civil. There were no arguments, no disagreements, no need for anyone to storm off, and there was no indication from Kasia that she felt uncomfortable and wanted to leave early. In fact, after the food had finished she'd gone into the living room with her cousins while Tomek stayed in the dining room to chat with the adults.

'Go on then,' he said, refilling his glass of Coke. 'Let the grilling commence!'

The look on the abashed faces suggested they didn't know where to begin, nor who was going to be brave enough to go first.

In the end, it was his dad. Perry Bowen had always been the complete antithesis to his mum. While Izabela was abrupt and cavalier in her words and attitude towards certain things, Perry was more sensitive, more understanding. Every relationship needed light to balance the dark, and that was his dad.

But tonight it was as though the roles had reversed.

'You're not seriously going to keep looking after this girl, are you?' Perry asked.

'I am.'

'Why? She's not your problem.'

'Of course she is. She's my daughter. We did a DNA test and everything. I've got the email on my phone if you want to read it?'

'But what about your work, your home life?'

'What about it? We've survived all right the past few weeks, I'll think we're over the worst of it.' Tomek took a sip of his drink to calm himself down. 'I brought her here in good faith, thinking that she would be accepted into the family. It's not like last time where she turned out to be a serial killer. This is different. This is my *daughter*.'

Perry opened his mouth but was stopped by a hand on his forearm.

'I guess what your dad is trying to say – *horribly*, I might add,' his mum began, casting a quick malicious glance in Perry's direction, 'is that we're all a little shocked. And, on behalf of all the family, we're all a little disappointed and hurt that you didn't tell us sooner. It's taken you over a month to tell us she exists.'

'Because I was worried this would be the reaction.'

'Well, you have my vote,' Kristina added with a weak smile.

Tomek offered her a half nod to show his appreciation, but it wasn't her support he was looking for. He turned to his parents.

'I just need to know that I have *your* support on this. I know I've never asked for it before, but in the past month I've had to do a lot of growing up. And I want you to be a part of her life, and I want her to be a part of yours...'

It didn't take them long to respond.

'Of course we'd love that,' Izabela said, placing a hand on his. 'We'd be delighted to welcome her into the family. She's a Bowen. We make sure no one gets left behind.'

If that were true, then this entire conversation wouldn't be happening in the first place.

CHAPTER
TWENTY-SEVEN

Tomek left his parents' house with mixed emotions. While they'd said that they would be happy to welcome Kasia into the family, he sensed a reluctance behind it. As though it was forced. That they felt obliged to say what they thought he'd wanted to hear. But on the other hand he knew his parents better than most and that was something they'd never done before. They'd always been straight-talking, brutally honest (that was the Polish side of the family) and never duplicitous. So he didn't know what to think.

Perhaps their hearts were in the right place, just not their heads.

Not yet, at least.

Yes, that seemed right. They would just need time to come to terms with the news.

God knew it had taken him long enough. And he wasn't sure he was even entirely all the way there yet.

'Did you have fun tonight?' he asked Kasia as he pulled away from their drive and turned into the darkness of the country lanes.

'Yeah, it was nice, thanks.'

She didn't look up from the screen as she responded, and she'd been on it ever since they'd left the house. He tried to not take it personally.

'Did you manage to count how many times the Little Piggy oinked?'

'Too many. I think I lost count after a while. Although I think you should know that the boys call you Little Piggy as well.'

Tomek's grip on the steering wheel tightened. 'That right? Who'd you hear that from?'

'The boys. They told me when we were in the living room. Said that Dawid's always calling you it to their mum.'

He tried to stifle the chuckle but was unable to.

That little bastard. Dawid the hero, lambasting his own brother's name like that. And in front of his own children, no less. He wondered what other things he said to his family, but then decided against probing. If it was anything like the comment Kasia had just said, then he could imagine the rest. Nothing he hadn't heard before.

As they merged onto the A12, a treacherous road notorious for being busy and responsible for several fatal crashes, Tomek turned the radio off and allowed his thoughts to drift off to Annabelle Lake and her killer. As far as he was aware – he'd checked his emails a handful of times while pretending to disappear off to the toilet – the team were no closer to finding the killer. They'd exhausted all leads, and there was still no reason for him to come back. So Nick had signed off for him to take another day's "rest".

I know now's a personal time for you, so take tomorrow off. We'll see you first thing Monday.

And then his thoughts turned to Kasia.

'Would you like to go shopping tomorrow?' he asked. 'We need to get a load of boxes and supplies for the move.'

Kasia moved a strand of hair away from her face and nodded. 'Yeah, that'd be fun.'

'Lakeside, all right?'

'It's for ten-year-olds.'

'You're only thirteen...'

'Do we have to?'

'They've got an IKEA there...'

'I don't care about IKEA.'

'What? I thought kids your age *loved* IKEA. Ten-year-olds don't like IKEA. But kids your age *love* IKEA. IKEA's where it's at!'

Kasia shook her head in derision. 'Please don't say that ever again. In fact, don't even think about saying anything like that ever again!'

'Too cool for you, am I?'

She rolled her eyes. 'You wish. I've seen pigeons on the street that are cooler.'

'Ouch. Burn. You stung me real deep, dawg. You stung me real deep.'

She dropped her face in her hands. 'Oh my God! Stop!'

The laughter dissipated a few moments after Kasia's phone had chimed. The loud *ping* echoed in the cabin of the car so loud it made Tomek jump and almost veer into the other lane of traffic.

'Who's that?' Tomek asked. At this time of night – 11 p.m. – Tomek could only think it would be one thing. Boys. The opposite sex. The dreaded "B" word. He hadn't broached that minefield of a conversation just yet, and he hoped he wouldn't have to for a long, long while to come. Even the thought of having to give the "birds and the bees" chat sent his stomach into a twist. Nobody had given it to him, and look how that had turned out – the product of his naïvety and inexperience and idiocy was sitting right next to him.

A few moments passed before Kasia eventually responded. In that time, Tomek glanced at her several times, and saw her expression gradually drop, until she shut the phone off and placed it face-down on her lap.

'No one,' she said.

Though it didn't look like no one.

'It was just one of those notifications you get when someone you follow has just posted something on Instagram.'

Tomek looked at her in mild disbelief. 'You can get notifications for that? I mean, I know the term is "follow", but that feels like as a society we're all one step behind turning up at someone's door and watching over their shoulder as they post it – then giving them a high-five instead of liking their photo.' Tomek turned his attention back to the road. 'I don't think I could ever hand out that many high-fives...'

Kasia may as well have spoken a different language to him. It was a world he was not familiar with in the slightest. He knew the fundamentals of each platform, how they worked, how they could be mistreated and used for criminal proceedings – but beyond that he was about as clueless as a baby was behind the steering wheel. He'd only created profiles so that he could follow Kasia on them all to ensure her safety. And now that she'd mentioned it, he made a mental note to set up the post notifications for her. That way it would be easier than checking sporadically and whenever he remembered.

'Speaking of which...' he said, then realised he hadn't voiced the thoughts in his head at all. 'Have you thought any more about learning Polish? To be fair, I'm surprised your gran didn't mention it.'

'She did.'

'Oh. When?'

'When it was just the two of us. I went to get a glass of water from the kitchen and she followed me.'

'Right. Okay. And what did you tell her?'

'I said I was still thinking about it.'

CHAPTER
TWENTY-EIGHT

Tomek awoke with a start. Panting, sweating.

The nightmares, the ones that had once plagued him almost every evening, had stopped entirely ever since Kasia had moved in with him.

Except for last night.

The bloody and brutal images of his dead brother lying there in the field had been replaced with nondescript cardboard boxes filled to the brim with the contents of his wardrobe. Of mess everywhere. Of the life he'd lived for the last thirteen years crumbling away in front of him. The reality of the move was growing ever prominent in his head. One of the most stressful things to do in life, he'd been told. Well, whoever had decided that had clearly never managed a murder investigation, been a single parent, and had the brilliant idea to move house in the middle of a terrifying housing market.

Now *that* was stressful.

Not to mention finding time for it all was part of the problem. And so he was extremely grateful to Nick and the deadbeats in HR for allowing him to have another day off.

Lakeside Shopping Centre was one of the most famous and

popular locations in Essex. Which made absolutely no sense to Tomek. It was a shopping centre for Christ's sake. There were dozens of them all over the country, each boasting the same assortment of shops as the rest. Except millions of people flocked to it each year in search of something new for them to waste their hard-earned money on.

As a result it was one of the only places in Essex he tried to avoid more than the rest. He hated everything about it. It was filled with chavs and ten-year-olds that thought they were the big dogs, bowling around the shops with their mates, kicking off, making nuisances out of themselves all under the misguided idea that they were being funny.

It was, however, a rite of passage for any teenager growing up in Essex to have spent at least a full eight-hour shift there with their mates. And Tomek couldn't say *too* much. He had been one of those ten-year-olds once. Trying to afford the latest clothes and shoes while attempting to eat copious amounts of fast food all on the little budget his parents had given him.

It was a rite of passage, all right.

And now Kasia had the privilege of completing hers with a forty-year-old man with no dress sense.

'You're so embarrassing,' she said, as she walked with her head low and shoulders stooped. The last thing she wanted was to run into someone from school and suffer the embarrassment of being out with him in public. There was nothing more humiliating for someone her age. But unfortunately for her she didn't have a choice.

'I haven't done anything,' he replied defensively.

'Just... you. I can't believe you chose to wear that.'

Tomek looked down at his light green Polo shirt that had shrunk a few sizes in the wash.

'It's my favourite.'

'It needs to go.'

'All right then,' he said. 'How about we both cull our wardrobes for the move?'

'And buy new bits?'

'No.'

The hope on Kasia's face disappeared. 'Oh...'

Tomek rolled his eyes. He was rapidly becoming a soft touch. 'Fine. You can get *two* new outfits today. *Two.*'

To highlight his point he thrust the V-sign in her face.

Whether he had enough money in the bank account to pay for them was a different kettle of fish altogether. Funding the move, and paying all the bastard solicitor and agency fees – which seemed to have add-on after add-on – was rinsing him dry, and he didn't think it would be long until he had to start sending Kasia off into the big wide world of work for her to pay her own way. Places like Lakeside, or any other retail outlet, were perfect for someone her age. A place to thicken her skin while she received verbal abuse from depressed and miserable shoppers for something that wasn't her fault. Learning the importance of punctuality and hard work.

One of life's greatest lessons. Shame she still had a few more years to go before she was legally able to do it...

Until then he'd have to spend the remainder of his savings to keep her happy.

The first shop they ventured into was Zara. The global Spanish fashion brand was filled with an overwhelming assortment of clothes. Far too much choice. And as soon as Kasia set foot in there her eyes illuminated before she sprinted off to one of the sections in the far corner. Tomek, blinded by all the lights and mirages of customers rushing past him, quickly lost track of her and became disorientated. Overwhelmed, dizzy at having to pivot on his heels every half a second, he took a step outside to reconsider his life.

Here was a man who'd seen dead people, chased after and caught criminals, and almost died on several occasions. And yet he couldn't handle a simple fashion store.

What was becoming of him?

Outside, he found a precious free space on a bench with the rest of the men who'd either become lost, disorientated, or bored, and pulled out his phone. Then he messaged Kasia to tell her where he was.

Just as he was about to have a quick check of his emails, the screen turned black and the name "HMP East Sutton Park" appeared at the top. Below it were two giant buttons. One red, one green.

His thumb hovered over the red button for a moment, then tentatively moved to the green one.

'Hello?' he said slowly, plugging his finger in the other ear to drown out the sound of children screaming and the unemployed shuffling their feet.

'Tomek, is that you?'

'Hello, Anika.'

'Why haven't you been answering my calls? I've tried to get through to you so many times.'

'I've been busy. Looking after our daughter. Or did you forget about that when you sent her to me?'

'That's why I'm calling. I want to see her. I miss her.'

'I'm sure you do.'

'Please, Tomek. I'm begging you. I need to see my little girl.' A pause. 'And I think we should have a chat, too.'

Tomek didn't want to comprehend the thought of meeting with her right now. In fact, he didn't even want to think about letting Kasia speak with her either. Until that moment, he'd been willing and open to letting Kasia meet with her mother. But after hearing her voice... after hearing her speak, it brought up a lot of emotions and reminded him of the reasons behind his initial reservations about the idea. The pain and hurt she'd caused him. How she'd unleashed her killer uncle onto him and been an accessory to dangling him over a train track.

They weren't the sorts of things you forgave or forgot easily.

'I'll have to think about it,' he told her. 'Please don't keep calling me. I'll make contact with you when the time's right.'

And then he hung up on her.

Afterwards he felt bittersweet. But before he could dwell on it too long, Kasia appeared in front of him, looking down at him with her puppy-dog eyes.

'Who was that?' she asked.

Tomek looked at his phone as though it would answer the question for him. His mind drew a blank. 'It was an Instagram notification,' he began. 'Telling me someone had just posted...'

'What?'

'Never mind... Did you find anything you liked?'

The momentary look of confusion swept off her face and was replaced with excitement. 'Oh my God, there's *sooo* much.'

'Two outfits' worth?'

'Three...?' The plea in her voice was not lost on him.

Tomek sighed and scratched an itch on his back. The toss-up between buying her three outfits or letting her see her mother was weighed heavily in one direction. If he chose the former then she might forgive him for the latter.

'Fine,' he said, hoping the reluctance in his voice wasn't lost on her this time. 'But the extra one counts as an early Christmas gift...'

'Fine. Absolutely. I understand.'

Then she grabbed his hand and dragged him back into the nightmare.

CHAPTER
TWENTY-NINE

The news of Jenny Ingles' disappearance landed on Tomek's desk first thing the following morning.

'Seventeen-year-old foster kid from Canvey,' Victoria began. 'Went missing forty-eight hours ago. Last time someone saw her was Friday night. She went out... and didn't come home.'

'And they waited until now to call it in?'

'The impression I got from the foster carer was that she only called it in because she knew it was the right thing to do.'

Tomek inspected the document in front of him.

'Canvey. Again?'

'Woah, woah, woah,' Victoria said. 'You're going to need to control your excitement for me there, Sergeant.'

Tomek snorted. 'Do we think it's related to Annabelle Lake in anyway?'

'Not sure.' Victoria shrugged. 'That's for you to find out.'

'Okay... But why? As in, why is this being given to *me*?'

DCI Cleaves, who'd been hovering behind Victoria for the duration of the conversation, stepped forward. 'Because Vincent Gregory's made his views on the matter very clear. You and Sean are working on this, meanwhile the rest of the team will continue their work on Annabelle Lake's murder. Your aim is to find Jenny Ingles while she's still alive.'

Assuming she still was.

Tomek shook his head. 'Can't believe you're letting him get away with it still, sir.'

'Neither can I. Maybe you should write a book about it. And then find someone who cares and get them to read it. Because right now I don't want to hear any more moaning.' Nick waved the comment away with a flippant flick of the hand and hurried back to his office. And that was that on the matter. Nothing more to say, no one left to listen to it.

It was good to see Nasty Nick was back to his wicked old ways. Pleasant and delightful over email, a real stubborn and miserable arsehole in person. But that was Nick, that was the way he was made. Something somewhere down the line had made him that way, and there was no changing him. And a part of Tomek didn't think the fabric of the team would ever be the same if he did.

Victoria offered Tomek an apologetic smile and shrug of the shoulders.

'You get used to him eventually,' Tomek said, though he was unsure why he was consoling her when it should have been the other way round. 'Sometimes you think he's a real fuck nugget, but others—'

'Sorry?'

'Which bit don't you understand?'

'The fuck nugget bit. What does that even mean?'

'You know...' Tomek paused. Thought of where he'd heard the phrase before. Drew a blank. 'You know when someone's a fuck nugget...'

'No, sadly. I don't. That's why I asked.'

'Well, you a know, a nugget...'

'A chicken nugget? A nugget of poo?'

Tomek's body tightened with tension. 'I feel like the moment's gone now. Shall we forget I used that word and just call him an arsehole instead?'

Victoria's eyes widened. '*Now* I understand what you mean. You should've just said that in the first place. But I completely understand where you're coming from.' She turned over her shoulder to check that Nick had left the room. 'He really can be a right little fuck nugget sometimes.'

Tomek clicked his fingers and fired a finger gun at her. They were now united in their sporadic dislike towards Nasty Nick. 'Now we're shooting the same shit, Vicky.'

Then he turned the document over in his fingers, reading the information that had been scribbled on it: the name, address and mobile number of Jenny Ingles' foster carer. Climbing out of the seat, he craned his head over his desk and searched for DS Campbell.

When he spotted him, he blew a whistle with his lips, disrupting the entire room from their studious work.

'You coming, big man?'

'Where?' Sean was so large he didn't need to pop his head over the monitor; his head jutted out from the horizon of computers like a skyscraper in the distance.

'Canvey.'

'Again?' said Chey Carter, butting into their conversation. 'You sure you're not property searching down there and just using work as an excuse, sir?'

Tomek shot the young man a wicked glare. 'At least I can buy a house down there, Mr Pepper. It'll be another twenty years until your mum finally lets you out of the home.'

The wide grin on Chey's lips fell flat.

Tomek made his way to Sean's desk.

'You coming, or am I going to have to drag you?'

'I don't think you have the facilities for that I'm afraid, little man.

You've been so used to being a stay-at-home dad for the past four weeks I don't think that little belly of yours will allow it…'

Tomek was speechless as his friend lumbered his bulky frame out of the chair.

'I adopt an SAS mentality on a daily basis, fuck you very much.'

'In what way?'

'Eat as much as you can because you never know when your next meal might be.'

'That only applies in the wilderness, or if you're getting shot at in the desert. Not when you've been on your arse all day every day with a McDonald's twenty yards down the road.'

CHAPTER
THIRTY

Alison Jones was the sort of woman you wouldn't want anywhere near an adult, let alone a teenager. She had a slightly unhinged look about her, as though she'd smoked too many crack pipes in her time and had spoken to enough celestial bodies to make her rethink her total existence. The walls of her house were draped in patterned satin sheets, and the smell of an eclectic array of incense candles burned throughout the property – there were at least three in the living room alone. Meanwhile, the carpets of the living room were filled with old newspapers and *Hello!* magazines that didn't look as though they'd been read. In her hand, Alison held a cigarette with no sign of an ashtray in the immediate vicinity. Tomek looked down by her feet and spotted the black charcoal stains on her carpet from where the ash had fallen and burnt a hole right through.

She was one cigarette away from lighting the entire place up. And he was certain that, if they weren't there, then she would almost certainly be smoking something stronger. Perhaps that's what the incense candles were for – an insufficient effort to mask the smell of weed for impromptu visits from the police or social services.

How she'd ever been allowed to take a child into foster care was beyond him. Though he hoped to discover a little more about her and Jenny's dynamic.

'You two wanta tea?' Alison asked after they'd already sat down.

'No. Thanks,' Tomek answered for them both. He was afraid what they might find sitting in the bottom of the mugs. Or what might be laced in the teabags.

'Suit yourself. You 'ere 'bout Jenny?'

'Spot on,' Tomek said, resisting the urge to fire his finger gun at her. Maybe he would save it for later. 'We just wanted to ask a few questions about the last time you saw her and where you think she might be.'

'Well if I knew that I wouldn't'a called your lot, would I?'

Your lot...

The words immediately got Tomek's back up. He hoped they didn't have another little racist fascist bastard on their hands.

'Of course not. We don't like time wasters any more than the next copper,' Sean said, his deep voice bouncing off the furniture. 'Do we, Tomek?'

'No, Sean. We certainly don't. You wouldn't happen to be wasting our time would you, Alison?'

She took a toke of her cigarette and held it there for a moment, before releasing the grey cloud of smoke into the air, making no effort to blow it away from their faces. 'What'd give ya that idea? Jenny went out Friday night but ain't come back. She ain't been back since.'

'Why did you wait so long to call us?' Tomek asked.

'Because this ain't the first time she done it, know what I mean?'

Another toke, another plume of stale, rancid smoke.

'How many times has she done this in the past?'

'Four or five, give or take.'

Give or take... as though she was referring to her age.

Seventeen years and five months, give or take.

She's only done a runner four and a quarter times, give or take, because that one time didn't really count.

'And has she always returned each time she's tried this in the past?' Tomek asked as he reached into his pocket book and began taking notes.

'Well, 'course she has, otherwise she wouldn't'a gone missin' this time, would she?'

She'd got him there, and to save his blushes, Sean jumped to his defence.

'What my colleague means, is whether you were ever concerned about her? Was she always contactable? Did you always know where she was?'

Alison shrugged, nonchalant. 'Most a times she was down the pub, got drunk and then went round a mate's. She was always round a mate's.'

'Do you know any of these mates?'

Another shrug. 'Can't say I recognise any of them, but I wouldn't mind a piece of some of them...'

Jenny Ingles' age flashed in his mind. Seventeen. Which meant she was above the legal age for consent, and hopefully so were her friends...

'Did she have her phone on her typically?' he asked, wanting to move the conversation along.

'Fucking hell, 'course she did. You seen teenagers now, ain't ya? Them bloody lot can't live without the bastard things.'

Until that point, he'd tried to separate the Jenny Ingles that had gone missing with the Kasia Coleman that was at school. But she had just changed that. Now they'd become interchangeable, and the images in his head of Jenny being trapped somewhere – possibly lying face down in a ditch somewhere near or in the Thames Estuary – had been replaced with Kasia. Only four years separated them, and she was closer to Jenny's age than she was Annabelle's. Which meant the Worry Thoughts were taking him full speed to Paranoia Central.

He didn't like thinking about these awful things happening to her. Not now, not ever.

'You got any more questions?' she asked.

'Yes,' he said, suddenly regaining his composure. He pretended to consult his notes, as though his next question was written in front of him when it was already in his head. 'What's the pub that she used to go to? I presume you've already checked there?'

'I popped in but couldn't see her. I know the landlord, that's why he always lets her stay for a couple of drinks. Likes to keep an eye on her.'

'What's the name of the pub?'

'Windjammer.'

Tomek made a note, though he knew Sean was logging the same information in his head beside him. The silent one, sitting there, judging.

Then he decided to change direction.

'How long has Jenny been under your care?'

'Seven years,' Alison replied. She answered so quickly that it sounded as though she'd come up with the number off the top of her head. It made Tomek dubious.

'And how has your relationship developed in those last seven years?'

'You know...' She paused even longer to take a drag of her cigarette. Probably coming up with more of what she thought they wanted to hear. 'It's had its ups and downs. She can be a right little brat sometimes. Spoilt little girl, ungrateful...'

Tomek was right. This was exactly what he wanted to hear. Whether she knew she should be saying it or not was a different matter. Her words were enough for Tomek to make a call into social services and get her taken away. That, and the weed and other drugs paraphernalia that was probably lying around the house somewhere. Only problem was, Jenny had already had the same idea; she'd taken herself away before anyone else could.

'To the best of your knowledge, has Jenny been in touch with her birth parents recently?'

Alison scoffed. '*To the best of my knowledge*? This some sort of law drama or something?'

By now she had finished the cigarette, but continued to suck on it, getting as much value for money as possible.

'Answer the question please,' Tomek said firmly.

'Not that I know of. But she don't tell me much now'days. All I know is she comes in, goes out, comes back in again and then she's off out again.'

'What about school... friends?'

'What about 'em?'

This was painful, but Tomek was thankful it would be over soon.

'Does she go to school, and does she have any friends?'

He felt the need to painfully spell it out for her.

Alison finally stubbed the cigarette out on the knee of her jogging bottoms and brushed away the debris with a flick of the hand. Now it made sense why she'd sucked the stick dry to within an inch of its life, though Tomek couldn't help think it would be less of a health and fire hazard if she'd invested the effort in using a mug or even a glass to collect her ashes.

Oh well, it was her funeral.

Maybe that was why Jenny had taken herself away before anyone else could. To avoid the excruciating pain of burning to death. Or to let the woman kill herself in the same way by accident.

'Jenny ain't been'a school for a while now,' Alison said, bringing him back to the room and away from thoughts of an inferno blazing in the darkness.

Tomek prodded the pen deep into the paper of his notebook as he added a full stop to his sentence.

'And what about you, Miss Jones...? Where were you Friday night?'

If she picked up on the insinuation behind the question, then she didn't let on. Then again, Tomek didn't think she'd be able to if she wanted to; whatever concoction of drugs she'd taken before their arrival was beginning to take effect.

'Wha' you sayin'?' she said, her words becoming slower, her voice becoming thicker, like treacle. 'You sayin' that I had somethin' to do with it?'

'Nope. Just asking a question, Miss Jones. All part of the process.'

She shook her head, but her movements were so slow and laboured it looked like she was being thrown about in zero gravity. 'I was out with some of my mates...' she said. 'We was at the pub... Quiz night in the town centre...'

'Different to the pub Jenny usually goes to?'

A nod. One that took at least thirty seconds to complete. Tomek then made a note of the pub before asking a few more questions. He wanted to get out of there as soon as possible. The stink – and the leftover smell of weed – was making him sick. And the less time he spent in Alison Jones' presence the better.

'Think a good old phone call's in order, don't you?' Tomek said as he headed back towards the car.

'To where?' Sean asked.

'The SS.'

'I don't think you wanna be calling back to the 1940s, mate. That's dangerous territory.'

Tomek chuckled. 'I bet Vincent Gregory would fucking love for them to come back, wouldn't he?' The thought of the man sent his cortisol levels spiking instantly. 'Not *that* SS,' he continued. 'Social services. I don't think she can look after herself, let alone anyone else. She's not fit for care and she needs to be struck off the register.'

'Maybe they can come live with you...' Sean said with a wide grin on his face.

Tomek gripped the car door handle. 'Someone woke up on the funny side of the bed today, didn't they?'

'Someone had to keep the banter going while you were gone. And it's just not been the same since you came back.'

Before Tomek could open his mouth to respond, a white van sped past him and tore through a puddle. A tidal wave of water burst into the air and splashed Tomek's legs and arse, soaking him.

His natural reaction was to swear, but when he saw a young child being pulled along the street by his mother, he stopped himself and instead looked down at the mess the van had made. And the uncomfortable day he had ahead of him.

Christ, he hated Canvey.

CHAPTER
THIRTY-ONE

The Windjammer was situated on the south of the island, hidden behind the sea wall that stretched along the coast and did its best to protect its inhabitants from the battering winds and rising sea levels. Sean swerved the car into the unmade car park and manoeuvred it into a makeshift parking spot, sitting beside an Audi Q7. For 11 a.m., the pub was surprisingly busy, with half a dozen cars parked as close to the entrance as possible. It was the first time Tomek had been to the Windjammer, and he was less than impressed. In his time, he'd been to several bars and pubs over the years (and had his favourites), so he liked to think he knew a thing or two. The building was a two-storey brick house that looked more like a function room than a pub. The lower floor was constructed from brick while the top half was made of black panelling that stretched across from one side to the other. A meeting room at the top, pub beneath.

Upstairs for thinking, downstairs for dancing, as his dad used to say. Repeatedly.

Even when Tomek had asked him to stop.

The first thing he noticed when he entered was the smell. That quintessential English pub smell. Of broken dreams, lost hope, and a smattering of ecstasy combined with the heady mix of alcohol and spilt beer. Then he noticed the floor. The garish patterned carpet that hadn't been replaced since its original instalment in the seventies, and had seen more spills than punters. Then there were the overhead wooden beams across the ceiling that Sean nearly knocked into as he shut the door.

The bar itself was situated in the centre of the building, penned in by four beams that were more for structural integrity than any sort of cool design feature. Tables and chairs were dotted around it like a horseshoe, with some sitting higher on a raised platform. Above the bar was a sign, stencilled in different shades of chalk, that offered customers a range of double shots for as little as £2. Vodka, gin, rum, tequila.

All of which had been Tomek's go-to when he'd been younger. Even as late as his mid-thirties. Going out, drinking with his old school friends, feeling like death the morning after. Promising he'd never drink again but then finding himself at the bottom of vodka Red Bulls the following day. And then something had switched. He grew up a little, and all of a sudden started to develop a taste for beer. Sophisticated, entering into adulthood. Since then he'd never looked back.

But he saw the appeal: two quid was insanely cheap for a double, and it was a wonder how the pub had managed to stay afloat for so long. But now it was beginning to make sense why Jenny found herself in here frequently.

That, and the clientele. Men who'd been working on site somewhere, builders still dressed in their high-vis vests and boots, giving young women attention they would never have received anywhere else.

Sean made his way to the bar first. He placed both hands on the counter and leaned forward, flagging the barman with his presence rather than any audible call.

'What can I get ya, fellas?'

Sean flashed his warrant card, and said, 'Two pints of Coke and a moment of your time, if that's all right?'

At the sight of the warrant card, the barman's eyes widened and his movements became laboured. He opened his mouth but for a few seconds nothing came out.

'Is there... is there anything wrong?' His eyes glanced towards a group of men propped against the bar, deep in loud discussion with one another.

'Does the name Jenny Ingles mean anything to you?' Sean asked.

Tomek helped stir the man's memory by holding a photograph of Jenny in front of his face.

'Yeah, I know her. That's Alison's girl. Well... not *girl*. I presume you...'

Sean nodded. 'We know about her adoption, yes.'

'Oh. Okay. Good. Then...' He swung his head round to the other side of the bar and pointed to an empty nest of seats tucked into the corner. 'Do you fellas wanna sit over there and I'll be over in a bit?'

Tomek and Sean made their way to the seats while they waited for their drinks. When the bartender arrived with them, he wore none of that exuberance in his expression that he'd originally greeted them with. Instead his face had fallen flat, and the crow's feet of his eyes deepened.

'What's your name?' Tomek asked.

'Terry Simpson.'

Though the way he'd said it made him seem uncertain of his own name.

'Is this... is this going to take long? As I'm... I'm the only one running the bar. Do I need to close up for a bit?'

'Shouldn't take too long,' Tomek replied with a smile aimed at putting Terry at ease.

'Okay. Good. You said this was about Jenny. Is she all right? Has anything happened to her?'

'We believe she's gone missing,' Sean said, taking control of this one. 'She was last seen by Alison Jones on Friday night. She's not been home since. We were informed that she usually comes here and we wanted to know if you've seen her at any point since Friday?'

Terry searched his memory, looking down at the table as he did so. Then he shook his head. 'She usually comes down here a couple of times a week. Nothing crazy. Sometimes she's alone, sometimes she's with friends.'

'You're aware she's underage?'

'Yes. But I let her in as a favour. Alison's an old friend. And at least this way I can keep an eye on her, stop her from getting involved in all that drug dealing stuff that's been picking up lately.'

'You ever seen her selling any drugs?'

Terry shook his head. 'Not *selling*. But I caught a couple of her mates doing lines in the toilets once. Think they had some heroin on them as well. I swear I never smacked someone so hard in my life. Almost sent him back to fucking childhood. Surprised I didn't call you guys, I was so...' He clenched his fist and visibly shook as he relived the events in his head. 'Most of the guys that come in here are in their fifties, right, maybe mid- to late forties. All they wanna do is come here after a long day of work, get away from the house for a bit and have a drink. But what they don't want – and what I don't want – is them lot coming in and starting trouble.'

'Was Jenny with them when you caught them in the toilets?'

'Yeah.'

'And how long ago was this?'

'About two weekends ago.'

'And was that the last time you saw Jenny as well?'

'Give or take...'

Tomek winced as he heard those words and was transported back to Alison's living room.

Give or take.

She's only done a runner four and a quarter times, give or take, because that one time didn't really count.

The conversation then moved on to what sort of girl Jenny Ingles was. For some reason Tomek thought they would get a better gauge of the girl from the man who saw her at her truest, with friends and a drink in her stomach. According to Terry, Jenny was a promiscuous sort of girl, flirtatious. Always coming up to the men at the bar and flirting with them, seeing how far she could push it to get a drink. Though, on a few occasions it had gone too far and Terry had heard stories of her going home with some of the men twice her age. He'd subsequently banned them from entering and made sure he kept a keener eye on her since. When she wasn't flirting with older men, she was always laughing and drinking with her friends, or sometimes sitting there on her own. She always looked glammed up and at least twice her age (which was the typical defence for some of the men who'd flirted back with her and bought her a drink).

Terry's parting statement to them was: 'As much I tried to keep her on the straight and narrow – I even offered for her to move in upstairs, but she didn't want to hear it – I think she may have got herself into something bad. Very bad.'

Tomek sensed where this was going but waited for Terry to elaborate.

'Someone came in the other day... Thursday, must have been, because the Europa League was on... and they said that they thought they'd seen Jenny on a street corner. That she... that she was going up to men in cars and waving them down.'

Terry's face fell as his gaze dropped onto the table, the pain and anguish on his face visible for them all to see.

'You've been a great help,' Sean told him with a warm smile. 'Massive, in fact. Thank you for your time.'

As Tomek left the pub, he felt slightly better about the place, and ever so slightly more confident about their chances of finding Jenny Ingles. The place had gone from a four to a seven in his estimations, aided greatly by Terry himself and his warm reception.

CHAPTER
THIRTY-TWO

The last place Tomek expected to find himself later that afternoon – as well as the last place he wanted to be – was outside Vincent Gregory's house. But the world worked in mysterious ways, and so did murder investigations. They had a funny way about them, serendipitous, that everything came back full circle at some point.

And now here they were, the two men that had been exiled by the sympathiser, standing on Vincent Gregory's doorstep, eagerly awaiting the vehemence and venom that would no doubt fall out of his mouth as soon as he laid eyes on them.

The door opened, and much to their surprise, it wasn't Vincent Gregory who opened it. Rather, it was Mrs Gregory, the as yet untitled wife of Vincent. She looked a delight, with a face full of plastic covered in make-up, and a set of eyebrows that had been tattooed on in such a position that made her look constantly surprised. Tomek couldn't take her seriously with a face like that, and wondered whether she shared the same beliefs as her husband.

'Who are you? You lot can't be here.'

He was wrong. She was just as bad, if not worse.

'Is Vincent in?' Tomek asked. He wasn't in the mood for pleasantries. Those had flown out the window a long time ago with this side of Annabelle Lake's family.

'He doesn't want you here...'

'Tough. We're here anyway. Is he in? We only want to chat.'

And then the messiah emerged. Behind his wife, gradually coming into the light as he moved closer to the front door.

'Who is it, love? Oh. *You*. What are you doing here? You can't be here.'

'I know. Your wife's informed us. Twice.'

'Then what are you still doing here?'

'We're here for the shits and giggles, until one of us giggles and shits... What do you think we're here for? We want to chat.'

Vincent folded his arms across his chest like a petulant child. 'Well, I ain't wanna speak to ya. I got nuffin' to say. Maybe if you bring some of the other officers on your team down then I will.'

A wry grin grew on Tomek's face. He'd been waiting for this part. The bit that knocked down the racist defences that Vincent had built around him and his family.

'We're not here regarding your niece, Mr Gregory,' he said, stifling the smugness in his voice. 'We're here to ask you a few questions about the disappearance of a seventeen-year-old girl, last seen getting into *your* car on Friday night.'

Boom. And there it was.

The slap across the face. The truth bomb that had well and truly knocked the wind out of him.

And the mother of all laxatives that had made him undoubtedly shit himself.

For a long while, Vincent said nothing. The colour had flushed from his cheeks, and they seemed to turn hollow, as though the life was being sucked from them in front of their very eyes.

'Shall we talk inside, or would you prefer to discuss this out here?'

Vincent's face didn't move, like it had been pumped full of plastic, similar to his wife's.

'No... I think... Please, come inside.'

Please.

Tomek wondered whether that was the first time the man had ever used the word. Now that he'd visibly calmed down, Tomek and Sean entered the house and made their way into the living room where they waited patiently for Vincent to make the drinks, while staring down the malevolent – and surprised – glares from his wife. After Tomek asked politely, she snapped that her name was Georgia.

Georgia Gregory.

Objectively speaking, she was much more attractive than Vincent – a couple of leagues ahead, at least, thanks to the multiple surgeries she'd had – and she looked as though she wore that burden every day. The burden of carrying him around, of pulling the waste of space along with her everywhere she went. The two of them made a mismatch he couldn't immediately get his head around. But, a lot like the world and murder investigations, love also worked in mysterious ways.

Vincent returned a few moments later with a tray of tea.

'Detectives...' Vincent began. 'I just want to say, I know nothing about a seventeen-year-old girl... Honestly. I have no idea what you're talking about.'

'So you didn't go out for a drive on Friday night?' Tomek asked. Now the tables had turned and he placed the vehemence and the venom in his voice. Now all he had to do was find a piece of skin juicy enough to inject it.

'No. I was home. All evening.'

'We both were.' Georgia reached across the sofa and wrapped her hand in Vincent's, the two of them together, unified.

Tomek reached inside his blazer pocket and pulled out his phone.

After unlocking the device and scrolling until he found the image he was looking for, he held it across the room for Vincent to take. The man surveyed the photograph for a while.

'Do you recognise that area?' Tomek asked.

'It's the chippy... on the high street.'

Bingo.

'And do you recognise the car?'

'It looks like mine, but...' He switched the camera angle for a better view. 'But it's not. Look – look at the alloys. Mine aren't blacked out like that. Those ones are. That's somebody else's car. Somebody else driving it. Nothing to do with me.'

Fuck. Their one hope for an easy win had just flown out the door. And Tomek knew that from here on in, Vincent would be a sanctimonious little bastard and insist on making their lives even more horrible than he already had.

Tomek did his best to ignore the fact that they had no right being there any longer, and chose to move the conversation along.

'Does the name Jenny Ingles mean anything to you?'

'Should it? I already proved to you that weren't me.'

'It doesn't matter. It's all part of our routine enquiries.'

Vincent shuffled uncomfortably in his seat. Caught in the balance of admitting the truth in front of his wife or lying to the police.

Though at this stage, Tomek had no idea of knowing which one was true.

'No. Sorry. Don't recognise the name.'

From the sounds of it, he did know the name and he knew it well. From the way Terry at the Windjammer had spoken about her, a lot of men on the island knew about her. And, if he was being honest, a small alarm in Tomek's head had bleated that Terry knew her better than he was letting on as well.

'You've never seen her before?' Tomek insisted.

'No. Never.'

Tomek turned to Georgia Gregory. 'And you?'

The woman who clearly spent more time on her make-up and appearance than with her husband in general briefly glanced at the photo before turning back to Tomek.

'No.'

'And you're sure?'

'Yes.'

'On a scale of one to ten?'

'A thousand.'

'Not possible, but thanks for taking part—'

Before he could continue, a sound came from the front door, the noise splitting the silence like a whip. All four of them jumped, waited for the footsteps and shuffling to come closer.

A fraction of a second later, they saw who it was.

Elizabeth Lake.

Beth with an F.

She entered the living room with as much force and familiarity as though it was her own living room, and caught herself as soon as she laid eyes on Tomek and Sean.

'Oh... *you're* here.'

Ladies and gentlemen, racist number three has just entered the building.

'Why are you here?' she asked, looking Tomek directly in the eye.

'I'm getting accused of kidnapping another girl,' Vincent hissed.

'No one accused you of anything to do with Annabelle's disappearance, Mr Gregory,' Tomek said sternly, attempting to disarm the incipient argument as much as possible.

'No, you just tried to make it look like I'd fucking killed her instead!'

'*Kidnapping*?' Elizabeth asked, joining the conversation twenty seconds too late.

'No,' Tomek said with a sigh. 'Not kidnapping, Mrs Lake.'

'Yes, kidnapping. Kidnapping a seventeen-year-old girl.'

'Who?'

'Jenny Ingles,' Georgia Gregory answered.

The last thing this conversation needed before the inevitable decline, was another member of the Lake-Gregory family getting involved.

'Don't know her,' Elizabeth said. 'Who is she?'

Tomek sighed. What had once been a hopeful visit was now beginning to descend into chaos. He raised in his hands in mock surrender.

'Right. Let's get some things straight. Nobody is accusing anyone of anything,' he began, even though they were. 'The description of a car matching Vincent's Ford Fiesta was spotted on CCTV picking up a young adult. We suspect the driver is the last person to see her alive. All we wanted to do was ask your brother some questions to remove him from our enquiries.'

'No you weren't!' Vincent yelled. 'You fuckers were tryna pin it on me! Again!'

'Ain't you done enough to hurt this family already?' Elizabeth asked.

The statement stumped Tomek. And he wasn't sure if he was in the middle of an *EastEnders* episode.

'What are you talking about?' he asked bluntly. His patience was rapidly wearing thin. They had another thirty before he lost it completely.

'Steven...' she said, as though that answered everything.

'What about him?'

Elizabeth reached into her pocket and produced a note that had been crumpled and scribbled on.

'He's gone...' she whispered, as though an emotion she'd forgotten she was supposed to show had just come through. To further enforce the message, she creased her face into a sob. 'I think he's... I think he's done something very stupid. I think he's committed suicide.'

Hearing those words, Tomek leapt out of the chair, snatched the note from her and read.

I can't do this anymore. I'm sorry, but without Annabelle... I can't.
Please don't blame yourself. I'm sorry.
   S x

Tomek read and re-read the words several times, turning them over in his mind.

'When did you find this?'

'Just now.'

'When was the last time you saw him?'

She searched her memory. 'This morning. He left for work early while I was still in bed.'

'And how did he seem?'

She shrugged, as though there was no sense of urgency. As though her husband wasn't about to kill himself.

'I dunno. I didn't hear him. I'm a heavy sleeper.'

'What about last night?'

'He seemed fine... normal.'

'And before? Over the weekend?'

She paused, running her finger over her enlarged lips. 'He's not been himself for the past couple of days. Neither of us have. But he... I found him crying the other day.'

'Crying? When? Where?'

'At home. In the bathroom.'

'Did he say what was wrong?'

She shook her head, though it didn't take a genius to work it out. The death of his daughter would have been more than enough to push him over the edge of whatever cliff he was walking.

'Do you know where he is? Do you know where he might be?'

More shaking. This time the urgency of the situation seemed to grapple her and shake her into submission.

'Have you tried calling him?' Sean asked from behind.

'I came here first. I wondered whether Vincent or Georgia knew anything...' She turned to her brother and sister-in-law, both of whom shook their heads slowly.

'He's probably gone into hiding,' Vincent said.

'From what?' Tomek asked before anyone else could. He wanted to control the conversation and make sure he was the only one speaking.

Then Vincent suddenly turned coy, afraid, scratching the back of his head. He glanced over at his sister several times, bouncing his eyes between her and the coffee table in the middle of the living room.

'I... I... I don't really want to say in front of Beth... I—'

'I'm sorry, but your brother-in-law is missing. You have to tell us. You can't say something like that and expect us to ignore it. What is Steven running from?'

More scratching, this time harder. The sound audible over the silence in the room. Vincent wasn't such a big man when he was put on the spot after all.

'He was having an affair. I found out the other day.'

The words manifested on Elizabeth's face and knocked her back into the door. Her body wiggled, as if lifeless. The wind had been knocked out of her.

And Tomek.

It wasn't what he'd been expecting to hear. A part of him had been waiting to find out that Steven Lake had been responsible for the disappearance and death of his daughter, not that he'd been caught having a bastard affair.

'That fucking arsehole...' Elizabeth whispered, staring vacantly into the middle of the sofa in front of her. 'How could he do this... To me, to *us*...'

Tomek didn't have time for this. Since being around the Lake family (if only very briefly), his radar for "impending domestic argument" had become finely tuned, and he sensed where this was going. It was time to get out of there before they built an effigy of Steven and burnt him to the ground in the back garden. Because right now the most important thing was finding Steven Lake and Jenny Ingles, two individuals who deserved to be more alive than the three in front of him.

CHAPTER
THIRTY-THREE

S everal hours later, and there was no sign of Steven Lake.

A small sailing boat, however, had been found on the River Thames, floating lazily on the water, drifting further and further into the estuary as the tide sucked it away from shore. According to his wife, Steven had inherited the *Annabelle* after his father's death a little over ten years ago and frequently spent his free time on the Essex waterways, meandering through the rivers and canals, sometimes taking Annabelle with him. Steven had grown up on the water and he had wanted Annabelle to experience the same sort of sensation. Currently, a team of experts, with the help of the coastguard, were searching for Steven Lake in the water, in the darkness and in the middle of the night.

The odds of finding him alive were looking increasingly slim.

With nothing more to offer, Tomek left the station feeling deflated. One dead child, another missing, and a possibly suicidal father who had gone AWOL. Not the perfect start to his return to work, admittedly. In fact, he thought it was one of the toughest weeks he'd had.

And as he was about to find, it was going to get a lot tougher.

Mercifully tonight Tomek had been able to find a parking spot within a few strides of the flat, something he never took for granted. And as he sauntered up to the flat, jangling the keys in his hand, trying to find the right one amongst the dozen or so he had on there, a figure caught his eye, further down the street. At first he ignored it and continued towards the front door; the faster he could get in, the faster he would get to safety.

Since his altercation with the stranger outside his house, Tomek hadn't seen anyone else surreptitiously hanging around the street – fingers crossed – but that didn't mean to say they hadn't been there. Watching in the shadows, reporting back their findings.

Had they come back for round two? He didn't want to stay around long enough to find out.

As he fumbled with the door key, struggling to wriggle it into the lock – the bastard lock! – he heard the sound of footsteps growing louder. Except this time they were lighter, more delicate.

'Mr Bowen?' came the voice. Light, delicate, same as the footsteps.

Though he couldn't place it.

Carefully, tentatively, he swivelled on the spot to see Bridget Holloway standing in front of him. Dressed in the same clothes Tomek presumed she'd worn to school – an ensemble of jeans, a dark blue blouse, and a denim jacket. At first there had been a distinct look of worry on her face, as though his presence had frightened her more than hers had frightened him. As though she'd made a mistake and stumbled across a criminal attempting to break in. But then as realisation settled in, her face warmed and turned into a smile.

'Christ on a bike, you scared the shit out of me,' he said.

'Sorry. It's not often I go up to people in the dark.'

'That's probably for the best...'

Tomek looked at her with mild confusion. As though the reason for her being there should have been obvious to him, when it was a complete mystery.

'Sorry,' he began. 'I completely forgot. Kasia... maths. Sorry, come in.'

Tomek stepped through the door but Bridget's arm held him back.

'That's why I'm still here. It's nine o'clock...'

The cogs in Tomek's fried and deflated brain had stopped.

'I was supposed to finish an hour ago, but I haven't seen her. I've tried ringing the doorbell but I've not heard anything.'

'She's probably got her headphones in or something. Thanks for sticking around for so long.'

Eventually, after a moment of staring into empty space, Tomek pushed the door open fully and climbed the stairs. When he reached the top, he called out Kasia's name. No response. Then he made a beeline for his bedroom – *her* bedroom – and opened the door without knocking, an action that was sacrilegious under usual circumstances. But something new, something he'd never felt before – something *innate* – told him this wasn't a usual circumstance.

The inside of the room was empty. The bed had been made but hadn't been touched since the morning. Her laptop lid was closed on the dresser and her headphones, the ones he'd prohibited her from taking to school because they cost too much money and he was worried she would have been listening to music in classes, were hanging from the wall (apparently she'd seen the design feature on TikTok somewhere and was adamant she was going to drill a hole in the wall to make his room – *her* room – appear more *aesthetically pleasing*).

'Aesthetically pleasing, my arse,' he'd said. 'It's all fun and games until you knock it and that hole becomes a two hundred quid problem to fix.'

And there was nothing aesthetically pleasing about it now. Not when he didn't know where Kasia was.

'When was the last time you tried calling her?' he asked Bridget who was standing in the living room, doing her best not to snoop at the furniture and mountain of boxes everywhere.

'About twenty minutes ago,' she replied.

'And nothing?'

'No. Maybe she's hiding behind one of those boxes...'

Tomek grunted. 'She'll want to be after I find her.'

He removed his phone from his pocket and tried her mobile. Three times. Each time unsuccessful, going straight to voicemail. Either her phone was off or she had no signal.

'Did it actually ring when you tried her?' he asked.

Bridget confirmed that it had. So that meant it was either off, she had no signal, or she'd blocked his number.

Again.

Pacing up and down the length of the living room, Tomek tried Sylvia's mother, Louise. She answered on the first ring.

'Louise, it's Tomek, Kasia's father. I don't suppose she's with you, is she?'

'No. I haven't seen her,' she replied. 'Let me see if Sylvia knows anything.'

Tomek waited a few moments which seemed to stretch like the resistance of a rubber band.

'Sylvia doesn't know anything either. She's just messaged Kasia so I'll let you know if she says anything.'

'Thank you. I appreciate it.'

Tomek hung up and then threw his phone on the kitchen counter. The device skidded along the surface and, just as it was about to slip off into the abyss of the solid stone flooring, Bridget leapt forward and caught it. Afterwards, she held the phone aloft like she'd just won an Olympic gold.

'Thanks,' he said. 'You're good at that.'

'Practice,' she replied. 'Kids are always throwing their phones about in class. Plus I'm always dropping mine.'

'At least you've got the ability to catch it, whereas all my motor neurone function falls out of the window and my fingers turn into vegetable oil.'

Bridget took a small step closer towards him. Then another, until she was by his side, only a few millimetres separating them. Definitely too close for comfort.

'Has she ever done anything like this before?' she asked, dropping her hands by her sides.

'No. We've only been dealing with... *this*, for five weeks. That's a terrible ratio. If she keeps this up I can expect her to escape at least ten times a year. Maybe even eleven after a short while... It'll come round like a leap year.'

Bridget raised her hand and brought it up to his, then moved it gradually north, tentative inch by tentative inch, until she came to his shoulder. 'Don't be so hard on yourself. These things happen. I'm sure she's fine. I'm sure she'll be home any moment—'

Miraculously, the sound of the front door opening drifted up the stairs, followed by a loud bang and the heavy stomps of footsteps on carpet.

Kasia appeared a moment later. Still in her school uniform. Tie halfway down her chest, top buttons undone, skirt too high, shirt untucked. The same way she always looked. Except for the black stains running the length of her face and the den of snakes that had swarmed her eyeballs.

Tomek's first thought was that something had happened to her. That she'd been attacked. That she'd been raped on the way home.

But then he saw her phone. Alive and working.

Which meant she'd gone for option three.

Which meant she'd blocked him.

Which meant he'd done something to deserve it.

'Kasia...' he began. 'Where have you been?'

Before responding, Kasia's eyes fell onto Tomek's arm. 'Are you two... are you two fuck—?'

'Language!' Rapidly becoming aware of Bridget's lingering touch on his arm, he shifted away from the kitchen counter and moved to the other side. 'That? No. That was— We— Nothing. Nothing was happening.' Then he realised that he was the one who should have been angry with her, not the other way round. 'We were worried about *you*. Where have you been? What have you been doing?'

Kasia's eyes narrowed and her brow creased. He wasn't certain, but he thought he saw a vein starting to throb on her forehead.

'What the fuck is this?' she yelled, waving her phone in front of him.

'Language!' he told her. 'Stop fucking swearing!'

'I don't give a fuck!'

She stormed over to him, unlocked the phone and thrust the screen in his face. There, staring back at him, was a photo he recognised all too well. One that had been taken of him without his consent. One that had been shared with an underage girl. And one that he hoped his daughter would never *ever* see.

CHAPTER
THIRTY-FOUR

'What the fuck are you doing with that?' Tomek asked, struggling to keep his voice together.

'Language!' Kasia said mockingly.

Tomek raised a finger to reprimand her, but then immediately realised that he didn't have a leg to stand on.

'Where did you get that from?'

The image of his penis had been taken by Charlotte Hanson while he'd been sleeping one morning. She'd taken the image on her phone and had sent it to a sixteen-year-old girl on a fake Instagram account that she had set up under his name without his knowledge. It had started out as an attempt to land the girl in trouble with her parents but had quickly ended with a formal complaint made against him. Not to mention the image now existed on the Internet, something he was now painfully aware – thanks to his job – was virtually impossible to remove. The image of his flaccid penis would exist forever, and so long as people still had it and knew about it, so would Tomek's pain at seeing it.

And now Kasia's.

'Someone at school sent it to me,' she said bluntly. 'They said it was your dick. What the fuck?'

Tomek babbled a moment. Trying to think of what to say. He never expected Kasia to see it, for it to end up on her phone. Which meant he didn't have a logical and thorough explanation, one that didn't make him sound like a sexual predator. There was no way he came out of this lightly.

'Yes,' he said. 'It is what you think it is. But it's not the way it sounds. Someone I know took it and sent it to someone in a different school. You still haven't explained how you got it.'

'I told you. Someone sent it to me.'

'Who?'

'I don't know. They "*AirDrop*ped" it to me.'

Tomek knew enough about the technology in his iPhone to know she was talking about the functionality that acted like Bluetooth, enabling users to send anything to anyone willing to receive it without the need to enter mobile numbers or copy links in an app.

'And you don't know who it's from?'

'No. That's how AirDrop works. They changed the name of their phone so I didn't see who it was from.'

He clearly didn't know everything about it, after all.

'Give it to me,' he said, reaching out for her mobile. 'I'll take it to work tomorrow. They'll be able to trace its source.'

Kasia pulled the device away from him before he was able to reach it. She then clutched it against her chest. 'You're not getting my phone! I won't let you.'

'Yes you will. I want to know who sent it to you, I want to know why.'

She tucked her phone in the breast pocket of her blazer. 'You–can't–have–my–phone!'

Tomek quickly realised this was a battle he was going to lose. Not unless he chopped her hand off and retrieved it that way. Instead he would have to think of other, more creative ways to find the source of the image. And then, randomly, he remembered that Bridget had been standing behind him, quietly listening in to their conversation. He slowly turned to face her.

Her face was rouged, clouded with second-hand embarrassment. She'd witnessed one of the most bizarre and uncomfortable arguments ever by being in the wrong place at the wrong time.

'Sorry you've had to hear all that,' he began awkwardly. 'This is an incredibly embarrassing thing that's happened to me in the past few weeks, and it's something I'll explain to you later—'

'Is that what's going to happen after Miss had finished tutoring me? You were going to show it to her in person?'

'*Kasia! Enough!*' Tomek's bark echoed around the living room and into the kitchen. He'd finally snapped. The first time he'd shouted at her like that. Guilt immediately attacked him and convinced himself he was a bad parent. 'Please,' he added, though the damage had already been done. 'Nothing's happened between us, and nothing was going to. You have to give it a rest.'

'Or what?'

The venom in her voice scared him. This was a completely different side to her, one he hadn't experienced before. It was rapidly becoming a night of firsts.

To defuse the situation, Bridget stepped into his line of sight, tiptoeing forward hesitantly.

'I think I'm going to go...' she started. 'I will see you at school in the morning, Kasia. If you could come to my office in the morning after first period, we can discuss who sent this to you. And, Mr Bowen, I'm sure we'll get to the bottom of this, don't worry. I know it's your job and I know you'd like to do it yourself, but leave it to us first.' She gently glanced between them, her bright eyes defusing the tension and putting Kasia at ease. 'I know this is a bit of a shock to both of you – as it is for me – but I think if you both take a moment to breathe and calm down, then you can sit and discuss what's going on. I don't need to know anything more than you're both willing to share. All right? Enjoy... enjoy the rest of your evening.'

Tomek thanked her and then showed her out. At the bottom of the stairs he placed a hand on her arm – similar to the way she had done only minutes before – and then thanked her again. As he waved her goodbye, he thought of the next steps. Of the best way to proceed. Of the best way to calm the stormy waters between them.

He looked up the steps and imagined each one was a phrase or sentence he could use to explain himself. And then he realised that it was futile. No amount of preparation or planning could prepare him for *this* conversation.

When he finally clambered up to the top step, ready to face the music, he walked into an empty room. Kasia was missing; all that was left was her bag, resting lopsided on the solid floor surface, the contents spilled onto the floor, and her coat that had been thrown over the back of the sofa without his realising. Tomek ignored the mess and made for his bedroom – *her* bedroom.

He pressed the handle and pushed without knocking. There was no time for knocking. No time for the manners. Not now.

When the door opened fully, he saw nothing. The room was exactly as it had been when he and Bridget had searched it earlier. The untouched bed, the make-up dresser, the headphones...

Everything was exactly the same. Except for the window. His bedroom window – *her* bedroom window – had been left wide open, and a cold gust of wind blew in, billowing the curtains like dancers in the night. He sprinted towards it and peered his head out, snapping his neck left and right as he searched up and down the street. In the pitch black, he saw nothing. Not even the dark orange from the street lamps was enough to illuminate the trees or surrounding vehicles. Or the silhouette of a thirteen-year-old girl.

'Kasia!' he called out to her, but there was no response.

She had gone.

CHAPTER
THIRTY-FIVE

As Tomek grabbed his car keys he realised he wouldn't need them. She couldn't have gone far. Not far enough to warrant them, anyway. Chances were she was within a few hundred yards at the very least, half a mile if she really put her mind to it. He'd witnessed her athleticism every time she carried the shopping upstairs, and he'd heard the constant stories of how much she hated PE and any form of physical exercise, so he knew the search net wouldn't have to be cast that far.

The first decision he faced when stepping out of his house, however, was which way to turn. Left or right.

Which way had Bridget gone? Had he been paying attention? Had he even seen, or did he just *think* she'd gone left, towards the seafront?

He turned the other way, in the direction of the town centre. Then his gaze lifted skyward, towards the bedroom window. It was positioned north, towards the town. If she'd slipped out while he'd been saying goodbye – which she must have done because he'd only been downstairs for a few seconds – then she would have gone in that direction, towards the light and civilisation.

Fifty/fifty.

Left or right.

Then he made his decision.

Right. Towards Leigh Broadway.

At this time of night, the small town centre was beginning to wind down. Couples and families going out for their nice meals had finished and were slowly making their way home, arm in arm, headed towards the taxi rank. Last-minute purchases had been made in the Co-op and were being hurried down the street. Even the pub-goers were beginning to call it a night.

As he stormed through the street, he tried Kasia's mobile number. Nothing.

His number was still blocked. And if it hadn't been before, then it certainly would be now.

No bother. Tomek had a solution to the problem. No, two solutions.

The first was typical, non-intrusive. The second was more questionable.

First, he unlocked his phone and opened the Find My Friends app. As soon as the software loaded, a small map of Leigh-on-Sea appeared, followed by a small bubble above his exact location. He pinched the screen to zoom out, and as more of Essex appeared, so did more bubbles. His brother in Chelmsford. His parents right on top of each other in their home. Same for Sean and Chey who were both still situated in the incident room. Even Bridget making her way back home.

But no sign of Kasia.

He considered the possibilities. Either she'd disabled the app, turned off her location settings, or switched her phone off completely.

He preferred the first two possibilities. Detested the last.

But there was a way to find out.

After closing down the app, he scrolled to his address book and found Sean's number.

The phone rang and rang. Until eventually his friend picked up.

'Sorry, mate,' Sean began. 'We can't come out to play just yet. Chey's mum says it's past his bedtime and he's got to go to sleep as soon as he gets home.'

The sound of Chey screaming at Sean to fuck off echoed through the speaker in Tomek's ear.

'Can you help me?' Tomek asked. 'I need help.'

Sean sensed the urgency in Tomek's voice and lowered his own. 'Course, mate. What's happened?'

'Kasia's gone missing. She's just left the house and done a runner. Can you put a trace on her phone to see where she might be?'

'Ermm...'

'Come on, pal. Help me out. I've got no fucking idea where she is and with what's happened to Annabelle Lake and Jenny Ingles, I don't want her being out here for too long.'

Tomek knew that pulling on Sean's heartstrings would work. But it was a desperate time. Needs must, and all that. And the worrying thing was he didn't even feel guilty about it.

A moment later, Sean confirmed that he would do what he could, and after handing Kasia's mobile over to him through the phone, Tomek continued storming through the town centre, searching for his daughter. He had never known such angst and anguish before, such desperation. Though he may not have shown it in the way he spoke or in the way he moved, he felt it deep down. The burning desire to return a loved one home, like the pain and shock you felt when you misplace your phone.

Now Tomek was beginning to understand how Steven and Elizabeth Lake had felt.

Sean called him back a few minutes later.

'I found her,' he said. 'She's on the seafront. Old Leigh. Somewhere between the beach and the Ye Olde Smack.'

Tomek knew exactly where she was. He thanked his friend, hung up and then hurried down to the seafront.

Old Leigh, so named because it had once been the town's buzzing high street several centuries ago before it had moved further inland, was a ten-minute walk – and a very steep decline – away. This part of town was famous for its beautiful walks along the estuary; its several docks filled with boats that looked as though they'd been uninhabited for several hundred years; its pubs that had been there as long as the boats; a small strip of sand that locals flocked to as soon as the sun made an appearance and the temperature reached fifteen degrees; and most importantly, its fish and chip shops, made from fresh fish from the local fish market along the promenade. Tomek had spent many afternoons there as a child, and many evenings there as a teenager. It had been one of his favourite places to escape to after an argument with his parents. Sometimes he'd stay there all night and come home in the early hours of the morning, his parents completely oblivious to his absence.

It was a miracle then that he hadn't thought of it first. That Kasia may have ended up there. Perhaps it was because the two of them hadn't walked along the path yet. They'd never made the journey from Old Leigh to Chalkwell all the way to Southend seafront.

As he crossed the footpath bridge that led to Bell Wharf beach, Tomek's phone chimed. Sean had sent him a photograph of Kasia's latest location. Just over a few hundred feet away, perched on the edge of the sand.

At the bottom of the steps he made a left turn and hurried towards the water. There, he found her, a figure in the sand, curled into a ball. Her body glowed an angelic shade of white as the moonlight bounced off her school shirt. The gentle sound of waves lapping against the shore echoed and immediately put him at ease. All stress and angst flooded out of him as he exhaled deeply.

Cautiously, he removed his shoes and socks and stepped onto the beach. It had been a long time since he'd last felt the sensation of sand on his feet, of it between his toes, of that tingle and burn. It immediately transported him back twenty years. Sitting there, with his friends, flirting, laughing, drinking, shouting, singing. It was a surprise nobody had called the police or complained.

Now it was different. The place was desolate. Perhaps it was the cold, too wet, too miserable. Or perhaps it was too early for the youngsters and revellers to make an appearance. Perhaps they were still enjoying dinner with their parents before slipping out and breaking underage drinking laws. Or perhaps it was just something they didn't do anymore. Now they were too busy with their video games, reality TV, and their fingers hardwired into the digital twenty-first century, they didn't need to do anything as reckless and slightly anti-social as spending the evening away from parents. Not when they could do that from the comfort of their own home.

'Hey...' he said softly and from a distance, so as not to disturb her.

Kasia, sitting on her school blazer to prevent the sand from getting into her tights, scrunched in a ball with her legs pressed against her chest, remained perfectly still.

'Can I sit down?'

She said nothing, but Tomek found himself a space a few feet from her anyway and sat with his legs in a similar position. For a long while he said nothing. Just listened to the sound of the water, of the wind, of the birds in the distance, of the train coming in from Benfleet towards Shoeburyness.

This was what it was about. Pausing, stopping all the chaos and madness to take a break, a breather. He hadn't appreciated it as a twenty-year-old. All he'd cared about was being cool, fitting in, and getting with girls. But now, now it was moments like this that enabled him to reflect.

'Do you want to talk about it?' he asked as he watched a small shipping container steadily float along the River Thames towards the Channel and beyond.

'No...'

'Okay,' he replied. 'Do you want to know the story behind it?'

She hesitated. Considered.

'No.'

'Fair enough.'

Tomek changed the grip on his knees as they began to sink into the sand. By now the shipping container had moved all of five inches, pootling along. Beyond it were the night lights of Kent to the south, sparkling amidst the fumes coming from the vessel. Overhead, the light cloud cover had begun to disappear and reveal the tapestry of the night.

'On a clear night, and with a very good camera, you can see the Milky Way,' he told her.

'No you can't,' she said in disbelief.

'You can,' he continued. 'You just need a very *very* good camera and a lot of patience.'

Intrigue piqued, Kasia craned her head towards the sky.

'I don't believe you.'

'Well maybe one day I'll have to buy you a camera and you can try it for yourself.' She tilted her heads towards him, a slight, gentle smile on her face. 'You take enough of them on your phone. How come you came here?' he asked. 'Of all places. I'm surprised you even knew where to find it.'

Kasia inhaled deeply before replying.

'I came here with mum once...' she started, then stopped herself. 'When I was ten. Just for the afternoon. It was my first time by the seaside. She said it was so I could get to experience the sea and the sand. But then she disappeared for an hour, left me in this exact spot. I didn't move the whole time she was gone, just stayed right here, waiting. I didn't cry, I didn't scream for help. Because I knew she'd be coming back.'

'And did she?'

Kasia dropped her head. 'Yes... but only after she'd got what she wanted...'

Drugs.

He wasn't sure exactly when Anika's habit had started – at some point after their break-up, he'd guessed – but it had come as a shock to him when he'd originally found out. Her uncle, a loan shark, had been responsible for killing two of his best friends, and Anika had narrowly avoided a prison sentence or any sort of charge. Her uncle on the other hand had been charged with murder and sentenced to life in prison. But that hadn't stopped her from keeping in touch with him and making use of his criminal underworld contacts. As a result, she'd developed a dependency for cocaine and heroin, and would do anything to get it. Like prostituting herself, beating people up, breaking and entering, and even committing GBH – all of which had led to her inevitable imprisonment in one of His Majesty's finest establishments, and Kasia coming into his care.

'Did you know at the time what she was doing?' Tomek asked carefully.

'I guess a part of me knew. That's probably why I stayed, because I knew she'd come back eventually.'

Until the day she hadn't. Until the day the drugs had consumed her and taken over her life.

'But why here?' he continued. 'Is it because you think she's coming back...?'

She lowered her legs, stretching them across the sand, creating little grooves with her feet. 'No,' she replied. 'I know that's never going to happen. I guess it's just... when I was standing here, I wanted to run away. I wanted to cry and run and scream for help. But I told myself to be brave. I told myself that everything would work out in the end. And in a way it did. I came here to remind myself of that.'

CHAPTER
THIRTY-SIX

When Tomek left the house the following morning, it was pitch black. Had been ever since he'd first lain down. No sleep for him, not unless you counted the two hours that had teased him between twelve and two. Since then he'd tossed and turned, unsettled. The thoughts in his head whirring. Scenes from last night playing in his mind.

He could only imagine how much more graphic and disturbing they were for Kasia. He wouldn't be surprised if she needed therapy or some sort of hypnotist treatment to make her forget everything she'd seen. But he knew that would be impossible. The image of his penis was firmly ingrained in her mind.

Which was a thought he never imagined would cross his head.

He'd also been kept awake for hours trying and failing to work out who'd sent it. At first he'd tried sneaking into her room to steal the phone from her bedside table and looking at it that way (he'd seen her enter her passcode to unlock the device several times, and much to his chagrin, it was the least inspiring number ever – her birthdate). But, as he'd slipped through the doorframe and tiptoed over to the table, he'd noticed that the phone was wedged between her and the duvet, a thin white cable protruding from the folds. Realising that she must have fallen asleep with it in her hands, he dismissed that idea and went back to square one.

Square one which was useless.

He could only imagine what inspiring thought he'd have for square two.

And then it had hit him. Social media. Rooting through Kasia's follow list and descending down the rabbit hole of people from her school. But that was a murky world he didn't want to get into. The majority of the children her age that he'd come across at work had little to no privacy or security settings, and so it would have felt weird for him to be scrolling through images of teenagers and underage children – and with his ineptitude at navigating the intricacies of social media interfaces, he just knew that he'd be prone to liking something or following someone by mistake. Or inadvertently sending them a giant image of a thumb. And landing himself in a shitstorm of trouble.

Instead, he'd lain awake, letting the thoughts and ideas fester in his head. Until the pressure had grown so heavy, so unyielding that he couldn't handle it anymore and rolled out of bed. By the time he left for work, he'd made Kasia her breakfast and lunch, and even written a little note to say that he'd left early and would be home late. He was old school like that.

As he made it to the end of the road, instead of turning right towards the station where he was due to attend a briefing at midday, Tomek turned left, in the direction of his new favourite place in the world.

◁▷

Vincent Gregory was apoplectic to see Tomek first thing in the morning. The man had barely woken up, and his hair was a mess, as were his eyes, still clinging to the remnants of sleep. He was dressed in a set of bed shorts, leaving his chest and a mat of curly hair exposed to the cold. It wasn't long before his nipples became erect, like two turrets sticking out of a spaceship.

'What the fuck are you doing here – *again*? How many times do I have to tell you, I don't want you here! I've already spoken with your boss and he said he'd take care of it – he clearly ain't doing shit if your stupid arse is still coming round unannounced!'

Vincent's voice had echoed up and down the empty and quiet cul-de-sac, and at the end of it he had treated Tomek to a view of his grime-stained teeth with a long yawn.

'Late night, was it?' Tomek asked, struggling to stifle a yawn of his own.

'Whadda *you* think? You're the cop. Thought yous was supposed to be all perceptive, n' that? Beff's been going outta her mind, worrying 'bout Steven all night.'

As far as he was aware, according to the case notes and files, her reaction to her husband's disappearance was more visceral than the one she'd had when she'd found out her daughter had been kidnapped and murdered. Strange... But then again, grief did work in mysterious ways.

'Do you think I could come in?' Tomek asked.

'No. Absolutely not. Fuck off! You have no right to be here.'

Tomek folded his arms across his chest and waited a few moments before continuing. 'It's about your car...'

That seemed to draw the aggression from his face, and he retreated a step further into his own house.

Despite the fact Vincent had managed to prove it wasn't his car that had been used to pick up Jenny Ingles, Tomek and Sean had requested a duo of Scenes of Crime Officers to come down and swab the vehicle for prints and DNA. Just in case, they'd told him. All part of their routine enquiries. To help them rule him out. But they all knew it was out of spite. A chance to get one over on the little racist fascist bastard. And who were they to argue if Victoria had signed-off the request without argument?

Sadly, it would be a while before the forensic examiners found nothing during their investigations, so he couldn't have the luxury of arresting Vincent on this cold and wet November morning. Instead the real reason for his visit was far more innocuous, far more benign. But so long as it continued to apply the pressure in the right direction, Tomek didn't mind. It was the least the little racist fascist prick deserved.

'What about my car?' Vincent asked carefully, as though if he said it any louder he might admit culpability.

'It's better if we discuss this inside...'

And just like that, he was in. The house was asleep, and the sound of Georgia Gregory's snoring rumbled through the building. Tomek headed straight for the living room and dropped himself onto the sofa.

'Well...?' Vincent began urgently, keeping his voice low. Though Tomek didn't think it necessary. 'What is it?'

'We found a few anomalies...' Tomek started. 'With the paperwork... It appears you've missed a couple of payments to the DVLA for your road tax.'

'You what?' Vincent's face turned red.

'You've been driving on the road illegally for the past four months.'

'What the fuck is wrong with you? Are you some sort of Polish cunt? You came all this way to tell me I've forgot to pay something. Nah... get the fuck outta my house, man. You're driving me round the fucking bend.'

Tomek chose to ignore the instruction. Instead, he remained where he was and simply smiled smugly up at Vincent. The response heightened the man's aggression, and in a flash he charged up to Tomek and reached for him. But then, at the final moment, he caught himself, and realised that he was about to put his hands on a copper.

'Not thinking of doing anything silly now, are we?' Tomek asked. 'You might not want me investigating your niece's death, but I'm still a serving police officer, and I can still flip you on your arse and squeeze your fucked-up little face into the carpet and arrest you if I want. So think very carefully about which way you want to do this...'

Indecision played on Vincent's face. And after a while, he gradually withdrew his hands and lowered them by his sides.

As a sign of dominance, Tomek brushed himself down (even though he hadn't been touched) and remained in his place. This was his seat now. This was his house. And Vincent was the one intruding.

'While I'm here,' Tomek began, 'I had a few questions I wanted to ask you about your brother-in-law, Steven...'

CHAPTER
THIRTY-SEVEN

Tara Moore lived alone in a three-bedroom house in South Benfleet, round the corner from the train station. Parked on the driveway were two cars: a BMW 4 Series and a Vauxhall Corsa. One for business, one for leisure. Before knocking on the door, Tomek checked his watch. 8:50 a.m. A more sociable hour to be calling. By now most of the kids were at school and all the workers had made the arduous journey into the city for the day ahead. Except for Tara Moore, one of the doctors at Southend Hospital.

In a bid to get rid of Tomek as fast as possible, Vincent Gregory had answered all of his questions in record time. That he had nothing to do with his brother-in-law's disappearance. That he'd been working the morning Steven had gone missing. That he'd only known about the affair for the past few days and was going to break the news to Beth with an F sooner, but owing to the current situation of her dead daughter, had decided that now probably wasn't the best time. Elizabeth Lake's world had just come crashing down on her.

Her daughter had gone missing.

Her daughter had been killed.

And then she'd found out that the man she loved – or, rather, the man she was supposed to have loved – had been having an affair.

For how long, Tomek didn't know and neither did Vincent. But he intended to find out.

A moment later, the front door opened. From the groggy look on her face, Tara Moore had only woken a few minutes before, and was hastily rubbing the sleep from her eyes. She was dressed in a light cardigan and a pair of jogging bottoms. She had a head of thick brown hair that fell perfectly on her shoulders, and thick eyebrows that angled downwards sharply at the edges of her face. Tomek had never seen the show properly, but he thought that she looked like a character from *Grey's Anatomy* – too good looking and polished to be a doctor. Too Hollywood.

'Can I help you?' she asked, her voice as weak and tired as she looked.

Tomek fished inside his pocket and flashed his warrant card. 'Tara Moore?'

She was too busy rubbing her eyes to look at the details of his card. 'That's me.'

'Can I come in, please? It's regarding Steven Lake...'

At that, she stopped rubbing. 'Is... is everything okay? Is he all right?'

Tomek brought her up to speed once they'd found a comfortable seat in the living room.

'I've been informed his boat was found yesterday evening...' he continued as he met her gaze and allowed it to wander about the room now and then when she wasn't looking. 'But sadly there was no sign of Steven. The vessel has been seized and is currently being investigated.'

Which reminded him, he had plenty of time until the midday meeting.

'Are you... And you...' Tears started to form in her eyes. She fought them off for as long as possible. Until she uttered the words that had been holding them back: 'You think he's dead, don't you?'

From there, it was relentless. Non-stop for a few minutes. In that time, Tomek helped himself to a wander around the bottom floor of the house as he searched for some tissues. In the end he used toilet roll from the bathroom.

'Here you go,' he said, as he handed them across.

Sniffling, she replied, 'Thank you.' Then began dabbing her eyes with the three-ply.

Tomek allowed her a moment to come to terms with the news. He let his gaze wander about the room again, this time studying the fixtures and furnishings in more detail. The house was considerably larger and grander than he'd been expecting – especially for someone who lived alone. Thanks to his recent move, he now considered himself an expert on the property market in the South Essex area, and guessed that her house was somewhere in the six hundred to seven hundred thousand pound arena. An extortionate amount of money for a household with two incomes, let alone one. But what concerned him more was the worrying amount of dolphin-related paraphernalia around the place. Pictures hanging from walls and photo frames on a cabinet in the living room; glass and mosaic ornaments on the window sill; graphics and illustrations on the side of mugs in the kitchen. She even had an enlarged painting of a dolphin breaching the water, silhouetted against the backdrop of a rainbow and cloudless sky, imprinted onto a tea towel.

Tomek didn't know where that particular fascination came from, but before he could venture into the deep psychological difficulties that she must have gone through to get it, Dolphin Lady finished crying and looked up at him.

'When they... when they find his body... will you tell me?'

'Of course.'

Tomek reached into his pocket and produced his notebook. While he had no intention of writing anything down, it was a masterful way of insinuating that he would and that he had some tricky questions he needed to ask. It typically helped the witness prepare themselves for what was about to come.

'I understand that the two of you were having an affair...' Tomek started.

She nodded gently, brushing hair from her eyes.

'Can you tell me how long you've been seeing each other?'

'Four months or so. We... I'm a paediatrician. I look after ill children. Annabelle's come in a couple of times over the past year or so, and I've been looking after her.' She paused, her face washed over as she played fond memories in her head. 'Then one day Steven and I just got talking. Nothing too salacious, nothing too spicy. Just talking. Friendly, like. He struck me as a soft, genuine guy, and there aren't many of those around nowadays – trust me, I've tried. Then he asked if I wanted to go out for a coffee or lunch one time.'

'And you said yes?'

'Mhmm.'

'Knowing he was a married man?'

She stopped herself before responding. 'I... From what I heard, and from what he told me, it wasn't a happy relationship at all. Otherwise why else would he have invited me out? I don't think the two of them got on. They were always arguing over Annabelle, and Steven wanted to get out of the family. He couldn't stand his brother-in-law. Vic... Vin...'

'Vincent—'

'That's the one. Couldn't stand him. They were always arguing. More than he did with Elizabeth. It was always over little Annabelle. The poor little thing was just caught up in the middle of it. I think it really got to him.' She rubbed her thumb up and down her fingers, massaging the cartilage and bone. 'You could see it on his face. Just... despondent a lot of the time. Hardly ever there. I'd talk to him and I'd have to repeat it a few times for him to actually listen to me, you know?'

Tomek did know. He knew that all too well: Kasia had been the same when she'd first moved in with him. Sitting there in silence, staring into space, saying nothing, taking forever to answer him when he asked her an innocuous question such as whether she wanted a tea or not. And then in the evenings she'd headed straight to bed without a word, and whenever he'd tried to open a dialogue with her, she'd stared dispassionately at him and turned in the other direction. The first two weeks had been like that, until something had eventually clicked. Perhaps she'd come to the devastating realisation that this was her new reality and that she was stuck with it.

'Did you ever spend any time with Annabelle?'

'Not much. Not much outside what I needed to at the hospital. Most of the time Steven came here, under the guise of being at work. Or he'd sometimes come to meet me in my lunch break if he was in the area.'

Now it made sense why Steven had been getting an extra load of work up in Southend.

'It's terrible...' she said, as though it was an afterthought.

'What is?'

'What happened to that little girl. It was disgusting. You should have seen him. He was in bits whenever he came over. I tried to console him but there was nothing I could do. He would just sit there on the sofa staring at the TV or lying in the bed pretending to be asleep. He thought about keeping himself busy with work but he said that he wanted to be around me, to speak with me.'

'Did you not have work?'

She shook her head. 'I've been on leave for the past two weeks. Back tomorrow, though. First time I've taken any this year and they forced me to do it. At least I'll be back in time for all the drunk kids in A&E over the Christmas period.'

Tomek tried to remember whether he'd been one of those drunk kids. Getting so paralytic that he could barely walk and had to have his stomach pumped by the generous folk down at the emergency centre. He couldn't recall any particular nights out.

'Do you know who did it yet?' she asked.

Tomek shook his head and apologised. 'We're working on every possible line of enquiry,' he said, repeating the slated response. 'What sort of thing did Annabelle used to come into the hospital for?'

There had been no mention of hospital visits in Lorna's post-mortem report. Nor in anyone else's report for that matter, which made Tomek wonder whether they'd been officially recorded.

'She...' Then hesitated. 'At first it was because she was being tested for learning difficulties. But then, as the time went on, I think Steven found reasons to come in and speak with me. A lot of the times he complained about her having a headache or something else benign, so I didn't think to record it anywhere.'

Tomek made a note of that, then thanked her for her time and apologised for spoiling her day. As she walked him to the front door, he turned and addressed her. 'Lastly...' he began. 'And you don't have to answer if you don't want to – but what's with all the dolphins?'

Tara chuckled. 'This place was my gran's. I inherited it when she died. A lot of them were hers, but I've added to the collection over the years. She used to work with them as an environmentalist, travelling the world and monitoring them. When I was younger she wanted me to become a vet, but I couldn't stand to work on dying or injured animals. So I chose to help sick children instead – the next best thing.'

CHAPTER
THIRTY-EIGHT

'You've had a busy morning.'

'Since when was that a crime, sir?'

Nick knitted his fingers together and cleared his throat. 'Sadly for you, it's when the word "harassment" gets thrown about.'

'Bullshit.'

'Vincent Gregory seems to feel otherwise. You've been to his house at least four times in as many days.'

Tomek shrugged. 'I really like him. He has a great personality. I think the two of us could be friends outside of a professional capacity.'

Nick pulled a face in disgust. 'Don't get smart with me, Tom. You know you're not supposed to go anywhere near his house. If he makes one more phone call I'll have to start sending you out on shift with uniform. Or stick you in a room with Lorna and you can spend the next month with dead bodies.'

'Might as well just shoot me in the head now,' Tomek replied.

'I might do just that. But first I think I'll give Vincent Gregory the gun.'

Tomek pursed his lips. 'Don't think he needs a gun, sir. Just give him a metal chain and he's all set.'

'What are you saying, Tomek?'

'I'd say it's obvious, sir. I think Vincent Gregory killed his niece and then killed his brother-in-law to make it look like a suicide.'

Nick sighed heavily. This time the air coming out of his nose was stronger than a jumbo jet's thrust. 'I take it this has nothing to do with the fact you don't like Vincent Gregory?'

'Oh, it has absolutely everything to do with the fact that I don't like him.' Tomek raised his hands in surrender. 'Make no mistake, I hate the cunt. But I also think he's killed a couple members of his family.'

'Why?'

Tomek sorted the sleeve of his blazer out before speaking. 'Because I think Annabelle and Steven were coming between his relationship with Elizabeth, his sister.'

'You *think*...'

'Yes, but—'

'Well, there's part of the problem, Tomek. You *think*. Until you actually *know* something, there's very little myself or Victoria can do about it. And last time I checked, you weren't even supposed to be worrying about Annabelle or Steven Lake – you were supposed to be focusing your efforts on finding Jenny Ingles. Have you forgotten that she's still missing?'

Tomek's shoulders bowed forward as he withdrew into himself. 'Erm... No, of course I haven't forgotten.'

'Sounds to me like you have. You've had such a hard-on for Vincent Gregory that you've completely neglected to ensure the safe return of a seventeen-year-old girl. What the fuck is wrong with you?'

Tomek wagged his finger in the air in protest. 'I don't think that's fair, sir. I've made enquiries into who she was as a person and tried to trace her last movements. We've even got Gregory's car being examined. I know that she was a troubled teenager, who'd got herself into the world of drugs and prostitution, and more than likely, this is a case of something... something going wrong.'

Nick sighed. Except it wasn't his usual sigh. There was none of the aggression or resentment in it. This time it was filled with shock and surprise.

'Did you really just say that? You're attributing her disappearance to a freak accident, a horny junky that took things a bit too far?'

Tomek opened his mouth, however nothing but air fell out. Nick was right, it was ludicrous to think that Jenny's disappearance could have been attributed to such an arbitrary way of thinking, and he felt ashamed for even acknowledging it by voicing it. He dropped his head and apologised.

'I'll put all my focus into it this morning, sir,' he said.

'Afternoon,' Nick corrected, then checked his watch. 'Victoria's meeting is in seven minutes. Plenty of time for you to get me a coffee and treat yourself to one as well.

The smug grin on Nick's face remained as Tomek closed the door behind him and headed to the coffee shop round the corner.

Tomek returned eight minutes later, coffees in hand. The barista in the shop had messed up his order. Twice. And so he'd been forced to wait longer than anticipated. Plus it was nearly lunchtime and the queue had been a joke.

He apologised for the delay as he entered, handed Nick the coffee (which immediately dissipated the anger on Victoria's face as she realised she couldn't pick an argument with him over it), and then settled himself at the back of the room.

Standing beside Victoria at the front of the incident room was DC Rachel Hamilton. The two of them were both dressed in similar smart trousers with dark tops tucked into their waists. Almost identical. As though they'd planned it. Tomek wanted to ask whether that had been the case but thought that now definitely wasn't the right time. Perhaps after people had stopped killing one another.

That'd be the day.

Victoria, as senior investigating officer, was first to speak. She cleared her throat before beginning, demanding the attention of everyone in the room.

'Good morning,' she started. 'I trust you're all well rested – as much as possible, anyway – and I trust that you're all prepared for what I'm about to tell you. As you will all know, Steven Lake's sailing boat was discovered just off the Thames Estuary last night, floating aimlessly a few miles off-shore. There was no body discovered at the time, and the coastguard – with the help of our marine unit – are still searching the waters for any sign of him.

'Thanks to Chey's report last night, I've been informed that Steven's phone was last used at a short distance away from where his boat was found. The last ping on the radio towers was 05:35. He left his house early morning forty-eight hours ago and didn't come back. The *Annabelle*'s anchor was discovered missing, and so we believe that he's used it to keep his body beneath the water. The boat was found in almost pristine condition, with no sign of leaking or damage from a collision with another boat. And the chances of finding his body in that water are almost nil. As a result, right now our working hypothesis is that he jumped in and drowned. We will however continue to do everything we can to find him – dead or alive.'

Victoria paused to let the news settle on the team. Tomek scanned the faces of his colleagues. Some, the more experienced members of the unit, wore blank, muted expressions. Whereas the youngest members of the team were ashen.

'Any questions?' Victoria asked after the moment had finished.

At once, several of the team's hands went up, as though they were in the classroom. It was the orderly way to do things in the office; otherwise it was complete chaos and nothing ever got discussed.

Victoria scanned the room, looking at the hands, quietly selecting her first victim.

'Tomek...'

He repositioned himself on his chair so that he was sitting a little taller. 'Do we know where he kept the boat?'

'Good question. Yes. He kept it in the marina on Canvey Island. It's just before the bridge that leads onto Benfleet.'

'Has anyone been there yet?'

Victoria nodded, but before she could open her mouth to speak, Rachel stepped in. 'A team of SOCOs went down there last night. They found Steven's car parked right beside the water's edge, next to a giant hole in the row of boats where he must have kept his. They're going to be combing their way around the boat over the next day or two, but the weather might put paid to that idea.'

Tomek nodded as he was eager to move onto his final question: 'Are you a hundred per cent certain he's topped himself?'

Victoria's eyes narrowed and her voice deepened. 'Yes. Well, I'm not far off. The evidence seems to point that way. Unless you have anything you'd like to offer?'

He shrugged. 'Nothing at all. Just wanted to make sure that we've covered all angles.'

'You're right. A fresh pair of eyes and ears goes a long way.' She turned to Sean, who was sitting beside Tomek. 'Anything you wanted to pick up on, Sergeant?'

Sean shuffled uncomfortably in his seat. Tomek wasn't sure if it was an awkward reaction to the question or to the person asking the question. It wasn't the first time he'd picked up on his friend's shyness around the new inspector.

'His financial records...' Sean said slowly as if the words were forming in his mouth as he said them. 'Have we... Have we...'

'Have we checked them?'

'Yes.'

'Yes, we have.'

'And?'

'There appears to be nothing abnormal about them,' DC Rachel Hamilton added gently. 'All his money's still there. But there have been no major cash withdrawals. No large payments made to any rogue bank accounts. Like we might typically expect if he was trying to fake his own death. Just a few payments to an account registered to a Miss Tara Moore.'

'His bit on the side,' Tomek added.

'Excuse me?' Victoria asked.

'This morning I spoke with Tara Moore. Doctor at Southend Hospital. She's been having an affair with Steven for the past few months. I informed her of his disappearance and suspected suicide.'

Victoria turned to Nick for support, for an explanation as to why Tomek had been interfering with the investigation when he shouldn't have. But when one didn't come, she returned her attention back to Tomek, however he was too busy silently yelling *I told you so* at Nasty Nick with a smug grin on his face.

'I've got all her details if you want to give her a call or pop round for a visit.'

'Where did you get this information?' Victoria asked.

'My good mate, Vincent Gregory.'

'I heard you two were moving in together,' noted Nadia.

'Almost,' Tomek replied, still keeping his gaze on Nick. 'But we couldn't agree on a few fundamental differences. Namely the whole racism thing. But, still, a stand-up guy, though. Not a bad word to say about him...'

I told you so.

I told you so.

I told you so.

Eventually Tomek pulled his gaze from the chief inspector and returned it to Victoria, who was standing with one hand on her hip, the other holding onto her lanyard as if for dear life.

'Thank you, Tomek. That's very thorough work.'

'A pleasure, ma'am.'

The team then turned their attention to Steven Lake's mental health. An in-depth search into his financial history indicated that he'd been paying for private therapy sessions to help cope with what Tomek suspected to be his depression. And after a quick meeting with his therapist, the team had learnt that she had referred him to a website called *The Man Club*, an online forum for adult men to share their thoughts and feelings with one another in a safe and friendly environment. According to his therapist he was an avid user, but had stopped sharing recently, and in their last few sessions he had stopped posting entirely.

Steven had started seeing his therapist four months ago. Right around the time he'd started seeing Tara Moore on a less professional basis. There were two conclusions that the team had drawn from that. The first being that the therapist had enlightened Steven and opened his eyes to the misery of his marriage with Beth with an F and inspired him to seek an affair; or his affair had already started with Tara and, upon seeing how miserable and depressed he was, she had diagnosed him and recommended he seek professional help. The perks of having a medical professional in your life.

Tomek was firmly in the first camp. That it had taken one meeting with an outsider for Steven to realise he was miserable and that the grass was greener on the other side – and certainly much greener away from Canvey Island. A massive fuck you to Elizabeth. And an even bigger fuck you to Vincent Gregory.

No prizes for guessing why Tomek liked the first option so much.

CHAPTER
THIRTY-NINE

After the midday meeting had finished, Tomek had been pulled by Nick into his office for a brief chat.

'What's your game plan for finding Jenny Ingles?' he'd asked.

No profanity. No aggression. No shouting.

Totally out of character for the chief inspector and, truthfully, a little frightening.

When Tomek had told him what he planned to do for the rest of the day, Nick had pointed his chubby little fingers at him and said, 'Well go and fucking do it. And if I see – or hear – that you've been stalking Gregory and climbing through the windows, then I swear to fucking Christ...'

He'd been unable to finish his statement, too overcome with frustration. But Tomek hadn't cared. He'd heard it all before. And he left the room with a wide grin on his face. Nasty Nick was back and there was nothing to worry about.

Nothing to worry about except crossing the bridge onto Canvey Island and spending yet another chunk of his afternoon on there.

While he'd been in Nick's office, being told to pull his finger out his arse, Sean had managed to come up with a name of the island's biggest drug dealer, the one they suspected Jenny Ingles had found herself working for.

William Morton.

An unemployed six-two high school dropout who owned the latest car and all the designer gear. Just from the look of him – with the chains and the watch and the shoes that probably cost more than Tomek's monthly mortgage payments – it was clear to see what line of work he was in. They found him in the car park of the Knightswick shopping centre in the middle of town, leaning against his Range Rover, smoking a cigarette.

The car park itself had always struck Tomek as overly ambitious. Way more spaces than they needed, and even more than anyone had ever asked for. And the building was even worse. Stuck in the late seventies, early eighties, with its dull, red brick fascia and drab tiled flooring. Management had tried to spruce up the place with some artificial light and plant pots dotted about, but it had little effect. What they really needed was to keep the doors shut and not let anyone in. Either that or knock it down entirely.

Tomek pulled the car to a stop and climbed out of the vehicle. Sean lumbered his heavy frame a few moments behind him.

'Mr Morton?' Tomek asked.

As soon as he heard his name, William threw the cigarette onto the ground and stubbed it out.

'Most people call me Billy,' he said, chucking his hands into his pockets, nonchalant.

'Good for them. Can we talk to you about something?'

'It's not about Jesus, is it? I already had one customer come in and tell me about that motherfucker.'

'Customer?'

Billy thumbed in the direction of the centre over his shoulder. 'Got a little barber's in there, haven't I?'

Tomek didn't know – but he did now. A drug-dealing barber... Was there anything more obvious than that? He may as well have put a large sign on the front of the shop saying: *Please come and launder your money here!* Tomek was willing to bet a lot of his own hard-earned cash that Billy's barbershop was usually quiet as well, with long afternoons spent on the chairs scrolling on his phone. He was also willing to bet that as far as the government and the tax man knew, he was running a very profitable small business indeed.

'We're not here to talk about Jesus,' Sean said. As a man of loose faith (he practised when he wanted and went to church when he could), he disliked it when someone joked about that sort of thing. Though Tomek's use of the phrase "Christ on a bike" was both allowed and encouraged. Which made little to no sense to him, but he complied anyway.

'We're here to talk to you about a friend of yours...' Sean continued.

His imposing figure and deep voice had started to have an effect on Billy, and he began to recoil, losing some of the bullish youthful arrogance that came with thinking you were the cock of the walk, Lord of the Canvey Island realm.

'Don't have many of those...' Billy replied.

'Shouldn't take us too long then, should it? We were wondering if you've heard from Jenny Ingles at all recently.'

A shock of recognition flashed across his face as he registered the name. But Tomek knew the next few words that would come out of his mouth. Was willing to put even more money on them.

'Don't know who you're talking about.'

Dingdingding! We have a winner!

'That's a shame,' Tomek said. 'Because we had a little wager. See, Sean said you'd say that. Whereas I had a little more faith in you.'

Billy Morton shrugged. 'Sorry to let you down. Didn't your mum never tell you not to gamble?'

'Did yours never tell you not to sell drugs? Oh. Have I said too much?'

Billy's mouth opened and closed like a fish.

'Cut the BS, mate. We know she's working with you. Or should I say *for* you. So why don't you just do us all a favour and tell us what we'd like to know?'

Before responding, Billy's eyes flitted over Tomek's shoulder several times. Tomek noticed it and turned round to see what the drug dealer was looking at: two adults, one scruffy with their trousers halfway down their arse, while the other appeared more respectable, wearing a polo shirt that highlighted thick, rounded muscles, approaching them.

'Customers, are they?' Tomek asked. Then checked again. There was something different about these two. They weren't walking in the usual depressed and zombie-like walk of a junky stuck in the chasm between wanting their next fix and finding it, but instead they possessed the swagger of people higher up the food chain. 'Or are we looking at your suppliers?'

Billy's eyes danced between Sean and Tomek, Tomek and Sean. His chest heaved, bouncing up and down.

'Doesn't look like you got long, mate,' Sean said. 'Big decision to make. Bet they're wondering who these big wigs dressed in suits are. Not your average customers, are we?'

'Please,' Billy babbled. 'I haven't seen her since Friday. I don't know where she is. And I don't know what she was doing.'

'Yes you do. And so do we.'

'Ermm. All right. Fine. She was working – not for me though. She doesn't work for me. She was working her own thing. Said she was looking for some guys to meet. For sex. Happens all the time down that way. Nothing to do with me. But she had a bag of heroin on her. I know that much.'

Billy probably didn't know why he'd felt the need to tell them that little nugget of information, but the good news was that he had. The pressure of the situation had opened the flood gates in his mind and told them a little more than he may have planned to.

And just in time too; as he finished talking, the two individuals approached within earshot.

Tomek decided to save the man from a potentially grisly death; the drug squad would get him at some point, which for people like him was a fate worse than death.

'So we go down the end of this road, left at the roundabout and then follow it past the arcades, and then do another left?'

Billy's eyes widened with confusion. 'Yeah. If you get to the pub then you've gone too far.'

'Mega,' Tomek said. 'Cheers, mate. And if we get lost, we'll know where to find you, won't we?' He burst into a fit of laughter that rolled across the car park, and then he slapped Billy on the arm. 'Have a good one, mate. And thanks again for the directions.'

As they turned their backs on him, Tomek registered the faces of the two individuals with a nod, then headed back to the car.

He wasn't exactly sure what do with the information that Billy had given him. If the video of her jumping into another man's car from behind a fish and chip shop in the middle of the night wasn't irrefutable proof that she'd been prostituting herself, then Billy's testimonial was. And now they knew that she'd been carrying drugs on her as well – an upgrade from the cocaine she and her friends had been using in the Windjammer. But now it confirmed Tomek's hypothesis, the one Nick didn't want to believe: that perhaps her abductor had been a heroin addict looking for a good time.

A good time that had gone wrong.

CHAPTER
FORTY

That evening, Tomek didn't look forward to putting his key in the front door to his flat. It had been nearly twenty-four hours since Kasia had run away, and they hadn't spoken at all. Sure, he'd messaged her on WhatsApp to let her know that he was coming home late and she would need to put her dinner on. But had she replied? Absolutely not. Instead she'd read the message and ignored him.

Left him on read, the kids were calling it.

And he disliked it. Not only was it rude and disrespectful, it was also hurtful. He had no idea what sort of situation he would be walking into. What her mood would be like. How hot or cold she'd be.

And this wasn't something he was willing to take a gamble on.

'Kasia?' he called to no one.

The living room was empty, and his bedroom door – *her* bedroom door – was firmly shut. The smell of cooked dinner lingered from the kitchen and the leftovers were still on her plate. Nearly eighty percent of the microwaveable chilli con carne meal. The same as the night before and the night before that. She wasn't eating properly, and he wondered if she'd eaten the lunch he'd made for her earlier in the morning.

He didn't want to use the term "eating disorder", but one thing he was becoming increasingly aware of – and taking actionable steps to educate himself on – was the increasing pressure placed on young girls Kasia's age to look like fitness models and wear next to nothing. The advent of social media had created a perpetual anxiety about weight and looking slim on impressionable children by bombarding them with images of skinny, scantily-clad models who were horrendously thin and sometimes appeared emaciated. He had even started to notice Kasia slimming down herself; most noticeably on her shoulders and arms.

Just another thing to worry about when it came to looking after a teenage girl. That and boys, drink, drugs, sex. All sorts of things he had no fucking idea how to handle.

Next he made his way to his bedroom – *her* bedroom. The soft sound of music came from the other side of the door. She was listening to it in her headphones so loudly that he could hear from his position. If she wasn't careful, she'd be part of a generation that would be deaf by the age of thirty.

He knocked but received no response.

He knocked again.

Still nothing.

Then, carefully, he opened the door and tentatively peered his head through the gap, looking directly at the wardrobe in front of him – lest he spot her in an uncompromising position.

The reality was much worse.

At first he noticed the smell. Fruity. Sweet. Like grapes.

And then he saw the giant white cloud of smoke vapour hovering in front of her face, gently moving about as the wind blew in from the window.

There she was, sitting on her bed, still dressed in her school uniform, smoking a vape.

'What the fuck are you doing with that!?' His voice reverberated around the room and through the headphones.

As soon as she saw him standing in the doorframe she yanked them off her head and chucked them on the bed, then proceeded to hide the vape under the duvet.

'You can't fucking hide it,' he told her. 'I fucking saw it. What do you think you're fucking doing, smoking in my fucking house?'

Kasia opened her mouth but he was too incensed to let her speak, let alone hear what she had to say.

'Where the fuck did you get it from? Who do you think you are? This is my fucking house and you go and do something like that as though you own the fucking place?'

Tomek paused a beat to catch his breath. He'd lost track of the amount of times he'd said the word *fuck*.

'It's...' Kasia started. 'I... Don't talk to me like that.'

'I'll talk to you however I like.'

'No you can't. You're not my dad!'

Tomek clenched his fist. His reaction to those words would come later, once he'd had a chance to process them.

'Yes I am! But I never asked to be your dad, did I? But look where we are!'

And his reaction to *those* words would hopefully come sooner, he prayed. Much sooner. Like, in the next thirty seconds.

Kasia crawled to her knees. 'I fucking hate it here!' she screamed, then scrabbled for the vape and puffed on it repeatedly.

She made it as far as the second attempt before Tomek was on her. He yanked it out of her mouth and stormed into the kitchen where he chucked it into the bin.

'What are you doing?' Kasia screamed after him, blocking the kitchen doorway. 'I paid for that!'

'With what money?'

Before she could answer, Tomek hurried over to the bookshelf in the living room and pulled open his favourite book. *The Picture of*

Dorian Gray. Inside should have been a secret emergency stash of a hundred quid, but when he opened it he only counted fifty left, made up of two twenties and a ten.

'Have you been fucking stealing from me?'

The smoking was one thing, but the stealing was a completely different ball game. He wouldn't tolerate either.

'I asked you for money the other day and you wouldn't give it to me!'

Had she? Didn't he?

He couldn't recall the conversation she was referring to, but it still didn't mean she could steal from him.

'Where did you buy the vapes?'

'The shop,' she said with all the belligerence you'd expect from a child who thought they were in the right.

'Which shop?'

'One round the corner.'

'Which corner? Here or the school? Actually, do you know what? I'll speak with them both and make sure they don't serve you.'

'What? That's totally not fair.'

'You're *underage*! You shouldn't even know about these things, let alone be smoking them. They're not good for you. We don't even fucking know what they do to your health. I don't want you smoking them anymore.'

'You can't tell me what to do...' She crossed her arms and huffed.

'Because I'm not your dad? Well, I am. And that's the situation we're both in. I've been trying my hardest here, and you're not giving anything back.' He placed his hands on his head and sighed deeply, dropping his gaze to the floor. As he exhaled, the tension in the room seemed to level slightly. 'Know what – I can't stand to see you right now. Get out of my face. Go to your room.'

Unsurprisingly, Kasia didn't need telling twice. The door slammed shut a moment after he'd said it. And then he remembered – the window. It was open.

'Fucker!'

She was quick; if he didn't act now, he might lose her again. He leapt out of the kitchen and over to the bedroom door. He burst through a fraction later and caught her, reaching into her blazer pocket for another e-cigarette.

'Nearly...' he said, considerably calmer this time, and outstretched his hand. 'But not quite. Give it here.'

A few decisions took place on Kasia's face: the first was whether to throw it out of the window (after all it would be better for no one to have it than for him to), and the second was to smoke it in front of him in a display of sheer arrogance like she had done a moment before.

Fortunately for him, she took too long in deciding and failed to recognise Tomek's hand reaching out for it. He took the small cardboard box and tucked it into his pocket.

'How many more have you got?'

'None.'

'Don't lie to me, Kasia. I don't want to have to check your bag.'

'Then don't.'

If ever there was an invitation for him to do it, it was that. In one long stride, he made it to the other side of the table dresser and found her school bag. Inside was a planner, a small pencil case, an assortment of school books, and a bottle of water. And, sitting right at the bottom, was the sandwich he'd made her wrapped in tinfoil for lunch, though he decided not to mention it. The vape debacle was more than enough for now. That was an argument for another time, something for him to keep locked away in his arsenal.

'How long have you been smoking these for?' he asked, the fight gone from his voice.

'Not... not long.'

'A day? A week?'

'A couple of days.'

'And did Sylvia get you into them?'

Something in him had switched. From angry, rabid Rottweiler to a calm, gentle Labrador.

'No. She doesn't like them.'

'Then how the fuck did you get into them?'

She didn't answer. Something in her had changed as well. Like him, she'd gone from a savage Jack Russell to a temperamentally obedient Golden Retriever.

Tomek decided that was enough for tonight. No more to discuss on the topic. No more shouting. But before he left, he closed the bedroom window and locked it with the key.

No more escaping into the night either.

As he shut the bedroom door behind him, he pulled out his phone and made his way to the sofa. His mind was awash with myriad thoughts. Of the argument. Of her not eating. Of her smoking. Of her becoming a troublesome and difficult burden on his time.

Of how she was beginning to fall down the same slippery path that Jenny Ingles had once followed. Of how he didn't want the same to happen to her.

Of how he wasn't cut out for this. That he was way out of his depth. That he was completely and utterly fucking clueless.

Of how he was desperate for help...

Sitting there, staring at his reflection in the black of the TV screen, he thought about that word: *help*. Of what it meant and where he could find it.

Then he unlocked his phone and scrolled to the "Recents" in his phone book. Saw the several missed calls from the unregistered number.

Anika.

Kasia's mum. The one person she probably needed more than anyone right now.

CHAPTER
FORTY-ONE

To say that things had started to fall apart would be an understatement. They were rapidly losing grip on the situation, and he didn't know where they went from here. But a part of him felt like they'd gone past the point of no return, so what was the damage if they continued on this reckless path? What was one more life?

He had never planned for it to be this way, but she'd insisted. And now he'd done things he wasn't proud of. Things that he would later regret.

The sum of which was lying on the floor in front of him. Half naked from the waist down, her underwear discarded to one side in a dirty mess. Her skin was covered in a layer of dense sweat and she shivered violently. She was semi-conscious, though from the vacant, washed over look in her eyes you might think she was dead.

If she wasn't already, then she would be soon.

On the floor beside her was a needle, evidence of its use staining the tip. Next to that was evidence of something else: their ineptitude.

Rather, *his* ineptitude.

Finding a vein and injecting the drugs into her system had been a steep learning curve (and even now he wasn't entirely sure he'd fully grasped it) but he'd learnt the basics, and knew that, when it came to heroin and other such drugs, getting it into the bloodstream was just about the long and short of it.

Easy really. Except it hadn't been. Not when his hands had shaken as he'd threaded the needle into her skin, almost shearing off a chunk of her flesh as he caught it.

After he'd eventually administered the drugs, she'd fallen into a coma-like trance, her mind and soul light years away while her body remained firmly with him.

Open.

Ready.

He wasn't proud of what had happened next (Christ, who could be?) but it had happened nonetheless.

And again shortly after.

Since she'd been with them, poor Jenny Ingles' body had become a plaything. A toy for him – *them* – to experiment and enjoy themselves with.

She *was* a prostitute, after all.

The only problem they had now, however – the big dilemma, the biggest fucking dilemma to ever have existed – was what to do with her.

They were rapidly running out of her heroin. And soon after it was finished, she would awaken and recognise his face. That opened a whole host of potential problems that they weren't ready for.

He'd known this would be a part of it – he'd agreed – but not like this. There were better ways to do it than this...

He glanced down at Jenny, sprawled across the floor. Disgusting. Could he use what little heroin they had left and hope for an overdose? That way they'd save themselves the mess.

Or could he just finish with her one last time and then do what needed to be done?

One last fuck.

One last disappointing and predictable ejaculation.

Before they moved on to the next phase.

CHAPTER
FORTY-TWO

Moo-Moos had been a mainstay on Leigh Broadway high street for the past twenty years, and it was also one of her favourites, so he chose that as a more appropriate venue to meet. Not to mention she wasn't the type of woman to be taken to the pub. Too high-brow. Too civilised.

Tonight the bar was quieter than Tomek had expected for a Thursday night. Though it contained the usual number of people: the two women who were smartly done up, sitting in the corner with their G&Ts, quietly slagging off their husbands and having a catch-up before they went back to the real world; a young couple looking for a quiet place to finish their date night before heading home to sit in silence; and lastly the group of five men, who'd obviously geared themselves up for a night on the pull but had ruined their chances by getting too drunk before they'd even ventured out to any of the clubs towards the centre of Southend.

The melting pot of the Essex gentry.

Tomek checked his watch. It was a little after 10 p.m.

Late, but not too late. Closing time would be in an hour or so, maybe a little more depending on how generous the owner was feeling.

While he waited, he spun the glass of beer on the table and watched the liquid sway from side to side. Until eventually the door opened and in stepped an old face, a *strange* face.

A face that had changed drastically in the time since he'd last seen it, and yet not changed at all.

His *help*.

As soon as Saskia Albright noticed him, her face beamed, and he was transported back to the last time he'd seen her: at his friend's funeral, almost thirteen years ago. They'd gone for a coffee after the service and reminisced about the stories between them all. Right before she'd flown back to Scotland to live with her parents and embark on the grieving process of losing her boyfriend.

'Tomek...' she said in a Scottish accent that had a slight Essex twang to it. 'It's so good to see you.'

Tomek didn't reply. Instead he stepped out of his seat, approached her and embraced her. Hard. Wrapping his arms around her small body and hugging as though she were a long-lost relative he'd once presumed dead.

'You have no idea how much I've missed you,' he said as he finally let her go. If she felt disturbed by the duration of the hug, her face didn't show it.

'Likewise, but there was nothing stopping you from calling or texting now and then – it was like you'd disappeared off the face of the earth!'

Tomek hesitated as he formulated a response. '*Likewise*. Scotland isn't that far off the end of earth.'

She flashed that little glower at him. The one that tried to hide the smirk on her face but failed miserably. The one that he loved, and tried to elicit from her at every available opportunity.

'Drink?'

'Please.'

'Same as usual?'

'Let's see if you remember.'

He had. A Disaronno and cranberry juice. He only remembered because it tasted like the Cherry Drops he used to buy from the local off-licence as a kid.

'I'm impressed,' she said as she sipped on the drink. Her lipstick left a stain on the straw.

'There are a few things I'm good at in life, and one of them is remembering my friends' favourite drinks.'

'But not remembering to call?'

Tomek sighed. 'You going to be like that the whole night? Otherwise I'll send you the bill for the drink now and we can call it a night.'

'You're the one who asked me here,' she said.

'I'm starting to wish I hadn't. What do you want from me? An apology? Fine. I'm sorry for not calling. I was a shitbag, and even shittier friend. But you're not completely innocent of the blame yourself, my friend...'

'I know, but it makes me feel better about the part I played in it as well.'

'Classic Saskia,' Tomek said, rolling his eyes mockingly.

For the next few moments, neither of them said anything. To fill the space Tomek took a sip from his drink and she did the same. Set it down carefully, more eye contact. They were stuck in that gap of finding a place to begin. Of knowing where to start to fill in the last thirteen years' worth of blanks.

In the end Tomek settled for the only conversation starter that came to mind.

'How have you been?'

'That's it, is it? Nearly fifteen years and all I get is, "How've you been"? Come on, Tomek, you can do better than that. Where's that charm of yours gone?'

Sucked out of him by the teenager who was currently locked in her room and under strict instructions to not do anything stupid.

'I was building up to it,' he told her. 'That's how it's done. You wouldn't go up to someone and immediately ask them to marry you. But I have to say, you look really good. You don't seem to have aged at all.'

'Well, thanks... I guess. You're not looking so bad yourself.'

'How are the parents?'

'Still alive. Just. Mum's been in and out of hospital with a hip problem and Dad's still got his dodgy heart, so it looks like I'll have the same thing in about thirty years.'

'Look on the bright side,' he started, 'at least you're not going crazy up in the mountains. All that wide-open space and clean air really can cause you issues. Must be horrible.'

'Is that why you've stayed down here for so long? Because it's keeping you grounded?'

Tomek nodded. 'That, and because I can't *stand* the accent.'

She mock-gasped and threw her hand to her mouth. 'You always said you liked my accent!'

'I did thirteen years ago. Back then it was subtle. Now it's much more prominent. I guess that means you'll have to stay down here for a few more years.'

'That's the plan.'

'How long have you been back already?'

'About six months.'

Now it was his turn to mock-gasp. 'And you didn't call? You've been back all this time, and nothing...? I'm hurt.'

'I was trying to avoid you as much as possible. But now you've got me cornered... I had no choice.'

'Six months is pretty good going,' he said. 'But there's no evading me. I'm like herpes – I just keep coming back, baby.'

Saskia shot him another of those glowers.

Two in such quick succession. This was going better than he'd expected.

After she'd finished giving him the stare, the conversation moved onto the world of work, filling in the gaps there. After returning to Scotland, Saskia had decided to become a teacher. Secondary schools mostly, focusing on teaching English Language to the majority of her children who didn't care about it. But now she was looking for another challenge, and had a new permanent position in a primary school on Canvey (at which point Tomek had threatened to leave). It had been a massive career change for her in the first place, but after a few months she'd felt settled. And now she was going through it all again.

'It's literally like moving to a new school when you're a kid,' she said. 'You don't know anyone and it takes a while for everyone to warm to you. You must know what I mean...'

Tomek did. And he cast his mind back to his early school days. Of being at the front of the classroom with no one to talk to while all the groups and cliques sat at the back. He'd sat there looking up at the teacher and the whiteboard, trying to decipher the hieroglyphs of the English language without asking for help. It had been that way for weeks until one day Saskia had come over to him and started speaking to him. Complete gibberish, in his mind. But friendly gibberish, polite gibberish. She'd always maintained that she'd wanted to be his friend because she thought he looked friendly and warm. But Tomek knew the real reason even if she wasn't willing to say it. It was out of pity. A suggestion that her parents had made one evening and she'd acted on it.

But he was grateful she had.

And now Tomek was beginning to realise he was grateful that Sylvia had done something similar to Kasia. That she'd made the jump and started becoming friends with a total stranger who'd been new to the school.

Sylvia was Kasia's Saskia, and Tomek was grateful for it.

'There's something big I need to tell you...' he started.

The colour rushed from her cheeks as her mind considered the worst.

'No, I'm not dying,' he said quickly to allay her fears. 'At least I don't think I am. No... it's just the small matter of recently finding out over a month ago that I'm now the proud father of a thirteen-year-old daughter called Kasia.'

For a while, nothing seemed to happen on Saskia's face. It was as though she'd been frozen in time and the cogs in her mind had frozen along with her. Even if she'd wanted to speak or react, she couldn't. Not until everything had begun to thaw.

While he waited Tomek finished his beer and went to the bar. He returned with another beer for himself and another packet of Cherry Drops for her.

'You look like you could do with another...' he said.

'I...' she began, but only made it as far as the first syllable. 'I think it's you who needs the extra drink...' Then Saskia shook her head as she came to. 'I have so many questions.'

'And such little time to ask them in.'

While he'd been at the bar, the bartender had explained to him it was last orders and that they'd be closing in another half hour.

'I never thought anything like that would happen to *you*,' she started. 'I mean, I knew what you were like when you were younger but I never pictured you with a child. I always thought it would have been... But if she's thirteen then that means she must have been born shortly after I left.'

Tomek nodded.

'And around about that time you were still with Anika... Which means...'

Tomek nodded again.

'You know, if you don't like this teacher lark, then I'm sure we can find a role for you in the police. You're quite astute.'

'But how? When? What? Where is she? Have you two been

together since? What about all that stuff with her uncle...? Patrick...? James...? The affair...?'

Tomek reached across and placed a hand on hers. She immediately calmed down as she looked at it a moment. Now, while she was in a state of semi-shock, Tomek explained everything. About how Anika had been pregnant during their relationship. How she'd hidden the news from him and raised Kasia on her own. How she'd fallen into her debilitating drug habit. How she'd sent the girl to him one cold afternoon in November.

How she'd been living with him ever since.

At the end of it, Saskia's mouth had opened and she ran her tongue over her teeth.

'Jesus Christ. That's fucked.'

'Exactly. So this is the new me: the grown-up Tomek. Because I've had no choice.'

'And how have things been between you two?'

That was where it got interesting. Tomek explained to her the difficulties the two of them had been having. How things had seemingly been going great in the past week or so and how they'd dropped off a cliff drastically in the last couple of days. Tomek had so much respect and adoration for Saskia, and so much trust in her, that he was open and vulnerable with her. He explained in full the details of his own faults and failings, and also Kasia's. He hadn't wanted it to seem like he was placing all the blame of their difficult relationship on her.

'She's gone through a lot...' he said. 'But it's just recently things have... they've started to backslide. I found her smoking vapes when I got home this evening.'

'Is that the reason for the call?'

Tomek nodded. 'I need help. You were the only person I could think to call.'

'Very kind of you. But is what she's doing any different to what you did at that age?'

Tomek considered. Saw the other side of the coin.

'It's arguably better... Depending which medical professional you speak to.'

'Well, she's thirteen. Things are happening to her. Her whole world is changing. Even more so considering how much it's already changed.' Now it was her turn to put her hand on his. Soft, gentle, familiar. 'She's just adjusting to everything. It's going to take her a while. You just need to give her some time.'

Time wasn't a problem. Time he could do.

It was the patience he was running out of. And he needed a quick fix, fast.

CHAPTER
FORTY-THREE

J enny Ingles' body was found shortly after 9 a.m. It was the first time that morning anyone had been brave enough to venture through the park since Annabelle Lake's body had been discovered there. It was as though an invisible and impenetrable forcefield had settled around the area, and the only time it lifted was as soon as the sun appeared over the horizon. The death of little Annabelle had gone viral and shocked the town. As a result, dozens of flowers and photos that had been shared on Facebook by Elizabeth Lake and Georgia Gregory littered the metal gates around the perimeter. Some had been brave enough to venture into the playground and leave their mementos on the swing where she'd lain.

But now it was the place where another body had been found, in exactly the same place and position as Annabelle Lake.

Though this time, Tomek didn't expect the fanfare to be quite as loud. Jenny Ingles' disappearance hadn't garnered so much as a murmur on the rungs of the social media ladder. Nobody showed any emotion or seemed to care about a missing girl who sold drugs and prostituted herself.

Terrible, really.

Surrounding Jenny Ingles' body – which had been hung from the top of the swing this time because her body was longer – was a unit of Scenes of Crime Officers. They'd been there before, they'd done the same job, and so they'd erected the tent in the same positions as before. Everyone in the team knew what they were doing and what they were looking for.

As Tomek watched them mooch about, taking photographs of potential pieces of evidence, he noticed one of the team crouching by the mural near the swings. The suited individual was in the middle of removing the demonstrations of love and grief, carefully placing them into evidence bags. One by one, the sound of rustling plastic quietened.

Tomek had come alone this time. Only because he hadn't wanted anyone to witness him potentially slipping over the same piece of mud as last time.

He eyed that spot studiously, telling himself not to approach it.

'Morning, Chief,' Lorna the Home Office Pathologist said. She'd stepped out of her forensic suit and was standing with him on the other side of the cordon. 'You look tired,' she told him.

'Yeah. Thanks.'

'Once you reach forty, it all starts to go downhill,' she added. 'You start to feel things a bit more.'

Tomek raised an eyebrow at her. 'Aren't you in your mid-thirties?'

'Yeah. I just wanted to make you feel a bit better about yourself, that's all.'

Tomek thanked her half-heartedly and then pointed to the tent. 'Tell me everything I need to know and more.'

'You already know everything there is. Killed in exactly the same manner as Annabelle Lake. Same manner, same time of death – and I'm willing to bet she's got the same stomach contents as little Annabelle.'

'When can you say for certain?'

'This arvo. I can push a few things back. Your killer's just one kill away from being classed as a breakfast. And I just know I'll have you lot on my hands *then*.'

It took Tomek a moment for the joke to make sense.

'You mean cereal killer?'

'Yeah. But when I have to explain it, it doesn't sound so good.'

'No, it doesn't. Maybe think of a better delivery next time.' Tomek ran his fingers through his hair. 'But, yes, with any luck, we'll be able to catch him before we get to a third victim.'

Though there was no hope in his voice, no hope in his soul. The killer had managed to stay one step ahead at all times, and now it was beginning to feel like he was pulling ahead...

Two steps.

Three steps.

Tomek couldn't allow him to reach a fourth.

With any luck, he'd slip up, make a mistake. And when he did, Tomek would be ready and waiting in the wet and muddy grass.

CHAPTER
FORTY-FOUR

While he waited for Lorna to send across her findings, Tomek decided to follow up an idea that he'd had.

It was 10 a.m. and the Knightswick Shopping Centre had been open for an hour already. But when he'd arrived outside Billy Morton's barbershop – aptly, and if a little lazily, named Billy's Barbers – he found it closed, with no sign of Billy himself or any of his other barbers on the horizon. Perhaps the money laundering hadn't been going well and he'd been forced to go into hiding. Or, on the flip side, business was extremely healthy and he could take days off whenever he wanted.

Fortunately, it didn't take long for Tomek to find out. After a few minutes of waiting patiently outside the shop like he was waiting for a date, the man eventually appeared. Trundling in through the shopping centre with a slight limp.

'Fancied yourself a lie-in, did you?' Tomek asked as the man approached. 'Business that good, is it?'

And then he spotted the large blotches of black on his face, the grazes on his knuckles and fists.

'Don't worry,' Billy said, noticing Tomek eyeing up his injuries. 'The other guy came off worse than me.'

'You sure? Because you look like shit. Who did this to you? Those two blokes in the car park?'

'No,' Billy said as he shook his head profusely.

The realisation that he was talking to a copper in the middle of a shopping centre, where anyone could walk in and recognise them both, seemed to assault Billy very quickly. He had gone from momentarily being open enough to discuss that situation, to sealed shut like the exit of a submarine.

'Nobody did this to me,' he added, as if to emphasise the point. 'I fell.'

'Have you been to the hospital?'

'Can't afford to. Got a business to run.'

'Not for much longer if they come back. Or should I say if you fall over again…'

'You ain't gotta worry about me. I can protect myself.'

'For some reason the bruises on your face and neck tell me otherwise.'

Billy shrugged his shoulders, wincing in pain as he did so, then shuffled past Tomek as stoically as he could. He moved to the front of the barbershop and opened the door. By the time he'd finished switching on the lights and turning on the music and TV in the corner, a small queue of teenage boys had formed outside the shop. Tomek didn't know if this was a part of his drug operation or whether they just wanted a haircut – though looking at some of them they were in desperate need of both.

Surely Billy wouldn't be so stupid as to offer the kids his drugs in front of a police officer?

Then again, drug dealers weren't known for being the smartest tools in the box.

'Sorry, mate,' Billy said a moment later as he hobbled closer to

Tomek. 'But if you ain't here for a haircut, I'm going to have to ask you to leave.'

'I'm not here for a fade or a short back and sides, thanks. I'm actually here to tell you that this morning Jenny Ingles was found dead in a park, dangling from a swing.'

Shock registered on Billy's face.

'You wouldn't happen to know anything about that, would you?'

Wide-eyed, Billy shook his head.

'Nah, man. I... I... I don't know nothing...' He paused. 'And you're sure it was Jenny?'

Tomek nodded.

'Damn, man. Fuck. Jenny... I... Fuck.'

'Where were you last night?' Tomek asked quietly, lest the people around them overheard their conversation.

'I was at the hospital, man. A&E. Fucking thought I'd broke my leg, when—'

'When you fell?'

'Yeah, when I fell. Was there until like three, four o'clock. Came home, went straight to bed.'

He nodded again, this time thoughtfully.

'Why didn't you say that in the first place?'

Tomek knew the real reason before he'd even mentioned it. Embarrassment. Trying to save face. Ego. Trying to hide the fact that he'd had the shit beaten out of him.

Before leaving Billy to it, he told the man to stay in the area while they continued their investigations.

'Oh, and get yourself a pair of proper trainers,' he added. 'None of those designer ones. They've got far superior grip and should stop you from falling over again. Also, they're good for when you need to run away from anything...'

CHAPTER
FORTY-FIVE

Since Jenny Ingles' initial disappearance, Tomek had spent hours trying to work out a possible link that connected her with Annabelle Lake. But no matter how hard he tried, the evidence didn't seem to point them to each other. The girls were different ages, from totally different backgrounds, and as far as he'd been able to make out had never met each other or knew of one another.

The connection had been in his mind. An intangible idea, a hope. Until later that afternoon, in the incident room, where his suspicions were confirmed. There *was* a link between the two girls' deaths.

'Aside from the obvious mode of death,' Victoria began, addressing the room as she read from Lorna's pathology report, 'Jenny Ingles' stomach contained a lot of fish, the same stuff that was found in Annabelle Lake's stomach. Secondly, the same composition of mud and sand and dirt was found on Jenny Ingles' feet – also matching that found on Annabelle Lake's.'

'So it seems they've both been kept in the same place and they've both been fed only fish for food...' Tomek noted aloud, more for his own benefit than anyone else's.

'Salmon and tuna, to be precise,' replied Victoria.

'Shame tuna's my favourite,' said Rachel. 'Sort of spoiled it for me now.'

'Actually, fish in general has quite a high mercury count, so you shouldn't eat that much of it anyway,' DC Oscar Perez said. Then he turned to Nadia: 'That's one for you to look out for as well, by the way. Pregnant women and newborns are heavily advised not to eat salmon or any type of fish.'

Nadia grunted and rubbed her belly. 'Thanks for that, Captain. I had planned on chucking her into the North Sea and letting her catch her own meals, but I'll have to let the little one down gently when she comes...'

The smile on Oscar's face suggested he was proud of his advice, regardless of the sarcasm that it had been met with.

'Can we get back on track, please?' asked Nasty Nick, sighing loudly enough for everyone to hear.

They all fell silent as they waited for Victoria to continue. Before doing so she gave a slight nod to Nick by way of saying thank you. Then she cleared her throat.

'The rest of the report does not make for such pleasant reading...' she said, her voice a little more than a whisper. 'In the events leading up to her death, Lorna reckons she was pumped full of heroin every waking moment of the day – possibly to seduce and stabilise her – and she was also raped, brutally raped, multiple times. She found bruising in and around the vaginal area, but no semen. Either our guy was wearing a condom or he... or he cleaned her out well enough for us to not pick it up.'

Tomek's shoulders sagged. He'd been hoping for some positive news. While yes it was great that they'd managed to connect the two cases, they were still no closer to uncovering the killer's identity. All they knew was that they were looking for the same person.

And yet one name continued to pop into his head.

Vincent fucking Gregory.

The little racist fascist bastard.

'Any word on Vincent's Ford that was swabbed, by any chance?' Tomek asked Oscar. The Captain had been managing the process of getting it checked out.

He shook his head, disappointed. 'Forensics found nothing. No evidence of Jenny Ingles ever being in his car.'

Tomek's shoulders sank even further. That meant the Ford Fiesta that had been used to abduct Jenny Ingles was still out there somewhere, and they needed to find it.

It also meant that perhaps it was time to leave Vincent Gregory alone and look at the case from a different angle.

Like Billy the Barber. And finding a link between the drug dealer, a seventeen-year-old prostitute, and a little girl. Something, or someone that connected them.

But that was easier said than done. Usually he would see these things, spot the connections sooner, but as it was, he couldn't even see the dots to join up let alone the numbers to help him put them in the right order.

The rest of the working day, what was left of it, was spent strategising, formulating their plan of attack. Now that the murders had been linked, Tomek and Sean were officially back with the rest of the team, the only stipulation being the same one they'd had before: under no circumstances were they to venture anywhere near Vincent Gregory's house. In the meantime, DC Anna Kaczmarek, the team's family liaison officer, had been to visit Alison Jones, Jenny Ingles' foster carer. She had informed the woman that her foster daughter's body had been found in the playground and that social services would be round in the coming days to investigate her suitability as a carer. Tomek and the team were confident she would never be entrusted with looking after anyone else again. Afterwards, Anna had tracked down Jenny's birth parents, a couple who lived in Grays, and explained to them that their daughter had died. Tomek couldn't imagine how that must have felt. Not to have heard from their daughter for years, to have stayed on the fringes of her life and have had no involvement in it whatsoever, only to receive a knock on the door one afternoon and find out that she was dead. The thought of it had sent his body cold.

Lastly on Anna's list was the Lake household. Before calling it a day, Anna had brought Beth with an F up to speed and informed her that her daughter's murder was being investigated with another as part of a double murder investigation. She was still mourning the loss of her daughter and husband, and Anna had reported that she'd listened despondently, her body present, her mind on another planet. But at least she had a strong support network – namely Vincent and his wife, Georgia. Though if Tomek had been in her position, he would have preferred to suffer alone rather than have those two there all the time.

He was aware that his hatred for Vincent was clouding his judgement, but he believed it was firmly justified. The man had singled him out and made him feel small and marginalised. He couldn't tolerate that.

Nor could he tolerate the attitude that had met him when he'd got home that evening. As soon as he'd walked through the door, Kasia had been blunt with him, snappy. She'd told him very little about her day and when he'd asked if anything had happened, she'd grunted, slammed the fridge door shut and told him to leave her alone.

The entire situation confused him. Surely she couldn't still be upset about the explicit image she'd received, could she? Or was it because she thought that he was being too hard on her for the vaping? Or perhaps it had been about his earlier comment, the one that had slipped out of his mouth accidentally, a Freudian slip of immense proportions: *I never asked to be your dad, but here we are, so we have to just suck it up and get on with it.*

He'd thought about that sentence ever since. How far he'd crossed the line and hurt her feelings. But at the time it had been true. He hadn't asked to be her dad, hadn't asked for the responsibility, hadn't asked for the burden. But now that he was beginning to find his feet, he was feeling glad that she had arrived on his doorstep.

He'd also thought about apologising, about being the bigger person, setting an example and the tone for their relationship going forward, but the only problem was he was a stubborn bastard and she was making it extremely difficult for him to want to say it.

What they needed was a fresh start. A route out of the arguments and bickering, all the immaturity and torment. With the move taking place in two days, it seemed like they had the perfect opportunity. A chance to bond and connect again, the same way they had when the packing had started – since then Tomek had resorted to doing the majority of it alone.

As he opened a bottle of beer and plopped himself on his sofa bed, he pulled out his phone and messaged Saskia, asking if she was free to help them unpack on the weekend.

She replied a few minutes later: not only would she be there to unpack, but she could also act as mediator and motivator. And maybe even be a receptive ear for Kasia to vent to. A friendly adult to hear her concerns.

Because God knew their relationship needed it.

CHAPTER
FORTY-SIX

Tomek had worked into the early hours of the morning while Kasia had stayed in her room. He had dived into the murky underworld of drug trafficking and prostitution on the island, searching the PNC and HOLMES 2 for references relating to Billy Morton. The man had a bigger role to play in this, but he wasn't sure how, or what – or why.

Sure, he could understand fitting Jenny Ingles up for failing to pay a debt or being caught stealing from him. But what did little Annabelle Lake have to do with it? Could it have been a case of being in the wrong place at the wrong time? Had she seen something she wasn't supposed to and had got caught in the crossfire as a result?

He'd mulled over that for a while, scribbling and doodling away in his notebook, dumping all the thoughts in his mind onto the page – like he was a paranoid author. Until he'd come across a name.

A name he felt like he recognised but couldn't place.

A name that, by the time he went to bed, he felt like he knew inside out.

Including the man's home address which, unfortunately, led

Tomek back to Canvey again first thing in the morning with a liveried police vehicle in tow.

Mercifully the man had been home and Tomek had invited him in for questioning at Canvey police station. A little less formal than going all the way back to Southend. Also a lot less of a ball ache, too.

Sam Dellas was a man of Greek heritage, and you could see it. When Tomek had first laid eyes upon him he was grateful for the extra support – and the fact he hadn't chosen to put up a fight. He was a builder by trade, but Tomek also got the impression he trained as a bodybuilder in his spare time. Not that he needed to – the helping hand of genetics and the manual labour involved in his job were more than enough to enable to him to grow to the size he was. The shapes of his shoulders and arms reminded Tomek of the domes from the Eden Project, while his forearms were as big Tomek's calves. Tomek liked to think he was a big lad, muscly, well defined in all the right places (except for the gut; he just loved beer and bad food too much), but this was on a different level. The bloke barely fitted into his shirt. Nor the chair for that matter.

'Why'm I here?' Sam asked.

'Because we understand you have a working relationship with Billy Morton and Jenny Ingles.'

A shock of fear flashed across the man's face.

'I take it you know those names?'

'I... Yeah.'

The internal battle that played out on his expression was over quickly: he'd decided that he wouldn't put up a fight, that he would take whatever was coming his way.

'I know them, yeah,' he added. 'What's this about?'

'We understand you're a regular down the Windjammer pub. That right?'

Sam nodded slowly. 'I go down there a couple of nights a week. After work. Just a few drinks with the boys.'

'Anything else?'

'Sometimes...'

'Particularly when Jenny Ingles is there? From what I hear she's a very flirty girl, always laughing and trying to seduce the older man. Ever fallen for her charm?'

Sam's cheeks flushed red and he began rubbing his thumb over the edge of his nails uncomfortably. 'It's been known to happen...'

'Ever got on so well with her that you thought you'd go back to your place together – or maybe hers?'

More flushing, more rubbing. 'It's been known to happen.'

'Did you ever pay her for anything while she was with you? Sex, drugs... maybe?'

And then his head dropped. He could no long meet Tomek's gaze.

'Let me guess,' Tomek began, 'it's been known to happen?'

A nod. A single, almost imperceptible dip of the head, confirmed what Tomek suspected.

'How many times have you slept with Jenny Ingles, Sam?'

The man looked up at him, and Tomek noticed tears forming in his eyes. Tomek had no sympathy. He knew what he'd done was wrong, and he'd taken advantage of her.

'Three times, I think. Maybe four.'

'Did you buy any drugs from her as well?'

Sam wiped his eyes with the back of his massive hand that seemed to swallow his entire face.

'Just some cocaine and heroin. It was all she had on her at the time. I never... I never used it though.'

'Heroin?' Tomek asked. The sirens were sounding in his head.

'Yeah,' Sam replied.

'And when was the last time you saw her?'

He shrugged, hesitated. And then stopped responding. The tears had stopped and his expression had fallen flat, his lips moving into two horizontal lines.

'When was the last time you saw her?' Tomek asked again, growing increasingly concerned with the man's silence.

'Has something happened to her?' he asked.

'She's dead, Sam.'

'When—? How—?'

'Her body was found yesterday morning.'

'I had nothing to do with it. I promise.'

'Then I'm going to need you to tell me where you were on the night of last Friday, and where you were last night.'

'I... I think I was at the pub last Friday. Yes. I would've been because I always am. You can check with the landlord, Terry.'

Tomek confirmed he would do exactly that.

'And as for last night, I was home. I was... just watching TV. On my phone, looking at Instagram. I didn't do anything in particular.'

'As for the early hours of this morning?'

'Went to work about six. We start on site really early.'

Tomek nodded and paused a moment. Currently, all fingers were pointing to Sam Dellas as having some involvement in her death. For someone who had paid her for sex in the past, it wasn't inconceivable to think that he'd abducted her and raped her as many times as he'd wanted without having to hand over a penny. And, because he hadn't answered the question about the last time he'd seen her, it was possible that Sam Dellas may have still had the heroin he'd bought from her in his house, easily accessible.

But a lot of it was circumstantial. There was no *real* evidence. That particular proof would take time to gather, and with his options and patience running out, Tomek wasn't sure how much of it he could spare.

And then there was the small matter of Annabelle Lake. And how she fitted into all this.

Noticing the silence in the room, Tomek pulled out an image of Annabelle and slid it across the room.

'Recognise her?'

Sam inspected the image, dwarfing it in his hands. 'I recognise her face from the TV. And I see it on Facebook, too. That's that Annabelle girl, isn't it?'

'Yes. Do you know anything about her death?'

Sam shook his head confidently. 'I only know what I've seen on Facebook.'

Tomek sighed internally. Finding evidence to convict him of Annabelle's murder, if it existed, would take longer and be much harder. If Sam's name hadn't appeared in any of the team's investigations so far, then chances were there may have been a reason for it.

So far it was looking like six of one, half a dozen of the other. Tomek had reasonable grounds to suspect him of the murder of Jenny Ingles, but nothing to touch him with for the murder of Annabelle Lake.

One girl was able to receive justice, while the other was not. And he knew what the fanfare would have to say about which girl received which outcome.

He tried not to think about that, about how the public might react to the prostitute's killer being caught while the case of the innocent schoolgirl was left unsolved.

As he sat there, staring at the man who outweighed and outmuscled him two to one, Tomek tried to listen to his intuition. To tune in to it as much as he could. It was something he'd neglected recently – namely because his intuition had told him that dating Charlotte Hanton had been a good idea. But now it was time to forget all that and listen to it.

And, unfortunately, it was telling him that this wasn't his man. That Sam hadn't abducted or killed either Jenny Ingles or Annabelle Lake. And if he wanted to prove it, it was going to take an enormous amount of digging to unearth the evidence they needed.

But it wasn't all doom and gloom. There was still some light left. For Jenny, in particular.

Because, at the very least, if he couldn't arrest him for her murder, then he could certainly arrest him for paying for sexual services from someone under the age of eighteen. And if any further evidence came to light about her murder, or Annabelle Lake's murder for that matter, then he would be the first one to jump on it.

CHAPTER
FORTY-SEVEN

Moving day. The biggest day of Kasia and Tomek's life as a family. The most stressful day of the year, supposedly. Except it wasn't; it had been all the other days leading up to this bastard moment that had been the most stressful. Completing the paperwork. Settling the deposit – and seeing that large chunk of money disappear from his account and into someone else's pocket. Collecting the keys. Changing the addresses on *everything* – his driving licence, passport, bills, his Amazon account. Everything. And if that wasn't bad enough, then there was still the monumental task of packing, throwing out, replacing, buying brand new. It had been a never-ending battle of To-Dos, incomplete tasks, and reminders.

At the end of it all, he couldn't wait to put his feet up and have a cold beer from the fridge. Providing the electrics worked and he didn't send the flat into darkness at the beginning of winter.

Despite the new house only being down the road, Tomek's small car wasn't large enough to transfer nearly a tenth of the mess they needed to, and he didn't fancy ferrying the car back and forth twenty times in one day. So instead he'd bitten the bullet and forked out the money for a removal lorry to do it for him.

The lorry, in all its articulated glory, arrived at the house a few minutes after them. Tomek had wanted the moment they put the key in for the first time to be special, poignant, the turning of a new chapter. But Kasia hadn't been arsed. She'd shrugged her shoulders and offered it back to Tomek. And after deciding that she wasn't going to change her decision, he'd slotted the key in and twisted.

At last, it felt good to use a lock that worked with ease. If that set a precedent for the rest of their time in the flat – that was still yet to be turned into a home – then he would take that as a good omen.

It took them a little over an hour to unload the boxes and furniture from the van and find a place in the flat to put them all. And by the time they were finished, Tomek's helping hand arrived.

'Good to see you again,' he said to Saskia as he hugged her.

'And you,' she replied with a warm smile. 'And you must be Kasia?'

The teenager grunted and returned her attention back to the boxes labelled with her name. She carried them carefully into her room and began unloading, focusing on the essentials first. Headphones plugged in, muted to the world around her.

'See what I'm dealing with?' Tomek noted as Kasia shut the door behind herself.

'She's very pretty,' Saskia said, absent-mindedly. 'Not sure where she gets that from.'

'Probably Anika,' Tomek replied.

'Oh, without a doubt. Definitely not you.'

Tomek frowned at her and then passed her the last box. The weight of it buckled Saskia's arms as he dropped it on purpose.

'Where do you want it?'

'Somewhere. Anywhere. Doesn't really make a difference. They're all gonna sit there for a couple of weeks while I'm at work anyway.'

Tomek shook hands with the van man, then waved him goodbye.

'You mean you don't have a system?' Saskia asked.

'A system? What type of system?'

'A system for unloading and unpacking...'

'One box at a time was my preferred method,' he started. 'But now I'm beginning to think you might have a problem with that.'

Saskia shook her head in disgust and carried the box into the flat. At the top of the stairs she placed it in a small free space on the coffee table, then placed her hands on her hips and surveyed the room. Tomek did the same, except his first impressions of it all were tainted by the monumental task in front of him.

Was it too early to have a beer now?

'You want to start with the most important bits,' Saskia said, though he wasn't paying much attention. Just thinking about the cold on his lips, the bubbles in his mouth, the taste down his throat.

'Things like cutlery, plates – something for you to eat from,' Saskia continued. 'Then your clothes, shoes, rest of the wardrobe. But only enough for a couple of days. You can do a wash every time you need to – you *do* have a washing machine, right?'

Tomek opened his mouth to respond, but she beat him to it and continued. 'Never mind. I'll sort it for you.'

'Sort what?'

'A plan. I'll put together a plan for you so you know which boxes to unpack first and where to begin.'

'Are you about to take the fun out of everything?' Tomek asked.

'*Excuse* me?'

'Do you take the fun out of your lessons as well?'

'I beg your pardon?' Saskia said playfully. 'My lessons are fun for everyone. I'm consistently told I'm the best teacher by a lot of my students.'

'Is that by just the teenage boys or is that the general consensus amongst everyone in your class?'

Saskia's glower returned, this time deeper. '*Everyone*, actually! But if you don't want my help then I think I'll go. I've got plenty of other things to be getting on with.'

'Like working out how to bore your kids to death? Sucking all the fun out—'

Saskia made for the doorway. Only thing stopping her was Tomek. He placed his hands on her arms and laughed.

'Relax! Relax! I was joking. Come on, don't be daft. I'm very grateful that you're here. That's why I invited you – so you could do the cerebral part of the job and I'll do all the heavy lifting.'

'I can do the heavy lifting too, you know.'

'I know you can. But if I don't have the heavy lifting, then I'm nothing. *Nothing* I tell you!'

A smirk. A faint, flicker of a smirk. One that reduced the glower by a fraction.

'I suppose you really aren't good for much else,' she said, the smirk rising.

'Exactly.' He fired his finger gun at her. 'So off you pop! Come up with a plan and I'll be in the corner with a beer.'

'No you won't. You don't get to drink until I do.'

So *she* was the boss. That was how it was going to be.

And that was how it went for the next four hours. Saskia plotting, planning, and then the two of them unpacking. Starting with the most important parts of the house, as she'd suggested. Meanwhile Kasia stayed in her room, silent. The only evidence they had to suggest that she was still there – and hadn't fled from the boredom of Saskia's routine – was the vicious sound of cardboard tearing and items falling onto the carpet.

By the end of the day, they'd accomplished quite a lot. A conservative twenty per cent of the work, in Tomek's immodest and wildly inexperienced opinion. Fortunately Saskia had backed up his estimation – though he'd half expected her to dock a few percentage points for the handful of spare and unnecessary tea towels that he'd thrown out while unboxing the kitchen.

To celebrate Tomek ordered a Chinese. Kasia's favourite.

'Mum got me into this,' she'd said, as she spooned a mouthful of egg fried rice into her mouth. 'Best thing she's ever done, to be honest.'

That was the most that Kasia had spoken the whole day – except for answering that she would like Chinese food in the first place and then giving Tomek her order – and Tomek was surprised to hear it. Things between them had been tumultuous in the past few days. Tomek had been spending more time at the office than they'd have both liked, and the few interactions they'd managed had been filled with arguments. Most of the time she locked herself away in her bedroom, plugged herself in and the spent the evening watching Netflix or Disney+.

'I think this is probably my favourite too,' Saskia said as she too shovelled chicken chow mein into her face. 'Nothing beats it.'

'Though an Indian comes close.' That was Tomek's favourite, as he and Sean always treated themselves to one if they'd had a heavy night at the pub and needed something to soak up the alcohol.

Shortly after, the conversation moved from the topic of food onto school. As a teacher, Saskia was fascinated to learn and understand what Kasia was enjoying, what she disliked, and what her favourite subject was.

'I don't really have a favourite subject,' she said quietly.

'That's not true. Miss Holloway said you were enjoying your English,' Tomek added.

'Miss Holloway says a lot of things...'

Tomek set his knife and fork down. 'What's that supposed to mean?'

'Nothing.'

'*Kasia...*'

'Nothing, all right! It means nothing!'

Tomek bit his tongue. He knew better than to start an argument with a guest present. The last time that had happened an image of his penis had been shown – and he certainly didn't want *that* particular topic of conversation to be brought up in front of Saskia. In the end, he decided to leave it and pick it up another time.

But before he could, Kasia pushed her plate across the table – which had been hastily placed in the centre of the living room with no thought as to its final position – and then left. Before heading to her room, she grabbed an empty glass from one of the cabinets in the kitchen and filled it with water. As the door to her bedroom slammed shut, Tomek continued to eat his food, sensing Saskia was watching him uncomfortably.

'Good thing we stuck to your list,' he said. 'I can see it paying off already...'

'Now...' she started, oblivious to what he'd just said. 'Now I see what you mean.'

Tomek grunted. 'Volatile little thing, isn't she?'

'A teenager, Tomek. She's a teenager.'

'Volatile little teenager then. That better?'

Saskia rolled her eyes and glowered at him, except this time it wasn't the typical, slightly flirty look she gave him. This one carried a lick of concern with it.

'Tomek...'

Here we go.

He knew what she was going to say before she'd even said it. That she was about to confirm his suspicions.

'I think the best thing that girl needs right now is someone who knows her. Someone who can get to the bottom of this.' She placed a hand on the back of his upper shoulder. 'I think that girl needs to see her mum.'

CHAPTER
FORTY-EIGHT

Tomek didn't like prisons in a professional capacity, let alone a personal one. They were dark, depressing places, and they reminded him all too much of work. Of the horrible deeds people had done, the crimes they'd committed to end up there.

Today was the first time he'd gone into one as a civilian visitor. The experience was virtually the same as when he'd visited prisoners in the past, but not wholly alike. The only difference was that he was treated with a little less respect, as though he was one of the criminals making his way into the visitor hall just like all the other inmates. That he was part of the latest shipment being herded in like cattle.

He hadn't been forced to wait long for Anika. She, along with all the other women prisoners in HMP East Sutton Park, Kent, had been let loose in the visitor hall a few minutes after his arrival. Anika had emerged from the middle of the pack and shuffled towards him.

Tomek hadn't known what to expect from today. What she might look like since he'd last seen her. What the effect of five weeks into a six-year prison sentence might have done to her already. How harrowed and hollow she might look. His estimation – of the serious weight loss, the bedraggled and messy hair, the complexion that had lost a few shades in the artificial light – had been spot on. She was leagues away from the Anika that he had once known – dolled up, full of make-up, someone who prided herself on her image, the way she looked, and the attention she got from it. At one point she'd been the prettiest girl in the school; now she was arguably not even the prettiest in prison.

What a fall from grace.

After recognising him, Anika sauntered over. She walked with her arms folded across her chest as though she were cold, even though the heating had been on full blast since Tomek's arrival and it was now warm enough for him to remove his coat. She walked carefully, slowly, as though conjuring the strength and power to make it all the way to him. She seemed reserved, embarrassed, shy. Not the loud outgoing girl he had once known.

But then again, he probably wasn't the shy, timid boy that she had once known either.

Time had changed them. It had been kind to one and not the other. Their lives had gone in separate directions, and if ever there was an advertisement for steering away from a criminal background for as long as possible, it was Anika Coleman.

Tomek didn't rise to greet her as she pulled the chair out from beneath the table and slipped her skinny little body into the gap. Instead he kept his hands placed on the table, his fingers knitted together.

'Hello, Anika.'

'Hi, Tom...'

The word made him wince. It had been a while since she'd last called him by that name.

'Where's Kasia? I thought she was supposed to be here...'

'Not today. Not yet. I wanted to speak with *you* first.'

Anika's eyes widened and she scratched the back of her head like a dog with fleas. 'Please...' she began. 'I miss my baby girl. I need to see her. I thought she was coming today...'

'She will do. One day. When she's ready. When I think she's ready.'

More scratching. More awkward, nervous movements.

'You can't... you can't control her like that. You can't tell her what to do.'

'Actually, as her legal guardian – as her *father* – I can do exactly those things.'

Tomek paused to survey her. The skin around her face and arms had fallen away from her body. Her teeth had started to fall out and the ones that remained had turned the colour of coal. Lastly the inside of her nostrils had started to decay.

'Besides,' he began, shaking his head, 'I don't want to bring her here while you're... you're like *this*.'

'Like what?' she hissed. The sudden sound echoed around the room and disturbed the visitors and inmates beside them.

'Coked out of your head. You're still using, I can tell you are. I know the signs. If you want to see your daughter, you're going to have get off the drugs. I won't have her seeing you while you're in this state.'

Anika reached a hand out to Tomek but he pulled away, narrowly avoiding her skeleton-like fingers from scratching him.

'Please...' she began. 'Please, Tomek... Please.'

Tomek sighed and placed his hands in his lap. 'I didn't come here for you to beg. I came here for some advice, some help...'

It was then that he realised that he'd played his hand at the wrong time. That he should have asked for the advice before prohibiting her from seeing her daughter. That the power was now in her hands. If she had any semblance of cognitive ability left, then she might have picked up on it, but...

'What's wrong? Is she... is she okay?'

Perhaps not.

'She's fine,' Tomek started. 'In a physical sense. She's healthy, as far as I'm aware. She started her period the other week, so that's all good. It's just...'

Tomek stopped and looked deeply into Anika's eyes. They were wide, glistening beneath the light. As though the life had returned as soon as they'd started to discuss Kasia. And it was then that he realised she *had* picked up on the power he'd placed in her hands, but she just hadn't acted on it. The maternal instinct within her, the instinct to protect and help her baby girl, was enough for her to push all that aside and do what she could to help. Right now it was the only thing keeping her alive while she was in there.

And then Tomek realised the power was still very much in his hands. And that it would be for a very long time to come...

'She's been acting strange,' Tomek began again. 'She's not eating. She's got an attitude on her that would probably see her survive a couple years in here unscathed. She's arguing a lot more with me. She locks herself in her room all night. She doesn't talk. She's coming home a lot later than usual. She's... she's just different.'

Despite the substances floating around inside her bloodstream, Anika was still able to pull off a wry, smug smile without Tomek noticing. A small win in the battle for Kasia's love and adoration.

'It doesn't sound like you're fit to look after her at all,' she said with some vehemence and venom. 'You're neglecting her.'

'Like fuck I am,' Tomek whispered, leaning closer.

This was about to get ugly, and if he wasn't careful he risked walking away without the information or advice he needed.

'I've been nothing but good to her...'

Except for the whole dick pic scenario, but Anika didn't need to know about that.

'It sounds like you have no control over her,' Anika began, her voice turning sour. 'It's your job. It was always your job. Neglecting her like you neglected me. You never made any time for me, and I bet it's the same with her. She probably feels lost and alone with no one to talk to.' She ran her fingers through her hair, scratching roughly at her scalp. 'I knew I should never have let her stay with you.'

'You didn't have a fucking choice. It was either she come to live with me or spend the next five years in care...'

At that moment an image of Jenny Ingles, swaying in the wind, chain wrapped round her throat, appeared in his mind.

Evidence of what could have happened to Kasia if she'd gone down that path. Evidence of the worst-case scenario.

And he wouldn't allow that to happen.

'I'm going to report you,' Anika said, the smile now more obvious on her face. 'I'm going to report you to social services and tell them you're unfit to look after my daughter.'

Tomek took a moment before responding. Anika had just played her hand, and he wasn't sure if he was ready to call her bluff. He knew the system, and he knew that, given the lengths he had gone to in order to accommodate and home her, that she didn't have a leg to stand on. Though he still wasn't willing to take the risk.

Tomek pushed himself from beneath the table, rose and then started to walk past her. Before he could make it any further, Anika reached out a hand and held him back.

'No! No! Stay... Please...' Her voice broke as she spoke. 'I... I don't want you to go. Stay. Please. Kasia, she's...' Anika dropped her head and lowered her grip on his arm. 'She gets like that sometimes... The best thing to do is...'

Tomek stayed where he was, waiting.

'The best thing to do is to talk to her. Have you tried talking to her...?'

Tomek didn't answer, as it was written on his face.

No, he hadn't tried to speak with her or address the problems she was facing directly. Instead he'd asked everyone else how to solve the issue. Everyone else except for the one person it was impacting. It was so obvious it was painful that he'd missed it. Perhaps he'd been too afraid, too cowardly to approach the topic and find out what had gone wrong for her. That he would find out that *he'd* let her down somehow. That it was all his fault.

Anika tightened her grip on his arm, pulling him out of his thoughts and back to the present.

'I... I can't make you bring her here, I realise that. But if you think it might help, then please do. I know it would help me. I'm not begging – I don't want to be like that anymore. But I want to prove to you – prove to you both – that I'm okay, that I'm all right. That she can come and see me. I promise... I promise I'll get off the drugs. I promise I'll...' She let out a deep, heavy sigh that deflated her entire body. 'I promise to *do* better. I promise to *be* better.'

CHAPTER
FORTY-NINE

Tomek was home by the time Kasia walked through the door from school – had been for a couple of hours. In that time he'd been unboxing and unpacking another twenty per cent of the flat, though he'd left her bedroom well alone. That was her domain.

Kasia came home a little after 4 p.m. Not too late so as to suggest she'd been up to something she shouldn't. Not too early to suggest that she'd come straight home, either. Perhaps she'd taken a leisurely stroll, the long route home. But he decided immediately he wasn't going to ask to find out. He didn't want to piss her off the moment she stepped through the front door.

As she closed it behind her, she dropped her bag on the floor and headed straight for her bedroom. She had her headphones plugged in and was staring down at her mobile so naturally she didn't see him wave at her, nor did she hear him call her name.

It wasn't until he climbed out of the sofa and made his way towards her that she recognised him. The scream that followed was so loud it felt like it burst his eardrum. In an attempt to defend herself, Kasia launched the phone at him and raised her fists.

'Jesus, fucking hell!' she screamed. 'You scared me!'

'I live here as well, you know,' he said, rubbing his right pectoral from where the device had hit him. 'And *no* swearing!'

Kasia rolled her eyes. 'Well, don't scare me like that then!'

Tomek bent down to pick up her phone and handed it to her. 'Did they teach you that at karate class?' he asked. But she didn't see the funny side of it and instead folded her arms across her chest. 'How was school?'

'Fine.'

Same as every day then, he thought. Fine. Always fine.

Never anything other than fine.

'Hey...'

His skin began to turn clammy and he placed his hands in his pockets, the nerves gradually taking hold of him.

'I think... I think we should have a chat,' he said finally.

'Do we have to?'

'Yes. Unless you don't want to eat tonight...'

'I've still got your card details saved on my phone. I can just order myself a takeaway whenever I want.'

He was sure she could. Much faster than he would be able to as well. Fucking kids and their technology. Soon they'll be coming out of the womb with a phone already in hand.

'Well maybe we can order another one tonight,' he said, then added: 'but only if you'll sit down with me now and discuss what we have to discuss.'

The internal battle inside Kasia played out on her face. On the one hand she wanted the prospect of eating a delicious takeaway. But on the other hand did she really want to sit down and talk about things, with her *father* no less?

In the end, she pulled the chair out from beneath the dining room table and perched herself on the end of it.

'*Yes*?' she said with all the attitude of a teenager.

Tomek was cautious in his movements, careful. Too abrupt and he might knock his own train of thought off kilter. When he eventually joined her at the table, he suddenly felt very high up.

'Have these chairs always been this high?' he asked, but received no response. Kasia was ready to get this conversation out of the way as fast as possible. And so was he...

'It's about you and me,' he started.

Get the ball rolling, he told himself. *Just say some things and then the rest will follow...*

'You're not in trouble, don't worry. You're not going anywhere either – so don't think you can start packing your bags yet. It's just... I've noticed a change in you. You've been acting strangely the past couple of weeks, and I don't like it. You're not eating properly, you're shutting me out, you're giving me way more attitude than you ever did when you first moved in.' He inhaled deeply, allowing his chest to inflate all the way. He held it there a moment before letting it all out again. 'If I didn't know any better, I'd say something's happened, or is still continuing to happen at school. If I didn't know any better, I'd say that maybe you were being bullied...'

The epiphany had come to him on the drive home. The sudden realisation that it could have been the 'B' word, the one that affected so many children – even more so with the advent of social media and online anonymity. A quick online search of some of the signs had confirmed his suspicions.

Now it was up to Kasia to confirm the actual thing.

But she had become withdrawn. Her shoulders had collapsed and her head had dropped. Beneath the table she picked at her fingernails and scratched her knee.

'Kase...' he began. 'You can tell me. I want to help. I *will* help. I'll speak with the school, get Miss Holloway to—'

'She already knows...'

The words stung him for many reasons. Firstly, his own daughter hadn't felt comfortable enough to tell him about it, and secondly, her teacher had also decided to keep it from him.

'When did you tell her?'

'Last week. She said that she would do something about it. That she would speak to the girl, but nothing's happened…'

And now it made sense. Kasia's earlier comments the night before regarding Bridget.

Miss Holloway says a lot of things…

Like promising to deal with the bullying. Like promising to speak with the bully.

But in reality doing nothing about it.

'Why did you go to her first?' Tomek asked, trying to hide the pain in his voice.

'I didn't,' Kasia replied. 'She saw it happen. I didn't have a choice.'

'What happened? Who is it? Who's bullying you? What are they doing?'

Tomek realised that the flurry of questions may have come across as too strong, but he was stuck in the no man's land between Dad and Sergeant. They both wanted the same thing, but there were different ways of getting the answers and information he needed.

'Sorry,' he said quickly after. 'I… I just want to help.'

Kasia nodded her understanding and lifted her gaze a fraction. She stopped playing with her fingernails.

'Her name's Crystal Redknapp. She's in my year. At first she started making fun of me in the classroom, whenever I asked a question or got a question wrong. But then… when my period started, she took all my clothes away from me in PE. I had nothing to wear and then I found them in the bin. It isn't just her… she's got some friends doing it as well. But it's mostly her. And when the image of your…' She couldn't bring herself to say it; and Tomek was grateful she couldn't. 'When the *image* went around school, it was because of her. She sent it to everyone.'

Tomek was quiet and patient as he listened, focusing more on trying to keep his cool than the meaning of her words. He felt a knot tighten in his stomach. A knot of guilt. He blamed himself. Not only for the image that had been shared around her school, but also because he had failed to notice the signs and symptoms straight away.

He'd been around broken and emotionally damaged children before, ones that had suffered years of abuse, and so he should have seen it, should have picked up on it.

He reached across the table and wrapped his hands around hers, enveloping them. He waited until her eyes met his before speaking.

'I'm sorry,' he said. 'You should never have been forced to go through that. I've let you down. I've disappointed you. But I'm going to get to the bottom of it. I'm going to speak with the school, I'm going to notify them of the situation and I'm going to tell them the police are involved.'

'No, you can't!'

'I can, and I will.'

'No, please.' She pulled her hands away from his and dropped them beneath the table again. 'I don't want you to.'

'Why not? She can't keep doing this—'

'Because if you do then everyone will know I'm a grass, everyone will know I'm a rat.'

'She can't keep getting away with it, Kase... Bullies need to be stopped.'

'You can't go to the school. Please. You can't.'

The plea in her eyes was overwhelming, almost to the point of forming tears.

Tomek grimaced and shook his head. He didn't like the idea of letting Crystal Redknapp slip through his and the school's fingers, but if she didn't want him to address the issue, then fine. He would respect her wishes.

'I won't go to the school. I won't speak to Miss Holloway. If that's what you really want...?'

She nodded firmly.

'Then all right,' he continued. 'I won't go to the school.'

But that didn't mean he wouldn't find more creative ways of dealing with the issue.

And he already had one of them in mind.

CHAPTER
FIFTY

E lizabeth Lake looked down at the small bed in front of her. The one that had been, up until a few weeks ago, the place she would have found herself on a night like tonight. Stormy, rainy, wet. Annabelle wouldn't have liked the rain thrashing against the window. It would have scared her. But everything would have been all right with mummy beside her, cuddling her, protecting her from the outside world.

But now there was nobody there. Her little girl, gone... Never to sleep in that bed again. Never to sleep in any bed again.

She missed the sound of her feet on the carpet, coming up the stairs. She missed the noise of excitement she made when she was ready for bed ahead of story time. She missed the way she brushed her teeth, almost scrubbing each tooth individually and with an extreme amount of care and attention.

Since Annabelle's death, Elizabeth had neglected to brush her own teeth. In fact, she'd neglected to do a lot of things. She hadn't washed her hair in a week. She hadn't shaved her legs or armpits. And the bush that was growing down below had already been out of control for weeks so that letting it grow a little more made no difference. She hadn't cleaned her ears. She hadn't trimmed her fingernails.

She hadn't done the washing up. She hadn't done the washing. She hadn't tidied the flat. She hadn't gone to work.

Instead she'd stayed indoors, staring blankly at the TV screen. Watching but not watching. Present but not present.

Wasting away.

Elizabeth pulled herself from Annabelle's bedroom and made her way to her own. To the place where she would have found her husband lying there on his phone, ignoring her. If he wasn't already asleep, that is. Most nights she found him passed out, but she knew he was secretly awake, pretending. And that, as soon as she closed her eyes and began to drift off, he would roll over to the other side and text on his phone for a while. Anything not to talk to her, anything not to communicate with her.

And now he was gone as well.

Just like Annabelle.

Despite the void that their loveless marriage had fallen into, and despite the divide that had been wedged between them, and despite the affair – despite it all – she still missed him. Still missed his touch, his warmth, the feeling of his body pressed against hers.

Now she came upstairs to a cold bed every night.

A cold bed in a cold, empty house.

A cold bed for a cold and malicious person.

As she rounded the other side of the bed, she pulled the curtains closed slightly and yanked the covers from atop her pillow. Then she slid onto the mattress and lay on her back, staring into the ceiling, her mind vacant, devoid of thought. The room was bathed in a bright orange glow from the lamp beside her, but summoning the energy to turn it off was difficult. Though she'd found in recent days that sleeping with the light on helped her. That it stopped the images and monsters appearing in the dark. That it silenced the noise in her head.

But tonight she felt different. Tonight she felt like turning it off. Tonight she felt like punishing herself for all that she'd done...

Just as she rolled over to the bedside table, she heard a noise. A small click. Faint, distant.

Coming from downstairs.

She held her breath as she waited, waited... Her pulse racing, chest rising.

Then the sound grew nearer. The sound of her fate coming to find her.

It appeared a moment later, the bedroom door opening. Standing in the doorframe. A set of keys glistening in the light.

Medical syringe in the other hand.

As she stared up at the figure in front of her, Elizabeth Lake was too afraid to speak. And her body remained perfectly still on the bed as the figure climbed over her and stabbed the syringe into her neck.

CHAPTER
FIFTY-ONE

Another morning. Another reason to be in Canvey.
This time for the disappearance of Elizabeth Lake.

The call regarding Beth with an F's disappearance had come in during the late morning from none other than Vincent Gregory, who right about now was hanging up picture frames on the walls of the interview room, Tomek had joked. The bloke spent so much time there he would have been surprised if Nick didn't offer him a room of his own to stay in.

With Tomek, in Elizabeth and Steven Lake's bedroom, was DC Rachel Hamilton, the crime scene manager, and a scenes of crime officer, busy studying the duvet and mattress. The syringe that had been left on the side of the bed had already been photographed and submitted as evidence, whereas the bed sheets might take a little while longer to examine.

'Now, I might go out on a limb here and say she's definitely been abducted,' Tomek remarked. 'Unless I've been taught wrong and heroin gives you a sudden burst of energy and sends you on a massive walk.'

'That's *some* walk,' Rachel replied.

From behind the face mask around her mouth, he saw the rise in her cheeks that suggested she was smirking.

'We don't know for certain it's heroin,' the crime scene manager said.

Tomek turned to face her. 'Given that it's been found in our latest murder victim's bloodstream, I'd say it's highly likely that it is.'

'We'll still examine it.'

'Of course. Thank you.'

Elizabeth and Steven Lake's bedroom was small, tiny really. Barely large enough to fit the double bed inside it; there was a small gap of a few inches around the perimeter of the mattress, and if you wanted to open the window, you needed to shuffle on tiptoes round the side of the bed, or climb over the duvet. Which, unfortunately for them, was something they couldn't do. As a result, Tomek and Rachel had been forced to stand pressed against one another just in the doorway, breathing on each other.

'Any sign of a break in?' Tomek asked, the thought occurring to him suddenly.

The crime scene manager shook her head. 'Nothing. No sign of forced entry in the front or the back. We've taken photos of the locks for further examination, but I'm confident you'll draw the same conclusions we did. As for anything that gives away who's done this... I'd say that's your biggest determiner. It was either someone she knew, someone she let in, or someone who had access to the house.'

Tomek and Rachel looked at one another.

Their main suspect, who ticked all those boxes, was exactly where he was supposed to be. Currently being grilled by some of the best officers in the business. As much as Tomek wanted to be there, to further apply the pressure on the little racist fascist bastard, he was beginning to have second thoughts. He knew Vincent Gregory wasn't the sharpest tool in the box, but was he really capable of abducting three individuals and killing two of them, all the while staying right in front of them, remaining at the forefront of the investigation at all times? Surely he couldn't be *that* stupid, could he?

Or perhaps that was why he'd got away with it for so long. The perfect disguise...

The thought troubled Tomek, but before he could think on it any further, Rachel nudged him in the ribs and gave him the look that signified it was time to leave. As he did so, he thanked the CSM for her time and told her that they'd be contactable on mobile if she needed anything. Then he turned his back on the room and headed down the stairs carefully, keeping his hands by his sides lest he be tempted to touch anything. At the bottom of the steps, he slipped out the front door and made his way to the car, where he stepped out of the outfit and stared back at the house. The road in and out of the cul-de-sac had been shut off, and access to and from the school was subject to a monitored police presence.

Tomek thought of Amelia Duggan, Annabelle Lake's school teacher.

The Two As.

He wondered whether it was possible for her to have had an involvement. She'd been present at the time of Annabelle Lake's disappearance – *seen* it, in fact, which made her the perfect witness to throw them off the correct line of enquiry. And she'd also been the one to *find* Annabelle. The perfect cover again. Wrong place at the wrong time.

Or was she in the right place at exactly the right time?

Tomek didn't know.

As he entered the car, he pondered it some more.

Of course, she would have to be working with someone. But who? And what was the connection between Annabelle Lake and Jenny Ingles? And why would she even have wanted to abduct and kill Annabelle Lake in the first place? From what he'd gathered, they were the best of friends (in Annabelle's eyes at least) and they adored each other.

It was then that it dawned on him they had absolutely no fucking idea about anything. They hadn't been able to determine a clear motive for Annabelle Lake's death, other than the wild possibility that she'd been abducted and rolled onto an assembly line for a human trafficking operation, but even that was a stretch. Canvey Island was a shithole, but it wasn't that depraved.

They didn't have a motive for Jenny Ingles' death either, aside from the idea it might have been drug related. But if that was the case, then why the connection to Annabelle Lake?

How could someone have been sick enough to abduct a poor, innocent little girl, house her while she was being held captive, ensure that she was properly fed – her favourite food, no less – and then kill her in such a manner? And then how could the same person turn their attention to a seventeen-year-old girl, rape her, pump her body full of heroin, and then kill her in the same way?

The treatment of both victims was completely different.

There had to be an obvious connection there somewhere.

Had to.

Tomek was sure of it.

And now Elizabeth's disappearance had been thrown into the mix as well. There was no doubt in his mind that she would end up the same way as her daughter eventually. Dead and dangling. But why?

What was the connection?

Tomek's gaze moved slowly along the houses in the cul-de-sac. From number twenty-three to forty-one. Until he stopped between forty-three and forty-seven. There, in the background, wedged between the gap in the two houses, was the back of Vincent Gregory's property.

The missing link? The missing connection?

Tomek still wasn't sure.

The man had no motive – he loved his niece and sister as much as anything, if not more than that. He'd always been acquitted of Tomek's accusations and he'd always had solid enough alibis for each of the murders. He stood to gain nothing from killing his own family members. Not to mention the lack of evidence implicating him in Jenny Ingles' death.

Vincent Gregory was a dead end.

A man who found himself in the wrong place at the wrong time.

Same as Amelia Duggan.

Tomek closed his eyes and placed his clenched hands on the dashboard. In his left hand, he released two fingers, forming the V sign; and on his right, he released his thumb.

Annabelle and Elizabeth Lake on the left.

Jenny Ingles on the right.

Then he conjured images of them in his mind, standing there in front of the car, on the pavement. The mother and daughter hugging while the lonely teenager braced herself against the cold.

Above them he tried to imagine the killer's face. In all its vague and mirage glory.

'Two sets of victims...' he whispered to himself, his lips flickering gently as he spoke. 'Two from the same family. One completely random.'

And then it hit him.

Two sets of victims.

Two killers. Working together.

One seeking revenge or retribution on the Lake family.

While the other acted on impulse and lust in the murder of Jenny Ingles.

'Tomek...'

At first he didn't recognise the voice. Didn't hear it, even.

'Tomek...'

Then he thought it was little Annabelle Lake talking to him, looking up at him, the chains still around her neck.

But when he felt a hand on his arm, he snapped out of his reverie. Holding onto him was Rachel, a worried expression written across her face.

'Sorry,' he said, chuckling awkwardly. 'Forgot you were there for a minute.'

'You good?' she asked. 'You look like you need some time to yourself. You've been sitting there for a while... Made me think you were having a stroke or something.'

Why did everyone keep saying that?

Tomek shook his head. 'No... No stroke. Just... deep in thought.' Then he added as a whisper, '*Seriously* deep in thought.'

'Anything interesting come up?'

Tomek turned to her and grinned. 'As a matter of fact, I think it did.'

CHAPTER
FIFTY-TWO

'You what?'

Nick sighed loudly enough for the whole room to hear.

Tomek raised his hands in mock surrender. 'Hear me out...'

'Okay. We're listening.'

Before explaining his theory, Tomek cleared his throat. He then told them about how there *was* a link between the victims, but not in the way they'd originally thought. They were connected by a duo of killers. Two evil compatriots working together.

'They call that a *folie à deux* in the business, sir,' Captain Actually added for effect. 'Like Fred and Rose West.'

'Yes, thank you for that, Oscar,' Nick replied, trying to keep the vehemence out of his voice.

'One of them will be telling the other what to do. It's typically two men, but can be a man and woman.'

Nick snapped his fingers and pointed at Oscar excitedly. 'Exactly!' he said. 'A man and woman. Vincent and Georgia Gregory. Husband and wife. Like Fred and Rose!'

Tomek hesitated, chewed on his bottom lip.

'You say that as though you know them personally, sir,' he said.

'Who? Fred and Rose or Vincent and Georgia?'

'Both.'

'Bullshit. We know almost everything there is to know about Vincent Gregory, but how much do we really know about *her*?' Nick asked Tomek, then opened the question up to the rest of the room when he realised Tomek had had little to do with Georgia Gregory in his investigations into Jenny Ingles' death. 'Anyone? Anyone?'

No one answered. Heads turned, searching for someone else willing to take responsibility for the question. In the end, Rachel fell on the team's sword.

'Not that much to be honest, sir,' she replied, coughing some resolve into her voice. 'She's been on the periphery of our investigations.'

'What do you mean periphery? She's slap-bang in the middle of the fucking thing. How has this not been picked up?'

Nasty Nick turned his fury towards Victoria who was about to experience his wrath for the first time.

'How has this one slipped through the net?' he asked, the calmness in his tone belying the rage on his face. 'It can't have been an oversight. You've all been twiddling your thumbs for the past week.'

Just as she was about to open her mouth to speak, Tomek leapt to her defence. He felt like he needed to. While she had to face up to Nick's music at some point, he didn't want it to be in the middle of a meeting, in front of everyone else – he'd been on the receiving end of a grilling like that, and it usually created a precedent that entitled Nick to think he could get away with it whenever he wanted. It was better to shut him off at source before things got out of control.

'With all due respect, sir,' Tomek began, but then slowed to a stop when he noticed Victoria raise her hand at him.

'Thanks, Tomek,' she started. 'But I can answer for myself.' Then she cleared her throat before doing so. 'The reason the team have missed Georgia Gregory from our investigations is because I instructed them to do so. We've spent that time focusing on the evidence.'

'What evidence?'

'Exactly. There's been very little. But from the evidence we *do* have, it's pointed us nowhere near Georgia Gregory. You can berate me as much as you want, but don't take it out on my team. That's been my oversight, and I accept full responsibility for that.'

Stunned silence drifted through the open door, climbed over the heads of everyone sitting down and then finally came to a stop in front of Nick, who looked sheepish. Tomek felt like standing to ovation and saluting Victoria. Many had tried to stand up to Nasty Nick in the past, but very few succeeded. Victoria had just added her name to that illustrious and minute list. And for that, Tomek's respect for her multiplied greatly.

Before Nick could respond, Victoria continued, moving the conversation away from her minor display of ineptitude and onto the task at hand.

'Rachel, after this meeting, I'd like you visit the island and find Georgia Gregory. Bring her in if you can. Find out what she knows and where she's been.'

Rachel nodded and made a note of the instruction in her phone. As Tomek watched Victoria pace from side to side at the head of the room, staring at the incident board in front of her, Tomek raised his hand.

Said: 'Can we get back to my theory now?'

'What's the point?' Nick asked. 'We've already debunked it.'

'No we haven't, sir. We know just as much about Georgia's involvement as we do Vincent's. I still don't think they're involved. I think Vincent's being set up.'

'You've changed your tune...'

'Don't get me wrong, he's still a racist fuckface, but ever since this whole thing started, it's been made to look like him. And now that I think about it, the signs have been there from the start – I was just a little blinded by the fact I hated him.'

'And now you don't?'

Tomek shrugged. 'Like I said, he's still a fuckface. But I don't think he's a criminal or deserves to be treated like one.'

But then again, neither had Tomek... neither had Sean. Both had been treated like criminals – being thrown off the team for the colour of their skin and their nationality – and they'd been forced to accept it. So how was it any different? Perhaps it was what the man deserved...

But that wasn't the right way to go about things. That wasn't what he'd signed up for.

He felt conflicted. On the one hand he detested the man for his views and opinions, but on the other hand he didn't think he should have been treated the way he was, even if Tomek had been largely responsible for such treatment in the first place.

'Right from the start, he's been made to look the scapegoat,' Tomek continued. 'The car that was stolen and used to kidnap Annabelle Lake – the same car as Vincent Gregory's. Even the car that had been used to abduct Jenny Ingles – his exact fucking car! And yet not a shred of evidence to suggest he'd been the one to do either.'

'That's all you're basing this on?' Nick asked. He wasn't prepared to let this go, and neither was Tomek.

Two brick walls meeting an impasse. Eventually one would have to yield. And it wasn't going to be him.

He turned to DC Carter. 'Let me ask you this, Chey. During the interview downstairs, has he given any details about where his sister is being kept?'

Chey shook his head. 'No. He's been quite upset by it actually. Like, really upset. Begging with us. Pleading with me to let him help. It's a bit strange.'

'They're very close...' Anna, Triple Word Score, said, beginning to weigh in.

'Exactly,' Tomek continued. 'They were in care together. They grew up together. I can't imagine for a second that he would have done anything like this to his own sister. And he treated Annabelle like his own daughter – why would he kill her if that was the case?'

Nick paused before responding. 'I could think of a dozen reasons why...'

Tomek considered calling the chief inspector's bluff, but knew that the subtle punishments afterwards would not be worth it.

'What about the fish in the stomach?' Nick was clearly clasping at straws now.

'It's possible we could be looking for someone who knows the family. Who knows Annabelle. Who knows them well enough to have a key...'

'Who?'

Tomek thought back to Amelia Duggan. The teacher who watched Annabelle Lake go home from school every afternoon. Who watched her insert her key into the house. Who watched her eat lunch during break time. Who spent almost every part of every day with her.

'I'm not sure right now,' Tomek admitted. 'But I will be soon. *We* will be soon. All I'm asking *right now* is that we let Vincent Gregory go. And if you're that worried about him, then set up surveillance on him. Get someone to watch his every move. In the meantime, bring Amelia Duggan and Georgia Gregory in for questioning. I think they might know a few more things than they're letting on.'

CHAPTER
FIFTY-THREE

Vincent Gregory had lost track of the emotions currently surging through his body.

Despair at having lost his sister.

Grief over the death of his beloved niece.

Anger and frustration at having been pulled into the police station for the third time in as many weeks.

Resentment for the people who were trying to find Elizabeth.

Guilt at not having been there to protect her, to stop this from happening to her in the first place.

Confusion at wanting to help the police in any way possible but not knowing how, and not trusting them to do it properly and without interviewing him every five minutes.

Hatred for the person that was doing this to his family.

Regret for not saying things he'd wished he'd said sooner.

He was a melting pot of human emotion. And he was beginning to feel like a teenager again. Back when he'd experienced the same sort of feelings. Back when Elizabeth had been there to help him through them. And when he'd returned the favour.

He remembered her touch on that night. Amidst the darkness of the room. Surrounded by the muted sounds of children in the foster house sleeping heavily. The way it had relaxed him completely, softened the tense muscles in his body.

How he wished they could go back to then. Back to when things were... simpler.

Vincent climbed out of his car and slammed the door shut. Over the fences to his house he saw the forensics vans and police vehicles still outside Elizabeth's. He fought hard with the decision to go round there and see what they were doing. If there was one thing he'd learnt from this entire ordeal, it was that the police didn't like him being so close to everything, him being at the forefront of the investigation. That made them suspicious.

Besides, he didn't know if he would like what he saw. What they might pull out of the house.

Instead he entered his own home and headed straight for the kitchen, where he made himself a cup of tea. White, two sugars. Anything less and it simply wouldn't taste right.

As he carried the drink into the living room, he suddenly became aware of the person standing in the corner, dressed in a white forensic suit, their features hidden behind a mask.

'Who the fuck are you?' Vincent asked slowly, feeling his body tense with adrenaline – another addition to the melting pot.

The figure said nothing.

'I said who the fuck are you?'

Still nothing.

Both stood there, separated by a few feet – easily within reaching distance, he estimated – just staring at one another. Both waiting for the other to make the first move.

Vincent gauged the intruder's build: slight, small, skinnier than him. Yet they were the same height, and there was *some* definition there. He couldn't underestimate that fact.

He tightened his grip on the coffee mug, feeling the ceramic slip against his sweating skin. Thought about throwing the contents of it over the person in his living room.

Seriously considered it.

But before he could even act on the thought, he heard a noise. The sound of the back door opening. Then the sound of the door closing, followed by footsteps moving towards the front door and locking them in the house.

Then another figure appeared, wielding a baseball bat in one hand.

At the sight of them, Vincent dropped the cup of tea. Scalding liquid splashed onto his legs and burnt his skin, but he felt nothing. He was numbed to the pain. Another addition to the melting pot.

The last and final addition, before he was knocked unconscious by the baseball bat, was surprise.

Surprise at recognising the other figure in front of him, despite the forensic suit protecting their features.

CHAPTER
FIFTY-FOUR

Tomek had chosen to stay longer than he was supposed to. He had a point to prove. Needed to find evidence that exonerated Vincent Gregory from having any involvement in the kidnappings and murders. And so far it was looking like he'd made a wildly inaccurate statement. No matter how hard he looked, no matter how hard he ventured away from the evidence, it was all still pointing to Vincent Gregory. To the one man who had been at the forefront of the entire investigation from the start.

'Any luck?' Sean asked as he approached Tomek's desk with a slight spring in his step.

'Like you wouldn't believe. I'm about to make an arrest now actually.'

'*Really?*'

'No, dumbass. Not really. I'm about as near to finding out who killed Annabelle Lake and Jenny Ingles as you are. And don't come over here with that smile on your face, eagerly awaiting to hear how miserably I'm failing.'

Offence gradually crawled across his friend's face.

'I actually wasn't,' Sean replied. 'I just came for a chat.'

'Now really isn't the time.'

Sean pulled the chair out from beneath the desk beside him. 'You look like you could do with a break...'

Tomek closed his eyes. He didn't want to think how red and tired they looked. Hour upon hour staring at the same screen, worsening the tension headache squeezing either side of his head. Perhaps his friend was right. Perhaps it was time for a quick break.

'How's the move going?' Sean asked flippantly. 'How's Kasia doing?'

A quick one, at least. Couple minutes.

Just enough to rest the eyes and allow the brain cells to recover.

'The move's been going well,' he said. 'I'd say we're about halfway there. Kasia's been doing most of it when she gets home from school – though she can only manage little boxes, nothing too strenuous.'

'And how is the little problem child? Still causing you problems?'

'Yes, but I found out the reason why...'

'Oh?'

Then Tomek told him that Kasia was being bullied, keeping his voice low in case anyone else in the office overheard. He didn't want them thinking badly of him, and he certainly didn't want them thinking badly of Kasia.

'I'm sorry to hear that, mate.' Sean looked down at his lap, deep in thought. 'Did I... Did I ever tell you I was bullied when I was a kid?'

'Fuck off,' Tomek replied. '*You*? You're the biggest bloke I know. Who had the balls big enough to come up to you and pick a fight?'

'A bunch of little racists, that's who.'

That shut Tomek up.

'They used to chase me round the playground screaming monkey chants at me and launching bananas at me in the classroom. I fucking hated it. Pricks, the lot of them. They made my life a living hell in school. Made me hate it so much I didn't want to go in.'

Tomek heard echoes of Kasia's bullying in Sean's story. The way she sometimes didn't want to get out of bed in the morning. The way she would do anything to get out of going into school – even going to the lengths of feigning illness.

'Don't get me wrong,' Sean continued. 'I beat the shit out of them multiple times, and I beat the shit out of them good. But that only made it worse. They always came back, sometimes with more of them.'

'Like an ambush?' Tomek was on the edge of his seat, tilted forward, listening to his friend's story. The story he was hearing for the first time, yet wished he'd heard much sooner.

'Of sorts. One time it was just me versus about five of them. They were much smaller than me, but still...'

'Five of them...' Tomek said, finishing his friend's sentence. 'Did you tell anyone about it?'

Sean nodded slowly. His gaze had drifted off into the carpet, staring vacantly into the middle ground as he relived the experiences of his childhood. 'My dad went ape shit once. Went round the house of one of the bullies and started beating the shit out of the dad. Nearly made it to the kid as well, if it hadn't been for me, pulling him away. But my dad... well, he didn't do much exercise – ate a lot of shit really – and not to mention he was in his fifties. Then he dropped dead. Just like that. There and then. Major heart attack. He was gone by the time the paramedics arrived and tried to resuscitate him.'

Tomek had known about his friend's father's death. About the manner in which it had happened. But he hadn't known the circumstances surrounding his sudden and traumatic passing. He listened intently, waiting patiently for Sean to continue.

'After that I became the man of the house, so for us to get by I had to start making money. So I started selling sweets and drinks at school. My very own black market – of which I only sold my stock to the white people who weren't racists, and some of the other black people in school. The bullying quickly stopped after that. After they realised I couldn't be touched... not unless they wanted everyone else in the school to come after them.'

Sean snapped out of his trance and slowly turned to face Tomek, pain and suffering written in the lines of his eyes and forehead. A slight shimmer of liquid had formed in the bottom of his eyes. He tried to blink it away but Tomek saw it for what it was; emotion, grief.

'All I'm saying is,' he continued, as though he felt like he needed to make some sort of point, 'is that Kasia will get through it the same way I did. Not only that, but it will shape her into a better, more resilient human being.'

Tomek smirked, nodding slowly. 'I guess you didn't turn out all that bad.'

'Better than you, you little deadbeat.'

He chuckled. 'But if it's all the same to you, and no disrespect to your dad, but I'd rather not have a massive heart attack while defending my daughter.'

Sean's lips flickered slightly into a weak smile.

'You only have to worry about that if you find the person who's doing it...'

Tomek turned to his computer, pointed at the screen. 'Shouldn't take me too long. One of the perks of the job, I'd say. Who used to bully you?'

Sean burst into a bout of laughter. A sudden, singular burst that echoed around the room. 'You wouldn't believe me if I told you.'

'Try me...'

Before Sean could answer, a name popped into Tomek's head. He blurted it out.

'Vincent Gregory?'

Sean wagged his thick finger in the air. 'Close, very close. But not quite. You're on the right path.'

Tomek considered a moment but then the well of names in his mind came up dry.

'Steven Lake,' Sean replied calmly, slowly, with no animosity in his voice.

The name stumped Tomek momentarily.

'Steven...?'

Sean nodded. 'The very same one who killed himself the other day. I recognised him as soon as I saw him the morning after Annabelle had gone missing. You don't forget a face like his.'

'Did he recognise you?'

'Course he did. The little coward wouldn't speak to me. Practically ran away whenever I went near him. It's funny...' Sean's gaze drifted off again. 'Funny how at one point I used to be so scared of him, so scared to cross him or any of his mates. But then... then it was like he was scared of me. The tables had turned and I had the power. *Again.*'

Tomek's mouth fell open as he struggled to process the information. 'But... but he seemed so nice in comparison to Vincent...'

'Don't let his looks deceive you. The bloke's a Class A cunt from start to finish. He was always a bit of a cretin.'

'Why didn't you say anything before?'

Sean shrugged, waited a moment before responding. 'I didn't want to give him any more airtime than he deserved. And it's not exactly a part of my life I like to relive, if I'm honest.'

Tomek could understand that. He had also been through something similar as a child, but nothing as traumatising and harrowing as Sean. Without saying anything else, Sean slapped his knee and rose out of his chair. Before leaving the conversation quietly, he placed a hand on Tomek's shoulder and walked off.

Leaving him to his own thoughts.

Thoughts that started off small, then suddenly began to roll downhill and grow in size and momentum.

Don't let his looks deceive you.

Sean's words echoed around his head.

He was always a bit of a cretin.

And then an idea hit him like a sledgehammer to the face. At once, he leapt out of his seat and hurried across to the other side of the office. Fortunately, while he was busy trying to find reasons not to assume the worst of Vincent Gregory, the rest of the team were trying to find Elizabeth Lake.

He found Nadia sitting at her desk, one hand on her stomach while the other was moving her computer mouse from one side of the screen to the other.

'Good evening,' he said. 'Shouldn't you be home?'

'I'm only staying another fifteen minutes,' she replied, craning her neck to see him. 'What can I help you with?'

'Steven Lake,' Tomek replied. 'I don't suppose we ever found his body, did we?'

She shook her head. 'Not that I've heard. As far as we're aware he's still floating about in the sea.'

Tomek smiled. 'Excellent! And the evidence found on his boat...'

'What about it?'

'Remind me...'

A moment later, Nadia had pulled up the list of evidence found on Steven Lake's boat, the *Annabelle*. To see the screen more clearly, she leant closer and lowered her glasses onto her nose.

'Says here they found his DNA on there, Annabelle's DNA... and traces of tuna.'

Tomek's face beamed.

'Do we have his laptop?' he asked.

'Somewhere. Do you want me to—'

'Never mind,' he said, then swivelled on the spot and left her without another word.

Buoyed by the revitalising thoughts floating to the top of his head, he made his way back to his desk and opened Google. In the search bar, he entered *The Man Club*, the name of the group for depressed men, and hit Return. Then he clicked on the first result that appeared on the page.

On the home screen of the forum was a list of different categories related to being a dad with depression, with between two and three comments beneath it before it had been clipped. The topics ranged from the specific to the broad, but Tomek didn't care about that. He was looking for something in particular.

Rather, someone in particular.

And he found it a few moments later.

In the category for "*dealing with the death of a child*".

There, at the bottom of the comments section was a post from Steven Lake's profile, S.Lake85.

Dated twenty hours ago.

CHAPTER
FIFTY-FIVE

'The slippery bastard's alive?'

Tomek nodded. 'He's been posting from beyond the grave, sir.'

'And you're sure?'

'I'm not a firm believer in ghosts, so I'm going to say that I'm *fairly confident*. And that's not all of it, sir. I also found this...'

Tomek removed the piece of paper he'd folded into his breast pocket and slid it across the table. Nasty Nick, who wasn't being so nasty anymore, picked it up and examined it, then handed it over to Victoria who was standing at his shoulder.

'Where did you find this?' she asked.

'His email. I found his laptop in storage and logged into his account. Something just occurred to me and I thought to follow it up.'

'How did we miss this?' she asked, even though she already knew the answer.

To save her blushes, Tomek said: 'He hid it pretty well in his inbox, several layers deep and in the most bizarre email folder... but not well enough. Besides, we probably never thought to look that far because we didn't consider him a suspect.'

'I...' Nick began as he read the document again. 'Oh, shit.'

Before finishing his sentence, Nick stormed out of the room and called an immediate meeting inside the incident room. Within a few moments, the rest of the team – those who'd stayed, including Sean, Chey, Martin, Rachel and Anna – quickly filtered into the room. All of them began to sense that this was going to be a long night.

'Right, you lot,' Nick said. 'It seems our missing dad, Steven Lake, is actually alive. He was last reported using the online forum, *The Man Club*, twenty hours ago. Now, unless Tomek's mistaken, that means he's hiding out somewhere. We need to find out where...'

'Has anyone got any ideas where to begin?' Victoria asked, stepping in. It was clear to see that she wanted to be at the forefront at this stage in the investigation. A chance to redeem herself.

'The dirt!' someone called.

Tomek turned to face the rest of the room and saw Martin's beady eyes gleaming with delight.

'Just this morning we got the composition report on the dirt and sand found on Annabelle Lake and Jenny Ingles' feet.'

Martin glanced around at a set of expressionless faces.

'I wasn't expecting it back for another week but it seems forensics managed to find the time to examine it,' he continued, but everyone was waiting for him to get to the point.

'It's been confirmed that the dirt on the girls' feet came from the same place,' he continued. 'And this morning, the SOCO team found small traces of the same mud and dirt and sand in Elizabeth Lake's bedroom.'

'That just tells us it's the same killer and that they were being held in the same place,' Tomek said. 'But it doesn't tell us *where* they are.'

'It does when we know who the killer is...'

It took Tomek longer than he would have liked for the penny to finally drop. For him to finally understand what Martin was alluding to.

But, much to his delight, it took the rest of the team even longer to figure it out.

'How quickly can we get down there?' Victoria asked.

'Us? About twenty minutes, depending how fast we're driving.'

'What about the nearest uniform?'

'Canvey Police can be there within minutes.'

Victoria turned to Nick. 'I think one of us should go. If things go... *wrong*, I think one of us should be there to defuse the situation.'

Nick considered a moment with a sigh.

There was a sigh for every mood, every reaction. But Tomek knew from experience this was a good one.

'I'll go...' he said.

'Why you?' asked Martin, sitting upright, clearly upset by the decision. 'Can't we all go? We all have as much right to be there as he does?'

Nick shook his head. 'Tomek's close to this investigation,' he said. 'Tomek's the right fit. Trust me...' He placed his hand inside his blazer pocket and pulled out the printout Tomek had given him. 'Trust me. Tomek's best suited for this.'

'Meanwhile, the rest of us need to prepare for interview,' Victoria said.

Nick clapped his hands and adjourned the meeting instantly. The room erupted into action, each of them filtering back to their desks. Except for Sean, Nick and Victoria who remained behind. Tomek decided to stay with them briefly.

'I'll sign out a car and get down there as quick as I can,' he said. 'I'll try my best to bring him back in one piece.'

Victoria nodded. 'We'll be waiting for you when you do.'

Tomek swivelled on the turn, but then stopped himself. 'Not sure if you've thought about it already, but I think Sean should be the one to interview Steven Lake when I bring him in.'

'Why?' asked Nick, whose head bounced between himself and Sean.

In response, Tomek reached for the printout and snatched it from the chief inspector, holding it aloft between the four of them. 'Trust me...' he said.

And that was enough.

As he left the room, he caught Sean's eye. The expression on his friend's face told him everything he wanted to say but couldn't.

CHAPTER
FIFTY-SIX

The boatyard located near the bridge that connected Canvey Island and Benfleet had always been a mystery to Tomek. He'd driven past it every time he'd made his way onto and off the island, but never truly understood what was there.

And now he found out.

After passing Benfleet train station, he and the convoy of liveried police vehicles made their way towards Benfleet Moorings, a small bank where a row of boats had been moored along the mudflats. On the other side of the Hadleigh Ray, the stretch of water sitting in the middle, was Canvey Island marina. To the right was a footbridge, joining the two together.

Tomek and the team pulled up beside the footbridge and immediately began fanning out. The suspected location that Steven Lake was keeping Elizabeth Lake hostage was a few hundred yards along the riverbank. Discretion and anonymity was key – the last thing they wanted was for Steven Lake to spot the bright yellow and blue of the police cars as the moonlight bounced off the panels.

Instead, they made the journey by foot.

Cars driving along Canvey Road sped past, eager to get off the island. The rustling noises of insects fleeing the scene sounded by his ankles. The rest of the silence was disturbed by the sound of their feet moving along the gravel, gradually closing in on their killer.

Tomek didn't know what to expect when they found him. Based on the injuries sustained to Annabelle Lake and Jenny Ingles, Tomek was expecting to find Elizabeth Lake in good health. Perhaps tied to a chair or bound at the feet and hands. But something told him that wouldn't be the case.

That they would be entering into something evil, something disturbed.

Especially after what he'd discovered in Steven's inbox.

A little further down, they passed a large boat that had been converted into a restaurant. Chairs and benches had been left on the grassy area outside and opposite was a car park.

Beyond that was the small boathouse they were looking for, if it could be called that. Rather, it was more like a shack, a small space possibly large enough for a small boat, nothing too extravagant. The perfect size for the *Annabelle*. Parked behind it, Tomek spotted a blacked-out Ford Fiesta, with a number plate matching that discovered in the CCTV shot on the night of Jenny's abduction.

As they approached the building, Tomek's phone vibrated in his pocket. A message had just come through from Nick, notifying him that Vincent Gregory had potentially gone missing. A team of uniformed officers had been sent to call round at his house, to check up on him and inform him that they were confident an arrest would be made soon. It had originally been Sean's idea; he'd sensed that Vincent Gregory's life would be in danger somehow. But he hadn't envisaged it happening this soon, so soon after Elizabeth had been kidnapped.

Not only might they potentially find one victim, now they might find two.

Steven Lake's vendetta against his wife and brother-in-law was strong.

Tomek looked at the officers behind him – six of them in total – and was grateful for the large number.

'This is for you, Annabelle,' he said as he pocketed his phone and approached the building.

In the darkness, he fumbled for the door, careful not to make any drastic sounds or disturbances. Once he felt the wooden panelling beneath his fingers, he paused, listened.

Sounds, murmurings echoed through the fibres. Life, coming from inside the building. That was a good sign. A very good sign indeed.

As he braced himself to open the door, wrapping his hands over the handle, he gave one last look at the team surrounding the building.

And then he entered.

CHAPTER
FIFTY-SEVEN

The first thing he noticed about the space was the smell. Rancid, putrid. The type that stung the back of your throat, got in your eyes and made you wince.

The smell of rotting and decaying faecal matter.

And then, after his mind had had a chance to process the smell, he took in the sight, the view immediately in front of him.

For one of the Gregory siblings it was too late. For the other, their life was hanging in the balance.

Hovering over Vincent Gregory was the mastermind behind the entire operation. Knife in hand, pressing it against the man's throat. Meanwhile, Elizabeth Lake was dangling from a steel a-frame, suspended by a piece of rope. Her belly and throat had been sliced open, and her blood continued to drip from her naked feet, gathering in the pool beneath it.

Splash.

Splash.

Splash.

'Steven...' Tomek said as he raised his hands in the air to suggest he meant no harm. 'Put the knife down.'

Tomek was acutely aware of the officers behind him, waiting for a command. But right now in his mind, it was just him, Steven and Vincent. Two men who perhaps deserved the outcome they were about to face. For Steven it would have been an arrest and a lengthy jail sentence. As for Vincent, it would have been death.

There had been a time – as little as twenty minutes ago after he'd find out about Sean's childhood – where he would have allowed the two of them to carry on, to let them play out their own fates...

But he couldn't do that. Not again.

He'd made that mistake with Tony. And he relived it almost every day.

The scene in front of him was a harrowing reminder of what had happened in the past.

Tony dangling from a wooden beam, bleeding to death, his genitals lodged in his mouth. Dying in a similar sort of place.

The parallels were too strong for him to ignore. He couldn't let anyone else die in a place like this.

'Put the weapon down, Steven,' Tomek repeated. 'Please.'

By now the initial look of shock and surprise on Steven Lake's face had withered and been replaced with a look of desperation and anger. And there was nothing worse than a volatile man with nothing left to lose.

'How did you find me?' Steven asked.

'It's our job,' Tomek replied.

'Get out. Leave here. I... I have unfinished... You can't be here.'

'But we are, mate. And we're going to need you to put the weapon down.'

Now it was time for Steven to turn the blade on Tomek. His eyes widened and he gritted his teeth maniacally.

'Get out. You have to get out. You can't be here!'

Tomek chewed his bottom lip. 'Can't do that, mate. I'm sorry. Best I can do is just me. The rest of these guys leave while I stay. How does that sound?'

Steven considered the proposition for a minute. Then realised it was a lose-lose. Whichever way the situation played out, there was no escape for him, no boat for him to hop in and sail away on. Nowhere else for him to hide.

'Fine,' he said eventually, choosing the lesser of two evils. 'You stay. But everyone else leaves. Now!'

Tomek turned to face the uniformed officers and gave them a slight nod. Within a few moments they were gone.

'There... How's that?' he said. 'Is that a bit better for you?'

He was aware of the patronising tone in his voice, but there was little he could do to help it.

'Why are you here?' Steven asked, still pointing the murder weapon at him.

'Because I'm doing my job,' Tomek replied. 'Something your brother-in-law accused me of not doing not so long ago.'

Vincent Gregory, who was tied to a chair in the middle of the boathouse, scowled at Tomek. As though blaming him for signing his death warrant, adding the final nail to the coffin and all Steven Lake needed to do was give it a whack. Or, more aptly, a nice clean swipe across his throat.

'I'm still going to need you to put the knife down though, Steven. And then maybe we can talk.'

'Talk about what? There's nothing to talk about.'

'I have a few questions I think I'd like some answers to.'

A few was an understatement – he had a whole file on the notes app on his phone containing them.

'Perhaps you could satisfy my curiosity a bit...'

Steven Lake hesitated as he considered his best route out of there. Tomek studied him for a moment. It occurred to him that here was a man who had no idea what he was doing. That he was panicking, reacting – the same way he'd been reacting to instructions given to him in Annabelle Lake's and Jenny Ingles' deaths. It occurred to Tomek in that moment that he wasn't looking at a mastermind at all.

That he was looking at the submissive, the second half of the *folie à deux*.

'Where's your partner in crime, Steven?' Tomek asked.

'My what? My...? What are you talking about?'

'I think you know exactly what I'm talking about, Steven. Where are they, and who are they?'

'I don't know what you mean. There isn't... there isn't anyone else. I acted alone. I've always acted alone.'

Classic, Tomek thought. The man was weak and feeble, and had been brainwashed into not giving his partner up. The answer lay within him somewhere, and if Tomek was going to get it out he would have to be clever about it.

'You still haven't put the knife down, Steven,' Tomek said, pointing at it. 'I'm really going to need you to do that, otherwise one of us is going to get hurt.'

'Yeah! And it'll be him!'

Before Tomek even noticed the movement, Steven swung the blade in front of Vincent and held it against his collar bone that had become exposed in an earlier scuffle. The man's chest heaved, bouncing up and down, the light from the lamp in the corner reflecting off the blade's surface.

'I get it...' Tomek said. 'I understand completely.'

'You what?'

'I didn't like your brother-in-law much when I first saw him. If I wasn't doing this job I'd probably be doing the same thing right now...'

The glare on Vincent's face turned to fear, as the nail in his coffin drew closer to being hammered home.

'What do you mean?' Steven asked, pure confusion lacing his words.

'Your brother-in-law, he got me thrown off the team looking into your daughter's disappearance. Because I'm Polish. Because he's a racist. And, even worse, he got my friend kicked off the team as well –

for the colour of his skin. But the funny thing is, I bet he's regretting that decision because if he didn't make that call to my boss in the first place then maybe he wouldn't be in this situation right now...'

For a brief moment, Tomek thought he saw a morsel of guilt flash in Vincent's eyes. But then he knew the man was too proud to do anything like that.

'I don't want to kill him because he's a racist...' Steven said slowly, as though the words weren't forming in his head properly.

I know you don't, Tomek thought. *Because* you're *a dirty little racist as well*.

'If not because of that, then what? Is it because of *this*?'

Tomek reached into his pocket and produced the printout that had stunned Nick and Victoria in the office.

'Where did you...? Where did you get that from?'

'Like I said, I was doing my job.'

Tomek turned his attention to the document. In the top corner was the name and logo of the company that had run the DNA test. Beneath it was the date of the letter and the reference number that had been assigned to the query. Beneath that was a small table highlighting the connections between the two DNA samples – one for Annabelle Lake, the other for Steven Lake.

Or rather in Steven Lake's case, the lack of connection.

There, in black and white, was the piece of evidence that had sparked Steven Lake's killing spree. The confirmation that Annabelle wasn't his daughter, that she was someone else's.

It didn't take a genius to work out whose...

'I know you hate him for what he's done,' Tomek began. 'But you can't kill him.'

'It was never about killing him,' Steven replied. 'I wanted to destroy him. I wanted him to witness everything he loved fall apart and burn right in front of him.' Steven turned to look at Elizabeth's lifeless body. 'And there she is. The one thing he loved... The one thing he loved most in the world. Loved her enough to fuck her...'

Tomek decided to stay quiet. To let Steven say everything he needed to. To tell him everything he needed to hear.

To satisfy his curiosity.

'I've always known they were close...' Steven continued, as though Vincent wasn't right in front of him, still alive, still breathing. 'They always have been. How could they be any different, given what they went through as kids? But I never thought they'd go as far as incest. I... I first suspected something was happening between them at a garden party one summer. I caught them in one of the rooms hugging. But it wasn't one of those sibling hugs, it was something deeper. They both denied there was anything more to it, but I knew it, I saw it. I *felt* it. Since then I couldn't let it go. I had to find out, but I was too afraid...'

'So you kidnapped her?'

Steven hesitated as he relived the events in his head. He lowered his gaze to the floor and stared into nothing.

'I... I...' Steven swallowed the lump in his throat hard. 'There's no nice way to say this, but... I've never been able to love Annabelle. I've never loved her as my own. I've always felt she was different to me – not just in looks but in personality. For that I've never allowed myself to *fully* love her. She's always been one step removed. She just... exists. She's just... there.'

'I get it,' Tomek replied.

At that, the man lifted his gaze and met Tomek's eyes for the first time in a long while.

'You... you understand?'

He nodded, shrugging his shoulders the way blokes do when they were too afraid to admit something embarrassing.

'I recently found out I was a dad after thirteen years. She landed on my doorstep one evening and she's been living with me ever since. She's come out the woodwork after all this time and all of a sudden I'm supposed to love her like my own? It's been difficult. We've struggled to say the least, but things are getting there.'

'That's not the same,' Steven said. 'Because she *is* your child.'

'It's not felt that way. And it still doesn't. At times she's felt like a complete stranger, because that's what she is... It's the first time I've met her in my life. That's what constitutes being a stranger. I imagine that's how you felt with Annabelle?'

Steven nodded.

'I did. Back then. But not anymore...'

The grief and guilt was clear to see on Steven's face, as his cheeks and lips began to scrunch up, as his eyes began to squint, as the tears began to form.

'I've not been able to forgive myself for what I did to her. I should never have done it. I should never have killed her. She didn't deserve it. None of this was her fault. That responsibility laid with Elizabeth and... and...' Steven suddenly seemed to remember the tied up man in front of him, and then his countenance changed. The humility and vulnerability that had been refreshing to hear disappeared and was replaced with fury again.

Fury at Vincent Gregory for sleeping with his wife – with his own sister – and for being the father of the child he thought was his own. That whole dynamic was a complete mindfuck to Tomek, one that he would need to process after this was over, but right now his immediate priority was to make sure no one else got hurt.

'Do you regret killing Jenny Ingles?' Tomek asked as he made a small step forward while Steven was distracted.

'What?'

'Jenny Ingles. Do you regret abducting her, raping her, and killing her?'

Steven dropped his gaze again. This time he dropped the blade to his side with it.

And there was the answer.

A man who regretted the things that he'd done but had felt compelled to do them anyway.

'Why did you rape her, Steven?'

'Because... because I could. Because I had the power to.'

Because Steven had gone past the point of no return...

There was no animosity in his voice, no evil undertones that hinted he was a bad person. Just a seriously confused and broken one.

Tomek didn't know if he already felt sorry for him, or if he wanted to feel sorry for him.

'Do you regret it?' he asked again.

Steven nodded gently, like a small child in the middle of being told off.

'Do you not think, then, that if you kill your brother-in-law you might regret that too? I don't think you're a bad person, Steven. I think you've made some mistakes in the past. I think you bullied my friend in school because your dad was a racist so that was all you knew. And I think you did these things because someone told you to. Someone was directing you.'

The look in Steven's eyes – of pity, sorrow – told Tomek he was right, but those weren't the words that came out of his lips.

'I did it all alone...' Steven said, though the weakness and hoarseness in his voice implied he didn't even believe himself.

'Then explain this to me,' Tomek said, taking another step forward. By now there was about three feet between them, short enough for Tomek to smell the rancid smell on Steven Lake's breath. 'How did you fake your suicide? How did you get back to shore after you ditched the *Annabelle*? When we found it, it was a mile or so out to sea.'

'I'm a good swimmer.'

'And I'm Brad Pitt. We can all say things that aren't true, mate... So why won't you tell me? I've believed everything else you've said up to this point. So why are you lying to protect them? *Who* are you trying to protect?'

Steven fought internally for the answer to that question. Do or don't. Tell all or say nothing. And Tomek watched it play out on the man's face.

In the end he got the answer he was expecting.

'I'm a good swimmer.'

———

It took a few more minutes for Tomek to completely deactivate the situation and convince Steven to drop the weapon. When he eventually did, the uniformed officers who had been waiting patiently outside charged in and arrested the man. A team of paramedics had been called and were on their way to tend to Vincent, who had been left in the chair, hands and feet still bound.

'Aren't you going to get me out of here?' he growled at Tomek as he approached.

Before replying, Tomek watched the uniformed officers usher Steven Lake out of the boathouse, hands cuffed behind his back.

'You're in shock,' Tomek replied. 'We don't know what sort of injuries you've sustained. We wouldn't move someone who's just fallen twenty feet in case they've broken their back, would we? It's the same with you.'

'The fuck you talkin' 'bout? I ain't fallen from nowhere.'

Tomek knew that. Of course he knew that. He was just fucking with the man. For one final time – because, and he hoped more than anything, that this would be the *last* time he saw him. And if that was the case, he wanted to soak up every moment of it, every uncomfortable and painful moment.

'I think we're going to keep you there until the paramedics arrive...'

'No, please don't. You have to get me outta here. I don't wanna stay... please.'

Tomek pushed the smug smirk away from his face. How the tables had turned.

'Need I remind you that I just saved your life? You'll thank me for making you sit down and process it all.'

Vincent contorted his face as he prepared himself to launch another verbal attack on Tomek, but then immediately thought better of it.

'I know. Thank you. I... I'm sorry for everythin' I did to... to you and your mate.'

A genuine apology. One that Tomek hadn't expected to hear, though it only counted for about eighty per cent of face value because he'd only said it under extreme circumstances. He doubted that Vincent would have uttered the words of his own free will, had it not been for the knife that had been pressed against his throat.

'You're lucky my colleague didn't come down here...' Tomek started. 'Otherwise I'm fairly confident he would have let you die and then probably ended up killing your brother-in-law afterwards.'

'I bet he fucking would, they're always the same, those—'

Tomek shoved his palm in front of Vincent Gregory's face. 'I beg you, please don't finish that sentence. You've just been given another chance at life and I'd hate for you to experience so little of it by continuing to be racist. And so, because you made it that far in your sentence, I'm going to leave you here. Maybe you could say goodbye to your sister.'

Whether that was a punishment or gratitude, Tomek didn't know. Either way he left the shack feeling pleased with himself, feeling a slight sense of retribution. He'd saved Vincent Gregory from death, even if the man hadn't deserved it.

As he made his way out of the building, a duo of paramedics were rushing to the scene. Tomek stopped them in their tracks and explained to them that Vincent was absolutely fine and that maybe he needed a couple more minutes' wait.

Five. Ten. The length was up to them.

CHAPTER
FIFTY-EIGHT

Following his arrest, Steven Lake had been put in a holding cell where he'd waited for his solicitor to arrive. From there, he'd been ushered into the interview room and had spent the next four hours sitting opposite DS Campbell.

Tomek had stayed to watch his friend drill into the story behind the murders for a couple of hours, before he'd eventually started to get tired and decided to head home. It had been fun watching Steven Lake squirm and look uncomfortable as he came face to face with the man he'd bullied as a child. He had hated every minute of it and Tomek was glad to leave on such a high. The only downside to the interview – after getting everything they needed out of him – was that he was still reluctant to share the name of the individual helping him. That particular nugget of information would require more resources, more time, more effort away from all the other investigations that had landed on the team's desk since Annabelle Lake's disappearance.

And if they were going to catch the individual, they needed to do it quickly. Word of Steven's arrest had been kept internal so far, but it was only a matter of time until his accomplice found out what had happened to him – the heightened police presence and forensics tent perched outside the small boathouse was a big enough giveaway.

The following morning, after only a couple of hours' sleep, Tomek dressed for work, dropped Kasia off at school for a change (to make up for some lost time recently), and then headed into the office.

'What are you smiling about?' Kasia had asked as he'd parked a few hundred yards down the road so none of her school friends saw her getting a lift from her boring old dad.

'Work,' he said, massaging the steering wheel with one hand. 'We made an arrest last night. But the hard work's not done. We've got another one to make.'

'Nice,' she said, smiling. A genuine smile, followed by an interest in his job: 'How long do you think it will be before you make the next one?'

Tomek looked at his watch on his other hand. 'I should say we'll be finished by the end of the day.'

'Wanna bet?' Kasia's eyes beamed excitedly at the prospect of getting money.

'You still owe me for the fifty quid you stole the other day.'

'I thought you'd forgotten about that,' she said, still smiling. 'Anyway. What do you say? A tenner?'

'Hang on,' Tomek said. 'Let me get this straight. Not only are you refusing to pay me back the fifty quid you *stole*, but you're betting against my abilities to make an arrest?'

'Yes. I guess so.'

'So you're saying that you want a killer out there on the streets for longer than they should be?'

Kasia's excitement fell from her face and she looked down at her phone. 'Well, when you put it like that...'

'Yeah. I do put it like that. Besides, you're too young to be gambling. I've tried and failed miserably several times, so take it from me it's not worth it. Now go on, get to school, I've—'

'Got a murderer to catch, I know.'

Tomek watched her leave the car and start towards the school gates with a fuzzy feeling in his heart. Not only was she talking to him about his job with an air of genuine interest and intrigue, but she was talking the way she had done a few weeks ago. It felt as though she had gone back to normal, her old ways, the way she used to be – or at least her personality from six weeks ago.

Things with her were looking up. Another reason to smile.

And as she hurried through the school gates, disappearing amongst the sea of black and red school uniforms, Steven Lake's words echoed in his head.

She didn't deserve it. None of this was her fault.

The same could be said for Kasia. None of this – being kicked out and being forced to live with him – was any of her fault, and so he needed to stop blaming her for upending his life. It wasn't her fault, and nor was it his. It was their new normal, one that he was looking forward to.

A life with his daughter.

CHAPTER
FIFTY-NINE

'What's got you so smiley?' Rachel asked as he entered the incident room.

'It's going to be good day today,' he responded, chucking his bag down by his desk and logging in. 'I can feel it. The sun's out. One murderer is off the streets. Another's about to be caught. And I've not even had my morning coffee!'

'Ugh,' she said, 'I hate overly happy people sometimes.'

Tomek spun on his seat and tilted back until she came into view from behind her computer monitor. 'And we hate overly grumpy people as well,' he replied. 'But the two of us must learn to live in harmony.' Then he meshed his fingers together and made a humming sound.

Rachel skidded the computer mouse across the desk and folded her arms. 'Who are you and what have you done with Tomek? The Tomek I know is a miserable bastard.'

'Welcome to the new me, baby! What have I missed? Any update on they-who-must-not-be-named?'

Before responding, Rachel stepped out of her chair and wandered over to his desk, coming to a stop by his side. 'Sadly not. Steven Lake's proving a tough nut to crack.'

'Looks like we need to get our thinking caps on, Watson!'

For a long moment, Rachel stared at him with a blank, bemused expression on her face. Then she grunted before sauntering back to her own desk.

Tomek chuckled as he watched her go, then he turned his attention to his computer. He needed to find a starting point, a place to look for their mystery accomplice. Fortunately, he'd spent the entire night thinking about it.

Ever since the start of the investigation, the seemingly random connection between Annabelle Lake's disappearance and Jenny Ingles' had concerned him. There must have been a reason. Must have. It didn't fit in with Steven Lake's motives to have randomly picked up a girl from the street, rape her, pump her full of heroin, and then kill her in the same way that he had his own daughter.

It didn't make sense to him.

Which meant there must have been a connection. Not between Steven Lake and Jenny Ingles, but between his accomplice and the teenager.

A connection that would be hidden deep within Jenny Ingles' history.

Sadly, because she was dead, he was forced to rule her out of helping him in any way. The same went for her poor excuse for a foster mother, Alison.

Which left only one possibility: Jenny Ingles' birth parents.

CHAPTER
SIXTY

K aren and Johnny Ingles lived in a small one-bedroom maisonette in Grays, a few miles outside the M25. Originally from Canvey Island, they had been forced to move to the area nearly ten years ago after losing custody of their daughter, Jenny.

That was about as much as Tomek knew about them. About as much as he wanted to know, as well. There was only so much he could learn from a piece of paper; he was hoping they would be able to fill in the gaps and tell him the complete story.

Perched beside their front door was a small plant. A snake plant, *dracaena trifasciata*. Tomek looked down and admired it, and thought of his own plants that were now sitting pride of place in the living room, and his bonsai trees on the window sill in his bedroom. As he bent down to inspect the soil contents and the general health of the leaves, he was oblivious to the sound of the door opening and the man standing over him.

'Can I help you?' Johnny Ingles asked.

Crouched on his haunches, Tomek looked up to see a man with neat hair and an even neater beard. He was dressed in a loose-fitting polo shirt and a pair of denim jeans that looked a few sizes too big for him. Upon first impressions, this didn't seem to be a man who was incapable of looking after a daughter, of having her taken away by social services. But he'd made that mistake in the past...

'Sorry,' Tomek said as he returned to standing. 'Detective Sergeant Tomek Bowen. Are you Johnny Ingles?'

The man immediately became defensive, his stance turning taut. 'I am...' Hesitance in his voice. 'What's this regarding?'

Tomek reached into his pocket and whipped out his warrant card. Smiling, he said, 'Is it all right if I come in?'

Johnny Ingles looked over his shoulder before granting Tomek permission to enter. 'It's a bit of a mess, but—'

'That's fine. I see a lot of houses. I see a lot of mess.'

But in this particular instance, Tomek wasn't sure what "mess" Johnny was referring to, because the house was almost pristine, flawless. His own flat was dirtier than this and he considered that to be in a decent enough, liveable condition.

Inside the living room he found Karen Ingles sitting on the sofa, playing games on her iPad. The sudden arrival of a stranger in her home panicked her and she swung her legs off the sofa before standing to attention.

'Honey, this is Detective Sergeant Tomek Bowen. Detective, this is my wife, Karen.'

Once they'd completed the formalities, and he had refused the offer of a cup of tea, Tomek found a seat on the sofa and rested his elbows in his knees. He was forcibly struck by how different the Ingles' family home was compared to the squalor Jenny had been living in with her foster parent.

'I'll try to keep this brief, but as you know, Jenny was murdered a short while ago. I'm here to tell you that we've made an arrest and that her killer is being charged this afternoon with her murder.'

A look of relief, mixed with grief, washed over their faces.

'But sadly we believe there is another killer involved with her death.' Tomek inhaled deeply, held it for a moment. 'I understand that this is a very difficult time for you both, but I was wondering if I could ask you some questions about your daughter and how you lost her...'

Sniffling, choking back the tears, Karen Ingles asked, 'Is it going to help you find out who else killed our daughter?'

Tomek nodded slowly. 'I believe so, yes.'

'Okay. Fine. Yes. What would you like to know?'

CHAPTER
SIXTY-ONE

Tomek knocked on the door and waited.

And waited.

It was nearly midday, and by now news of Steven Lake's arrest had started to emerge online and on the television and radio. Not the exact details, but enough for his accomplice to know that their time was up.

Very soon.

As soon as they opened the door, in fact.

When they finally did, he was met with the presence of someone he'd only met once and subsequently completely forgotten about. They hadn't been a part of his thought processes, nor had he thought to include them in them. They had remained on the periphery of the investigation from the start. And now, knowing what he knew about them, commended them for their ability to stay well out of sight.

'Detective... What are you doing here? Is it about Steven? Have you found him?'

'I think you know we have, Doctor. Might I come in?'

Situated on the road outside Tara Moore's house was a handful of police officers, ready and waiting for anything unexpected. He'd asked them to give him some time with her before they entered.

'May I?' he asked.

The doctor had little say in the matter and stepped aside. Since Tomek's last visit, the number of dolphin and unicorn decorations had dwindled drastically, and a lot of furnishings in the house seemed to have disappeared.

'Going somewhere?' Tomek asked as he peered through the various rooms branching off the hallway.

'Only for a quick holiday to Cornwall.'

'Am I not right in thinking you've been on leave for the past two weeks already? Surprised they let you take the extra time off.'

Tomek came to a stop in the living room; she paused in the doorway, glaring at him.

'I can be very persuasive when I want to be.'

'So I've heard,' Tomek said as he seated himself on the edge of a coffee table, his head still pirouetting around like a lighthouse.

'Is there any particular reason you dropped by, Detective? Only I've—'

'We found Steven,' Tomek said, keeping his gaze on every part of the house except for her. 'Turns out he was the one who abducted both his daughter and Jenny Ingles, then killed them. He's looking at a long time in prison. But you'll be pleased to know that he's not given you up... He's stayed silent in that regard.'

It was a while before she said anything.

'He's not giving *me* up – what's that supposed to mean?'

'Oh, come on, Tara. We both know what it means. We both know you've been the one helping him this entire time. The one who stole Bradley Baxter's car. The one who picked up Annabelle that day after school. The one who surgically cleaned it after ditching it in the farm. The one who looked after her while she was in that shack. The one who fed her her favourite meals to make it look like Vincent Gregory had been giving them to her. The one who convinced and manipulated Steven Lake into doing this entire thing. The one who suggested he do the DNA test in the first place.'

'That was a lie.'

The statement took Tomek by surprise. Her words contained no hint of empathy in them. Instead she said with them pride, with defiance. And Tomek sensed he was about to hear a lot more...

'I altered the DNA results email,' she said.

'How?'

'Well, I made it up. I've seen a couple of them in my time, so I know how they work, and I know what they look like. All I had to do was find a blank template, input the right names, the right information I wanted, and then send it to him from a fake email address. He wasn't going to know any different, was he?'

The revelation floored Tomek. This meant that Annabelle Lake *was* Steven's biological daughter. That he had abducted and killed her for all the wrong reasons. By mistake...

Tomek took a moment to absorb the information.

'Why?' he asked eventually. 'Why did you make him believe she wasn't his?'

'Because you didn't have to hear him. Constantly moaning and complaining about Elizabeth's relationship with Vincent, how close they were, how much he felt like something had gone on between them. It was never ending and got on my nerves.'

'So you convinced him to destroy his own family as a result?'

She shrugged, nonchalant, as though the context of the question was as innocuous as whether she wanted ketchup with her chips: "Yeah, if some's going, I'll have some..."

'Sometimes all you need to do is give people the gun and they're willing to do the rest...'

'But not when it came to Jenny Ingles, surely?'

'Steven took a little more convincing when it came to her. I had to convince her that this was what she deserved, that she got what was coming to her.'

'No she didn't. Your issue was with her parents. Not her. Jenny had nothing to do with your dismissal, and you know it.'

The glare in Tara's expression seemed to recede a little. At Karen and Johnny Ingles' house, they'd told him about their broken and non-existent relationship with their daughter, which had all been a result of Tara's neglect and unprofessionalism. Before she'd worked at Southend Hospital, Tara had been doing the same job as a paediatrician at the hospital in Basildon. Jenny Ingles had been one of her patients, but after a disagreement with her parents, Tara had found herself under investigation and sacked from the hospital. After eventually convincing her manager at Southend, who happened to be a good friend, she quickly found herself in the same job in a different hospital without anyone noticing. Meanwhile, she'd notified social services of Karen and Johnny's ineptitude as parents, and campaigned against them to lose their daughter. So while she managed to lose a career and get it back, the Ingles were losing the one thing they held dear in life.

And that's what this whole thing had been about. Revenge, retribution on Karen and Johnny Ingles for almost destroying her career.

'She was a misfit, a drug dealing whore who deserved it,' Tara hissed.

'And who do you think is to blame for that? You created her. You made her go down that path. If you hadn't interfered with her life or her parents, then none of this would have happened.'

Tara smacked her hand on the door, so hard it swung round and bounced off the wall. 'If they hadn't got me sacked then none of this would've happened!'

It wasn't common for Tomek to feel threatened and uncomfortable, but as he stood there inches from this cold and calculating killer, he was beginning to feel a little unnerved. There was something unhinged about Tara Moore that scared him. That she might flip at any moment and launch herself on him. But he wasn't finished yet. He still had more questions he needed answers to.

'Whose decision was it to rape Jenny?'

'Steven's.'

Tomek didn't believe her. He'd watched the way the man had admitted to it the night before, the way he'd felt ashamed and remorseful for his actions – not the behaviour of a man who had done so because he *could*, because he'd had power over her. Instead he'd behaved like a man who'd been instructed to do so.

'I think you did it,' Tomek continued. 'I think you convinced him to do it because you thought that's what she deserved.'

Tara simply shrugged, back to being nonchalant again.

'And so what if I did? She deserved it all.'

'And the heroin?'

'She already had that on her. Saved me having to raid the medicine station at the hospital. Steven tried a couple of times but it was an absolute mess. He couldn't find a vein if it was labelled. So I had to step in and do it, the stupid bastard.'

'Stupid bastard? How can you say that?'

Tara scoffed. 'Oh dear, Detective. Did you really think I loved him? No, of course I didn't. It was just easy getting to him because he was so caught up about his family. I knew from the moment I met him he was weak and would do whatever I told him to.'

That was all Tomek needed to hear. As soon as she'd finished, he let out a long, heavy sigh that deflated his entire body and mind. Then he reached into the back of his trousers and unclipped the handcuffs from his belt.

'Tara Moore, I'm arresting you for the abduction and murders of Annabelle Lake and Jenny Ingles. You do not have to say anything...'

―

And she hadn't. She had remained silent the entire journey back to the station. As soon as she'd got into the interview room, she'd explained every intricate detail of their plan like it was story time. As though she was showing off to them, demonstrating how clever she'd been.

By the time the interview had finally finished, Tomek and some members from the team went for a drink at the Last Post. Only the one though, because they all had responsibilities they needed to get back for. And as he headed back to his car, the contents of the alcohol beginning to swish around in his brain, he spotted a figure in the car park. His immediate suspicion was that it was one of Charlotte's criminal friends coming to send him another message. He was pleasantly surprised then, when he saw that it was Vincent Gregory. The man wore a black hoodie, except this time the hood was pulled low over his eyes to hide the bruises on his face.

As Tomek approached, Vincent removed the hood and held out his hand. Tomek ignored it and placed his own in his coat pocket.

'Good to see you,' he said. 'You don't look as bad as I thought you might.'

'I... I just wanted to say thank you. Thank you for everything your lot done. And... and sorry for the way I behaved. I should never of judged you the way I done. And I'm sorry.'

Tomek was blown away, and before he could think of a response, the man pulled his hood back over his head and disappeared off towards the train station, like a superhero disappearing into the night.

As he watched the man go, Tomek thought to himself that the past twenty-four hours had been healthy, positive. There were now two fewer killers on the streets.

And now he could add a racist to that list as well.

CHAPTER
SIXTY-TWO

One of the perks of being a police officer was that he had access to a lot more resources than the average citizen. Resources that enabled him to locate with ease the address of the girl who had been bullying Kasia.

Was it an ethical use of those resources? Probably not, but bullying wasn't an ethical practice either, and yet people still did that – and a lot of things that were way worse.

The house they were looking for was at the end of the road somewhere. On the right-hand side. Number one-four-seven. Google Maps suggested it had a black panelled door with a large handle running down the length of it, and a white garage to the right.

'One-four-one...' Sean said, counting down the house numbers while Tomek looked for the front door. 'One-four-three... One-four-five.'

'One-four-seven.' Exactly as Google had told him it would be. Now he hoped the occupants would be exactly as his computer systems said they would be.

'There you go, mate. She's all yours.'

After finding a parking space a little further down the street, Tomek left Sean in the car and made his way to the front door, straightening his tie as he went. It was a weekend, so he expected everyone to be home – or at the very least *someone*.

Fortunately, he was right. When the front door opened he was greeted with the presence of a woman who was well into her fifties and yet was trying her hardest to cling onto her twenties. Her hair had been straightened and curled, her skin tanned a few shades too dark as though she'd been on the sun bed for too long. Eyelash extensions and copious amounts of make-up caked on. And a small amount of Botox in all the usual places.

'You must be Mrs Redknapp,' he said.

'Do I know you?' Helen Redknapp replied, her voice deeper than he expected.

'No. My name's Tomek. I was wondering if your daughter Crystal is home at all?'

Helen looked over her shoulder and peered into the house. Apparently concerned that there was a forty-year-old man at her front door asking for her thirteen-year-old daughter, she called her husband, a large brute of a man, who came bowling his way to the door. His shoulders and muscles were so wide – evidence of never having done anything else in his life other than lift weights – that they meant he could barely fit through the doorframe.

'Who're you?' he grumbled, gesturing with a slight flick of the head.

'I'm Tomek. I wondered if I could speak with your daughter, please?'

'What you gotta do with my daughter?'

'Nothing. I just wanted to talk to her.'

'What you gotta say to my daughter, you can say to me.'

'That's exactly what I plan to. Have you got any other family members out there who might want to come and join the conversation? A brother, a sister, perhaps? I only need the three of you but everyone else is welcome, I guess. The more people who know what your daughter's been up to the better.'

Without warning, Axel Redknapp muscled his way past his wife and squared up to Tomek. The man was a few inches shorter, but what he lacked in height he more than made up for in width and strength – four times over. On his breath were the traces of a banana smoothie.

'The fuck you here for, bro?'

Then he raised his hands to touch Tomek.

'I really wouldn't do that if I were you,' he said, calm, quiet.

'Why the fuck not?'

'Because I'd like to speak with your daughter before I arrest you for assaulting a police officer.'

The smug smile Tomek flashed at Axel incensed the man, but the warrant card in his pocket was enough to cool him down. It had needed to be otherwise he would have found himself pinned to the ground with his arms behind his back, being restrained as he was thrown into the back of a police car.

'There, that makes a little more sense for you all doesn't it?' Tomek said, making no effort to hide the gloat in his tone. 'Now, where's your daughter?'

'What has she done?' Axel asked.

'You're about to find out. Helen, if you could go and find her I'd really appreciate that. I don't want this to take up too much more of all our time.'

Helen didn't need to be told twice. At once, she turned her back on them and sprinted into the house. The sound of her calling her daughter's name echoed through the hallway all the way to the porch. A moment or two later, both women appeared.

Crystal was the spitting image of her mother, and it was clear to see who was trying to emulate who. The young girl was wearing a thick green hoodie and a pair of loose-fitting tracksuit bottoms that were tucked neatly into a pair of thick white socks. He was seeing more and more of that nowadays, in particular with Kasia. Perhaps it was the fashion... something he'd never understood.

'The family's back together again, great.' Tomek clapped his hands and stepped forward, waiting for Axel to move out of his way. 'This will be short and sweet for everyone. There's no need to take it inside. If your neighbours overhear, then that's your problem, not mine. I'm only going to say this once, and that's it. Are you all ready?'

The question was rhetorical, but they all nodded their heads anyway. It was clear to see they were afraid, concerned about what he had to tell them. And he was enjoying this – and he was determined to enjoy it more than Crystal enjoyed fucking with his daughter.

'Helen, Axel – it's come to my attention that your daughter has been in receipt of a certain image of myself. She can explain the logistics and backstory behind that, but what I'm here to let you know is that sharing said image to the rest of the school is considered revenge porn and is a very serious offence and can result in a lengthy prison sentence.

'It's also come to my attention that your daughter has been bullying my daughter at school. Stealing her clothes during PE. Humiliating her in front of the whole classroom. Making her call in sick and wish she didn't have to go in. Now, I can tolerate the image thing, that's taking the piss out of me. But when it affects my daughter, and you choose to target my daughter with things like that and everything else you do to her, that is something I will not tolerate. So I have come here in good faith to warn you to stay away from her. And if I find out that this has been continuing, then I will be back. And I will be back with an arrest warrant.'

'Why? You can't arrest her for bullying,' Helen hissed.

'No. Very true. But I can arrest you both for your connections with Billy Morton and the drug ring he's operating on Canvey Island.

I'm glad we bumped into each other the other day in the car park at Knightsbridge, Axel – it made it much easier to recognise your face.' Tomek paused to survey the house. 'This is a *very* nice property you've got,' he said. 'Not cheap, I imagine. And your Range Rover Sport is a lovely car as well – I'd love to own one for myself one day, but for now I'll just stick with my car. But I would love even more to know how you paid for it all. Perhaps we could discuss it in an interview room one day...?'

'Th-Th-That won't be necessary...' Axel babbled, his voice weak and hoarse.

'Excellent. Then I hope we're all in understanding with one another. Crystal will stay away from my Kasia, and I will stay away from you. Enjoy your afternoon, guys. And don't do anything uncharacteristic – we tend to pick up on things like that...'

Tomek offered them a piss-take of a wave and an overwhelmingly smug smile that threatened to consume his face. He walked with a marked spring in his step back to the car, and as he slumped into the passenger seat, he began chuckling.

'Positive result then?' Sean asked as he started the engine and slipped it into first.

'You were right,' Tomek replied. 'I would never have had as much fun if I'd beaten the shit out of him.'

'Not like you'd have been able to, mind,' Sean said. 'You saw the size of the guy, right?'

The smile dropped from Tomek's face. 'Fuck off. Now take me home. I've got an afternoon I'd like to spend with my daughter.'

━━━

By the time he was dropped off at the flat, Kasia had finished baking the cake they'd prepared in the morning.

'Smells good!' Tomek said as he entered the kitchen.

She had her phone lying on the side, music blasting from the tiny speakers, and was jamming away to the sound of Harry Styles.

'It tastes even better,' she replied, small crumbs of cake stuck around her mouth.

Then she handed him a piece. An overwhelming assault of lemon hit his senses and sent his tastebuds into overdrive.

'You're right, that is delicious. Did you learn how to make this in food tech?' Tomek asked.

'Pfft. Please. Mrs Shaw wishes she knew how to cook as good as this...'

'Then I think we've found your passion,' he replied as he took another slice of cake. 'This is one of the best I've had in a long time.'

'Well I can't make it every day, otherwise you'll get fat. And at your age, you—'

'Yes, yes. That's enough of that, thank you.'

Tomek reached across the counter, tapped her phone screen and then reduced the volume on the speakers. It was good to hear his own thoughts again.

'Did your meeting go okay?' she asked.

For a moment it took Tomek a while to figure out what she was referring to. But then he remembered. The little white lie he'd told her.

'Very well, thank you,' he said. 'Better than expected.'

As Tomek reached over for another slice, unable to control himself, she slapped him on the back of the hand with a wooden spoon.

'Dad, *stop!*'

At first he wasn't sure he heard her properly. But then as the realisation and embarrassment settled on her face, he knew she'd said what he thought she had.

'Did you just call me *Dad*?'

Warmth swelled in his body.

'No. No, I didn't...'

The smug grin he'd worn outside the Redknapps' drug-funded house returned, bigger, brighter and bolder this time.

'You did. You said *Dad*. You said, "Dad, stop!"... *Dad*...'

He didn't think this day would come. He didn't think she'd ever feel comfortable enough to call him that word. But she had, and she did. Something must have changed, something inside her must have thought it was a good idea, that he was deserving of it.

He didn't need to know what or why; he was content in letting that information stay with her. Just the fact she'd said it was enough.

That their relationship was moving in the right direction.

Dad...

Which reminded him. For every dad there was also a mum.

'I was thinking,' he started, massaging the back of his hand. 'You've not said anything about going to see your mum recently. Is that something you were still interested in doing?'

Kasia didn't need long to make a decision. She chewed on her bottom lip, pushed a strand of hair from her eyes and shook her head.

'No, I don't think so,' she said confidently.

'Sure?'

'Positive.'

'Well, if you ever change your mind, just let me know and I'll arrange something.'

Smiling, she stepped forward, wrapped her arms around his waist and hugged him.

'Thanks,' she said.

'Pardon?'

'Thanks...?'

'What are you missing?'

She looked up at him and rolled her eyes.

'Fine. Thanks, *Dad*.'

'That's better.'

'You're not gonna let it go now, are you?'

'You bet your arse I'm not.'

'Erm. Language!'

'Arse is fine. You can say arse. I'm in a good enough mood to let that slip.'

He wrapped his arm over her shoulder and pulled her in closer against his chest.

'Aww,' she said. 'Thanks, Dad. You arsehole.'

DEATH'S TOUCH

Tomek Bowen returns in...

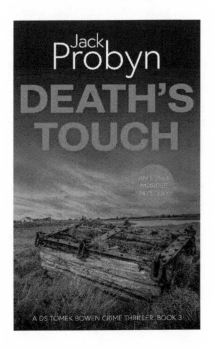

When the fog clears one December morning in Essex, the body of a teenage girl is discovered lying face down in a field.

The victim, Lily Monteith, was murdered in a peculiar and unique way — so unique that it could have only happened to her.

As a result, the case quickly lands on DS Tomek Bowen's desk who, while trying to juggle his newfound life as a single parent to a thirteen-year-old daughter, must unearth the deadly sequence of events and bring the truth to light.

But as soon as the investigation begins, Tomek discovers Lily's death may be linked to a killing spree that has lain dormant for many years — with no one ever being brought to justice for it.

And, if that's the case, he fears another killing spree, this time years in the making, is yet to come.

Read Now

ALSO BY JACK PROBYN

The DS Tomek Bowen Murder Mystery Series:

DEATH'S JUSTICE

Southend-on-Sea, Essex: Detective Sergeant Tomek Bowen — driven, dogged, and haunted by the death of his brother — is called to one of the most shocking crime scenes he has ever seen. A man has been ritualistically murdered and dumped in an allotment near the local airport. Early investigations indicate this was a man with a past. A past that earned him many enemies.

Download Death's Justice

DEATH'S GRIP

Annabelle Lake thought she recognised the Ford Fiesta waiting outside her school, and the driver in it. She was wrong. Her body is discovered some time later, dangling from a swing in a local playground on Canvey Island.

Download Death's Grip

DEATH'S TOUCH

When the fog clears one December morning in Essex, the body of a teenage girl is discovered lying face down in a field. But as soon as the investigation begins, Tomek discovers Lily's death may be linked to a killing spree that has lain dormant for many years — with no one ever being brought to justice for it.

Download Death's Touch

The Jake Tanner Crime Thriller Series:

Full-length novels that combine police procedure, organised crime and police corruption.

TOE THE LINE:

A small jeweller's is raided in Guildford High Street and leaves police chasing their tails. Reports suggest that it's The Crimsons, an organised crime group the police have been hunting for years. When the shop owner is kidnapped and a spiked collar is attached to her neck, Jake learns one of his own is involved – a police officer. As Jake follows the group on a wild goose chase, he questions everything he knows about his team. Who can he trust? And is he prepared to find out?

Download Toe the Line

WALK THE LINE:

A couple with a nefarious secret are brutally murdered in their London art gallery. Their bodies cleaned. Their limbs dismembered. And the word LIAR inscribed on the woman's chest. For Jake Tanner it soon becomes apparent this is not a revenge killing. There's a serial killer loose on the streets of Stratford. And the only thing connecting the victims is their name: Jessica. Jake's pushed to his mental limits as he uncovers The Community, an online forum for singles and couples to meet. But there's just one problem: the killer's been waiting for him... and he's hungry for his next kill.

Download Walk the Line

UNDER THE LINE:

DC Jake Tanner thought he'd put the turmoil of the case that nearly killed him behind him. He was wrong. When Danny Cipriano's body is discovered buried in a concrete tomb, Jake's wounds are reopened. But one thing quickly becomes clear. The former leader of The Crimsons knew too much. And somebody wanted him silenced. For good. The only problem is, Jake knows who.

Download Under the Line

CROSS THE LINE:

For years, Henry Matheson has been untouchable, running the drug trade in east London. Until the body of his nearest competitor is discovered burnt to a lamppost in his estate. Gang war gone wrong, or a calculated murder? Only one man is brave enough to stand up to him and find out. But, as Jake Tanner soon learns, Matheson plays dirty. And in the estate there are no rules.

Download Cross the Line

OVER THE LINE:

Months have passed since Henry Matheson was arrested and sent to prison. Months have passed since Henry Matheson, one of east London's most dangerous criminals, was arrested. Since then DC Jake Tanner and the team at Stratford CID have been making sure the case is watertight. But when a sudden and disastrous fraudulent attack decimates Jake's personal finances, he is propelled into the depths of a dark and dangerous underworld, where few resurface.

Download Over the Line

PAST THE LINE:

The Cabal is dead. The Cabal's dead. Or so Jake thought. But when Rupert Haversham, lawyer to the city's underworld, is found dead in his London home, Jake begins to think otherwise. The Cabal's back, and now they're silencing people who know too much. Jake included.

Download Past the Line

The Jake Tanner SO15 Files Series:

Novella length, lightning-quick reads that can be read anywhere. Follow Jake as he joins Counter Terrorism Command in the fight against the worst kind of evil.

THE WOLF:

A cinema under siege. A race to save everyone inside. An impatient detective. Join Jake as he steps into the darkness.

Download *The Wolf*

DARK CHRISTMAS:

The head of a terrorist cell is found dead outside his flat in the early hours of Christmas Eve. What was he doing outside? Why was a suicide vest strapped to his body? And what does the note in his sock have to do with his death?

Download *Dark Christmas*

THE EYE:

The discovery of a bomb factory leaves Jake and the team scrambling for answers. But can they find them in time?

Download *The Eye*

IN HEAVEN AND HELL:

An ominous — and deadly — warning ignites Jake and the team into action. An attack on one of London's landmarks is coming. But where? And when? Failure could be catastrophic.

Download *In Heaven And Hell*

BLACKOUT:

What happens when all the lights in London go out, and all the power switches off? What happens when a city is brought to its knees? Jake Tanner's about to find out. And he's right in the middle of it.

Download *Blackout*

EYE FOR AN EYE:

Revenge is sweet. But not when it's against you. Not when they use your family to get to you. Family is off-limits. And Jake Tanner will do anything to protect his.

Download *Eye For An Eye*

MILE 17:

Every year, thousands of runners and supporters flock to the streets of London to celebrate the London Marathon. Except this year, there won't be anything to ride home about.

Download *Mile 17*

THE LONG WALK:

The happiest day of your life, your wedding day. But when it's a royal wedding, the stakes are much higher. Especially when someone wants to kill the bride.

Download *The Long Walk*

THE ENDGAME:

Jake Tanner hasn't been to a football match in years. But when a terrorist cell attacks his favourite football stadium, killing dozens and injuring hundreds more, Jake is both relieved and appalled — only the day before was he in the same crowds, experiencing the same atmosphere. But now he must put that behind him and focus on finding the people responsible. And fast. Because another attack's coming.

Download *The Endgame*

The Jake Tanner Terror Thriller Series:

Full-length novels, following Jake through Counter-Terrorism Command, where the stakes have never been higher.

STANDSTILL:

The summer of 2017. Jake Tanner's working for SO15, The Metropolitan Police Service's counter terrorism unit. And a duo of terrorists seize three airport-bound trains. On board are hundreds of kilos of explosives, and thousands of lives. Jake quickly finds himself caught in a cat and mouse race against time to stop the trains from detonating. But what he discovers along the way will change everything.

Download Standstill

FLOOR 68:

1,000 feet in the air, your worst nightmares come true. Charlie Paxman is going to change the world with a deadly virus. His mode of distribution: the top floor of London's tallest landmark, The Shard. But only one man can stop. Jake Tanner. Caught in the wrong place at the wrong time. Trapped inside a tower, Jake finds himself up against an army of steps and an unhinged scientist that threatens to decimate humanity. But can he stop it from happening?

Download Floor 68

JOIN THE VIP CLUB

Your FREE book is waiting for you

Available when you join the VIP Club below

Get your FREE copy of the prequel to the DS Tomek Bowen series now at jackprobynbooks.com when you join my VIP email club.

ABOUT THE AUTHOR

Jack Probyn is a British crime writer and the author of the Jake Tanner crime thriller series, set in London.

He currently lives in Surrey with his partner and cat, and is working on a new murder mystery series set in his hometown of Essex.

Don't want to sign up to yet another mailing list? Then you can keep up to date with Jack's new releases by following one of the below accounts. You'll get notified when I've got a new book coming out, without the hassle of having to join my mailing list.

Amazon Author Page "Follow":
    1. Click the link here: https://geni.us/AuthorProfile
    2. Beneath my profile picture is a button that says "Follow"
    3. Click that, and then Amazon will email you with new releases and promos.

BookBub Author Page "Follow":
    1. Similar to the Amazon one above, click the link here: https://www.bookbub.com/authors/jack-probyn
    2. Beside my profile picture is a button that says "Follow"
    3. Click that, and then BookBub will notify you when I have a new release

If you want more up to date information regarding new releases, my writing process, and everything else in between, the best place to be in the know is my Facebook Page. We've got a little community growing over there. Why not be a part of it?

Facebook: https://www.facebook.co.uk/jackprobynbooks

Manufactured by Amazon.ca
Bolton, ON

37825392R00213